Grand Deceptions

By

G S Willmott

ISBN 9781925283532 (pbk)

ISBN 9781925283549 (ebook)

Grand Deceptions is a work of fiction. Any resemblance to real persons, living or dead, is purely coincidental.

ACKNOWLEDGMENTS

Anna my wife

Preview Readers

Bill Simpson

Ian Jones

Kim Krarup

Tony Pittard

Previous Books by G S Willmott

The Other Side of the Trench

Brothers in Arms

Escape

Red Lights on the Somme

You Forgot the Sauce

Survival

Soul Survival

Boy's Own War

Serendipity

The Importance of Being Ivy

Contents

Fox on the Run

Chapter 1

November 1, 1855

The horseman was riding his stallion through the Kent countryside. The land belonged to his family's estate. He had been newly appointed as The Master of Foxhounds, and the objective of his ride was to determine suitable ground to conduct a foxhunt. The hunt was to be the first in over a century at Abernethy Manor, and the young man was committed to making his first hunt as Master of the Foxhounds a success.

Mathew Abernethy was born in 1833 to wealthy parents named Julia and Samuel; the family had been the custodian of Abernethy Manor for over three hundred years. Henry VIII had gifted the estate, including 2,000 acres, to Lord Abernethy in 1532 as a reward for the support given to the Tudor king during his fight with the Vatican.

Mathew was twenty-one, a tall, blond young man with blue eyes and an engaging manner. He was liked by all, especially the young women of the village.

Mathew never tired of riding over the green hills of his family's property. There were patches of oak forest and winding streams dotted throughout the estate. Stone walls bordering the paddocks would make for excellent jumping.

The primary source of income for the estate was sheep. The Abernethy fleece was known for its fine wool, which was not only prized by the English mills but also by mills in France and Italy. The purpose of the foxhunt was not only sport. The foxes killed lambs on a regular basis, and therefore, eradicating them was sound farm management.

Satisfied with the course, Mathew returned to the manor. He was to join his family for dinner and his elder brother Joseph, his younger sister Rosie, and his parents were waiting for him in the conservatory.

The young man entered the beautiful greenhouse where everyone was enjoying a sherry and discussing their day's activities.

'Hello Mathew. Were you successful in plotting a route for the hunt?' asked his father.

'Yes sir, I think we'll have a very successful day.'

'Excellent. Where on the estate will you be leading the hunters?'

'We'll follow the river to the stone bridge then cross over and enter the forest area. With luck, we'll flush the little blighters out onto the moors where the dogs should be able to run them down.'

'Well, that sounds like a good plan, in theory anyway.'

'You sound a little sceptical, Father.'

'Do I? I don't mean to, but we all know how difficult it is to catch these cunning foxes.'

'Yes, I understand, and I've organised some of the workers to go out in the early morning to stop up the holes of their dens. That should force the wily creatures to find shelter above ground during the day. That will make it easier for the hounds to track them.'

'Clever thinking, Mathew.'

'What time do we start out?' asked Joseph.

'We will all meet here at the manor ready to begin the hunt at eleven.'

Joseph nodded and turned to their sister. 'I assume you'll be joining us, Rosie?'

'I wouldn't miss it for the world.'

'What about you, Mother? Will you be joining Father in the hunt?'
'I'm afraid not, son. My fox hunting days are well over.'

November 16, 1855

At 11 a.m. a hundred and fifty riders assembled, with over fifty hounds.

Mathew, being Master of Hounds, was in charge of the hunt; supervising the field, the hounds, and staff. The huntsmen, who had bred the hounds and worked with them, took charge of the pack during the hunt.

When Mathew was satisfied that all was in order, he instructed the huntsmen to lead the pack of hounds out over the estate's meadows, hoping to flush out a fox. When the fox was flushed out into the open, the group would pursue their quarry with the huntsman and the hunting party. The field would follow at a gallop and watch the hounds chase down the fox. When the animal was cornered, the hounds took over.

In this particular case the fox eluded the hunters, the riders and hounds returned to the manor house without the trophy they sought. Waiting for the group was a banquet of food and drink on the lawns of Abernethy Manor. Mathew was congratulated by the former Master of Hounds, his father Lord Abernethy, for the excellent hunt despite the lack of success.

June 23, 1856

Lord Abernethy was sitting in his office, which was adjacent to the manor's extensive library.

He was waiting for his son to meet with him as arranged the previous day.

Mathew entered the office, wondering what the purpose of the meeting was. It was unusual to receive a summons from his father. They usually talked at dinner or when working around the estate.

'Ah, Mathew, please take a seat. Can I pour you a whisky?'

'Yes thank you, sir.'

Lord Abernethy poured two generous malt whiskies from a 16th century decanter, and added, 'I suppose you're wondering why I asked you here.'

'Well, yes, I don't believe I've done anything wrong.'

'Of course you haven't! I just thought it was time to discuss your future.'

'My future?'

'As you are aware, Joseph as the eldest son will inherit my title and the entire estate. Your mother and I want to make sure that you are in a position to build your personal wealth.'

'Thank you, sir. What are you proposing?'

'What do you know about Australia?'

'Well, I know it's on the other side of the world.'

'True, it is certainly a long way from here. However, it offers great promise of prosperity. It is rich in resources, including gold, and boasts the highest standard of living of anywhere on the globe.'

'Father, are you proposing I immigrate to Australia?'

'I am suggesting it; there is no pressure whatsoever. I will bequeath you £25,000[1] to establish yourself.'

'That's a significant amount of money.'

'Yes, it is, more than enough to create a very comfortable life in the colonies.'

'Do I have a choice, Father?'

'Yes, you do, but the money will not be available to you if you decide to stay. Understand, Mathew, it's not that we want to get rid of you. Your mother and I love you. It's just that we think this would give you an enormous opportunity to create your personal wealth.'

'May I think about it?'

'Certainly, take your time.'

Mathew decided he had no other choice, so he accepted his parent's offer and made preparations to sail to Australia.

---

[1] * Equivalent to $3,500,000 in 2016

The Pain of Seduction

Chapter 2

January 1, 1856

George Griffith was preparing to celebrate his 21st birthday. His parents, Harriet and Harold, had invited one hundred guests to their home in Somerset for a party to end all parties, doubling as a New Year's celebration. George was regarded as handsome with black hair and dark brown eyes and his posture was such that he appeared taller than his 5 feet 10 inches.

'So, George are you looking forward to the festivities?' asked Harold.

'I am Father, and not just to the party but to coming of age.'

Harold looked at him thoughtfully. 'Yes, son, you are now a man with all the responsibilities that entails.'

'Like earning a living, you mean.'

'Yes, that's part of it. Have you given any more thought about what you would like to do?'

'I'm still considering your offer of joining you in the bank, but I'm still not sure.'

'Well, George, you'd better decide soon.'

'Yes, I know.'

Harold laid a hand on his son's shoulder. 'We'd better get organised. Your guests will be here any moment.'

'I purchased a new outfit for the occasion, so I'd better get changed.'

'Did you? I'm just wearing the same old thing I wear every New Year's Eve.'

'Hardly the same old thing sir! I've always admired that Savile Row suit.'

'Yes, I must admit I always feel special when I'm wearing it,' Harold admitted.

The two women of the house were also getting themselves ready for the big occasion Harriet had chosen a low-cut velvet dress, while her daughter Jane had chosen satin with the same fashionable neckline.

They both looked beautiful as they made their way to join the gentlemen in the foyer ready to greet the first guests already arriving to wish George a happy birthday as they presented him with gifts.

Soon the house was filled with the sound of conversations and laughter. At midnight the guests sang *Auld Lang Syne* and immediately after that, every guest present shouted *Happy Birthday George*.

When George finally made it to bed at 3.30 am, he was exhausted but euphoric.

The next morning, the young man decided to try and clear his head by taking a walk along the River Brue which bordered his parents' property.

As he walked, he noticed young Cathy Haines swimming in the river. He stopped and called out to attract her attention. 'Good morning, Cathy! I can't believe you're swimming… it must be very freezing in there.'

The girl rolled over on her back and regarded him with an impish smile. 'It is when you first get in, but you get used to it. It's very invigorating, George. You should join me.'

George didn't hesitate but disrobed and jumped in the freezing water which almost took his breath away. 'Blimey, Cathy! It's freezing.'

'Don't be such a Nancy. Come over here and I'll warm you up.'

As George began to swim over, he could see Cathy's ample bosom floating in the water.

'Come on, George, put your arms around me and I'll warm you up,' she urged.

George's loins were stirring and despite the chill, he felt very amorous. 'Cathy, I think I've had enough. I'm getting out.'

'I'll join you.'

The two young people found themselves on the riverbank naked, and naturally attracted to each other. George leant over and kissed the young women. Cathy responded enthusiastically and they made love.

George bade farewell to the buxom maiden from the village and made his way home.

June 1, 1856

George had just returned home from his father's bank where he had been working for the past five months.

Waiting at the rear entrance was Cathy Haines.

'Hello, George.'

'Hello, Cathy. I haven't seen you for a while.'

'No, not since we went swimming together on your birthday.'

He grinned. 'Yes, you were my most memorable present.'

'I'm glad you think so, as actually the second part of your present is arriving shortly.'

His grin faded. 'What do you mean?'

'George, I'm with child.'

'Oh my God.'

'I'm here to ask you to marry me. I don't want to bring a bastard into this world.'

'Cathy, I don't know what to say. You're going to have to leave it with me for a while, so I can determine the best course of action.'

'There is only one course of action,' she said.

'Leave it with me; I will get in touch with you shortly. Now I'll have to ask you to leave. My father is due home any time now.'

'Well, don't take too long, George. The baby is due in September.' The young woman walked away leaving George in a state of shock.

George went to his room, and lay upon on his bed staring at the ceiling, his head spinning. He had no idea what to do.

Should he marry this peasant girl? What would his parents think? Would he be cut off without a penny?

The clock struck six. He was due at the family dining table, so made his way slowly down the stairs and entered the ornately decorated room.

'Hello, George, you're a little late this evening. That's unlike you,' said his sister.

'Yes, I had a few things to take care of.'

The maid served the family roast pheasant with vegetables. Their next-door neighbour James Whitmore had been hunting that day and bagged several birds, so he gave two to the Griffiths.

Pheasant was a general favourite, but tonight George just picked at his food.

His father noticed his son's lack of appetite. 'What's the matter George? Aren't you feeling well?'

'Not really Father, in fact, may I be excused?'

'Yes, you may. Is there anything we can do to help?'

'No, I'll just go to my room and rest for a while.'

George left the table and returned to his room where once again he lay upon his bed. He had no idea what to do. He decided to retire early. Maybe he would wake up with a solution.

The next morning, he woke to the same conundrum. He decided the only option open to him was to divulge his situation to his father. Therefore, after breakfast, George asked his father if he could have a conversation with him in the study.

Harold motioned him in and they sat down. 'Well, son what is it you wish to discuss with me?'

'Sir, I have been a fool. It seems I have made one of the girls in the village pregnant.'

'Oh my God, do you love her?'

'I hardly know her.'

'What's her name?'

'Cathy.'

'Does she have a last name?'

'Sorry, yes, of course, Haines.'

'Did you know her father's one of my tenants? He's one of my best.'

George sighed. 'So, what do you think I should do?'

'You don't have too many options. You either marry the girl or pay her off.'

'I don't want to marry her. She's below my station.'

Harold frowned. 'You don't have much of a station in life at this very moment, George.'

'No sir, I suppose I don't. Would you lend me the money to pay her off?'

'How much were you thinking?'

'I'm not sure." He looked helpless. "Do you think £1,000 would be enough?'

'Well, if I were her I'd refuse,' Harold said dryly. 'I would think a figure more like £2,000 would be appropriate.'

'That's a lot of money, Father. I'm not sure how I could pay it back.'

'Don't worry about that now. What you need to do immediately is contact the girl and make the offer.'

'Thank you, sir, I appreciate your support.'

'Don't thank me, George, I'm doing it for your mother and myself more than anything.'

George rode into Yeovil next morning with the intention to make the offer to Cathy. She worked at the village bakery, and as George entered the shop, she was bringing a tray of pies out from the wood-fired oven. She saw George and indicated that he should meet her at the rear of the shop.

'Hello, George. Have you decided to make an honest woman of me?'

'Not exactly.' Before she could respond, he stumbled on, 'Cathy, I am willing to pay you £2,000 to assist you in raising the child. You will be able to buy a cottage and have money left over.'

'When do I receive the money?' she asked. Her face gave nothing away.

'I will get an agreement drawn up by my solicitor. You will have the money as soon as you sign it.'

'Let it be so.'

'I'll inform you when the document is ready to sign. It shouldn't be more than a week.'

The two young people bade one another farewell. George returned to the bank and Cathy returned to the bakery.

Cathy couldn't help thinking about the money all day. She was champing at the bit to finish work so she could see her true love and give him the news. The payoff would enable them to get married and have their baby in wedlock.

Cathy's deception would alter George's life forever.

The following week, George arranged to meet Cathy and she signed the agreement, ensuring she and her child would make no further claim.

The same day Harold summoned his son into his study. 'George, I hope this has been a lesson to you.'

George nodded sheepishly, but his father hadn't finished.

'Your lack of judgment has concerned both your mother and me. We have decided that a reasonable course of action will be for you to immigrate to Australia.'

'Australia? Why there?'

'My business contacts inform me it is a land of opportunity. It doesn't have to be a life sentence. Once you've made your fortune you can return home to England.'

'I have no money, Father. How will I live?'

'We have decided to gift you the sum of £5,000, which will be your inheritance. Don't waste it.'

'So when should I depart?'

'Here is a first-class ticket on the *SS Great Britain*. It is reputed to be the most modern and fastest ship afloat.'

The Launch of SS Great Britain

George boarded the ship September 1, 1856, bound for Melbourne, Australia, together with the other 120 first-class passengers. The majority of the passengers, 580 in all, were housed in less salubrious quarters.

In God We Trust

Chapter 3

Oxford University 1856

John Davies was the son of a Church of England Minister, the Reverent James Davies. His parish was King's Walden in [2]Hertfordshire.*

St Mary's King Walden

James was very proud of his church, which had been constructed in the 13th century. He was also proud of his son John, who was studying theology at Christ College, Oxford. James's father was the previous minister at St Mary's; therefore, the minister had the expectation his son would follow the family tradition.

John was a tall, slim man with red hair and blue eyes. He enjoyed University life, and although theology wasn't his first choice, he felt he owed it to his parents to continue the lineage at St Mary's.

---

[2] The author's ancestors lived in King's Walden from the 1600s

John was an active sportsman, playing in the college rugby team in winter and the first eleven in the cricket team in summer. Another interest John had was chess; he became a chess master in his second year; consequently, he was appointed team captain leading Oxford in the annual chess tournament against the traditional foe, Cambridge. Oxford won for the first time in ten years under John's leadership.

The other extra curricula activity John enjoyed was being a member of the Oxford theatre group. He had roles in a number of Shakespearean plays, including *The Merchant of Venice* where he played the role of Shylock. He also played Lady Macbeth, due to a shortage of female actors at the time.

The aspiring minister also developed a love for playing cards, in particular; five-card poker. Every Friday night a poker game was held in one of the college's student union halls. To allay suspicion, they called themselves *The Oxford Bridge Club*.

John won significantly more than he lost, and he banked his winnings in a private bank account accumulating interest over the three years at university.

After three years studying theology and coming first in his year, John completed his degree.

James and his wife Sarah were very proud of their only son, so they arranged a celebration in the church hall, inviting parishioners and a few of John's friends from the village.

August 6, 1856

Sixty villagers attended the graduation party and John, although not keen to be there, greeted everybody with believable enthusiasm.

The time came for his father to address the group. 'Welcome friends! As you all know, we are gathered here tonight to help my son John celebrate his graduation. Our family has a long history at St Mary's. Some of you would remember my father who was the minister at this church for over forty years. The Davies family has worshipped at St Mary's since the fifteenth century. It is our hope that John will become minister here in the future and carry on the Davies family tradition. May I ask you all to raise your glasses and drink to his future.'

Everyone in the hall raised their glass saluting the graduate and wished him well.

The next morning, John requested a meeting with his father in the rectory's office.

'Father I know you have high hopes that I will succeed you as minister of St Mary's in the near future. However, I have decided not to be ordained... or at least not yet.'

'I don't understand, John.'

'I'm still young, sir. I want to experience life before committing to the ministry.'

'So, what are your intentions?'

'I'm going to go to Australia, sir.'

'Australia! That's half a world away! Why Australia?'

'I believe I can make my fortune there.'

'So, money is more important than God.'

'No, not at all, I still intend to return to England and become a minister at this church. I'm just not ready for it at the moment.'

'Do you have enough savings to travel there and live until you find gainful employment?'

'Yes, I have saved a reasonable amount.'

'When do you intend to sail?'

'September 1. I've already purchased the ticket.'

James frowned. 'That's only a few weeks away. You haven't given us much notice.'

'I'm sorry, Father. I did think this over.'

'You can announce your intentions to your mother at dinner tonight.'

'Yes, sir.'

John waited until the evening meal had been consumed before raising the subject of his departure to his mother. She was also stunned by the news, and even after her son explained his reasons she was no more accepting of his plan. Nevertheless, James and Sarah knew they had no alternative but to accept that their son would be living in Australia for who knows how long before returning to England and the church.

John had saved £2000 from his poker playing over the previous three years and he felt comfortable arriving in Australia with sufficient funds.

We are Sailing to the Antipodes

Chapter 4

September 1, 1856

A beautiful carriage pulled by two jet-black horses arrived at Liverpool wharf. Inside were Lord and Lady Abernethy, their two sons, Mathew and Joseph, and daughter Rosie. The family had come to say farewell to Mathew who would be sailing on the *SS Great Britain* to Australia and a new life.

The family alighted from the carriage and the two grooms unbuckled the sea trunk from the back of the carriage and carried it to where the luggage would be loaded.

'Well, son, it's time to say farewell and safe passage. I have two things to give you as a parting gift.'

Lord Abernethy passed Mathew a beautiful oak box, in which lay two Hollis & Sheath pistols.

'I hope you have no need for them but better be safe.' He then handed over an envelope containing a bank draft for £25,000 from the Glyn Mills Bank London to be redeemed at the Union Bank of Australia.

A Glyn Mills director also sat on the board of the Union Bank. Therefore, the two banks had a strong business relationship.

Finally, Lord Abernethy gave his son another envelope, in which was £2000 cash. 'This is for spending on your journey and when you first arrive in Melbourne.'

'Thank you, Father, I won't disappoint you and Mother, I promise.'

'I know you won't Mathew. Godspeed.'

The two men shook hands. Mathew then kissed his mother and sister and shook hands with his brother. He strode up the gangplank to begin his adventure.

Another carriage arrived just as Lord and Lady Abernethy's carriage departed the dock. In it was George Griffith together with his parents and sister Jane. George's father had handed his son a bank draft for £5,000 before they left their estate that morning, and he intended to redeem it with the English, Scottish and Australian Chartered Bank in Melbourne. The young man had savings of £1,500, which he carried in a wallet on his person.

'Make the most of this opportunity, George. Go and make your fortune,' said his father. George boarded the ship with great trepidation.

John Davies was already on board the ship and he watched as George and Mathew bade farewell to their families.

John had made his farewells in Kings Walden before he boarded a coach to transport him to Liverpool; a journey that took ten hours. He was interested in meeting these two strangers, as they appeared to be about his age. He had hoped he might meet new friends on the long and arduous journey to help make the trip more tolerable.

John was shown to his cabin upon embarkation. It was small, but at least he didn't have to share like those poor blighters in second and third class.

He left the main deck once the ship had made its way out into open water and retired to his cabin. He unpacked his sea chest, placing his clothes in a chest of drawers. There was a small wardrobe where he could hang a few pieces of clothing, including his woollen overcoat.

SS Great Britain

At 7 pm John entered the ship's saloon, looking forward to a whisky before dinner. He was delighted to see one of the men he observed on the dock sitting at the bar. He approached the man, introducing himself and asking whether he could join him.

First-Class Saloon Lounge

He was received gladly by the man who said his name was Mathew.

'So, why are you immigrating to the Great Southern Land, John?' asked Mathew.

John smiled and shrugged. 'I have just completed my degree in theology. It was expected I would take over the family business from my father.'

'What do you mean?'

'My father and his father were both parish ministers at St Mary's in Kings Walden. I was next in line. I felt I needed to experience life outside the church before I settled into the ministry.'

'Well, you couldn't get more outside than Australia.'

'No, I expect you are right. What about you, Mathew? What's your motivation to immigrate to another land?'

'I come from a wealthy family. My father is a peer. I'm the younger son, so my brother inherits the title and the estate. My parents gave me the choice; immigrate or become a pauper.'

'Well, I can think of worse fates. My research tells me Australia is the land of opportunity.'

'Yes, so I believe. I suppose time will tell.'

'Would you care to join me for dinner?'

'Yes, John, I would.'

The two men finished their drinks, and then entered the elegantly decorated dining room and were shown to a table for four by the headwaiter.

First-class Dining Room

After they were settled, Mathew noticed another young man enter the room. He looked a little lost.

'We should ask that chap if he cares to join us for dinner,' he suggested.

'Yes, by all means.'

John called the waiter over and instructed him to invite the young man to join them at their table.

He accepted their invitation.

'Thank you so much; I was dreading eating alone. My name is George Griffith.'

John and Mathew introduced themselves.

'Tell me, George, why are you sailing to the antipodes?' asked John.

'To make my fortune.'

John nodded and grinned at Mathew. 'So are we all.'

The first-class passengers were always assured of fresh produce as the ship carried livestock on board. This comprised a hundred and twenty-six sheep, four lambs, thirty pigs, two bullocks and a cow. Besides these were five hundred and ten fowls, two hundred and eighty-six ducks, sixty-five geese, thirty-two turkeys, and six rabbits.

The dinner served to the three new friends included soup followed by a choice of pigeon or pork pies and a selection of various puddings, tarts and blancmange. A cheese platter was served with their coffee and port. Mathew had chosen a French Cabernet to accompany the meal. The three men all agreed the standard of dining aboard ship was excellent.

Some passengers complained of the constant animal noises emanating from down below, but they didn't complain about the fresh produce served in the dining room.

The not so fortunate were the passengers below deck in steerage they had a small galley where they would prepare their meals with food usually reserved for farm animals back home.

Mathew, George and John became good friends over the following few weeks. They dined together and quite often joined each other for breakfast and lunch depending on what activities they were involved with during the day.

George, Mathew, and John

Mathew suggested to his two friends that they indulge themselves in some clay pigeon shooting from the stern of the ship. Shooting was an activity popular with both male and female first-class passengers.

'Yes Mathew, I enjoy shooting particularly grouse and deer. However, a clay pigeon will have to do, I suppose,' said George.

'What about you John? Would you like to join us?' asked Mathew.

'Yes, why not? I wish I'd brought my shotgun with me. I prefer using my own gun.'

'You can both use one of my Purdeys if you like.'

'A Purdey, well now that's what I call a gun.'

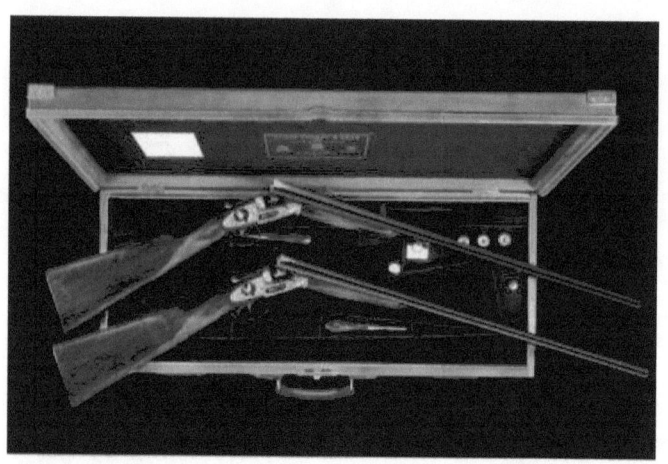

A Pair of Purdey Shot Guns

The hand-crafted Purdey shotgun equates to gun making excellence going back over two centuries. The founder, James Purdey the elder, was apprenticed as a gun maker in 1798. After joining master gunsmith Joseph Manton, he went on to forge a gun making dynasty that would surpass all others.

A Purdey 'Best' gun is a gun that cannot be bettered. No extra time or expense can bring further improvement. From the very first measurement, it is designed to perfection.

The weather was good, and the seas were calm; perfect for shooting clay pigeons.

The second officer oversaw the shoot and two of the seamen operated the traps for launching the targets.

The officer invited Mathew to be the first shooter. He called for the trap and the clay disk was hurled into the air. Mathew fired one barrel, missing the target. He called for the second and shot it out of the sky.

He passed his gun to George who missed both pigeons.

Finally, it was John the minister's son turn to try his hand. He called for the first target, hitting it instantly. He called for the second and that clay pigeon met the same fate as the first.

'Where did you learn to shoot like that?' asked Mathew.

'My father taught me.'

'I thought your father was a Church of England minister?'

'He is, that doesn't mean he can't shoot. He's a keen hunter back home in Hertfordshire.'

'Well, that's amazing.'

Each shooter had ten attempts. At the conclusion of the competition, John had successfully shot seventeen targets. His closest competitor was Mathew with twelve, and George finished with ten.

After a week of sailing, the young men were looking for things to occupy their evenings.

Mathew enrolled in several lectures on Australia and also attended a lecture on Charles Darwin's book *The Origin of the Species*. Mathew was intrigued with evolution and borrowed the book from the ship's library.

George and John joined a poker group in the saloon lounge where a total of six gamblers played poker into the wee hours every night after dinner.

Forty days into the voyage, John had increased his cash reserves to £4,500, an increase of £2,500 over and above what he brought on board at the beginning of the journey.

On the other hand, George had lost £2000, leaving him well short of what he estimated would be required to begin a new life in Australia.

George had a decision to make; he could keep on gambling in the hope he would win back the money he had lost or stop playing immediately and make do with the £3,000 reserve.

He decided his luck would change, and continued.

Storm and Tempest

Chapter 5

The *SS Great Britain* was into its 50th day of the voyage to Australia. The ship was now sailing in the Southern Ocean, known for its treacherous seas and high winds. The route taken by Captain Grey meant all going well they would arrive in Melbourne after 60 days at sea.

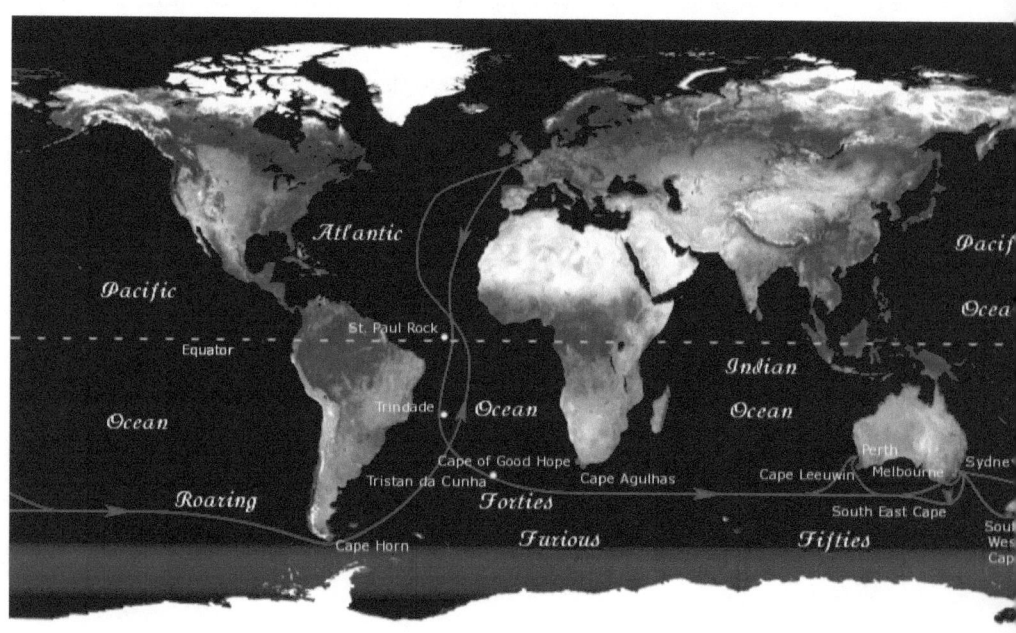

October 20, 1856

The first officer, John Crane, was on the bridge while Captain Grey was in his cabin resting. The seas halfway between the Cape of Good Hope and the West Coast of Australia were high without being menacing.

The second officer, Malcolm Turner, was responsible for monitoring the weather. He used two barometers to ensure his readings were always correct.

Ship's Metallic Barometer

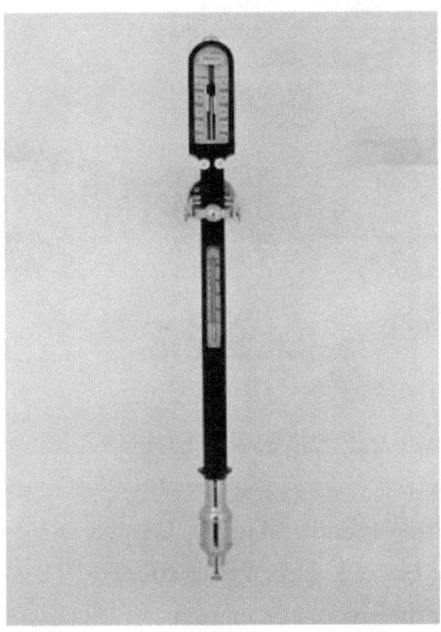

A Steel and Brass Mounted Marine Stick Barometer

He checked the barometers every hour of his shift. The last reading at 3 pm was reading fair but at 4 pm the readings indicated a sharp drop in the barometric pressure. A storm was looming. He informed the First Officer of the impending storm. Crane decided not to disturb the Captain, but ordered the second officer to make the passengers aware of the inclement weather. The first-class passengers were in a relatively safe position being on the upper decks; not so the second, third and steerage passengers. Depending on the ferocity of the storm, they could well be flooded. Latrines could be knocked over with the effluent swirling around the flooded decks.

The sky began to darken. The clouds swirled above, and seagulls could no longer be seen trailing the ship for scraps discarded by the kitchen crew. The sea began to rise, smashing into the *SS Great Britain*, rolling the largest ship afloat from starboard to port side.

The Captain was now well and truly awake, having been thrown out of his bed by a huge wave hitting the ship.

Below deck, the three friends, Mathew, George and John, were in the saloon lounge holding onto the bar rail with all their strength. They dared not try and make it to their cabins for fear they would be injured.

The second and third-class passengers plus steerage below were having a much worse time of it. Sea water was swirling around them up to their knees. Various objects were floating past, including the odd hen and duck.

The Captain and crew fought hard to keep the ship afloat throughout the storm. Morning finally broke and so did the storm. The calm seemed like a dream to all.

The crew were ordered to clean up the ship, ensuring there was no effluent or rotten foodstuffs remaining.

The pumps operated for the next twenty-four hours without reprieve, and then finally the ship was back to normal, and the passengers and crew could continue the journey in relative comfort. Not so the steerage passengers.

Steerage Passengers

Life on board returned to normal. Mathew continued to read books from the library including *Great Expectations* and *A Tale of Two Cities* by Charles Dickens. The final book he read was *Moby Dick*, by Herman Melville.

The other two continued their regime of playing poker after dinner. By journey's end, John had increased his winnings to £6,000 while George's purse had decreased to £1,500; hardly enough to begin a new life in the colony.

Charles Harmsworth at the Table

The poker player who seemed to win George's money on a regular basis was a professional gambler. He was an older man with a full beard and was quite debonair in appearance. His name was Charles Harmsworth. He claimed to be a lord, but most of the other players doubted this was true.

This man would have a significant influence on the three young men's lives in the colony.

Melbourne

This will be the place for the village
John Batman 1835

Chapter 6

Port Melbourne November 1, 1856

All passengers were on deck; even those relegated to steerage. The *SS Great Britain* was approaching the port of Melbourne, their final destination. There was an air of excitement among the passengers and crew. The voyage had taken sixty days, and they had not placed their feet on terra firma for the entire journey.

Port Melbourne 1856

Mathew, George, and John thanked the Captain and the ship's officers before disembarking down the gangplank where they waited for their luggage to be stacked on the dock.

Once all three had retrieved their sea trunks and assorted bags, they shared a horse-drawn taxi into Melbourne seeking suitable accommodation.

They chose Mac's Hotel, based on the recommendation of the driver of the taxi. It was regarded as the finest coaching hotel in Melbourne, and it also housed the gold run crews. These crews transported the gold from Ballarat and surrounding districts.

The three men decided to stay in Melbourne for the first month and then take a coach to Ballarat where they intended to settle initially.

Melbourne 1856

The discovery of gold led to a huge influx of people to Victoria, most of them arriving by sea at Port Melbourne. The town's population doubled within a year. In 1852, 75,000 people arrived in the colony and this, combined with a very high birth rate, led to rapid population growth. The concurrent dispossession of the Aboriginal tribes in country Victoria was equally rapid.

In 1853, work began on the Yan Yean Reservoir to provide water for Melbourne. Piped water started to flow in 1857. Victoria's population reached 400,000 in 1857 and 500,000 in 1860. As the alluvial gold became scarce, many of the miners moved to Melbourne or became unemployed in cities such as Ballarat and Bendigo. Significant pressure was placed on the government to make available lands in rural Victoria for small plot farming. In 1857 a Land Convention was held in Melbourne.

The accelerated population growth and the enormous wealth of the goldfields fuelled a high growth economy lasting forty years, which ushered in the era known as *Marvellous Melbourne*. The city spread eastwards and northwards over the surrounding flat grasslands, and southwards down the eastern shore of Port Phillip. Wealthy new suburbs were established. These included South Yarra, Toorak, and Kew while the working classes settled in Richmond, Collingwood and Fitzroy.

The influx of educated gold seekers from England led to rapid growth of schools, churches, learned societies, libraries and art galleries. The first telegraph line in Australia was erected between Melbourne and Williamstown in 1853. The first railway in Australia was built in Melbourne in 1854. Also, in 1854, the government offered four religious groups land on which to build schools. These included the Wesleyan Methodist Church and the Anglican Church and resulted in Wesley College and Melbourne Grammar School being built in St Kilda Road a few years later. The University of Melbourne was founded in 1855 and the State Library of Victoria in 1856. The foundation stone of Saint Patrick's Cathedral was laid in 1858 and that of Saint Paul's Cathedral in 1880. The Philosophical Institute of Victoria received a Royal Charter in 1859 and became the Royal Society of Victoria. In 1860 this Society assembled Victoria's only organised attempt at inland exploration, the Bourke and Wills expedition.

In December 1854, discontent with the licensing system on the goldfields led to the rising at the Eureka Stockade; one of only two armed rebellions in Australian history (the other being the Castle Hill convict Rebellion of 1804).

Eureka Stockade

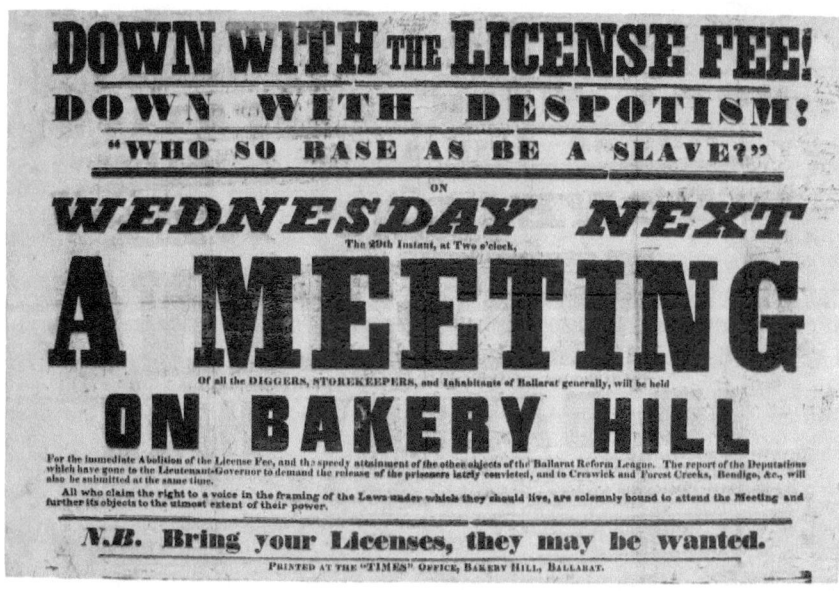

In November 1856, Victoria developed a constitution in 1857 a parliament was formed.

Parliament House was known for its magnificent architecture.

The boom fuelled by gold and wool lasted through the 1860s and '70s. Victoria suffered from an acute labour shortage despite its steady influx of migrants, and this pushed up wages until they were the highest in the world. Victoria was known as *the working man's paradise* in these years.

Melbourne November 2, 1856

The three Englishmen settled into their rooms at Macs. They ate their first meal in Melbourne at the hotel's café, where they all chose lamb cutlets with potato and vegetables.

The next day the three friends went their separate ways, agreeing to meet up again at 5 pm.

Mathew made his way to the top end of Bourke Street where he intended to investigate what hotels were available for sale in Ballarat. The offices he sought were Morgan & Davey Real Estate Agents.

He discovered their offices at 134 Bourke on the second floor. He entered the foyer where a young woman was busy filling out an official looking form. She ceased her writing and asked Mathew how she could help.

'I believe Mr Morgan is expecting me; my name is Mathew Abernethy.'

'Oh, I see. Please take a seat, Mr Abernethy. I'll inform Mr Morgan of your presence.'

Mathew only had to wait five minutes before a short, stocky man in his fifties appeared.

'Mr Abernethy, I'm pleased to meet you. I'm Horace Morgan. Please come into my office.'

The two Englishmen entered the small but tastefully decorated office and Mathew was offered a chair in front of the rosewood desk.

'Now Mr Abernethy, I believe you are interested in purchasing a hotel in Ballarat. Is that correct?'

'Please call me Mathew, and yes, I consider it would be a good investment.'

'Call me Horace,' responded his host. 'Yes, it certainly would be as long as you chose the right one.'

'Do you have any on your books at the moment, Horace?'

'I do, of varying sizes, but it does depend on how much you wish to invest.'

'I haven't a set figure in my mind. I'd rather examine what listings you have and then make a decision.'

The realtor reached for a large leather-bound book, opened it and began to show the young investor the hotels he had listed. Some were in the main street; others not. There were five in all.

One particular hotel took Mathew's attention.

The Golden Nugget Hotel

'This looks like a splendid establishment Horace why is it for sale?'

Horace responded, 'The publican has a desire to return to England as apparently his father is in poor health.'

'May I examine the books?'

'Yes, certainly I have a copy of them here.'

Mathew scanned the financials. All looked in order and the profit figures were more than acceptable.

'May I enquire the purchase price?'

'He is asking £10,000.'

'Will he consider an offer?'

'Possibly; what figure did you have in mind?'

'I have £8,500.'

'I think it would be worth me submitting your offer, Mathew. There's no guarantee he will accept it, but we can only try.'

The two men shook hands with Horace assuring Mathew he would contact him at Mac's Hotel when he received an answer from the current owner of the hotel on offer.

Mathew returned to his lodgings where he lay on his bed and imagined himself as the proud owner of the Golden Nugget Hotel. He decided not to mention his impending purchase to his two friends until contracts were exchanged.

George also headed for central Melbourne where he hoped to purchase the equipment needed to work a gold stake close to Ballarat.

He entered Wilson & Son, a large general store in Elizabeth Street. It stocked everything he thought he would need to become a successful gold miner.

He noticed a familiar face in the store but couldn't place where he had seen this man. It could have been aboard the *Great Britain,* but somehow, he didn't think so. The young man noticed George looking at him and approached the novice miner.

'Hello, George! Fancy seeing you here of all places.'

'Hello. I'm sorry, I can't remember your name.'

'It's Henry Baynes; we went to school together in Somerset.'

'Henry Baynes, my goodness of course! How are you?'

'I'm well George, but may I ask what you are doing here in Melbourne half a world away?'

'With luck, I'm here to make my fortune in the goldfields. What are you doing here?'

'The same as you, old friend.'

'I'm staying at Mac's Hotel so why don't we meet there at say 5 pm and have a drink and catch up on each other's news?'

'That sounds like a splendid idea. I'm staying quite close to you at The Royal.'

John wished to make a purchase also but not for gold mining equipment. He headed for the finest men's outfitters in Melbourne; A. G. Hodgson in Little Lonsdale Street. He desired to buy a fine English suit, which he would wear to the poker games where he sought to increase his wealth. Mr Hodgson measured John and assisted the young man in selecting the right English cloth. John was informed that the first fitting appointment would be in three days. All going well, the suit would be completed in seven.

The theology major had decided he could make more money at the high stakes poker table than breaking his back on the goldfields.

George was sitting in the saloon lounge at Mac's waiting on his old school friend Henry. At 5 pm, Henry entered the bar and approached George who was in a booth at the far end of the saloon.

'Good afternoon George, can I buy you a drink?'

'Thank you, Henry I'll have a stout please.'

'I think I'll join you.'

Henry approached the barmaid and ordered two stouts, returned to the booth with the drinks and took his seat.

'To your health George.'

'To your wealth Henry.'

'I'll drink to that.'

'So, Henry you're intending to become a miner. What makes you think you can find gold while so many others have failed?'

'I suppose there are no guarantees, but having a degree from Cambridge in geology will improve my odds somewhat.'

'I didn't realise you studied geology.'

'Yes, my initial ambition was to travel to South Africa working for a diamond company but decided gold and Australia was a better option.'

'From what I hear you've made the right choice.'

'I sincerely hope so. What about you? Why did you make the decision to immigrate here?'

'Without going into too much detail, Henry, let's just say I didn't have too many options.'

'I see. I've been thinking… why don't we become partners? I believe the whole is greater than the sum of the parts.'

'I must admit I have been thinking along the same lines.'

'We can pool our resources to purchase the right equipment, and we split the profit down the middle.'

The two old school chums shook hands and that gesture became their bond.

November 4, 1856

Mathew was in his room at Mac's when an envelope was slid under his door. He opened it and read the letter from Horace Morgan.

Dear Mathew,

My client has rejected your offer of £8,500; however, he is prepared to accept a counter offer of £9,000.

I believe this is a reasonable amount for such an excellent hotel. If you wish to submit a revised offer, I will arrange to see him immediately.

Please inform me of your intentions as soon as possible.

Yours Sincerely

Horace Morgan

Morgan & Davey Real Estate Agents

Mathew was delighted, as he was prepared to pay the full asking price of £10,000. He decided to catch a taxi from outside his hotel and visit Morgan in his office. On the way, he stopped at his bank and arranged a draft for £9,000. He arrived at Morgan & Davey at 11.30am and by 5 pm the Golden Nugget was effectively his. The settlement was arranged for December 15. The purchase included all stock and furniture, in what Morgan termed "walk in walk out."

John soon discovered that a high stakes poker game was held in room 306 of Mac's every Friday night; the room belonged to the owner of the hotel, Frank Gardener, and it was more an apartment than a hotel suite. It comprised of five rooms; a parlour, a dining room, a bathroom, and two bedrooms. The young professional gambler enquired if he could join the group. Frank, always on the lookout for fresh blood, readily agreed.

John continued his winning ways and although he had his bad nights he ended the month £2,000 better off. His wealth was now £8,000, so he was considered a wealthy young man.

George and Henry decided their quest for gold and riches would best be achieved if they dug a shaft. Alluvial gold had started to become scarce and consequently, miners turned to digging deep holes, or shafts, in the ground. These shafts would be approximately one metre squared and could be up to 50 metres deep. The miners would prop timber along the sides of the shaft to stop it from collapsing and would use a windlass or winch to bring up buckets full of soil.

George (left) & Henry Working Their Shaft

They had purchased most of their mining equipment in Melbourne, arranging it to be transported to the goldfields outside Ballarat by horse and dray.

Henry decided to register their claim close to a major mining operation where the geology seemed right, and the two novice miners began the long and arduous task of digging the shaft. Every six feet they placed wooden boards around the walls to ensure there were no cave-ins.

After two months digging, they had reached the required depth, forty feet. They took turns on being lowered down the shaft, digging the rock, while the other winched up the bucket. When they had removed a suitable amount of rock and dirt, they would wash the soil in the cradle, extracting any gold they found.

For the first three months, they found enough gold to encourage them to keep going but not enough to make them rich.

March 1, 1857

George was on winching duty one day when Henry shouted out to winch up the bucket. George complied with the request. God knows how many he had raised that day. As he tossed the rock onto the pile to be washed later in the day, he noticed a particular rock that seemed to gleam in the sun.

That rock has got some gold in it, he thought.

He decided to wash it immediately and as he scrubbed the sizable rock, the mud and dirt disappeared, exposing a solid nugget. He estimated the weight as around a thousand ounces. They were rich, filthy rich.

He called casually, 'Henry, I suggest you come up. I've got something interesting to show you.'

'Can't it wait, George? I think I might have found a new seam.'

George didn't want to bring attention to himself in case the miners close by may get wind of their find, so he replied, 'All right, whenever you're ready.'

George wrapped the nugget in an old blanket and placed it next to an old gum tree. He found it extremely difficult not to yell *EUREKA*.

Eventually, Henry yelled out to George to bring him up. Once he was back up, George grabbed his arm and led him to where he had hidden the nugget.

'Henry, I want you to promise me not to yell when I show you what's hidden under the blanket.'

'Why George; have you got a body under there?'

George slowly pulled the blanket back, exposing some of the nugget.

'Bloody hell – how big is the bugger?'

'It's huge; maybe 1,000 ounces.'

'George we're rich. Bloody rich.'

'We have to sneak this thing back to Ballarat without anybody noticing. If word gets out, we could be in real danger.'

'You're right; we'll have to move it in the dead of night.'

'I don't think we can delay it; should be tonight… we can't leave it here. Besides, if we did, we would have to guard it, which would only raise suspicions.'

'So, we need to load her on our dray and take her back to Ballarat?' said Henry.

'Maybe we should take it directly to Melbourne. No one would suspect a 1000-ounce nugget to be loaded in a back of a cart and driven to Melbourne,' said George.

'You might be right. The only thing that concerns me is leaving our mine unattended for a week or so.'

'Yes, I agree, so why don't you take it to Melbourne? You being a geologist will convince the bank that we own the thing, and all is legitimate.'

'Sounds like a reasonable course of action. I need to load up some provisions for the trip and hitch up the horses. I should be able to leave about midnight.'

The two gold diggers lifted the sixty-two-pound nugget onto the dray, covered it with a clean blanket and placed provisions on top to try and disguise their precious cargo.

'Good luck Henry. Watch out for bushrangers. Send me a telegraph once you have been successful in selling it to the bank. How much do you think we'll get for her?'

'I would estimate £10,000 more or less.'

'We really are rich, aren't we?'

'We are.'

Henry said his goodbyes and began his twenty-four-hour journey to Melbourne.

The Colour Yellow

Chapter 7

China 1857

Two brothers, Zhang Wei and Wang Wei, lived with their parents and sister in a small village in Guangdong province north of Hong Kong island. The family grew vegetables on a reasonably large scale by Zhuhai standards. Zhuhai was the village they resided in, located on the magnificent Pearl River.

The last two seasons, however, had been very lean due to a drought that had affected the Sze Zap region of which Guangdong was a part.

Wang and Zhang loaded their junk with the produce they were able to grow during the previous two months. It was their intention that Wang would sail the vessel to Hong Kong where he intended to sell the vegetables at the market.

Once they had completed the task, the junk headed down the river in the direction of Hong Kong. Wang was a master sailor, so the journey presented no problem to the young Chinese man.

The trip took a day, and when he tied up at the market wharf and unloaded his produce he was fortunate enough to be able to sell his entire cargo to a wholesaler.

As was his custom when he had finished his day at the market, he would go to his favourite teahouse, the Lotus Flower, where he would not only drink fine tea but also catch up with the latest gossip and news from around the region.

On this day, Wang entered the fine establishment and as usual; it was packed with Chinese merchants plus many men from outlying areas. Once the young man had found a seat, he ordered his tea. The conversations circulating the teahouse were about a land called Australia and how it was made of gold. Wang asked a friend he knew from the market what this gold talk was all about.

'Li, do you know anything about this land of gold everybody is talking about?'

'Yes, Wang it's true! This place called Australia has a mountain of gold! People are going there from all over the world and getting rich and then returning home as rich men.'

'Is there anyone from China going?'

'There are thousands; an English ship left Hong Kong this morning bound for a place called Ballarat. It had five hundred Chinese on board.'

'How can they afford it? It must cost a lot of money.'

'There are several entrepreneurs who are lending the gold diggers their fare plus living costs when they arrive.'

'Where's the catch?'

'There's no catch, Wang. They simply take a share of the gold. It's easy.'

'Are you going to go?'

'Yes, I am. I leave in a week's time.'

'I wish you well, my friend. I'd better get back to my junk and prepare to return home.'

Wang was thinking the entire journey back about his friend Li and the thousands of his countrymen travelling to this strange place made of gold. When he arrived back in Zhuhai he pulled his brother Zhang aside and told him about Australia and the mountain of gold.

'If this is correct, Wang, maybe we should go. We would come back to China rich.'

'That's what I've been thinking, brother. We could look after our family and grow the vegetable business.'

The two brothers decided they would travel to Australia and make their fortunes. They were dubious of the loan system, deciding to fund the adventure from their savings.

The announcement was made to the family next night and although concerned, both parents agreed it was an incredible opportunity.

The two brothers sailed to Hong Kong in the junk, captained by their father Zhao. Upon arrival they said their goodbyes and watched their father as he started his journey back to his home in Zhuhai.

They purchased their tickets for £10 and boarded *The Rose of Julpha* bound for Port Phillip Bay. Their quarters were commonly known as "steerage".

Wang and Zhang found a spot where they could store their bags and claim a bed on a three-tier wooden bunk. Their conditions were superior to what the earlier migrants were forced to endure; captains eager to make the most profit from their human cargo overloaded the ships, which resulted in dangerous sailing conditions as well as unsanitary and uncomfortable living conditions for the Chinese passengers.

The government introduced the "British Passenger Act" to guarantee the safety of the passengers. The act stipulated ships could carry only one passenger for every two tonnes of weight. Other conditions included allowing the passengers to exercise on the upper decks, medical staff available to the Chinese, and providing adequate food and water.

The two brothers survived the two-month journey in relatively good condition, landing at a place called Robe in South Australia, not in Port Melbourne as they had been promised. The reason for disembarking in Robe was that the Victorian Government had set a restriction on the number of Chinese migrating to Victoria. The formula they used was one Chinese for every ten tonnes of ship's cargo.

The government also imposed a £10 per head tax on every Chinese entering any Victorian port. The ship owners advised the Chinese passengers that they could avoid the tax by landing in South Australia and taking a leisurely walk to the Victorian goldfields.

The so-called leisurely walk turned out to be a very difficult three-hundred-and-ten miles. During the first six years of the Victorian gold rush, 16,261 Chinese migrants arrived in the land of plenty to seek their fortune.

A European man offering to guide them overland to the goldfields approached Wang and Zhang. 'I can show you the way; it's near impossible to find your way without a reliable guide.'

'How much would you charge us?'

'The going rate is £10 a head.'

'That's how much it cost to sail all the way from Hong Kong.'

'Well, my little yellow friend, that's the fee. Take it or leave it.'

'I think we'll try on our own thank you.'

'Please yourself. Others have tried and died.'

A Chinese man overheard the conversation and approached the two brothers. 'Hello, my name is Lee. I have a map with instructions in Mandarin which will enable you to conduct the walk in relative safety. It marks where the water wells are along the route and the best places to camp.'

'How do we know the map is accurate?'

'I've travelled the route myself and I'm now heading back home to China.'

'Were you successful in finding gold, Lee?'

'Yes, I was. I've transferred the money back to Hong Kong. I will be very comfortable when I arrive back home.'

'How much for the map?'

'It's £1— much cheaper than the £10 a head that fellow was asking.'

Wang and Zhang agreed to buy a copy of the map, which they thought was a much better option; they handed Lee the £1.

The following day they began their epic journey. Their objective was to walk twenty miles a day carrying their provisions.

Other Chinese prospectors followed them on the trek and by the time they reached Ballarat, over a hundred fellow Chinese were part of Wang and Zhang's group.

When they arrived on the goldfields, Wang and Zhang and the other Chinese from their village worked as a team. They immediately built shelters and slept crowded together as was usual at home in Zhuhai. Teams were organised to mine, to cook and to tend vegetables. Their mining methods proved different to the Europeans' in that they seldom tackled new ground and usually avoided deep mining, as they feared that the mountain gods would be offended. Instead, they preferred to go over the ground which had been abandoned by European miners. In their haste, the Europeans were often careless as they sifted through the dirt. The Chinese were prepared to take more time, even sweeping the floors of abandoned huts, where they often found gold which earlier Europeans had missed. They soon learnt to keep quiet about this as it made many Europeans angry.

The two brothers from Zhuhai created a market garden not far from their camp and with their vast experience, they were able to not only feed their group but to sell vegetables to the diggers on the goldfields.

After six months in Ballarat, the brothers found they were making more money from their produce than from digging for gold. They erected a large tent where they established a store selling produce grown in their market garden.

'Wang, I think we should start importing Chinese herbs and medicines to supplement our green groceries. With the number of our countrymen here I'm sure we would do very well.'

'I think you're right,' agreed his brother. 'Why don't I travel into Melbourne and speak to the shipping companies? Father could order the goods from a wholesaler in Hong Kong.'

The Wei brothers imported their first shipment in January 1860. They were required to place another larger order in March. The foundation for The Chinese Emporium had been laid, and after twelve months they leased a shop in Ballarat, selling all things needed by the Chinese diggers, including hardware and clothing.

Many Chinese returned to their homeland their pockets filled with gold. This caused resentment amongst the other miners who felt Australia had been plundered.

Wang and Zhang never returned to their village of Zhuhai, however. They continued to grow the business and became two of the wealthiest Chinese citizens in Victoria.

Change of Fortune

Chapter 8

Ballarat March 7, 1857

Mathew was in his office counting the day's takings. He had been the proud owner of the Golden Nugget for five months and in that short time had increased the hotel's revenue by 25%. One of the innovations he had introduced was a high-stakes poker game. The house, i.e. Mathew, charged a 10% commission on all winnings which over the past few months had generated a significant amount. The game was held in a private apartment on the rooftop dome every Friday night. He was expecting a good result this particular night as several professional gamblers, including his good friend John, would be participating.

Friday 8 pm Golden Nugget

John Davies arrived at the Golden Nugget at 7 pm and made his way to Mathew's office to say hello to his friend.

'Hello, Mathew counting your money again I see.'

'Hello John. Yes, just about to place the day's takings in the safe.'

'I take it you're pleased with your purchase?'

'Oh yes, it's the best thing I've ever done. Would you care to join me for a wee dram before you head up for your game?'

'Yes, thank you, Mathew, BUT just a wee one. I don't want to impair my judgment tonight.'

'Do you know who's playing?'

'No. I suppose Doctor James and Robert Kelly will be present they're the regulars. I don't know why as they rarely win.'

Mathew warned, 'There's a new player joining the game. Harmsworth is his name apparently, and he has quite a reputation.'

'Charles Harmsworth? He was on our ship and he cleaned up poor George many times.'

'Well, you'd better make sure he doesn't clean you up.'

'Oh, I can handle Charles Harmsworth. He's good but not that good.'

'It's time you made your way up. I wish you well and I'll drop in, later, to see how you're going.'

'Thank you, Mathew, I'll see you in a little while.'

John climbed the red cedar stairway to the top floor and entered the suite where Dr James and Robert Kelly were already seated at the table, keen to begin the game. John greeted them both and took his place. A young waitress who had been assigned to care for them through the night asked whether he would like a drink. He declined.

Five minutes after John's entrance, another player arrived. He was unknown to the others at the table and he introduced himself as Victor Worthington. The last player arrived soon after. This was Charles Harmsworth, the professional gambler John remembered from the *S S Great Britain*.

As the first dealer, John dealt five cards to each player. His cards included a king of spades and an ace of spades. He kept those two cards and threw out the remaining three. His next three included a king. It wasn't a strong hand, but a pair of kings could win the hand.

Dr James, Harmsworth, and Worthington folded, leaving Robert Kelly and John to play out the hand. John bet £5, Kelly raised him £5 and John saw him. Kelly had a pair of queens; first blood to John.

The following ten hands were evenly matched, and all players were about even for the night.

Charles Harmsworth was the next player to deal a hand. John looked at his cards and saw he had Q♥ J♥ 10♥ 5♠ 4♠. He threw out the spades and called for two more cards. Harmsworth dealt the cards without taking his eyes off John, hoping to see a reaction. John looked at his cards and found 9♥ 8♥. He had a queen high straight flush, which was almost unbeatable. John knew he didn't have enough money in front of him to make the appropriate bet. Mathew had entered the suite a few minutes before the hand was dealt to see how the game was progressing. John called him over and requested a £5000 guarantee. Mathew knew his friend had sufficient funds in the bank to honour the debt.

John bet £1000, Harmsworth saw him and raised John £1000. John saw him and raised Harmsworth £1000 until eventually the stake was £5000; a small fortune. Harmsworth finally said, 'I'll see you.'

John laid out his cards for all to see, a straight flush. He was preparing to scoop the cash in the middle of the table. Harmsworth just stared at the cards, not saying a word. Eventually, he looked at John and said, 'That's a great hand John.' He laid out his own cards. A♦ K♦ Q♦ J♦ 10♦ and added, 'However, it's not good enough to beat a royal flush.'

John was stunned. He had just lost £5,000 in one fell swoop.

The game was over, and the players dispersed, leaving only John and Mathew.

'I can't believe the odds of a straight flush and a royal flush in one hand. It's almost impossible,' lamented John.

'Maybe it is impossible without cheating.'

'What do you mean, Mathew? Do you think he cheated?'

'I'm pretty sure he did. I believe he had cards up his sleeve. I also think that Worthington fellow was part of the ploy.'

'Why didn't you say something at the time?'

'If you make those types of accusations without solid proof you're likely to get shot. Come with me, John. I've got an idea.'

The two men entered Mathew's apartment and sat in the lounge room.

'Can I get you a whisky, mate?'

'Yes, please I think I need a double.'

Mathew poured two generous glasses and sat next to his good friend. 'I think I know how you can get your money back.'

'How? Steal it back?'

'That's right, we steal it back.'

John stared at him. 'Are you serious? If we get caught we'll both end up in gaol.'

'If we're smart we won't.'

'So, what are you proposing?'

'Come with me. I've got some things to show you.'

Mathew entered his bedroom and gestured to the foot of the bed where there was a large captain's trunk. He opened it and John couldn't believe what was in it. There were several long wigs, women's underwear and various items of outer clothing.

Mathew hastened to explain. 'When I purchased the hotel, it was what they call WIWO which effectively means everything in the hotel at the date of settlement stays. This trunk was one of the things included.'

'So, how does this help us get my money back without being caught by the police?'

'If we're about to become bushrangers we need to have a bloody good disguise, and if we dress up as women, they will never suspect us.'

'So, you're suggesting we dress up as girls and bail up the Cobb & Co coach that Harmsworth will be travelling on to Melbourne.'

'Yes, that's exactly what I'm proposing. Once we rob the coach, we change back, and no one will be the wiser.

'So why would you put yourself at risk for me?'

'Because I lack adventure in my life and I hate seeing you, my friend, being cheated out of your life's savings.'

'Thank you, Mathew, I appreciate it.'

'Well, I don't think we have much time to get organised. You need to find out what coach he will be on and his time and day of departure.'

John nodded. 'I'm sure I can discover his travel details.'

'I'll sort out our disguises and have two of my best horses at the ready in the stable.'

John said farewell to his friend and headed back to his cottage in Bradshaw Street to reflect on the incredible events of the evening. If he and Mathew could steal back his money his life would get back to normal; or so he thought.

John knew a fellow who worked for Cobb & Co in Sturt Street, so he walked down to the staging post the next morning and approached his friend.

'Hello Frank, are you keeping busy?'

'Always busy John. People coming and going every day.'

'That's good, mate. I have a favour to ask of you.'

'Oh yes, and what's that?'

'I am trying to contact a good friend of mine. He told me he intended to return to Melbourne, but I'm not sure if it was tonight or tomorrow.'

'What's his name?'

'Charles Harmsworth.'

'Hold on. I'll look up the passenger list.'

Frank scanned the names on the passenger list. 'Here we are, John, he's booked to leave for Melbourne at 3 pm today.'

'Thank you, Frank, much appreciated; I should be able to catch him before he leaves.'

'My pleasure, and by the way, let's have a game soon. I'd like the opportunity to win back some of the money you won from me last time we played.'

'Yes, let's organise something soon.'

John walked briskly to The Golden Nugget. 'Mathew, may I have some of your time please?'

Mathew was at the front desk checking the hotel register.

'Hello John, yes, certainly; come into my office.'

'I've discovered that Harmsworth is due to depart Ballarat by Cobb & Co coach at 3 pm.'

'Good work! We need to move quickly. Come up to my apartment. I have our disguises ready.'

The two novice bushrangers climbed the stairs to Mathew's suite. The wigs and clothes were laid out on a Chesterfield lounge.

'Try this wig, John. It needs to fit your head tightly. We don't want it falling off while we are in the middle of our dastardly deed.'

John placed the long brown wig made from human hair on his head and shook it furiously; it stayed on.

'You look rather pretty mate. Now, I've created a pair of breasts for each of us to wear.'

Mathew had two tin bowls which he had drilled holes on either side so that a thin rope could pass through and tied at the back. When a shirt was worn over them, they looked like a fine pair of breasts.

Mathew opened his safe and withdrew the wooden box with the two Hollis & Sheath pistols his father had given him. He ensured both were loaded and had sufficient ammunition for the mission.

The two men placed their disguises and weapons in a bag and headed for the stables where their steeds were waiting.

2 pm

Mathew and John had decided on a secluded part of the Melbourne Road about ten miles out of Ballarat. It was heavily wooded, which would allow them to remain out of sight until the last minute.

They arrived at the site at 4 pm estimating the coach would arrive at 5 pm. This gave them plenty of time to get into their disguises, including tin breasts and long wigs. They intended to wear hats and a bandanna as a mask. By the time they dressed, they did look like a couple of female bushrangers.

Mathew decided John had the more convincing female voice. Therefore, it would be John who would do the talking.

They sat on the old log they intended to block the coach with and waited nervously. They knew if things didn't go to plan they could be arrested or worse still, shot and killed.

'John, I think I can hear the coach. Quick, mount up and draw your pistol.'

'This is it, Mathew, good luck mate.'

'You too John.'

The Cobb & Co coach came into view and the two bushrangers rode into the middle of the road, pistols drawn.

'Stop, nobody move, or you'll be shot!' yelled John.

The coach driver pulled his horses to an abrupt halt and put his hands in the air as did the co-driver.

'Everybody out of the coach.'

Eight passengers got out including Charles Harmsworth who stood there glaring at the two female outlaws.

'You in the fancy vest, come here.'

Harmsworth slowly walked forward standing in front of the two women.

'Give me your wallet please.'

Harmsworth was surprised by the politeness of the demand. He handed the bushranger his wallet.

John handed it to Mathew, who counted the notes, £200.

'Which suitcase is yours?'

'You work it out,' he said defiantly.

Mathew fired his pistol, narrowly missing the gambler's right foot.

'Cooperate, or she'll shoot you where it hurts.'

'All right, it's the red one.'

'I should have guessed.'

Mathew grabbed the suitcase and opened it on the road, while John kept his pistol aimed at the group.

'Well, look at this, a suitcase full of £20 notes. That's an awful lot of money to be carrying around in your luggage.'

'I don't think we need any more loot than this, Betsy. Let's get out of here.'

The two bushrangers mounted their horses but before they rode off, John addressed the victims. 'You can tell everybody you were bailed up by the Banshees.'

They then rode at full gallop away from Ballarat to confuse the onlookers.

A couple of miles down the road, they stopped and hid in the bush until they saw the coach pass. They then returned to Ballarat, taking off their wigs and female attire before returning to the hotel.

Once safely in Mathew's suite, they opened the case and began the pleasant task of counting the money. The total amount was £7,467 a significant haul for their first heist. Mathew counted out £6233 and handed the bundle to John.

'So, John, you have your £5,000 Harmsworth stole plus an additional £1233 which is your share of the booty. What are you going to do with all that money?'

'My big loss last night would be known by everyone in the town by now. If I turn up to the next game with plenty of dosh, it could arouse suspicion.'

'I think you're right. John, may I make a suggestion?'

'Of course, what is it?'

'The hotel turns over a significant amount of money each week. If I hold your cash and bank it then feed it to you each week, it will alleviate any suspicions.'

'If it were anyone else I'd decline the offer, but seeing it's you, I graciously accept. Thank you, Mathew.'

'I think we've earned a whisky. What do you say, John? Or should I call you Betsy?'

'Yes, where did you get that name from?'

'I just thought the name suited you. While we're discussing names where did you get *The Banshees?*'

'Don't you like it? I just thought Banshee encapsulated a couple of female bushrangers instilling terror along the Melbourne Road.'

'Don't get me wrong... I like it. If we ever do another bail up, I think we should use it.'

John bade his fellow bushranger goodnight and returned to his cottage feeling very pleased with himself.

Trust

But Always Verify

Chapter 9

March 4, 1857

George continued working on his own for he didn't want to arouse suspicions. He could not descend into the shaft alone, so he worked on the tailings from previous digs. He did find a small amount of gold but nothing like the nugget they had uncovered.

Henry had been gone for four days. George had hoped he would have received a telegram by this time, but nothing had been received thus far.

The digger kept working for another five days and still no word from Henry. George began to worry that bushrangers had bailed his partner up. He decided to visit his good friend Mathew and ask his advice on what to do. Although he implicitly trusted his friend, he chose not to divulge to Mathew the size of nugget.

'I'm at a loss, Mathew. My partner Henry took a sizable nugget into Melbourne to sell nine days ago, and I haven't heard a word.'

'That is strange. If he'd been robbed we would have heard about it by now. I suggest you take one of my horses and ride into Melbourne and see whether you can find him.'

George decided to take Mathew's advice after his friend assured him he would have one of his employees keep an eye on his mine in his absence.

March 10, 1857

The following morning George began his two-day journey to Melbourne he arrived at 9 am 12 March he ate breakfast in a café in Bourke Street and then headed for the English, Scottish and Australian Chartered Bank where the partnership's account was held. He requested to speak with the manager Mr Simpson.

'Good morning Mr Griffith; this is an unexpected pleasure. Don't tell me you've uncovered another enormous nugget.'

'So you are aware of the nugget we discovered?'

'Why yes; of course. Your partner Mr Baynes brought it into the bank last week. It took two of my tellers to carry it.'

'What value did the bank place on it?'

'Surely, Mr Baynes would have informed you we put £10,300 on it?'

George said grimly, 'Mr Baynes has not informed me of anything. He has not communicated with me since departing Ballarat ten days ago.'

'Oh dear, would you like me to check the balance of the account?'

'Yes I would, thank you.'

The bank manager excused himself, retiring to the back office to view the ledger. He returned ashen- faced. 'Mr Griffith, I don't know what to say. The account has a nil balance.'

'It is as I expected. He's stolen the entire amount.'

'I'm sorry, Mr Griffith… if there's anything the bank can do…'

'I think you've done enough already.'

George left the bank in a daze. His big opportunity to create wealth and possibly return home to England was gone.

After walking the streets of Melbourne for a few hours trying to determine what, if anything, he could do, he decided to check the shipping reports. He made his way to Port Melbourne. Ironically the *S S Great Britain* sailed for Liverpool on March 6. He approached the shipping company and requested to view the passenger list. Surprisingly they agreed, but after scanning the list he could not find Henry Baynes. His conclusion was the bastard had used a false name, or he was still in Australia somewhere.

The following day, a dejected George departed Melbourne for Ballarat. His only hope was to find another nugget like the one Henry stole, although he knew the chances were minimal. The other conundrum he faced was finding another digger he could trust to work the shaft with him.

Once back in Ballarat, he returned the horse to the Golden Nugget stables and sought to meet with Mathew.

He found him in the manager's suite and this time he told Mathew the entire story, including the value of the stolen nugget. Mathew was flabbergasted.

George left his friend and returned to his digger's hut close to the mine to contemplate his future.

George's Hut

Mathew sent a message to John to meet him at the hotel that night at 7 pm. John obliged, and they met in Mathew's suite.

Mathew started in without preamble. 'John I've just seen George after his return from Melbourne. The poor bugger has been cleaned out by his partner.' Mathew described what had happened to their good friend and how he had been left with nothing. 'The bastard not only stole the nugget which he sold for £10,300, but he also cleared out another £2000 they had in their joint bank account.'

'What can we do to help him?' asked John.

'Are you willing to carry out a few more robberies?'

'I don't know mate. I could justify getting my money back from that card cheat, but I'm not sure I could bring myself to rob innocent people.'

'No, neither could I.'

'So, what do you mean?'

'I'm talking about the gold shipments.'

'Do you think we could handle that?'

'Sure, it's the same as robbing a stagecoach except the stakes are higher. Plus, we'll have three of us.'

'Have you discussed it with George yet?'

'No, I wanted to talk to you first. Are you in?'

'I'm in if George agrees.'

'All right, why don't I arrange dinner here tomorrow night, and we can discuss it then?'

'That sounds fine with me. What time?'

'Let's make it 7.30 pm. I'll contact George and see whether he can make it. I'll tell him 8 pm. I want him to walk in and see us both sitting at the table in our disguises.'

John smiled faintly. 'Well, that will shock him.'

Mathew walked the mile to George's cottage where he found his friend sitting in front of the fire, staring at the flames. 'Hello, George how are you feeling?'

'Not particularly good at the moment.'

'Well, I can certainly understand that. George, I'd like you to come to my place for dinner tonight. John will be joining us.'

'Thank you for the offer, Mathew, but I don't feel like socialising right now.'

'I think John and I have a solution to your problem and we'd like to discuss it with you over dinner.'

'Well,' allowed George, 'that sounds promising. I suppose I'd better come.'

'Excellent, we'll see you there at 8 pm.'

Mathew left his friend wondering about what possible solution his two friends had devised.

The Banshees were in their full female regalia when George knocked on Mathew's door.

'Come in George.'

George stared at the sight before him. 'My God, what's going on?'

'Do you think we look pretty, George?'

'Bloody hell! Pretty is not a word that springs to mind.'

Mathew laughed at his expression. 'Sit down at the table, and we'll explain what's going on.'

The two men explained why they were dressed as females and how they had robbed Harmsworth of all his wealth after he'd cheated John of £5,000.

'So, George, would you care to be the third Banshee? We will only steal the gold shipments, depriving the banks and the government of their ill-gotten gains.'

'I don't know. It sounds risky.'

'If done correctly the risk is minimised significantly.'

'Well, I suppose this is my best option to get back on top. Actually, my only option.'

'So, you are in?'

'I'm in.'

'Excellent! Well John, we'd better get out of these outfits before they bring in our dinner.'

Gold

It's there for the taking

Chapter 10

The three comrades began planning their next robbery. One lesson learnt from Mathew and John's experience of bailing up the stagecoach was they needed two guns each. This would make their appearance more intimidating and, they hoped, would deter the police from firing on them.

Mathew was able to purchase the additional weapons on the basis he needed them to protect the hotel. The pistols he chose were .31 Colt Revolvers acquired from the gun dealer; Ninnis of 82 Little Bourke Street East. He paid £15 each, a sizable sum.

George was assigned the task of observing the loading of the gold security boxes onto the coach. He discovered over a period of three weeks that the gold run was always on a Thursday departing at 3 pm. He also concluded that the weak link in the steel boxes was the Chubb padlocks.

John purchased several of the locks in Melbourne to determine how they could be broken open. He discovered that an American tomahawk would accomplish the task with relative ease. John purchased two from the local general store.

After the initial robbery, the word had spread from Ballarat to Melbourne that there were two female bushrangers calling themselves the Banshees bailing up stagecoaches along the gold route. Most of the diggers and the police were sceptical; surely, they wouldn't strike again? After all, they were women.

April 30, 1857

The three friends met in Mathew's suite to determine their preparedness for the next robbery.

They had made a list the previous meeting, and now it was time to tick off all the items.

Purchase four pistols √

Buy ammunition √

Determine how the strong boxes can be accessed √

Acquire three pack horses or mules √

Discover what day and what time coach departs Ballarat √

Fit up George for his disguise √

Determine bail-up point on the Melbourne Road √

All the points were ticked off, and they all agreed they would bail up the gold coach the following Thursday, 4 May.

May 4, 1857

The first banshee, George, rode out of town on the Melbourne Road at midday. No one paid any attention to him as he was obviously heading to Melbourne for supplies with the pack horse accompanying him. He rode for two hours until reaching the rendezvous point; a bend in the road with a large rock formation on the side giving the bushrangers significant cover.

The other advantage of this site was a large cave one mile inland where they could break open the strong boxes and distribute the gold. They would then change back to their street clothes and head back to Ballarat the following day.

The next to leave Ballarat was John who departed at 1 pm with a packhorse in tow. He arrived at the bail up point at 3 pm.

Finally, Mathew rode out at 2 pm, so all three banshees would rendezvous at 4 pm giving them ample time to get into their disguises and wait for the coach.

All were nervous, particularly Mathew. He was concerned that the coach had an escort of four police officers, making it entirely different from the first robbery.

Five pm came and went without any sign of the coach at 5.30 they were becoming concerned that it wasn't coming at all.

'Where is the bloody thing? it's way overdue,' fretted Mathew.

'Maybe there wasn't enough gold to take into Melbourne. They may have cancelled the run,' said John.

'I bloody hope not,' said George.

John held up his hand. 'Hold on, I think I hear something.'

'You're right!' George said. 'I can hear wheels on the road. Quick, pull the log across the road.'

Mathew said with suppressed excitement, 'Mount up boys; this is it.'

The coach rounded the bend then pulled up quickly to avoid the obstruction. From behind the rocks came the three Banshees wielding their Colt pistols.

'This is a bail-up! Everybody get out of the coach,' yelled John in his best female voice.

A shot was fired by one of the policemen, missing the three bushrangers. Mathew responded immediately firing a shot into the coach, wounding a policeman in the arm. The police decided enough was enough and alighted from the coach with their hands up. The Banshees confiscated their manacles and handcuffed them all to the spokes of the coach. The driver and co-driver were told to get into the cabin of the coach.

After grabbing the six strong boxes, the men tied them to the packhorses. The Banshees mounted up and shouted, 'Tell them the Banshees bailed you up.'

They then galloped off down the road, and after a mile, the bushrangers headed inland to their secret cave.

The three Banshees arrived at the cave, tied up the six horses, removed the heavy boxes from the packhorses and carried them into the cave.

'Right, John, I hope you're right about these tomahawks.'

'Only one way to find out, Mathew.'

John swung the small axe with significant force, hitting the padlock square on. It didn't break, so he swung it again and again and finally the lock sprang open. John eagerly opened the lid and stared at the contents, as did his two companions. The box was full of gold nuggets and bags of gold dust.

He handed the other tomahawk to George while he continued to open the other boxes. The two men cracked open all six in thirty minutes. Every box was the same; full of gold.

The Banshees waited until 1 am before heading back to Ballarat. They arrived at 4 am, the return journey slower due to the weight the packhorses were required to carry. They quietly stabled the horses, relieving them of their heavy load. John went ahead to ensure the way was clear, and the three men carried in one box at a time. Eventually, all six were safely stacked in Mathew's suite. When weighed the estimated value of the haul was £15,000.

'We have to be careful, boys. If we start spending this booty foolishly around town we'll bring suspicion upon ourselves. My suggestion is we use George's mine as a ploy. We'll bring the gold up from the mine in small amounts; word will get around that George has a winning shaft.'

'You never know, when we've finished our bushranging careers I might be able to sell the bloody thing for a handsome figure.'

'You wouldn't deceive an innocent miner would you, George?' said John.

'Don't forget, mate, this bloody shaft produced a sixty-two-pound nugget. It could do it again.'

'Let's hope we find another one, then we could cease putting our lives on the line,' said Mathew.

July 15, 1857

Mathew heard two Cobb & Co-drivers who had too much to drink talking in the bar about a big shipment leaving for Melbourne on July 17. He called a meeting of the Banshees in his suite that night.

'I think this might be the shipment we've been waiting for. It's been ten weeks since the last one.'

'As you know, the gold we plundered last time has been signed and accounted for by the Gold Commissioner. As far as he's concerned our gold is legitimate,' said George.

'So what you're intimating, George, is it appears the mine's gold has dried up,' suggested Mathew.

'Exactly. If we don't keep the flow of gold coming the other miners will think it's a dead shaft.'

'So we're all in agreement? We ride again in two nights' time.'

'Agreed.'

'Have we got any idea when the coach is due to depart Ballarat?' asked Mathew.

'I'll find out and report back,' said John.

'I wouldn't be surprised if it was the same old 3 pm. These fellows don't seem to be very imaginative,' said George.

John wandered down to see his friend at Cobb & Co. He hoped he would be cooperative, considering John let him win at poker the last time they played.

'Hello, Frank. How are things with you?'

'G'day John. Are you here to try and get your money back?'

'No, you won fair and square, mate.'

'What can I do for you?'

'I was hoping to catch the coach to Melbourne tomorrow.'

'You're in luck. There's one leaving at 10 am.'

'Oh, I'm afraid I won't be able to catch a morning coach. Have you got one departing in the afternoon?'

'Sorry, mate, the only afternoon coach is leaving at 3 pm tomorrow but it's closed to passengers.'

'Oh, that's a shame. I'll have to delay my trip. Thanks anyway, Frank. See you at the next game.'

'See you John, and sorry I can't help you.'

John headed for the Golden Nugget to inform Mathew of the tidings. He found him in his office. 'Busy at it I see,' he observed.

'Hello John; yes, there's always paperwork to take care of.'

'I was hoping to catch the Cobb & Co coach to Melbourne tomorrow afternoon but apparently it's not taking passengers.'

'That's a shame, mate. What time is it leaving?'

'Three pm apparently.'

'Can I shout you a beer, John?'

'Thank you, but no, I've got some things to take care of.'

John headed back to his cottage to prepare himself for the big night.

John's Cottage

The three friends arrived at Mathew's suite at 7 pm. The object of the meeting was to go over their plans for the following night.

Mathew had reconnoitred the road soon after the last hold up to discover a suitable place which would allow the Banshees cover. It was important to change their bail up locations to ensure the element of surprise. The location he chose was only an hour out of Ballarat. What the bushrangers didn't know was that the Victorian Police Commissioner, Francis O'Connor, was due to be riding in the coach with four of his finest; Edward Reilly, William Campbell, John McNally and Robert Strahan. This gold shipment would be the most valuable transported to Melbourne to date, valued by the Gold Commissioner at £25,000.

July 17, 1857

The modus operandum remained the same. George, leading a packhorse departed first at 1 pm. John left thirty minutes later and Mathew at 2 pm. They all met up at Leigh Creek where they changed into their disguises and waited for the coach to round the bend just before the bridge. A large log had been placed across the road.

At five minutes past three they saw the coach coming down the road. The driver sighted the obstruction, pulling up the four horses just in time.

The Banshees rode out in front of the coach yelling in their shrieking voices that it was a bail up.

The three female bushrangers were brandishing their pistols and demanded that the police get out of the coach with their hands up.

Constable Edward Reilly leant out the window and shot at George causing a flesh wound to his left arm. John reacted immediately, shooting Reilly, who received a mortal wound. O'Connor instructed his men to vacate the coach with their hands up for he didn't want any more casualties.

While George covered the police, Mathew and John unloaded the ten strong boxes from the roof of the coach. After securing the police to the wheels of the coach they apologised for the shooting, justifying it as self-defence.

'Rest assured you will be caught and hanged for this outrageous and brutal crime,' said the Police Commissioner.

John approached the commissioner and looked into his cold dark eyes. 'If your man hadn't tried to kill us he'd still be alive.'

The Banshees mounted their horses and led away their packhorses, which were struggling with the weight of the strong boxes, filled with gold.

They arrived at the cave an hour later and proceeded to break open the boxes. They were delighted at what they found.

Retirement

It's not at what age you retire it's when you have sufficient funds

Chapter 11

The decision was made to bury eight of the ten boxes in the cave, so it would be less conspicuous returning to town. When the first box was taken from the mine shaft and assayed, one of the Banshees would return for the next box this procedure would continue until all the gold had been legitimised by the Gold Commissioner. Mathew estimated it would take twelve months at least before all the booty had been assayed.

The Banshees resumed their street clothes, staggering their return over the next four hours. Mathew was the first to return to the hotel, carrying a strong box. He hid it in the stables until his two friends returned with the other box. They agreed to meet at the hotel the following night to discuss their plans for the future. John was quite shaken up by the shooting of the constable.

When Mathew went down to the breakfast room in the morning, the place was abuzz with talk about the robbery and how a policeman had been murdered.

The hotel proprietor agreed with his guests, condemning the vile act and suggesting that these murderous thieves should all be hanged.

The entire town of Ballarat was talking about the heinous crime including the diggers on the goldfields.

At 7 pm John and George arrived at the Golden Nugget and proceeded immediately to Mathew's suite. It was a strange atmosphere. On the one hand, they were euphoric with the amount of gold they had amassed from the robbery and on the other hand they were distressed that Reilly had been killed.

'Gentlemen we have obtained [3]£47,467 in the three bail ups we have conducted this year apart from George's flesh wound we have all come out of our adventures unscathed,' Mathew said. 'My strong recommendation is we retire, disbanding the Banshees forever more. We will naturally launder the gold through the regular

---

[3] £47,467 equates to $4,000,000 in 2016

channel, and when that exercise is completed, we get on with our normal lives; all very wealthy men.'

'I agree entirely. We quit while we are ahead,' said George.

'What about you, John? You seem very pensive,' said Mathew.

'I agree now is the time to call it quits. I'd like to donate [4]£2,500 to the widow of Constable Reilly. At least it should help her raise her two children.'

'I think we should all contribute, John. It wasn't your fault,' said Mathew.

An anonymous donation was made to Reilly's widow via the Victorian Police.

George and John continued the charade of working the mine for the next twelve months. They had become known as the most successful gold miners on the Ballarat goldfields.

One night a week, usually Friday, John would partake in a poker game at the Golden Nugget. He continued his winning ways and although he did suffer some significant losses he was well up overall.

The Golden Nugget continued to prosper with Mathew being regarded as one of Ballarat's most esteemed businessmen.

1 August 1858

Mathew was enjoying his dinner in the hotel's dining room with a young woman, Elizabeth Gallbally, who was visiting from Melbourne. She came from one of Melbourne's richest and distinguished families which had developed large cattle and sheep properties in the Gippsland area. Mathew had been introduced to Elizabeth by his good friend the Chief Magistrate of Victoria, Sir William Foster Stawell. The two men had met at a race meeting at Flemington Racecourse and later purchased a yearling filly together.

The publican heard a woman yelling in the reception area. He excused himself to determine what the fuss was all about.

'Madam, what on earth is the matter?'

'There's a woman being attacked in the room next to mine! You need to save her or I'm sure she will be murdered.'

'What room number are you in?'

'I'm in 206 and she's in 208.'

---

[4] £2,500 equates to $190,000

Mathew moved fast. 'Harry, take this lady into the saloon bar and give her a drink to calm her down. Sam, come with me.' He went to his office, opened the safe and took out his Hollis & Sheath pistols. He gave one to Sam, his senior porter. As they climbed the stairs to the second floor, they could both hear the screaming coming from room 208.

'Open the door or we'll break it down!' yelled Mathew.

There was no response.

'Sam, break down the door.'

Sam stepped back and took a flying leap at the hotel room door, hitting it hard. He was thrown back against the opposite wall. He got back up and was about to try again when Mathew stopped him. 'You'll never do it Sam I'll shoot the lock.'

Mathew aimed the pistol and fired at the lock, shattering it and leaving the door ajar. The two men raced in, pistols drawn, only to find a young woman on the bed with two babies still connected by their umbilical cords.

'My God, are you all right, madam?'

The woman gasped and tried to sit up. 'I think so… how are my babies?'

'Well, they're crying; that's a good sign.' Mathew hoped that was right.

'Can I see them, please?'

Mathew picked up one baby at a time, one boy, one girl and placed them on the young woman's chest.

'They're beautiful, thank you.'

'Sam will stay with you. I'll go and get someone that will be able to help you. What's your name?'

'Annabelle.'

'You've done very well Annabelle. I won't be long.'

Mathew went downstairs and instructed one of the waitresses to call on Doctor Higgins to come quickly to check both the mother and her babies.

The doctor arrived thirty minutes later. He examined Annabelle first and then the twins. Having satisfied himself that all three were well, he severed the cords and cleaned the babies.

'Well, young lady, where is the father?' asked Doctor Higgins.

'He died in a mining accident three months ago.'

'Oh, I am sorry to hear that. How are you going to support these children?'

'I can't. I'm going to put them up for adoption.'

'That is a shame but practical nonetheless. I can help you arrange the adoption if you like.'

'Thank you, doctor; I'd appreciate your help.'

'Why did you choose my hotel to give birth?' asked Mathew.

'I didn't have anywhere else to go. I was evicted from my cottage two weeks ago.'

'Did the landlord know you were about to give birth?'

'He did, but I was four weeks in arrears.'

'What's his name?'

'Stuart Spencer; do you know him?'

'Yes, I know him, and somehow I'm not surprised at his callousness.'

Doctor Higgins arranged for his nurse to pay a visit to Annabelle and the twins and to bath all three and dress the mother in a clean nightie. The babies were wrapped in baby blankets.

Mathew and his good friend Doctor Higgins went downstairs to partake in one of Mathew's fine malt whiskies.

'Young Annabelle informed me her intention was to give the babies up for adoption as she has no means to support them,' said the doctor.

'That's a shame. No mother would want to lose her child,' said Mathew. 'David, would it be possible for a single man to adopt a child?'

'That depends on the man and his circumstances. Why do you ask, Mathew?

'Looking at those babies and considering the lives they may have in an orphanage makes me wonder if I should adopt them.'

'Well, with your background and wealth I don't think the adoption agency would have too many objections, Mathew. Are you sure you would wish to adopt both of them?'

'No, probably not. Just the girl. I don't think I could manage with two. I would hire a full-time nanny to help take care of the child.'

'Do you want me to approach the agency?'

'Yes, if you could, David, that would be excellent.'

'Leave it with me, Mathew. I'll get back to you as soon as I know anything.'

David Higgins got back in touch with Mathew the following week.

'I have good news! Although the agency is always reluctant to adopt a child to a single parent, they are willing to make an exception in your case.'

'What do I need to do?'

'You will need to sign the adoption papers as will Annabelle. They have also asked me if you would be willing to make a donation to the orphanage the boy will be going to.'

'Yes, of course. Let me think about how much would be appropriate.'

Mathew placed an advertisement in the Ballarat Star the next day, hoping to find a suitable nanny quickly. He received ten responses and having interviewed six candidates, he chose a woman of twenty-five who had recently arrived in Australia from England. She came from Surrey, next to Kent where Mathew was born and raised. She had been a nanny to two children of the Guilford family for the previous five years and came with excellent references. Her name was Sarah Anderson and the fact she was pleasing to the eye had nothing to do with Mathew's choice.

Mathew donated £2000 to the Ballarat and District Orphanage, a non-denominational institution managed by an independent board of management. It would be here where the boy would be placed. Mathew never inquired about the boy's name. It was of no real interest to him.

The Ballarat and District Orphanage

Annabelle Huston moved to Bendigo where her family resided. She never saw her twins again. The last and only influence she had on the babies after the birth was naming them Emma and Gordon. Gordon was taken to the Ballarat and District Orphanage where he endured a life diametrically opposed to the privileged life Emma would enjoy.

A Tale of Two Orphans

Chapter 12

Where can we hide in fair weather, we orphans of the storm?
Author: Evelyn Waugh

It is health that is real wealth and not pieces of gold and silver.
Mahatma Gandhi

The Advantaged

Mathew arranged for the second bedroom in his suite to be converted into a nursery. The third became Sarah's room.

Mathew was besotted with Emma. He would visit her on his lunch break and could hardly wait for his day at the hotel to end so he could spend time with her. No longer did he drink in the bar with patrons and rarely ate in the dining room with friends.

As the little girl developed his love for her grew by the time she reached five years old she was ready for her first day at school.

February 1, 1863

'Emma, are you ready? We need to leave in five minutes?' Mathew called out.

'Do you think I look pretty in my new uniform Nanny? I want to please Daddy.'

'You look splendid, Emma. Come on, grab your school bag, and we can show Daddy how pretty you look.'

Sarah and Emma entered the parlour where Mathew was sitting on the chesterfield going over some papers.

'How do I look, Daddy?'

'Darling, you look beautiful. I like your plaits.'

'Nanny did them for me.'

'I don't know how Emma and I would cope without you, Sarah.'

The nanny smiled. 'It's my job.'

'I think it's more than just a job, Sarah.'

'You're probably right.'

Emma had been enrolled in Queens Grammar School, a newly created Anglican school servicing Ballarat and surrounding areas.

Queens Grammar School

Mathew's hotel was within walking distance of the school and they began their journey to a new life together. Mathew held Emma's right hand, Sarah, her left, as they approached the impressive building and entered the front gates. Emma had some trepidation, Mathew was full of hope, and Sarah was concerned she may soon lose her job.

There was a blackboard in the foyer directing first-year pupils to proceed to classroom 1B. When they entered the classroom, they were confronted with some boys and girls crying, begging their parents not to leave, but the majority of pupils were quietly seated at their desks.

The teacher, Miss Woods, welcomed Emma to Queens and suggested she sit next to a girl who also had her hair plaited. Her name was Jane.

The first day at school mainly comprised of Miss Woods reading *The Water Babies* by Charles Kingsley.

The class also partook in some very messy finger painting; fortunately, they were all given smocks to wear.

At 3 pm, Sarah along with the mothers of the children who waited outside the classroom to walk their children home.

'Is this your mummy?' Jane asked. 'Emma, she's pretty.'

'No, she's my nanny. I don't have a mummy.'

'How come?' asked Jane.

'My mummy died when having me.'

'Oh, that's sad.'

'My nanny makes up for it. She takes care of me.'

Mathew felt it was best to keep Emma's history a secret from her. He hadn't decided whether he would divulge the truth when she was much older.

When Emma and Sarah arrived back at the Golden Nugget Mathew was waiting for them with a surprise to announce.

'So, young lady how was your first day at school?'

'It was good thank you, Daddy.'

'Well, tell me all about it.'

'We did finger painting. Here, I brought you my painting. The teacher also read to us.'

'Did you make any new friends?'

'Yes, Jane. She's my best friend.'

'That's wonderful! Do you feel like going for a walk with me now? I've got something to show you.'

'Yes, that sounds exciting.'

'I'd like you to come with us Sarah. I'd like you to see it as well.'

'Sounds interesting, Mathew.'

The three of them walked down the main street of Ballarat and then turned into Lyons Street where Mathew stopped in front of a beautiful home.

'So, ladies, what do you think?'

'It's beautiful, Mathew,' said Sarah.

'Who lives in there, Daddy?'

'You do darling! This is our new home.'

'Really? Can we go inside?'

'Of course we can. It's our house.'

'You never cease to amaze me, Mathew,' said Sarah, shaking her head.

They all walked up the front path... well, Emma ran up the pathway.

As they approached the front door, Mathew turned to Sarah and said, 'I've decided to call the residence Abernethy House after my parents' estate in England.'

'I've heard of Abernethy Manor. Is that your family estate Mathew?'

'Yes, it's been in my family since Henry VIII's rule.'

'Again, you never cease to amaze me.'

'Come on Sarah, I'll show you through.'

The house was magnificent. It boasted a large living room and dining room and also an extensive library. There were six bedrooms including the master, plus a large kitchen with two wood-fired ovens.

'Emma, which bedroom would you like, darling?' asked her father.

'I don't care as long as it's next to yours, Daddy.'

Both Mathew and Sarah laughed.

'What about you, Sarah?'

'I don't mind as long as it's next to yours.'

They smiled at one another.

'Seriously do you have a preference?'

'Well, I think I should be close to Emma just in case she needs me through the night.'

'Right, well, that's settled! Everybody is happy with their sleeping arrangements. We move into Abernethy in two weeks' time, so we'd better all get organised.'

As they were walking back to the hotel, Sarah enquired why Mathew had decided to purchase the house.

Mathew shrugged. 'I just thought it was time Emma grew up in a normal environment. Living in a pub is hardly normal.'

The Disadvantaged

Gordon Huston, Emma's biological brother, took an entirely different path after his mother gave up the twins. Soon after birth, he was taken to the Ballarat and District Orphanage to be cared for and housed.

He received no real attention. The only time he felt the touch of another human being was when he was given his bottle at feeding time or his nappy was changed.

As he developed into a toddler, he began to experience the wrath of his carers. Beatings were not uncommon for the simplest of misdemeanours.

In winter, he slept in a cold, dank dormitory with thirty-nine other orphan boys. Ballarat had a reputation for being freezing cold in winter and stifling hot in summer and the orphanage was not designed to handle either.

At the age of five, he attended the orphanage school where he learnt to read and write at a very elementary level. The administration wasn't much interested in their charge's education as they preferred the children to work in the vegetable gardens and care for the sheep and cattle. This farming enterprise raised significant funds, which were not invested back into the running of the orphanage. The money went straight into the staff's pockets.

At night, if one of the masters heard a boy crying, he would order every boy to get out and stand at the end of his bed. He would then examine every boy's eyes to determine who the cry baby was. Once discovered, the boy would be beaten with a cane as punishment.

This was the environment Gordon suffered under. At the age of ten, he was sleeping soundly in the dorm when he felt a hand down the front of his pyjamas. He gasped, but a large hand covered his mouth.

'Shut up you little grub, or I'll make life hell for you.'

The master abused the young boy for the next thirty minutes doing unspeakable things. He then left Gordon crying into his pillow, fearing he would be beaten.

The next morning Gordon knew what he needed to do. He was not going to report the abuse as he was aware other boys had been abused for years. He needed to escape from the orphanage, never to return.

He started to formulate his escape plan and after considering the options, he decided his best chance was to make the break when he was in the sheep paddock. Once he got through the barbed wire fence he'd make his way to the railway station where he intended to sneak onto a freight wagon heading for Melbourne.

July 3, 1868

Gordon woke at 6 am as usual, dressed and headed for the sheep paddock where he was required to ensure the sheep had sufficient water for the day. He also fed the flock with fresh hay. This was part of his daily routine, but climbing through the fence and running towards Ballarat was not.

The young fugitive arrived at the station at 7 am and hid amongst the rhododendrons which lined the platform. He'd been in his hiding place for fifteen minutes when he heard the steam train approaching. The locomotive pulled into the platform, slowly blowing its whistle as it came to a stop. Gordon waited until he heard the second whistle alerting passengers it was about to depart. The young boy quickly ran to the freight wagon, slid the heavy door opened and jumped inside just as the train was moving off.

He hid behind two bales of wool, and the gentle rocking of the carriage put him to sleep. He woke to the sound of voices. Railway employees were unloading the cargo at Spencer Street Station, Melbourne. Gordon knew he would need to make a fast exit, so he jumped up and ran for his life. Despite the demands to stop, he just kept running through the exit, past the ticket inspector and out into the street. As he ran through the streets of Melbourne a feeling of freedom overtook him; nobody knew who he was or where he came from. He was anonymous, and he was free.

Gordon had saved some money from the paltry allowance he had been paid for his work at the orphanage, but it was not enough to live on. His next challenge was to survive on the streets.

Gordon would join the hundreds of street kids nicknamed "Street Arabs" who roamed the inner city of Melbourne. These kids used their cunning to prey on unsuspecting adults, stealing money and food, enabling them to survive and in a few cases, thrive.

The young fugitive from Ballarat was inducted into a gang of forty boys and girls calling themselves "The Melbourne Gang" who he met while sleeping in the Botanical Gardens.

They used all their cunning in robbing from the more fortunate including dropping a gold ring, which was previously stolen at the foot of an unsuspecting victim. One of the gang members would point to the ring, suggesting it had been dropped by the gentleman or lady. When the victim denied the ring was theirs the street urchin would insist they keep it. Once it was accepted, the street kid asked for money and usually an argument would erupt. During the fracas, another gang member would pick the gentleman's pocket or steal the lady's handbag and run off.

A more common but unsophisticated scam was begging in the street. The gang usually seconded the youngest boys and girls to perform this task.

The older boys tended to work in pairs. One would distract the victim while the other pickpocketed the gentleman's wallet.

All in all, the gang made enough to survive. They slept in the Botanical Gardens, finding shelter in the rotundas that were located around the gardens.

Gordon was happy for he no longer was beaten or sexually abused and kept company with kids that came from similar backgrounds.

Gordon

General George

Chapter 13

England is a Nation of Shopkeepers
Napoleon Bonaparte

August 1860

George and John had exhausted the gold from the shaft and the Banshees had been successful in laundering all the stolen gold through the mine. It was now time to close it down, though it had earned the reputation as the most lucrative gold mine on the Victorian goldfields. As soon as they walked away, there was a rush to secure a claim from expectant diggers.

George had decided to use his share of the loot to open a large general store on the main street of Ballarat, Lydiard Street.

Lydiard Street Ballarat 1860

He simply called it "Georges". It was a triple fronted two-storey store, stocking everything from miner's supplies to women and men's clothing, kitchen equipment and furniture. From the beginning, George ensured the business lived up to its motto of *Quod facimus, Valde facimus* (What we do, We do well)

Georges became the place to shop in Ballarat. It was profitable from year one.

After the fourth year of operation, George decided to open another store this time in Melbourne. He leased a beautiful building in Collins Street right in the middle of the "top end of town".

Georges Department Store

George had gone from being a gold miner left penniless by his crooked partner to high society retail magnate. His social status in Melbourne society was at an all-time high and the young society women showed significant interest in this confirmed bachelor.

One young lady, Mary Branson, caught George's attention. She was a beautiful redhead with steel blue eyes and alabaster skin. She had been well schooled at Queens Girls Grammar and could hold an interesting conversation.

George decided if he was ever to marry, this was the woman he would commit his life to.

The Governor's Ball was to be held at Government House on December 1, 1868. George was delighted to receive an invitation. He wrote a letter to Mary and got his butler to hand deliver it to her residence in Toorak where she lived with her parents and younger brother Arthur.

Mary's mother Anne answered the door and took the letter. The butler waited for an answer.

Anne called, 'Mary, come downstairs dear! There's a letter for you, hand delivered I'll have you know.'

'Who from, Mother?' Mary called back.

'I don't know. You'll have to open it and see.'

The young beauty descended the stairs and took the letter from her mother. She opened it while the butler and Anne looked on.

November 1, 1868

My Dear Mary,

I would be honoured if you accompanied me to The Governor's Ball on the night of December 1.

Could I ask you to either accept or reject my invitation by writing your answer on this card.

My butler will return it to me.

Yours Sincerely

George Griffith

Mary asked for a pen and wrote:

I would be delighted to partner you to the ball, George.

Thank you

Mary

Mary handed the envelope to George's butler who bowed his head and departed.

She described to her mother the contents of the letter, rather excited as George was one of the most eligible and richest bachelors in Melbourne.

December 1, 1868

Mary was almost ready when George's carriage pulled up outside the Branson home in St Georges Road Toorak. He was asked by the maid to wait in the foyer of the magnificent house. Mary's father entered and introduced himself as Sir Frederick

Branson. As it happened, Sir Frederick was being quite informal as he could have introduced himself as Chief Magistrate.

'So, I believe you're a shopkeeper, George?'

'Yes, sir I suppose I am.' George mentioned his store and its address.

'I've been inside your establishment. Very impressive I must say. How's business?'

'Beyond all my expectations sir, as is the Ballarat Emporium.'

'Oh, so you have two shops?'

'Yes, sir, I began in Ballarat, and after four years of profitable trading, I decided to open the Collins Street store.'

'Excellent. Well here she is, looking as splendid as ever.'

Mary glided into the foyer as though she was on ice. Her hair was arranged up with a diamond tiara and she looked beautiful in her emerald green ball gown. George was so totally captivated the only word he could utter was 'hello'.

'You two have a very enjoyable time if you get to meet the governor, say hello from me,' said Mary's father.

The handsome young couple walked down the front steps and into their waiting carriage for the short trip to Government House.

Once seated in the carriage, George began to relax and conversed freely with the red headed beauty. The carriage made its way down the long gravel driveway, pulling up outside the impressive building. Two footmen assisted them out of the carriage and they were ushered into the Grand Ballroom where other distinguished guests were present drinking champagne and talking among themselves.

Soon after they arrived and were offered a glass of champagne, the governor, John Henry Thomas Manners-Sutton, 3rd Viscount Canterbury GCMG KCB, together with his wife Georgiana entered the room. Once they were announced, they began to mingle with their guests.

John Henry Thomas Manners-Sutton

Eventually, the Governor and his wife approached George and Mary and began a conversation.

'I must say you are a handsome looking couple. May I inquire of your names?' said the Governor's wife, Georgiana.

George introduced Mary and himself.

'So, Mary, your father is the Chief Justice. I know him well but had no idea he had such a beautiful daughter,' said the Governor.

'You flatter me, Your Excellency.'

'And George, it is George isn't it?'

'Yes, Your Excellency.'

'George, what do you do?'

'I'm a retailer, sir; I own Georges in Collin Street.'

'Then I congratulate you as it is a fine establishment. My wife and I have both shopped there. Incognito of course.'

The Governor and his wife moved onto the next couple leaving Mary and George quite pleased with the conversation they had with their illustrious hosts.

It was a lovely night. George and Mary danced as though they had been dance partners for years. It was a natural connection, not only on the dance floor but also in their conversations throughout the evening.

The night came to an end when George's driver drove the couple back to Mary's home. He got out of the carriage and opened the door for her. When they reached the top of the steps, George asked for permission to kiss Mary goodnight. She agreed.

George was in a euphoric mood upon returning to his luxurious apartment on the top floor of his department store in Collins Street.

By the time he entered his bedroom he had decided that he would do all in his power to make Mary his wife.

God Help Me

Chapter 14

John continued to gamble despite the money he had accumulated with the Banshees. He enjoyed the challenge and the cunning required to be a successful poker player.

Mathew had opened another hotel in Ballarat called the Duke of Wellington. It was even more salubrious than the Golden Nugget. It was here where John used his poker skills every Friday night.

September 23, 1865

John was in his bedroom dressing for the card game. He had acquired a reputation of being one of the best-dressed gentlemen in Ballarat. He had purchased a home not far from Mathew's. It was not as luxurious as his close friend's, but it was regarded as one of the better homes in the city.

King's Walden

He named it after the village in England where he was born.

The Duke of Wellington was within walking distance from his home but he always arrived by carriage due to the amount of money he needed to bring to the game.

John made his way to the poker room on the top storey, calling into the hotel office to greet Mathew on his way. Mathew would always inform his friend who would be joining him in the game.

'Good evening, Mathew. I trust you are well?'

'Absolutely John, and you?'

'Splendid. How's Emma?'

'She's well—enjoying school and doing quite well. She's now having piano lessons and apparently is showing great promise according to her music teacher.'

'Excellent! Did you purchase the instrument in Melbourne?'

'No, I bought it from Suttons Music here in Ballarat. They're as good as any music store in Melbourne.'

'Well done.'

'Who do we have playing tonight?'

'The usual group plus one.'

'I see and who would that be?'

'Police Commissioner, Francis O'Connor.'

John stared at him, his usually urbane expression slipping. 'You're kidding.'

'Don't worry, John. There's no way he can recognise you. The last time you met you were dressed as a woman with a mask over your face. Not only that, but you spoke with a high voice.'

'I suppose you're right, although I still think I'll be nervous.'

'You've never missed a game and if you decided to pull out now it would bring suspicion upon you. Just act normally, and you'll be fine.'

'You're right. Wish me luck. I'm not going to let the bastard win.'

John made his way up to the game where the other players, including the Police Commissioner, were already sitting at the table.

'I'm sorry gents, I got held up,' said John, not missing the irony of his words.

'John, we have a new player; Francis O'Connor,' said Robert Kelly.

John nodded to the Commissioner. 'I'm pleased to meet you, Francis.'

'Have we met before, John?'

'No, I don't think so.'

'I never forget a face or a person's eyes, and your eyes seem familiar to me.'

'Hmm.' John pretended to consider. 'What is your occupation, Francis?'

'I'm the Police Commissioner.'

'Are you? Well, I'm sure we have never met. I'd remember if we had.'

'May I suggest we begin, gentlemen?' said Dr James.

The game lasted two hours and, as usual, John was the biggest winner. The Police Commissioner came a close second with Dr James being the big loser.

As all the players departed Francis pulled John aside. 'I know I've met you before, John and it will only be a matter of time before I remember under what circumstances. I hope for your sake it wasn't a police matter.'

'I can assure you, Francis, we have never met. Now if you'll excuse me, I must go.'

John descended the stairs to the ground floor, seeking Mathew's council.

'Mathew, the bastard recognised my eyes.'

'What do you mean, *recognised your eyes?*'

'He told me he never forgets a felon's eyes.'

'Did he say *felon?*'

'Well, no, but he intimated that he was on my case.'

'Don't worry, John, he can't prove a thing so just go home as though nothing happened.'

Back in his own house, John poured himself a generous whisky. He sat down in front of the fire in his living room and the memories of the bail up where he shot the policeman came flooding back. He had never got over the fact he killed another human being. The more he tried to justify the shooting, the more depressed he became.

John didn't sleep well that night, and by the time the sun rose next day he'd made his decision. He would be ordained a minister and devote the remainder of his life to caring for orphans and street children.

John wrote a letter to Charles Perry, the Anglican Archbishop of Melbourne, requesting he be ordained. After three weeks, he received a letter back inviting him to join the Church and be ordained at the next ordination ceremony in Melbourne to be held in February 1866 at Saint Paul's Cathedral.

John invited his two closest friends to dinner at King's Walden to announce his decision and, he hoped, receive their blessing.

Mathew and George arrived together as George was staying at the Duke of Wellington having travelled from Melbourne that afternoon. They all exchanged the usual pleasantries before dinner enjoying one of John's fine sherries.

After the main course of Beef Wellington and before to the dessert of plum pudding the host raised the subject of his pending ordination.

'Well, John, you have obviously given it a lot of thought,' said Mathew.

'You're right Mathew, I have. I've decided it's time to give something back to the community.'

'I thought your plan was to return to England and become the Minister at St Mary's? To carry on the family tradition as it were?' said George.

'You're right, George; that was my original intent, but an enormous amount has happened since I landed at the dock in Port Melbourne all those years ago.'

'You feel you will be content being a minister in a small parish initially?'

'No, Mathew that's not what I intend. I'm going to convert King's Walden into a home for homeless boys and girls.'

Mathew frowned. 'But there's already the Ballarat and District Orphanage looking after the orphans of the district so why would there be a need for an additional home?

'My home will be different; it will be much smaller, obviously. My objective is to house ten boys and ten girls. I have visited the orphanage many times and my perceptions are they are more interested in working the children rather than educating them. I also believe there is a certain amount of abuse taking place. My objective will be to ensure their education is paramount as well as grooming them to be good citizens.'

'Your cause is noble John, but you have no experience. How do you know your methods will be effective?' asked George.

'That's an excellent point, George. I intend to start slowly. I'm going to Melbourne next week and select a street child, a boy, and bring him back to Ballarat to test my theory.'

'Why not a boy from here?' asked Mathew.

'I want him away from the environment he knows. If he feels he can easily return to the streets he may do so without hesitation. In Ballarat, he has more of an incentive to improve his lot.'

Mathew nodded, agreeing. 'Well I know I speak for George also John, and we wish you well and if there is anything we can do to assist you, please let us know.'

'Thank you, I may well call on you both for assistance.'

Melbourne March 1865

John had been ordained as a minister the previous month. Charles Perry, the Anglican Archbishop of Melbourne, had given him the church's blessing to open a refuge for homeless children in Ballarat.

He was now walking the streets of Melbourne at night looking for a suitable candidate to be the first homeless child to be housed at King's Walden.

He had to admit to himself that every homeless boy could easily be the one. They all looked filthy, dressed in rags and had sorrowful looks on their faces.

In Spring Street, at the top end of Collins Street he found a boy he thought might be suitable. 'Hello, lad what's your name?'

The young boy looked at John and said nothing, turning his head away.

John tried again. 'My name is John. I'm a Church of England Minister and I'd like to be able to help you.'

The boy looked up and met John's eyes. 'How?'

'I have a beautiful home in Ballarat. I'd like you to come home with me, and I'll care for you.'

'I was born in Ballarat and I don't want to go back.'

'Were you living at the orphanage?'

'That stinking place? Yeah I was there, but I escaped. I'd rather live on the streets than return to that shit hole.'

'Well I can assure you King's Walden is nothing like the orphanage and I can guarantee you an education and a much better way of life.'

'Why would you want to do that for me? You don't even know me.'

'It's part of the promise I made God.'

'There's something else I don't believe in. If there were a God he wouldn't let adults hurt children, would he?'

'Did that happen to you at the orphanage?'

'Yeah, that's why I escaped.'

'What's your name?'

'None of your bloody business! Now if you don't mind, piss off. You're stopping me from begging, and I need the money to buy some food.'

'I'll go if you insist, but I may not be back. Think about what I've offered you, an education so you can make something of yourself, clean clothes and a safe, warm place to live.'

'Hold on, when would you want me to go with you?'

'You can come with me now if you like.'

'I'd want to say goodbye to the other kids, so how about tomorrow?'

'Tomorrow is fine. Why don't I meet you here at midday?'

'Right, midday it is.'

'I still don't know your name.'

'My name is Gordon.'

'Right, I'll see you tomorrow, Gordon.'

John walked away full of hope for the young boy.

As arranged, he returned the following day, but Gordon was nowhere to be seen. John waited for an hour but the boy didn't turn up.

Dejected, John began to walk away but just then, Gordon appeared out of a cobblestone laneway.

'You looking for me?'

'Gordon, I thought we had an agreement to meet at midday.'

'Sorry, I couldn't make it. I had some things to take care of.'

'Gordon, in the future I expect you to keep your promises, is that clear?'

'I said I was sorry. If you're going to come down hard on me for every silly little thing then maybe we should forget it.'

John shrugged. 'Let's forget it then. There are plenty of other boys.'

'No wait, I'm sorry, I really am, it's just that one of the kids I run with got beaten up last night, and I tried to get a doctor to help him.'

'Were you able to find a doctor?'

'Yeah, but we all had to pool our money to pay the bastard before he'd look at him.'

'Sounds like a nice caring doctor.'

'That's what it's like living on the street.'

'Not any more, Gordon. Come on, we've got a Cobb & Co coach to catch. Before we can do that, we need to get you cleaned up and buy some new clothes and a pair of shoes.'

Back to Old Blighty

Chapter 15

Ballarat
September 1,1868

Mathew was enjoying his new life in Australia, particularly living in Ballarat. He had prospered and was regarded as one of the most esteemed citizens in the community.

Two experienced hotel managers, Mr Andrew Phillips and Mr Samuel Jones, now managed the two hotels, the Golden Nugget and the Duke of Wellington. This allowed Mathew time to pursue other interests including racing a stable of horses. One of his steeds, Shenandoah, came third in the 1868 Melbourne Cup and the horse owner's ambition was to win the prestigious race.

Mathew had been considering returning to England, not to live but to visit his family. It had been twelve years since he departed England for a new life in the colony.

He made inquiries and discovered the *SS Great Britain* was embarking on its final journey to England on October 8 that year. He booked three tickets First Class for Sarah, Emma, and himself. His return journey on the *Flying Cloud* was booked for May 1, 1889.

Over dinner that night Mathew announced to Sarah and Emma that they would all be sailing to England for an extended holiday. They were both elated, particularly Sarah who would take the opportunity to visit her parents and siblings in Surrey; something she thought she would never have the opportunity to do.

October 8, 1868

The trio arrived at the train station ready to take the three-hour journey to Melbourne where they would board the *SS Great Britain* to Liverpool, a journey expected to take sixty days weather permitting.

Sarah and Emma shared a double cabin while Mathew occupied the cabin opposite.

Once the voyage was underway the three passengers from Ballarat fell into a routine. In the mornings after breakfast, Sarah would tutor Emma until lunch. In the afternoon the schoolgirl had free time to pursue other interests such as playing badminton with other children whose parents were travelling first class. She also loved spotting whales and dolphins gliding through the ocean.

Sarah spent her free time sewing needlepoint while Mathew spent time reading books from the ship's library including *Crime and Punishment* by Fyodor Dostoyevsky and *Les Misérables* by Victor Hugo. He could relate to both novels.

They were fortunate with the weather; the ship did not encounter any fierce storms like the one Mathew endured on his trip out to Australia. It was rough rounding the Cape of Good Hope and consequently Emma suffered seasickness, but overall the journey was a smooth one.

December 2, 1868
Liverpool

Many small boats came out to greet the *SS Great Britain* as it was her final voyage. The grand ship looked majestic as she neared the Liverpool wharf.

Mathew stood at the handrail looking over the sea of people, trying to find his family but to no avail. He and the two young women made their way down the gangplank and politely pushed through the crowd. At last, they could see the black highly polished carriage with Mathew's father standing beside two white horses.

Mathew held Emma's hand while striding over to greet his father. Sarah stayed back as was her station.

'Hello, Father, you look well,' said Mathew, shaking his father's hand.

'As do you, Mathew, the colony has treated you well.'

'I would like you to meet your granddaughter, Emma.'

'Hello, Emma welcome to England.'

'Thank you, sir.'

'I think you should call me Grandfather, don't you?'

'That would be nice.'

'Excellent then, Grandfather it is.'

Mathew looked about. 'Where are Mother, Joseph and Rosie?'

'Your mother is at home. As soon as we can collect your luggage we can be on our way, and you can see her.'

'I'll go and chase it up. I'll get Sarah to help me.'

'Who's Sarah? Not a wife we know nothing about?'

'No, she's Emma's nanny and teacher.'

'Oh, I see.'

Mathew found their luggage and organised a porter to carry the bags to the carriage where the driver fastened them on top of the horse drawn vehicle.

The journey to Abernethy Manor in Kent would take four hours by train and the carriage headed for the Liverpool railway station.

Lord Abernethy had arranged for another carriage to meet them at Gillingham Station to take them to the manor. The journey from the station to Abernethy Manor took thirty minutes.

As the carriage wound its way through the extensive grounds with deer grazing, Emma was astounded. She had never seen deer before. There were plenty of kangaroos and wombats but no deer.

Lady Abernethy waited under the classic portico waiting to greet her son and his daughter. She was excited on the one hand but sad on the other.

Mathew and Emma alighted from the vehicle and he hugged his mother, kissing her on both cheeks.

'Hello, Mother it's so good to see you.'

'Hello, Mathew darling, it's wonderful to see you after all this time. And who's this beautiful young girl?'

'Mother, this is my daughter Emma, your grandchild.'

'Hello, Emma, welcome to Abernethy. I'm sure you will enjoy your stay.'

'Hello, pleased to meet you.'

The family entered the magnificent home where servants had prepared an afternoon tea. It was served in the conservatory.

'May I inquire where Joseph and Rosie are?' Mathew ventured.

'Rosie will be joining us shortly. She's out riding.'

'How about Joseph?'

'I'm afraid he won't be joining us today,' said Lord Abernethy.

'Oh, is he away?' Mathew was disappointed.

His father said briefly, 'Yes. I'll tell you more about it later.'

Lady Abernethy broke in, 'You must be all exhausted. Why don't I get James to show you to your rooms?'

'Thank you, Mother. You're right, I think we could all do with a rest.'

James the butler showed Mathew to his old room and Emma and Sarah to theirs, close by.

Mathew was lying on his bed his eyes closed when there was a knock on the door. It was his father.

'Sorry to disturb you, son, but I need to talk to you.'

Mathew sat up. 'Come in Father. Is there anything wrong? You look grave.'

'I'm afraid I have some very sad news, Mathew. Your brother Joseph has passed away.'

'No, when, how? Oh my God!'

'He took over from you as Master of Hounds and kept that position up to three weeks ago when he had a fatal accident while on a hunt.'

'I don't know what to say... I'm devastated.'

'We have organised a memorial service for this Friday. We held his funeral a week after his passing as there was no way to wait for your arrival. He now lies in the family mausoleum on the grounds.'

'I can only try and imagine how you and Mother feel.'

'I'm afraid I am also obligated to raise the subject of your inheritance. You will now inherit my title and the Abernethy estate.'

'Thank you, Father, but I'd rather not think about that at this moment.'

'I understand. Why don't you rest for a while? I'll have you called for dinner later on.'

'Thank you, sir. I need some time to myself to reflect on what you have told me.'

Mathew had mixed feelings about the news. On the one hand, he was grieving for his brother, but on the other, he was thinking about becoming Lord Abernethy and all that came with the title. He was deep in thought when he heard a knock on his bedroom door. He assumed it was the call to dinner but in fact, it was Emma, his daughter.

'Hello, Daddy, can I come in?'

'Yes, of course, you can darling.'

'Has something terrible happened?'

'Why do you ask, sweetheart?'

'I went downstairs earlier, and I heard Grandma crying.'

'Yes, something terrible has happened Emma. While we were on our way here, your Uncle Joseph had an accident, and he died.'

'I didn't even get to meet him.'

'No. I'm sorry about that.' Mathew hugged his daughter, consoling her. Even though she had never met Joseph she could feel her father's pain.

Together they went downstairs to join the family for dinner. Sarah joined them. Although strictly speaking she was hired help and would normally join the servants in the kitchen, Mathew and Emma regarded the nanny as part of their family and she therefore always ate with them.

Rosie, Mathew's sister, was standing next to the fire when Mathew, Emma and Sarah entered the magnificent dining room. She walked quickly to Mathew and hugged him until he thought she would never let go.

'Mathew, it's wonderful to see you after all these years. You look in very good health. Are you indeed well?'

'I am, Rosie, although very much saddened by the news of Joseph's passing.'

'We all are. He was a very good man and a loving, caring brother.'

'May I suggest we all be seated? Dinner is about to be served,' said Julia Abernethy.

The family took their places with Samuel at one end and Julia at the other. The place where Joseph would normally sit was vacant. The symbolism was not lost on the other members of the family.

James, the butler, carried in the roast pork and proceeded to carve it, while Lucy, one of the family's servants, served the vegetables. Once all the family members had been served their meals, James offered wine to all except young Emma who was given apple juice.

'I would like to propose a toast to Joseph,' said Lord Abernethy.

'Hear! Hear!' was the unified reply.

Over dinner, there were many questions about life in Australia. Mathew was enthusiastic in his response, praising the young country. Emma enthused about the wildlife, including kangaroos and wallabies.

'Mathew, we have decided to conduct a fox hunt in Joseph's memory on Friday week. Would you be interested in acting as Master of Hounds?'

'I would be honoured, Father although it's been many years since I had that role.'

'You'll have no difficulty. Have you done much horse riding in Australia?'

'Indeed I have.'

'Excellent, then that's decided.'

Mathew turned to the nanny. 'Sarah, would you care to join us?'

'It sounds very exciting! Yes, I'd be pleased to join the hunt.'

'Can I go Daddy?'

'I'm sorry Emma. You're too young.'

'Well, that's hardly fair.'

'Don't worry Emma, you'll grow up quickly enough,' said her father.

December 12

The memorial service was held in the manor's gardens overlooking the family mausoleum. Over two hundred people from London, and the village, Charing, and surrounding areas, attended.

After the service a wake was held in the grand ballroom, and it was a memorable event.

The following days were spent riding the horses from the Abernethy stables around the two thousand acres belonging to the estate. Mathew, Emma and Sarah were all accomplished riders and enjoyed the estate's trails. The foxhunt would be conducted on these grounds but would avoid the place where Joseph met his demise.

December 16
The Foxhunt

The unspeakable chasing the uneatable
Oscar Wilde

Mathew was nervous about replacing Joseph as Master of Hounds. It was a role his brother had performed skilfully over the past twelve years since replacing Mathew when he was dispatched to Australia

At 11 a.m. a hundred and twenty riders assembled, including Rosie Abernethy and Sarah. Accompanying them were over forty hounds.

Mathew, being the new Master of Hounds, was in charge of the hunt; supervising the field, the hounds, and staff. The huntsmen, who had bred the hounds and worked with them, took charge of the pack during the hunt.

When Mathew was satisfied all was in order, he instructed the huntsmen to lead the pack of hounds out over the estate's meadows with the intention to flush out a fox.

When a fox was flushed out into the open, the group would pursue their quarry, with the huntsman leading the group. The field would follow at a gallop and watch the hounds chase down the fox. When the animal was cornered, the hounds took over.

Once again, the fox eluded the hunters, the riders and hounds returned to the manor house without the fox tail they were all hoping for.

Waiting for the group was the usual banquet of food and drink on the lawns of Abernethy Manor.

Mathew approached Sarah, who was enjoying a glass of wine and admiring the magnificent view from the large patio.

'So, Sarah, did you enjoy the hunt?'

'I did thank you, Mathew, very much so.'

'It's a pity we didn't catch a fox.'

'To tell you the truth I was quite pleased we didn't. I feel sorry for the animal.'

'You wouldn't say that if you saw a sheep after it had been savaged by the little blighters.'

'Everything has its place in this world, Mathew.'

'Yes, I suppose you're right. Will you excuse me? I'd better mingle with the guests. I haven't seen them for a while.'

'Yes, certainly.'

Mathew wandered off to greet some of the guests; he was hoping he would catch up with some of his old friends.

'Mathew, how are you, old chap? Congratulations; that was a well-executed hunt,' said a man he recognised as an old school friend.

'Good heavens, it's Howard Windsor! How are you?'

'I'm very well, and all the better for seeing you again.'

'What are you doing these days, Howard?'

'My father died five years ago, and being the eldest, I inherited the estate.'

'Well, Darlington is a fine estate. Do you still run cattle and sheep?'

'We most certainly do. In fact, we've increased the herds and flock by twenty-five per cent recently.'

'That's excellent Howard. I wish you well.'

'Tell me about Australia and what you've been up to over the past twelve years.'

Mathew briefed his friend about Ballarat, the hotels and racing stable. His friend was suitably impressed.

'Are you able to partake in fox hunting over there, old boy?'

'I'm afraid not. Australia is bereft of foxes.'

'No foxes! How inconvenient. So what animals can you run hounds with?'

'None, the native fauna would not suit such a hunt.'

'May I suggest you take back a fox and vixen and let them breed? Then you could organise a proper hunt.'

'That's a good idea, Howard; I'll look into it. Now if you'll excuse me, I'd better mingle. I'm not due to depart for Melbourne until May 1 so maybe we can catch up again before I go.'

'That would be splendid, Mathew.'

Mathew moved amongst the hunters greeting many people and swapping small talk. Finally, it was time for the hunters to depart, at last, the family had some quiet time together.

A New Life For Gordon

Chapter 16

March 15, 1865, Australia

The Cobb & Co Coach arrived at the Ballarat Depot at 4 pm. Kings Walden was only a short distance, and considering Gordon had no luggage John decided they should walk. Gordon hadn't worn a pair of shoes for some time, so he was finding it difficult but nevertheless soldiered on.

On arrival, John showed the young boy his room. It was quite large, with a three-quarter sized bed and ample wardrobe space. Two walls were covered in wallpaper.

Gordon just gazed at his room. He couldn't believe he had gone from sleeping in a park to this opulent bedroom.

'Well, Gordon do you approve of your room?'

'It's great, but where's the catch? What do I have to do?'

'There's no catch; you just need to behave yourself.'

'I promise you I will.'

'Come on, I'll show you the rest of the house.'

Gordon was amazed how big the house was as the only other building he had known had two hundred kids crammed into cold, stark dormitories.

'I suggest you go back to your room and rest up for a while. It's been a long day. Dinner will be at 6 pm.'

Gordon did as he was told. He took off his shoes and rubbed his aching feet. He lay on the bed staring at the ceiling.

'This is too good to be true. I bet the bastard comes into my room tonight and makes me do what that fucking master made me do,' he muttered.

John had given the young lad a pocket watch and at 6 pm he left his room and tried to find where the dining room was located. After several wrong turns, he entered the dining room where he found John already sitting at the table. As soon as he sat down, Mary, the cook, brought in a platter with roast lamb and vegetables. Gordon had never seen a dinner like it, and once Mary served the two of them

Gordon began to eat furiously. John told him to stop and place his utensils next to his plate.

'Gordon, we say Grace before we eat in this household. Close your eyes and put your hands together in prayer.' He waited for the boy to obey before continuing, 'For food in a world where many are in hunger; For faith in a world where many walk in fear; For friends in a world where many walk alone; We give you thanks, O Lord. Amen.'

He smiled at the boy and said, 'Now you can eat; tomorrow I will begin to teach how to hold your knife and fork properly. For the time being enjoy your dinner.'

After the meal, John read a book to his new houseguest, choosing *Moby Dick*, by Herman Melville. Gordon was captivated with the story of the white whale.

At 9 pm, John suggested Gordon visit the bathroom and then go to bed. A nightshirt had been folded and left on his pillow.

Once the boy settled into the clean, crisp sheets, he lay there trying not to close his eyes for fear of falling asleep. He lost the battle and was soon in a deep sleep, not waking until 7 am.

The next morning after breakfast, Gordon was introduced to his tutor, Miss Margaret Collins. John had advertised and appointed a schoolteacher to teach not only Gordon but the other children he intended to introduce to Kings Walden Home for Gifted Boys and Girls.

The schoolhouse was at the rear of the main house in converted stables. It had all the facilities required for a schoolroom, including a large blackboard. A toilet block had been constructed at the rear.

Gordon began his schooling with very limited enthusiasm but as the months rolled by, he became more and more committed to the lessons. Miss Collins was very pleased with his learning, reporting back to John on his progress at the end of each month.

John was also committed to teaching his young protégé manners and correct speech and by the end of his first year at Kings Walden Gordon was speaking like a student from Melbourne Grammar. The filthy Street Arab John had found in rags twelve months before had become an excellent student who spoke well and was very polite. The minister was now convinced he could do the same for other unprivileged children. His ambitious dream was becoming a reality.

John began the search on the streets of Melbourne, looking for children who were refugees from the orphanage system. Children like Gordon had been used and abused by a cruel system of child detention. Within a month he had discovered five girls and five more boys who were willing to give Kings Walden a chance.

John made a request to the church to help fund the new children's home and travelled to Melbourne to meet with the Bishop who was responsible for care organisations. Bishop David Chambers met with John in the officers adjacent to Saint Paul's Cathedral in Flinders Street.

'Hello, John welcome to Saint Paul's. How can I help you with your project?'

'Well, as you know, David, my ambition is to create a small home for boys and girls using my own home as the initial centre.'

'Why do you think it is required? Ballarat has an existing orphanage, and by all accounts, it's a very effective institution.'

'I think you have hit the nail on the head, David; it's an institution. My aim is to raise these children in a home-like environment. I want to not only educate them. My ambition is to teach them life skills.'

'What makes you think you can achieve this?'

'I *have* achieved it. I took a young street urchin in one year ago. He had no education, he spoke badly and had no trust in adults. In just twelve months his school results are exceptional, he has improved his vocabulary, and he is starting to trust me and the other adults he has encountered. If I can replicate the same results in the other children, our mission will be achieved.'

'Why are you calling the home King's Walden Home for Gifted Girls and Boys? Why gifted?'

'I want the children that come to the home to feel special. These poor kids have been abused and thrown out or escaped to fend for themselves. Saying they are special will give them some hope and encouragement.'

'John, the church admires your commitment to these children and what you are going to do for them, but we don't have the resources to support you. We will acknowledge the home, but we cannot fund it.'

'Well, that's very disappointing David. I have donated my substantial home and my time and money to this cause. I thought the church could have contributed. I bid you farewell, Bishop.'

John walked out of the Bishop's office into Flinders Street. He walked the mile to Spencer Street Station and caught the train to Ballarat, all the while thinking how he could make his dream of a series of homes throughout the colony come true. He could continue self-funding King's Walden for only another five years.

April 1866

John had found additional boys and five girls and they were now living in King's Walden.

Gordon had evolved as the senior boy, helping the other children cope with their new lives. John relied on Gordon to be a good example. King's Walden was diametrically opposed to Ballarat and District Orphanage. Rather than constant criticism and corporal punishment, John and his staff encouraged the children. If punishment was deserved, it involved denying the child privileges for a period of time, not the cane.

Mathew and George showed genuine interest in the home, visiting on a regular basis as well as supporting John financially.

July 1868

John invited his two closest friends to King's Walden for lunch to discuss the home's future. His objective was to convince Mathew and George to help fund a new home in Melbourne where there was a great need.

Mathew and George arrived together as George was Mathew's guest while staying in Ballarat.

'Hello, gentlemen how are you both?' said John to his two friends standing at the front door.

'Hello John, you look in rude health,' said George.

'As do you, George, it's been a while since we saw each other.'

'It has my friend, too long. My emporium keeps me in Melbourne I'm afraid.'

The three friends retired to the dining room where Mary served them roast beef and vegetables.

'So, John you obviously invited George and me for a reason, not just as good friends getting together.'

'You're right, Mathew. I'm very encouraged in what we have achieved at King's Walden. The boys and girls are being educated at the highest level, and they are now socially acceptable. I firmly believe they will leave here good citizens. Even though I'm very proud of what has been achieved I know much more needs to be done. When I visit Melbourne, I see children living on the streets just as the King's Walden kids were. They are dressed in rags and steal so they can eat. My ambition is to open several homes around Melbourne based on the Kings Walden model. The problem I have is funding; the church has refused help, and my resources will run out shortly.'

'I think I speak for both of us John… we both admire what you've done to help these children and will endeavour to help you as much as we can, but we do not have unlimited resources. George has two large retail enterprises, and I have the hotels and the stables. We are also considering a joint venture, which we aren't at liberty to discuss right now. May I suggest George and I think about a possible solution?'

'Rest assured, John we will find a way to help you because your cause is a very worthy one,' said George.

Happily Ever After

Or So the Saying Goes

Chapter 17

August 1868

George was busy running both stores. He now had seventy staff and turned over £50,000 per annum— a sizable amount. He also had the ambition to invest in Melbourne's most luxurious hotel, the Grand, with Mathew. The hotel had been constructed only two years previously, but the owner had gone bankrupt having overspent on its development. The construction and fitting out amounted to £120,000. Mathew and George had offered the receivers £70,000. All indications were that their offer would be accepted.

On September 15, 1868 settlement for the Grand took place.

Grand Hotel

The other issue occupying George's time and thoughts was Mary. He had been courting the red headed beauty for eight months and had been planning on asking her father for her hand in marriage.

His initial intention was to purchase a house for them to live in. He had his eye on a beautiful Georgian house close to where she lived with her family in Toorak. He had decided to delay this purchase because of the imminent acquisition of the Grand Hotel. They could either live in George's apartment in Collins Street or occupy the penthouse apartment at the hotel. Neither option was exactly roughing it.

George had discussed with Mary John's need to raise funds to continue his work with homeless children and she, in turn, broached the subject with her parents. They agreed to hold a charity evening in their home, inviting Melbourne's wealthy elite in the hope they could raise a considerable sum for the King's Walden Foundation.

Invitations were sent out, and they received over one hundred acceptances. The Melbourne Chamber Orchestra had agreed to donate their time. Walter Montgomery, the American actor who was acting in *Macbeth* at the Royal, also agreed to read some Shakespeare.

John was delighted not only for the anticipated donations but the opportunity to expose the guests to the work of King's Walden, which could mean ongoing support.

The King's Walden Home for Gifted Boys and Girls Charity Night was to be held on16 October 1868. Both the *Argus* and *Advocate* newspapers ran stories about the home and the excellent work it was doing.

Many politicians, professionals, and socialites attended together with some church dignitaries including Bishop David Chambers and Archbishop Perry.

The weather was fine and mild, allowing the recitals to be held in the gardens. Champagne flowed, and the food was superb.

John was mingling with the guests, answering questions about King's Walden Home and the work he was involved with when he felt a tap on his shoulder. He turned to find the Police Commissioner, Francis O'Connor.

'Hello, Reverend Davies, we meet again.'

John looked puzzled. 'Good evening. I'm sorry… I don't believe we've met.'

'My name is Francis O'Connor we met at a poker game at the Golden Nugget in Ballarat some time ago.'

'Oh, I remember. You're the Police Commissioner, aren't you?'

'That's right Reverend. May I ask you to have a quiet word?'

'Well, yes, I suppose so, but I can't leave my guests for too long as you would appreciate.'

The two men entered the magnificent house retiring to the library.

'Reverend.'

'Francis, please call me John.'

'Of course, John. Do you recall me saying I never forget a person's eyes?'

'No, I don't remember you saying that Francis, after all, I believe I played poker with you back in 1865, that's a long time ago.'

'I understand. Well, let me reiterate I told you I never forget a person's eyes. When I saw you again tonight, I remembered where I had seen you before.'

'And where might that be Francis?'

'On the Ballarat to Melbourne Road. You were dressed as a woman.'

John managed an incredulous laugh. 'You're ridiculous, Francis! A Minister of religion dressed as a woman?'

'You had just murdered one of my best men while executing a gold robbery.'

'I have to object! Your accusation is preposterous. Now if you don't mind I should return to my guests.'

'I will arrest you one day and see you hang.'

'I bid you goodnight, sir.'

John, although shaken returned to mingle with his guests. He knew there was absolutely no way this policeman could prove his guilt.

When the last guests left, John tallied the money and pledges. He was delighted that the event had raised over £3,000.

The next major function to be held at the Toorak mansion was Mary and George's wedding. George had purchased a two-carat diamond and emerald ring from Melbourne's finest jewellers, Kozminsky's. He had got down on one knee and proposed after they had attended the theatre. George had asked for Mary's hand in marriage the previous night and her father Sir Frederick Branson agreed to George's request.

21, July 1869

George asked Mary if she would be happy for John to conduct the service. She agreed without hesitation. The service was to be held at Saint Paul's Cathedral, a fitting venue for the Chief Magistrate's daughter.

George requested Mathew to be his best man. He had only just arrived back from another trip to England. Mary's brother, Arthur, was the groomsman.

One hundred and fifty guests and family attended the service. It was by far the largest congregation John had addressed.

The reception was held at Mary's parents' Toorak Manor. Mathew provided the catering from his hotels and over two hundred bottles of Mercia champagne were imported from France.

George was satisfied that his management group was more than capable of running his growing retail empire while Mathew and his staff would ensure the Grand would be managed efficiently. It was with this in mind that he and Mary decided to take a six-month honeymoon to England and France.

George and Mary departed on their honeymoon on the same ship Mathew sailed home on, the *Flying Cloud*, the swiftest clipper afloat.

The newlyweds enjoyed the trip, dining on the finest cuisine and drinking the best French wines. Much of the voyage was spent in their first-class cabin getting to know each other.

George was a regular participant in clay pigeon shooting and had improved his skills over the years.

After fifty-five days at sea, the Flying Cloud berthed at Liverpool. George took possession of their sea trunks and hailed a horse-drawn taxi to transport them to the railway station. The journey would take six hours to reach Somerset.

George's parents, Harold and Harriet, were waiting on the platform when the locomotive pulled into the station. Both were excited as they hadn't seen their son for thirteen years.

When Harriet saw George and Mary alight from the carriage, she started to cry. George approached his parents holding his new bride's hand. He kissed his mother and shook his father's hand.

'Mother, Father I would like you both to meet my wife, Mary.'

'It's so nice to meet you, Mary, George has told us so much about you in his letters.'

'I think he underplayed your beauty,' said Harold.

'Thank you, Mr Griffith, however, I think you exaggerate.'

'I don't think so, Mary. Right, let's collect your luggage and make our way home.'

The journey took just twenty minutes. Mary was impressed by the green countryside and the hedges on either side of the road as this was much different from the Australian landscape she was used to.

When the carriage stopped outside the Georgian house, Mary was amazed how similar the architecture was to her family home in Melbourne.

'May I suggest you two go to your room? Your mother will show you where it is. I'm sure you'll want to freshen up after your journey. Let's all meet for pre-dinner drinks on the patio at six pm.'

'That sounds like an excellent idea, Father; we'll see you soon.'

George and Mary retired to their room, which was quite large with a four-poster bed and a bay window looking out to the meadows.

'George, I think your parents are lovely, so warm and welcoming.'

'I'd forgotten how much I'd missed them.'

'You don't think you'd like to return home to England, do you?'

'God no, I have the retail stores and now a half share in the Grand Hotel. Besides, I'm sure you wouldn't want to leave Melbourne, would you?'

'No, I wouldn't, but having said that, I'd follow you anywhere my love.'

At breakfast, Harriet suggested to Mary that she join her on a shopping trip to Bath. Mary agreed. Bath was known for its excellent shops and Roman architecture.

George took the opportunity to travel into the local village Yeovil, to try and find Cathy Haines, the mother of his child. He enquired at the Post Office and discovered she lived at 10 Brue Lane. George thought it ironic it; was on the banks of the Brue River where he and Cathy made love.

He made his way to Cathy's house. Number 10 was a cute thatched-roof cottage with a colourful garden.

He couldn't believe how nervous he felt now he was about to meet the child he walked away from all those years ago.

He knocked on the front door and after a few minutes Cathy answered. She looked at George as though she had seen a ghost.

'Hello, Cathy. After all these years I would have thought a hello was warranted.'

'George, what are you doing here?'

'Well, Cathy if you invite me in I'll tell you.'

'I'm sorry, yes— please come in. Would you like a cup of tea?'

'I would, thank you.'

Cathy suggested George take a seat in the parlour while she prepared the tea.

Cathy was shaking. What if he had discovered Mary was not his daughter and demanded his money back?

She carried in the tray and placed it on the table.

'Do you take sugar, George?'

'Yes, one, thank you.'

Once the niceties were over George explained why he had contacted her.

'Cathy, as you know I now live in Australia. I recently married and have travelled home to introduce my wife Mary to my parents and familiarise her with where I was raised. For the past thirteen years, I've wondered if I had fathered a son or a daughter and how the child has developed. I have no intention to reveal my relationship, but I would like to meet my son or daughter... by the way, was it a boy or a girl?'

'A girl.'

'What's her name?'

'Ruth'

'Where is she?'

'She's at school. However, she should be home shortly.'

Just then, they both heard the front door open and Ruth entered the room. She had bright red hair. Neither George nor Cathy had red hair in their family genetics.

'Hello, Ruth, this is Mr Griffith who is visiting from Australia.'

'Hello,' the girl said politely.

'Hello, Ruth, it's lovely to meet you. You have beautiful red hair.'

'Thank you. It's the same colour as my father's.'

Cathy put in hastily, 'Ruth why don't you get a glass of milk and do your homework in the kitchen?'

'Yes, Mother.'

After the girl had gone, Cathy looked at George with a guilty look on her face. 'I'm sorry, George. I had no alternative.'

George sighed. 'If it weren't for your deception I would never have immigrated to Australia. I am very content living in Melbourne. I am a wealthy man and regarded as a model citizen. I am married to a beautiful woman; a redhead as it happens. I hold no grudge.'

'Thank you, George. I have always felt guilty.'

'Well, there's no need to, Cathy. I'll now take my leave.'

George left the house feeling relieved. He had always felt guilty about not marrying Cathy and caring for his child and he now had a clear conscience.

He returned to the family home, poured himself a whisky from his father's drink cabinet, and retired to the conservatory to contemplate what he had just discovered. He was convinced everything had worked out for the best. He also decided he'd like to take Mary on a trip to Cornwall, one of his favourite places in England. He could teach her to sail. It had been many years since he had taken a yacht out from St Ives; something he did every summer when he was a boy.

Harriet and Mary returned at 4 pm laden with parcels they had acquired on their shopping trip to Bath.

'Hello,' said George. 'You two look as if you have had a very successful day.'

'Hello darling! Yes, it was marvellous. We had a very good time and I did buy you something.'

'Did you and what, pray tell?'

Mary unwrapped a beautiful jumper knitted with an argyle pattern.

'Thank you, darling. I like it.'

'Well, we'd better put these parcels away before Harold gets home. He gets upset if he thinks I've spent too much,' said Harriet.

'Will we all meet in the conservatory before dinner?' enquired Mary.

'Yes, that sounds like an excellent idea,' said Harriet.

George and Mary went to their room with George carrying the majority of Mary's purchases. He broached the idea of travelling to Cornwell for a few days. Mary was enthusiastic. They then made love and bathed together before getting ready for the evening.

September 15, 1869

George and Mary bade farewell to Harold and Harriet at the railway station. They were bound for St Ives, a four-hour train journey. On arrival, they made their way to the Queens Hotel and checked into a beautiful suite overlooking the azure blue ocean.

Cornwall is renowned for its excellent seafood and the couple enjoyed eating out at the Mermaid restaurant on their first night.

The next morning George made enquiries about hiring a small yacht. He successfully found a suitable craft to teach his wife the fundamentals of sailing.

'Mary, make sure you dress sensibly. It can get wet inside the yacht.'

'I only have summer frocks. Do you think they will be suitable?'

'I suppose so but don't be upset if you get wet.'

'I'm sure I'll be fine. Let's get going— I'm looking forward to getting out on the water.'

The honeymooners walked to the pier where their yacht was waiting. George got in first and then helped his bride into the bobbing vessel. Once she was seated, he set the sail, and they began their adventure out into the Celtic Sea.

George was an experienced sailor, but it had been some years since he held the tiller.

After an hour of sailing along the coast, George decided to move further offshore in the hope he could find stronger winds. The couple were so enjoying the sailing neither noticed the ominous black clouds moving in from their stern. Eventually, they realised they were close to a storm as the sea became rough with waves breaking over the side. George did his best to head back to shore but as he tacked, a massive wave engulfed them. It took all of his strength not to be swept overboard. Mary was not so fortunate.

George couldn't see her in the swirling water, so he decided to jump in, despite not being a strong swimmer. He kept calling out to Mary but there was no reply. Eventually, realising the hopelessness of the situation, the distraught husband swam back to the yacht. George kept calling out to her knowing the likelihood of her drowning was high.

After a couple of hours, he knew he needed to get back to shore before dark the storm had subsided to the point he could sail the yacht.

Despite the inclement weather he finally managed to coax the small craft back to St Ives where, once moored, he made his way to the police station to report his beloved Mary missing.

The police officer took down the details but couldn't offer George any real help until there was calmer weather. George shuffled his way up to the hotel, tears streaming down his face. As he opened the door to the suite, the first thing he saw was a dress laying on the bed. He collapsed onto the bed crying hysterically. How could he live without his Mary?

The next day, the police arrived at the hotel informing George a woman's body had been found washed ashore two miles from St Ives.

'Sorry sir, but I have to ask you to accompany me to the police station to identify the body.'

'I don't think I could, officer.'

'I'm afraid you have to sir, it's the law.'

George reluctantly went with the policeman.

'Please wait here while I ensure everything is in arranged correctly,' said the policeman.

George didn't answer. He just nodded.

A few minutes passed when the police officer returned. 'Right Mr Griffiths, if you could follow me, please?'

George followed the officer into a room at the back of the station. In the middle of the room was a table with a body covered by a white sheet.

'Sir, when the sheet is pulled back all you have to say is, *yes that is my wife*. Is that clear?'

George nodded.

The policeman pulled back the sheet to reveal Mary's face. Is this Mary Griffiths?'

George didn't utter a word. He just let out a guttural sound.

I'm sorry Mr Griffiths, you must identify your wife.'

George could not speak. Finally, he uttered a single word. 'Mary.'

'That's sufficient. Come on sir, we'll get you back to the hotel.'

George was accompanied back by a police officer who made sure he was settled back in his hotel room. George had never felt so utterly alone.

The next unenviable task was to send a telegram to Mary's parents in Melbourne.

After consultation, her parents and George decided Mary should be cremated in England and her ashes returned to Australia.

Life would never be the same for George. He returned to his parents' home in Somerset where he was comforted by his mother and father.

He thought long and hard about his future over the following weeks. Should he stay in England, selling up his assets in Australia, or should he return and immerse himself in the business? Finally, he decided to return.

Gordon

Chapter 18

December 1875

John treated Gordon like a son, and in turn, Gordon regarded John as his father. The first boy introduced into King's Walden had been transformed from a dirty street kid who stole from the wealthy citizens of Melbourne so that he could stay alive into an intelligent, well-mannered young gentleman. He had been in residence for seven years when finally, the time had come for both John and Gordon to make a decision. Gordon could look for a suitable job, more than likely in a bank, or enrol at Melbourne University studying law or medicine. His grades were high enough to embark on either career. After much discussion, it was decided that the young man would study at university majoring in law.

John was able to find a place on the campus for Gordon to reside and it was now up to Gordon to study hard and qualify as a lawyer in three years' time.

'So Gordon, how do you feel leaving King's Walden and moving to Melbourne?' asked John.

'To be completely honest sir, I'm feeling a little nervous.'

'No need; you'll be fine once you've settled into university life. I remember my first day at Oxford. I didn't know where the toilets were let alone the lecture halls. By the end of the first week, I was relishing the life.'

'Yes, I'm sure I'll be fine. I hope I get on with my roommate.'

'Just take one step at a time, Gordon, and make sure you spend enough time studying and not playing cards in the student lounge.'

'Like you did.'

'Do as I say and not as I did, young man.'

'Just joking.'

Gordon boarded the Melbourne train at 9 am Saturday, suitcase in hand. He had been to Melbourne frequently since he lived there as a street urchin and enjoyed its wide tree-lined boulevards and many shops. He had worked during his Christmas holidays at Georges and several times his father's good friend had taken him under his wing. George had offered Gordon part time work while he was studying, and he gratefully accepted.

The young student stood out in a crowd. He was six feet tall with golden blond hair and piercing blue eyes, and he also had olive skin. Another appealing feature was his deep mellow voice. All these attributes made him very attractive to the female students on campus.

Gordon enjoyed a very active extracurricular life. He played cricket in the summer and he was regarded as the fastest bowler in the University First 11. In the winter he played half-forward in the University's football team. One other activity he enjoyed and excelled at was playing poker just like his mentor, John. Gordon also was able to accumulate significant savings at the expense of his playing partners.

His law studies were also progressing and at the end of his first year he came dux of the law school.

Gordon had known Emma, Mathew's daughter, for some time as she and her father would visit John at King's Walden on a regular basis. The two always got on well, but there was never any romantic interest from either of them.

At the end of Gordon's second year, the university union decided to organise a student ball to be held at the Melbourne Town Hall. There was no shortage of willing partners to accompany Gordon, but he decided to ask Emma, just to be safe. She willingly accepted his invitation as she loved to dance, and she hoped he was an accomplished ballroom dancer. He was.

Gordon arranged to collect Emma at her father's magnificent townhouse on St Kilda Road. Mathew stayed at the villa during his frequent trips to Melbourne. Gordon had borrowed John's carriage and a driver and they pulled up outside the residence. When he knocked on the front door, Mathew opened it and invited him in. Gordon had been to the house often, so he felt quite comfortable.

'So, Gordon you're taking my princess to the ball?'

'Yes sir, I promise I'll have her home by midnight.'

Mathew laughed. 'I'll give you a little leeway on that.'

Emma entered the room and both men admired her appearance.

'Hello, Emma you look beautiful.' Gordon smiled at her.

'Thank you, Gordon; I must say you look very handsome dressed in that dinner suit.'

'Well, you two, you'd better get moving,' George said. 'You don't want to be late.'

Gordon took Emma by the arm and escorted her to the carriage where the driver waited. He opened the door and helped his companion into the cabin.

The two young friends just made small talk on the way and it wasn't long before the carriage entered the portico. Gordon alighted and went to the other side of the carriage. He opened the door and assisted Emma out. They walked into the large foyer and then into the grand hall. It was wonderful sight; ladies in their ball gowns and men in dinner suits with an orchestra playing on stage.

Gordon located their table, but they didn't sit down as the music inspired them to join the couples dancing on the floor.

'Gordon, you surprise me! You're an excellent dancer.'

'Why does that surprise you? Did you think I'd fall over my own feet?'

'No, silly but being such a splendid sportsman. Well, you know what I mean.'

'Yes, I know what you mean. Or maybe you are such an excellent dancer you hide all my faults.'

Emma and Gordon danced, laughed, danced some more and laughed some more throughout the evening. They both enjoyed the night and departed reluctantly back to Emma's home.

'Thank you, Gordon, I had a wonderful night.'

'As did I, Emma. May I ask to kiss you goodnight?'

Emma didn't answer. She leant across, kissing her partner on the lips.

Gordon was taken back for it was the warmest, most passionate kiss he had ever experienced.

'I'd better escort you to the door, Emma,' he said.

When they said their final goodnight, Gordon got back in the carriage and headed back to the campus. His head was spinning, and his heart was pumping. He didn't sleep well that night. Should he endeavour to enter a relationship with his childhood friend or should he concentrate on his study without distractions? By the time the sun rose, he'd decided on the latter.

Emma was now infatuated with Gordon. Despite her knowing him as a family friend for many years, she now saw him through different eyes. She hoped each day after the ball for another invitation it never came.

The next time she saw him was at the Christmas party Mathew held each year two weeks before the 25th December. They were cordial to one another without being enthusiastic in their greetings. Three weeks had passed since the university ball and it seemed like three years to them both.

1879

Gordon approached his final year at law school with vigour, but still participated in cricket and football and was still known as the poker player to beat. He had the odd dalliance with a female student or two but nothing serious.

Emma worked initially on the reception desk at the Grand, working her way up to assistant manager. Mathew, her father, was very proud.

Gordon completed his degree and was named Dux of the law school. John was delighted. His experiment with Gordon had paid handsome returns. He regarded the young lawyer as his only son, but he hoped some of the other children now residing at King's Walden would follow his example.

Gordon was approached by one of Melbourne's most prestigious law firms, Corr & Corr, to join their practice. He didn't have to think long before accepting.

The young lawyer was highly regarded by the two partners who saw him as a future partner in the practice. He had been working at the firm for two years when he received a letter of offer from a London firm, Allen & Ovary, to join them in their corporate division. This was a unique opportunity to practise law in London; a place regarded as the epicentre of English law. He didn't cogitate too long before sending his acceptance by telegraph. The partners at Corr & Corr were disappointed but understood why their star lawyer would want to leave. Gordon negotiated a handsome package and set sail for what he hoped would be an adventure of a lifetime.

1880

Ormuz

The sea journey took only thirty-five days on the new ocean liner the *Ormuz*. Gordon enjoyed the first-class amenities including the saloon lounge where he played poker most nights. He won over £1,000. What shortened the trip extensively was going through the newly opened Suez Canal. Gordon and the other passengers were amazed at the technology used to achieve such an engineering feat.

June 1, 1880

The *Ormuz* berthed at Southampton at 9 am. Gordon had been told via telegram that someone from the firm would meet him. The newly arrived solicitor disembarked from the ship and began to look for someone holding a sign with his name on it. Eventually, having made his way through the large crowd on the wharf, he noticed a rather youngish fellow in a pinstriped suit holding up a sign.

'Hello, I'm Gordon Huston. I believe you may be looking for me.'

'Yes, hello, Mr Huston, my name is Cedric Cook. I'm an articled clerk for Allen & Overy and I've been instructed to take you to your hotel.'

'Excellent, Cedric. I just need to retrieve my sea trunk and a bag.'

'I'll get them for you. Have you got your luggage tag?'

Gordon handed over the tags and waited for young Cedric's return. After fifteen minutes he spotted the young man struggling with the trunk. Gordon approached him and gave him some assistance. Cedric called a taxi and after loading the luggage headed for the train station where they would catch a train into central London.

It was midday before they entered the foyer of the Savoy Hotel where Gordon would stay until he found suitable accommodation.

Mr Avery, the firm's senior partner, organised one of the law clerks to assist him in finding suitable permanent accommodation. The young Australian lawyer settled on a ground floor flat in South Kensington.

It didn't take long for Gordon to immerse himself in a case involving what the law in later years called a Ponzi scheme.

The first notorious Ponzi scheme was orchestrated by a man named Charles Ponzi in 1919. The postal service, at that time, had developed international reply coupons that allowed a sender to pre-purchase postage and include it in their correspondence. The receiver would take the coupon to a local post office and exchange it for the priority airmail postage stamps needed to send a reply.

With the constant fluctuation of postage prices, it was common for stamps to be more expensive in one country than another. Ponzi hired agents to purchase cheap international reply coupons in other countries and send them to him. He would then exchange those coupons for stamps that were more expensive than the coupon was originally purchased for. The stamps were then sold as a profit.

This type of exchange is known as an arbitrage, which is not an illegal practice. Ponzi became greedy and expanded his efforts. Under the heading of his company, Securities Exchange Company, he promised returns of 50% in forty-five days or 100% in ninety days. Due to his success in the postage stamp scheme, investors were immediately attracted. Instead of actually investing the money, Ponzi just redistributed it and told the investors they made a profit. The scheme lasted until 1920 when an investigation into the Securities Exchange Company was conducted.

The scheme Gordon was working on entailed a gold mine in Australia. The perpetrator had stolen over £100,000 from investors.

Gordon not only enjoyed his work but immersed himself in London life, mixing with the famous city's elite. He had considered staying in England but after three years he was becoming homesick.

Revenge

Chapter 19

January 1870

George decided he would spend a week in London before departing England for Australia. He hoped this time would help him heal his spiritual wounds. There wasn't a minute in an hour or an hour in a day that the widower didn't think of his beloved Mary.

George caught the train from Somerset having said his farewells to his parents. He booked into the Strand Hotel, then decided to take a walk through the streets of London. He strolled up to the Strand and turned into Southampton Street, leading him to Covent Garden. He enjoyed the crowds milling around the famous district. George purchased a mohair coat, something difficult to buy back home.

He eventually tired of walking and returned to the hotel, intending to rest before dinner.

The following day, George decided to visit Westminster Abbey and light a candle for Mary. As he was walking along Abingdon Street towards the Abbey, he passed a gentleman who looked strangely familiar. He stopped and looked back at the man. It then dawned on him who he was; it was Henry, his one-time partner in the gold mine.

The scoundrel who stole his share of the gold nugget was walking towards Westminster Abbey. George turned and followed him. He kept his distance so as not to alert Henry of his presence. Finally the thief entered a magnificent house at Howick Place quite close to the Abbey.

George stood outside the house trying to determine the right cause of action. Should he confront the bastard now, or should he take his time and devise an appropriate plan? Ultimately, he decided to think about it.

George returned to his hotel to cogitate over his next move and finally he decided to confront Henry, demanding he would be compensated for his loss. George would make a veiled threat if Henry resisted.

The next morning George rang the doorbell of Henry's house. A maid answered the door.

'Good morning, my name is George. I'm a very old friend of Henry's… may I see him please?'

'Come in sir, I'll let Lord Baynes know you are here.'

George was shown into the front parlour where many photos of Henry with various dignitaries were displayed. These included William Gladstone, the current Prime Minister.

Well, the bastard has done all right for himself, George thought.

Eventually, Henry strode into the room. He looked at George and stopped dead in his tracks.

'George, what are you doing here?'

'Well, Henry, I could ask you the same question. The last time we saw each other, you were driving a wagon into Melbourne with a very large nugget on board.'

'George, I can explain.'

'Can you Henry? Can you explain how you left me penniless?'

Henry looked sheepish. 'Well, actually, I can't explain. When I reached the bank, and received all that money greed took over. I figured if we found one huge nugget no doubt you'd find another one.'

'As it turns out, my old friend, I did recover and am now one of the wealthiest men in Melbourne. However, that doesn't excuse you.'

'No, I understand that, George.'

'Do you? What you need to understand, Henry, is that if I don't receive a bank draft for £15,000 by tomorrow, I will let the press and your peers know what a crook you are.'

'That's more than your share.'

'With interest, inflation and the pain I went through, £15,000 should cover it.

'Where do I deliver it to?

'The English, Scottish and Australian Chartered Bank. Deposit it in this account; B129.753. When I have notification the money has been deposited I will consider the matter closed.'

'I understand.'

'Good, I'll bid you farewell. By the way, congratulations on your peerage.'

George showed himself out and as he walked down the street he felt a sense of achievement. He would feel even better when he saw the money in his bank account.

The next day George arrived at the English, Scottish, and Australian Chartered Bank right on opening time where he enquired if £15,000 had been deposited into his account. It had.

He could now return home albeit without Mary.

George boarded the RMS *Siam,* bound for Melbourne. The return journey was very different from the voyage to England. He spent most of his time reading as well as writing a diary about his life since he first left England. It included all the aspects of his colourful life.

For Fox Sake

Mathew had arrived back in Melbourne just as George and Mary were leaving. Mathew had brought some very precious cargo with him; a pair of mated foxes. His objective was to breed the foxes and let them loose in the Australian bush. His intention was to establish a hunt club so that they could enjoy the pleasure and excitement of foxhunting on Australian soil. He envisaged he would be The Melbourne Foxhunt Club's first Master of Hounds. Mathew also imported two breeding pairs of beagles. The club was located just outside Ballarat and hunted foxes over the extensive pastures surrounding the very rich town.

Mathew advertised for members in both *The Age* and *The Ballarat Star*. He stipulated that correct clothing and tack was required. Georges of Melbourne was the only retailer stocking such attire.

Mathew was surprised at how many people both men and women applied for membership. He closed the list when it reached one hundred.

March 1870

The inaugural hunt began on the grounds of Ercildoune Homestead. The owners of the estate, the Livingstone-Learmonth brothers, had offered to provide the grounds for the hunt. The two foxes were released on the estate the week before.

Ercildoune Homestead

The Estate

At 10 a.m. a hundred riders assembled, with over twenty hounds.

Mathew, being Master of Hounds, was in charge of the hunt, and supervised the field, the hounds, and staff. The huntsmen, who had bred the hounds and worked with them, were in charge of the pack during the hunt.

They rode off into the extensive farmland in pursuit of the fox and vixen but despite the hunters' best efforts the foxes eluded them. The riders returned without the trophy they had been hoping for.

The foxes enjoyed their new home. They had plenty to eat, including sheep and began to breed with gay abandon. This was the genesis of Australia's fox problem and they were soon labelled vermin.

Mathew organised a foxhunt each month during the spring and summer. They did catch and destroy some foxes but their prey constantly outfoxed them.

The day after the first hunt, Mathew caught the train into Melbourne. The purpose of his trip was to meet the *SS Siam* and escort his good friend back to his apartment. Mathew knew George would need all the support he could muster.

Mathew's carriage entered the Port Melbourne dock precinct. The *SS Siam* had docked that morning and the wharf was a hive of activity. Cargo was being unloaded and packed onto drays to be distributed to various warehouses around the city.

Mathew caught a glimpse of George disembarking down the gangplank and he quickly walked over to greet him as he stepped onto the wharf.

'George, hello old friend, welcome back to God's own country.'

'Hello Mathew, it's kind of you to meet me. I appreciate it.'

'Not at all George, it's the least I could do.'

The two friends shook hands warmly.

'John was hoping he could make it, but he's got some important business in Ballarat to attend to. He assured me he'd come in tomorrow to see you.'

'That's good. I'll look forward to seeing him.'

'Do you know where your trunk is?'

'I believe it's at the far end of the wharf.'

'I'll get my driver to go down there and load it up, then he can pick us up on his way back.'

'Thank you.' George smiled. 'It really is good to see you, old friend.'

'I wouldn't have missed seeing you for the world.'

The carriage pulled up beside where the two men were talking. They boarded and began their journey into central Melbourne where George's apartment was located.

George was carrying a leather bag. He declined to have it packed with his other luggage and would not let it go.

'Is that bag stuffed with English pounds, George? You're hanging onto it as though it's your entire fortune.'

'It holds my most prized possession, Mathew. Mary's ashes.'

'Oh my God, George. I'm so sorry.'

'You weren't to know.'

The two men fell silent for the remainder of the journey. At last, the carriage pulled up outside Georges Department Store. The driver and an employee of the store carried George's luggage up to his apartment.

'Would you like to come up for a cup of tea Mathew?'

'No, I won't thanks. I have some things to take care of. May I suggest we meet at the Grand for dinner? You'll be interested in some of the changes we've made while you were away.'

'Yes, that would be excellent. What time?'

'Say 7 pm?'

'Yes, that would be fine. I'll see you then.'

George looked around his apartment; the home he'd intended to share with Mary until they bought a house together. Mary had moved her clothes and some decorative objects into the apartment prior to their honeymoon. George looked at the vases and burst into tears. How could he live without his Mary?

At 6.45 pm he began the short walk to the Grand Hotel, his business venture with Mathew. As he neared the magnificent building, he began to feel more positive about his future. The hotel and his burgeoning retail empire would become his life.

He entered the ornate foyer. Guests were checking in and people were in the café. The hotel had a sense of success about it.

George approached reception and asked if he could see Mr Abernethy. The receptionist requested George's name and the reason why he wished to see the hotel's owner. The employee went into the back office where he knew Mathew was going over the daily ledger. Mathew came out, welcoming George to his hotel, then called the front office staff together and introduced George as the half-owner of the hotel. George would no longer have to announce himself upon entering the Grand.

Mathew and George entered the Victoria restaurant, an elaborately decorated establishment.

The headwaiter approached them immediately; word had spread amongst the staff as to who the other owner of the hotel was. He showed them to their table and enquired if they would care to have a drink before they ate. Both men chose a twenty-year-old malt whisky.

'I must congratulate you, Mathew. The hotel has a fantastic atmosphere.'

'Thank you. Yes, it is operating very well. We have spent an enormous amount of time on staff training from reception through to the maids.'

'I'm also pleased to see the occupancy has risen significantly. I appreciate you telegraphing me the figures while we were away.'

The word *we* had an impact on both men.

'George, are you comfortable talking about what happened over there?'

'No, I could never be comfortable about reliving it, but I will tell you.'

George recounted the fateful day including identifying the love of his life. Both men had tears in their eyes by the time George had finished.

'When are you going to visit Mary's parents?'

'Tomorrow. I'm taking Mary's ashes with me. They need to have a say as to what should be done with them.'

'What do you want to do?'

'I'd like to keep them with me.'

'Are you intending to hold a memorial service for Mary?'

'I'll discuss that with them tomorrow.'

The two friends ordered their dinner, which was, as you would expect, delicious. George said farewell to Mathew and walked back to the empty apartment.

The next day George made the trip to Mary's parents' house, full of trepidation. He thought they might blame him for their daughter's loss.

The hansom cab pulled up outside the beautiful Georgian mansion. George disembarked, walked slowly up the garden path and rang the doorbell.

Lady Anne and Sir Frederick greeted him and the three bereaved made their way to the formal lounge room.

'I can't tell you both how sorry I am. Losing Mary is the greatest sadness in my life.'

'We understand. As you would expect it has been a terrible blow to Mary's mother and me.'

'I explained what happened in my letter to you both, but I'm willing to recount it now if you like.'

'I don't think that would serve any real purpose, George. Have you decided what to do with Mary's ashes?'

'Well, naturally you should have a say in it. My preference would be to keep them with me.'

'I think she would have preferred staying with you George; after all, you were her husband.'

'Thank you, I appreciate it.'

'The next thing we need to discuss is her memorial service. Both Lady Anne and I would like a ceremony befitting her standing in the community.'

'Yes, I agree. What were you thinking?'

'Charles Perry, the Anglican Archbishop of Melbourne, has agreed to conduct the service at St Paul's Cathedral.'

'That would be excellent, sir. I do have one request.'

'What is that?'

'My dear friend John Davies in a Minister in the Church of England and I would like him involved in some way. He thought the world of Mary.'

'I don't see a problem with that. I'll talk to the Archbishop.'

March 20, 1870

Mary's memorial service was due to begin at 10 am. Mourners began to arrive as early as 9 am. The family expected two hundred people to attend but they underestimated Mary's popularity. The cathedral could hold four hundred worshipers, and another one hundred mourners were required to stand outside the cathedral.

George and Mary's immediate family occupied the front pews. The service was very moving, and when George delivered the eulogy there wasn't a dry eye to be seen in the church.

The last time John had preached to such a large congregation was at George and Mary's wedding just eight short months previously. The irony wasn't lost on the young priest.

A wake was held at Sir Frederick and Lady Anne's Toorak home.

John and George were enjoying a sherry when the Police Chief, Francis O'Connor, approached them.

'My condolences, George, she was an intelligent, beautiful woman, and congratulations, John, the service was excellent. We will certainly use your expertise when you are incarcerated at Pentridge Gaol before you go to your execution.'

'If your accusations weren't so ludicrous, Francis, I'd hit you on that big bulbous nose. Now if you don't mind, you interrupted an intelligent conversation I was having with George, so we will take our leave.'

The two friends walked away from the police officer and found a quiet spot in the Chief Magistrate's library.

'What was that all about John?'

'For years he's been accusing me of the murder of the police officer I killed during the gold robbery on the Ballarat - Melbourne Road. He says he never forgets a felon's eyes and he's sure I was the one who pulled the trigger.'

'My goodness John, aren't you concerned?'

'How is he going to prove it?'

The Police Chief had followed the two men to the library, ensuring he wasn't spotted. He stayed outside the door but could hear every word of their conversation.

I knew it was him! Now all I need to do is prove it. That's not going to be easy, Francis thought.

The pursuit of John would continue not only through the Police Chief's career but also his retirement.

A Lawyer in Love

Chapter 21

London July 1881

Gordon wrote to his old law firm in Melbourne, Corr & Corr, enquiring whether he could re-join the firm. The partners were not only agreeable; they offered him a junior partnership. Gordon was delighted. He gave notice to the London firm who were sorry to see him go. He made arrangements to sail back to Australia.

The ship he returned to Melbourne on was named *Gunga;* a steam-powered vessel that reduced the time to make the arduous journey to thirty-five days non-stop.

S S Gunga

Gordon arrived at Port Melbourne Wharf on 18 August 1881. His guardian of old, John, was there to welcome his protégé home. The two men hugged each other warmly, John put his arm around Gordon and led him to his carriage. They didn't stop talking either on the way to Spencer Street Train Station nor on the train to Ballarat where Gordon would be staying at King's Walden for the first few weeks before taking up his appointment.

John had arranged a dinner to welcome Gordon home. Mathew and Emma and George were invited as well as Kate, another orphan John had taken in and metaphorically speaking, adopted. She was now twenty-four, and a qualified nurse.

Gordon and Emma were very pleased to see one another again. Gordon had forgotten just how beautiful the young woman was and how eloquent she was in her dinner conversation.

At the conclusion of the evening, Gordon suggested to Emma they attend a play at the newly constructed Princess Theatre. Janet Achurch, on tour from England, would be performing in Ibsen's *A Doll's House*.

She accepted Gordon's invitation without hesitation and they agreed on a date suitable to both. Emma would stay at her father's townhouse.

Janet Achurch

Princess Theatre

Gordon began his new role at Corr & Corr on September 1. It was an easy transition as he knew most of the staff and partners from his first experience with the well-respected firm.

He was assigned a complex case almost immediately. It took all his time and after two months was concluded successfully. The partners were well pleased with Gordon's work.

His private life was also proving to be fruitful. He and Emma continued going to the theatre and having picnics at various beautiful locations in the Ballarat region. After twelve months of courting, Gordon asked Emma to marry him and she had no hesitation in accepting his proposal. Mathew and John were delighted as both men had hoped the relationship would culminate in marriage.

The date was set for Saturday, January 22, 1883, and the service would be held at St John's, Ballarat. John decided he wouldn't conduct the service as he felt he would be too emotional. Instead, the minister asked his good friend the Reverend Michael Cooper to conduct the wedding.

Mathew and John organised an engagement party at Mathew's residence, Abernethy House. Over one hundred guests attended, including the society elite from Ballarat and Melbourne Victoria's Governor, Lord Normandy and the Premier, James Service, were there.

The *Argus* sent a reporter and a photographer to cover the upcoming wedding of Ballarat's elite; a group photo was taken of the young couple, and Mathew and John that took an entire page in the newspaper's social pages.

Wednesday, January 10, 1883

Mrs Phillip was sitting in her parlour drinking tea and reading the *Argus* newspaper, something she enjoyed doing every Wednesday the day the paper was published. She lived a privileged life in Bendigo where her husband, James Phillip, was regarded as one of the richest men in Victoria. He made his fortune importing and selling large-scale machinery to the mining industry. His company, Phillip's Industrial Equipment had offices in Victoria, New South Wales and Queensland. The company had recently begun manufacturing mining equipment in its own facility in Bendigo, which was proving to be very profitable.

As she turned the pages, she came across the article about Gordon and Emma's engagement. She dropped her cup and saucer on the floor, spilling the tea over the fine Persian Rug.

Saturday, January 22, 1883

Emma's two bridesmaids, Alison and Elizabeth, two friends she had known since her school days at Queens Grammar School, were assisting the young bride to be. Melbourne's most prestigious dressmaker Vivian's of Collins Street, had tailored her dress. The gown was white with pearls sewn over the bodice. A short train meant the bridesmaids were not required to assist the bride when she entered the church. Mathew had arranged for two white carriages pulled by two white horses. One would transport the bride and her father the other was designated for the bridesmaids.

'How are you feeling, Emma? It's not too late to pull out, you know,' said Alison.

'Don't be silly. He's the man I wanted to marry the first time I laid eyes on him.'

'I was just kidding.'

'Emma, what have you got that's old, that's new, borrowed and blue?' asked Elizabeth.

'I have a blue garter and new shoes, but nothing old or borrowed.'

'Well, wear my diamond ring. It was my grandmother's.'

'Thank you, Elizabeth.'

'And borrow my pearl earrings. They will suit your dress,' said Alison.

Mathew, Emma's father, called out to the three women that it was time to go. They quickly checked their outfits and hugged and kissed each other. Emma knew this would be the best day of her life.

The carriages looked magnificent and once boarded, the bridal party began their fifteen-minute journey to the church.

Gordon's best man and groomsman were colleagues from the law firm, James Kelly and Michael Smith.

The young lawyer thought how nice would be if some of his old friends from the streets of Melbourne could attend but he knew that was impossible as he had no idea where any of them might be now.

'Are you feeling nervous, mate?'

'Not at all, James. I'm looking forward to it, I know this will be the best day of my life.'

'Well, you certainly look the part. That morning suit looks great on you.'

'Thank you, and the same goes for you two gentlemen. I think we'd better leave. I certainly don't want to be late; that's the bride's privilege.'

The three men walked out of King's Walden and into the carriage waiting to take them to St John's. The journey took only ten minutes, and as they arrived they could see the guests milling outside.

The groom and his groomsmen walked up the steps of the beautiful bluestone church, greeting guests. As they entered the church they admired the white bows tied at the end of each pew. The flower arrangements were magnificent.

The guests began to enter the hallowed ground, taking their seats on the appropriate side. After about fifteen minutes all was ready for the bridal party to arrive.

The organist began to play *Here Comes the Bride*. Gordon looked around to see Emma walking down the aisle on the arm of her father, her veil covering her beautiful face.

Mathew withdrew, leaving the bride and groom facing the minister.

The minister faced the congregation and said these words:

The grace of our Lord Jesus Christ,

the love of God,

and the fellowship of the Holy Spirit

be with you

The congregation responded;

And with you

Various hymns were sung and prayers recited.

It came time for the declarations and the minister addressed the congregation.

'I am required to ask anyone present who knows a reason why these persons may not lawfully marry, to declare it now.'

A woman's voice rose from the back of the church. 'I believe these two people should not be married.'

The entire congregation turned to see who had the audacity to utter these words.

'You are required to state your reasons madam and identify yourself,' said the bewildered minister.

'My name is Annabelle Phillip, nee Huston. I am Emma's natural mother. I'm also Gordon's mother. They are the twins I was forced to give up at birth.'

'Madam, I suggest you and the bridal party plus Mathew and John meet with me in my office so we can determine an appropriate course of action.'

The five confused people followed the minister out of the church and into the manse. The congregation were completely flabbergasted.

Mathew had to admit what had happened in his hotel all those years ago. Emma was shocked as she had grown up believing her mother had died giving birth. Gordon knew very little apart from being placed in the Ballarat orphanage as a baby. The other telling fact was that Emma and Gordon shared the same birth date and age.

'I'm afraid I cannot continue the marriage service at this juncture. If Mrs Phillip's claim can be proved to be false I'm happy to marry you, Emma and Gordon, however, it does seem unlikely. I'm sorry.'

Further investigations proved without a shadow of a doubt the two lovebirds were, in fact, siblings.

Gordon and Emma were both devastated. Of all the people in the world to fall in love with, they chose their sibling.

Gordon decided he needed to get as far away as possible, not only from Emma but also Melbourne. He sailed to England on September 6, 1883. He never returned to Australia but married an English woman, Sarah Henderson, who produced two sons. Establishing his own law firm enabled him to create significant wealth.

Emma decided to pursue a career in retail and George offered her a position in his Collins Street department store.

Magnificent Deception

Chapter 22

Melbourne 1885

John was feeling forlorn. He'd had great hopes for Gordon to be living in Melbourne for the remainder of his life, happily married to Emma and raising a family. Now his life felt empty. Gordon had immigrated to Britain and he felt awkward when he saw Emma.

The minister totally engrossed himself in operating the King's Walden home. His ambition was to open additional homes in Bendigo and Melbourne. In the two years after Gordon had left Australia's fair shores, John had taken in, and graduated, over fifteen children. He knew this was only a drop in the ocean. He visited Melbourne often to see Mathew and George, and during these visits he would come across countless homeless children. John wished he could take them in, but King's Walden wasn't large enough to accommodate more children.

It was during one of his Melbourne visits that both Mathew and George suggested he take out a mortgage on King's Walden. They would both help the minister in raising donations to make the venture viable. The two businessmen were unable to contribute financially as all their funds were tied up in a new venture.

John decided this would be the correct cause of action. He made an appointment with a lending office from the Commercial Bank of Australia.

July 8, 1885

John had prepared a business plan, which had been vetted and amended by Mathew and George. This plan he carried in his Gladstone bag to the head office of the bank.

Commercial Bank of Australia

Upon entering the impressive building, John was ushered by a bank employee to the first floor where Mr Harold Trembath's office was located. John waited the customary twenty minutes before Mr Trembath's assistant asked him to follow her into the large office.

'Good morning, Reverend, please take a seat.'

'Thank you, and please call me John.'

'As you wish, now how can I be of service?'

John went through his plan in detail with the banker, including the valuer's estimate of King's Walden. The property market had been booming for a number of years, so the property value was impressive. It was more than enough to guarantee the loan of £30,000.

'Well, John, I think I have all the information I need to assess your loan application. You'll receive a letter from the bank in due course.'

'Thank you, Harold, I'll look forward to hearing from you.'

John left the bank not knowing if he would be successful or not. Time would tell.

Two weeks later he received a letter from the bank approving his loan. John was ecstatic. He could now implement his long-term plan to get kids off the street and educated.

Melbourne 1891

Mathew and George had owned the Grand Hotel for over twenty years. It had become the preeminent hotel in the city, and as a consequence, its value had skyrocketed from £70,000 to £350,000. Mathew still owned the two Ballarat hotels, the Golden Nugget and the Duke of Wellington and they also had increased significantly in value. Mathew was acknowledged as one of the richest and most highly respected businessmen in Melbourne, as was George. Both men were members of The Melbourne Club, regarded as the most prestigious men's club in Australia.

The Melbourne Club 1891

Mathew and John were having lunch in the Melbourne Club dining room when their long-time acquaintance Lord Archibald Abbott entered the room. The two men indicated to the esteemed businessmen to join them.

'Hello, Archie. We haven't seen you in here for ages,' said Mathew.

'No, I've been overseas for the past year.'

'Where have you been, Archie?' asked George.

'America.'

'What took you there?'

'I purchased a gold mine in Colorado.'

'A gold mine?'

'Yes, in a little place called Cripple Creek. I thought it might have a mine life of a couple of years, but as the mining continued, we've found amazing gold seams. The potential is endless.'

'So, why aren't you over there running the show as it were?'

'I need investors so we can exploit the mine completely. I'm unknown over there, so I came back to raise capital.'

'What sort of returns do you believe you can offer?'

'I know this sounds extraordinary, but I am guaranteeing a 25% dividend in the first year, increasing to 35% over the following years as the gold yield increases.'

'My God, that is extraordinary Archie!' George said.

'Well, gentlemen, I have to leave you. I'm meeting a potential investor.'

'Are we permitted to ask who?'

'Keep it to yourselves, but it is John Adrian.'

'The Governor?'

'Please keep it quiet. If the press found out there could be implications for the Governor.'

'You have our word, Archie.'

The businessman made his farewells and went to meet with the Governor in a private room.

'That sounds unbelievable George... 25% in the first year! What other investment can guarantee those returns?'

'None that I know of.'

'I think we should consider investing in this Cripple Creek mine,' said Mathew.

'The problem we have, my dear friend, is all our resources are committed to completing the construction of the Windsor Hotel.'

The Windsor Hotel would become the most lavish and prestigious establishment in Melbourne.

'Yes, but we have enough equity in the hotels and your stores to be able to approach the bank for a sizable loan.'

'I'd want to examine the mine's books and geological reports before we made that sort of commitment,' said George.

'I couldn't agree more. Why don't we ask Archie to meet with us and bring along any supporting documentation he has available?'

'It certainly couldn't hurt.'

'I'll contact him tomorrow,' said Mathew.

Mathew was able to get hold of Archibald and arranged to meet him and his business partner at the Melbourne Club the following Tuesday. He contacted George and informed him of the arrangement.

'Who is Archie's business partner?' asked George.

'You know him, Sir William Bannister.'

'The financial expert? That is encouraging.'

Sir William Bannister was the founding partner of the chartered accounting firm Bannister and Irving, regarded as the preeminent accounting firm in Victoria. He was an advisor to the Treasurer and sat on the board of the Commercial Bank of Australia.

Mathew and George arrived at their club at 1 pm, the time agreed to meet for a private lunch with Lord Archibald and Sir William. The two prospective investors were shown into a private dining room where Archie and William were already seated going over some papers.

'Good afternoon Archie, and it's good to see you again, Sir William,' said George.

'Hello Mathew, George, please take a seat. Sir William and I were just going over the audited financials provided by the company's American accounting firm, Hislop & Co,' said Lord Archibald.

'Excuse our ignorance but who are Hislop & Co?' Mathew queried.

'Sir William recommended them to me when I first purchased the mine.'

'They're regarded as the most trusted firm in America,' said Sir William.

'Excellent, we can trust their figures no doubt,' said George.

'Gentlemen, we also have the geologist's report for you both to peruse.'

Mathew and George were given the reports and began reading. The key figure they discovered was that 50,000 ounces had been extracted at 2000 feet in 1888, and the forecasted yield for 1892 was 200,000 ounces at 3000 feet. Based on these projections the mine's turnover would increase £16,000,000.

'These projections are very promising, but do you honestly believe you can increase the mine's output by 200% in two years?'

'We do, based on the geologist's report. He also believes by following the gold seam down to 5000 feet the yield will increase 200% per year for the next five years at least.'

'How much investment are you seeking from us, Archie?' asked George.

'That's completely up to you. Our overall objective is to raise £5,000,000.'

'That's a lot of money to raise.'

'It is but we are very close to closing the offer. We've had an incredible response.'

The two potential investors looked at one another, knowing if they didn't act quickly they would miss out on the investment of the century.

'Would you mind if we left you for a short time so that we can discuss our options?' asked Mathew.

'Not at all. Take your time,' responded Archie.

Mathew and George sat down in the lounge, reflecting on what they had just seen and heard.

'So, what are your thoughts, George?'

'It probably goes against my cautious nature, but I think we should invest.'

'Yes, I agree with you. It now comes down to how much should we invest.'

'Considering we will have to borrow the majority of the capital I think a total of £100,000.'

'I think you're being a little too conservative I was thinking £200,000.'

'Why don't we meet halfway, and say £150,000.'

'Done, come on let's go and inform them of our decision.'

Mathew and George returned to the dining room where they found Lord Archibald and Sir William sharing a bottle of wine.

'So, gentlemen have you arrived at your decision?'

'We have we would like to invest £150,000 in your gold mine.'

'Congratulations! I can assure you both you won't regret it. I haven't shown you a photo of the mine, have I?'

'It looks very impressive, and bloody cold by the looks of it,' said George.

'Oh yes, Colorado gets very cold in winter.'

'What size is the workforce Archie?'

'Currently fifty.'

'Will you need to increase it by much to exploit the expansion?'

'No, the beauty is we won't have to increase the workforce at all.'

'That's excellent; that will maintain the bottom line, Sir William,' said Mathew.

'It will improve it.'

'Well the only thing left to do gentlemen is deposit £150,000 into the Denver National Bank in Colorado. Once the money has been received, I will issue you with the share script.'

'Thank you for the opportunity, Archie. It has been a pleasure doing business with you both.'

'The pleasure has been ours. Now if you will excuse us we have another meeting to attend.'

When Mathew and George left the Melbourne Club, they decided to go to George's apartment and celebrate the deal with a fine malt whisky and a cigar.

The two investors agreed to confirm with their bank the need for a secured loan of £150,000, using their vast asset base as security. The Commercial Bank of Australia, the same bank where Sir William sat on the board, approved the loan and transferred the funds to Colorado.

Mathew and George looked forward to the first dividend payment due on 1st July 1892. The time arrived to check their joint bank account, and to their delight, an amount of £18,750 had been deposited by Cripple Creek Mining Company.

Both men toasted the dividend with a glass of French Champagne in the Melbourne Club.

1893 Crash

Chapter 23

Through the seventies and into the eighties Melbourne had been dubbed "Marvellous Melbourne". Australia's economy was second only to Great Britain.

During the 19th century, Australia's population grew from a few thousand to more than three million Europeans. Nobody knew the size of the Aboriginal population, as they weren't included in the census; in fact, the indigenous people were classified as fauna along with the wombats and kangaroos.

British investors funded roads, railroad tracks, and building construction. Banks flourished, and factory jobs multiplied.

However, things began to change.

During the late 1880s and early 1890s, the outback areas of New South Wales, Queensland, Victoria and South Australia were heavily overstocked. Large numbers of settlers had arrived in the previous thirty years. Their methods of farming led to a loss of vegetative cover and erosion and many native edible plant species vanished with devastating consequences. Between 1895 and 1903 there was a major drought that affected most of the country and became known as the "Federation Drought". The Federation Drought sent Australia spiralling into economic depression. This was the same year Mathew and George invested in the Cripple Creek Mining Company.

With a decreased demand for wool, public works projects fell like dominoes and banks closed their doors. That same year protests to improve working conditions became charged when the military was called in to deal with 30,000 strikers. Within three years the recession was global and had caused the total collapse of Australia's economy. Widespread unemployment set in, and many Australians faced homelessness and hunger. It would take years for the economy to wean itself off wool. In time, the wheat industry took root along with gold and silver mining in the west, ultimately helping to get the country back on its feet.

Between 1890 and 1893, this severe economic depression caused the closure and collapse of many banks. The Federal Bank of Australia ran out of money and closed. In August 1893 the Commercial Bank of Australia, Mathew and George's bank, suspended operations. Twelve other banks soon followed. Those who had put their savings into building societies, as well as those who had borrowed heavily to fund their own speculative investments, found themselves in desperate straits. Mathew and George were among them. Businessmen, pastoralist farmers and land speculators weren't able to pay their overdrafts, and thousands of small and large investors were ruined. The partners were determined not to collapse, and they needed to come up with a plan. They knew they could rely on the enormous dividends from Cripple Creek. The only issue was whether the Commercial Bank foreclosed on the loan. The first dividend cheque had been paid directly off the loan, so the bank could see their good intent. The next payment, £52,500, was due 1 July 1893 and they contacted the bank and informed them of the imminent payment. The bank was pleased, indicating all was well and the payment was welcome. True to their word the two investors paid the dividend directly against the loan balance, not keeping a penny. Two weeks later the bank suspended operations.

Over the following twelve months, the two businessmen played a juggling act between keeping the hotels operating as well as Georges Department store and keeping the bank's administrators at bay.

The third dividend cheque was critical in keeping the two businesses liquid. It was due on 1 July 1894, but it wasn't deposited. They waited a week and then began to panic. Mathew attempted to contact Archie but was informed he was no longer with the company. The reality was the company no longer existed. The gold had dried up four years previously. The photo of the workforce was that of another mine. Archie and Sir William had organised a massive fraud. The initial two years' dividend came from other gullible investors. It was determined the two crooks got away with as much as £2,000,000 each. The authorities had no idea where they had disappeared.

The desperate friends met at Mathew's home to discuss the situation and determine what options were available to them.

'Well, fellows, I think we all know we're in a spot of bother,' said Mathew.

'I'd describe it a bit more strongly than that, Mathew. I'd say we're buggered,' said George.

'Not while there's hope.'

'What hope have we got?' said John.

'I've been giving it quite a bit of thought, chaps; I believe the only hope we have of recovering is to bring back the Banshees.'

'You've got to be bloody kidding! Dress up as women and rob stagecoaches? I'm sorry, but I'm too old for that,' said John.

'Hold on, John, that's not what I'm proposing. It has come to my attention that a ship called the *Cygnet* will be sailing along the Victorian coast before sailing out into the Southern Ocean on her way to England.'

'What makes this ship so special?' asked George.

'The fact it will be transporting 60,000 ounces of gold dust makes it special.'

'Are you suggesting we become pirates?' asked John.

'Yes, that's exactly what I'm suggesting.'

'You obviously believe we could pull it off, Mathew?'

'With the proper planning and resources, yes I do. I have been constructing a plan over the past few weeks.'

'Forgive my ignorance, but how much would all that gold be worth?' asked George.

'At today's price about £12,000,000.'

'My God, this is sounding better all the time.'

'Do we all agree that we at least develop a plan and determine what resources we need to accomplish our goal? Once we've done that we can decide whether we go ahead.'

'How much time have we got? When's the ship sailing?' asked John.

'She's due to sail on 2nd October.'

'That gives us three weeks,' said George.

'That's right, George, time is of the essence. I suggest we get together daily. Each of us will be assigned tasks which need to be signed off on time. We cannot afford to waste a minute of any day.'

'What day do you think will be the cut-off point to make our final decision?'

'No later than a week before sailing; in other words, gentlemen, we have two weeks to finalise the plan and arrange for any resources that are needed.'

'George, we may need to use your cruising yacht as part of the operation. Are you all right with that?' asked Mathew.

'Yes, although if you are thinking, we can catch an ocean-going steamer with *Mary* you're very much mistaken.'

'No, that's not what I had in mind.'

Pirating We Will Go

Chapter 24

The Banshees met again the next day and Mathew outlined his proposed plan to George and John.

'As we all aware the *Cygnet* is due to depart Port Melbourne on 2nd October. She will follow the Victorian coastline until she reaches Portland where she will head out for open seas and the Southern Ocean. We need to stop her before reaches open sea, I suggest off the coast of Port Fairy.'

'Why Port Fairy?' asked George.

'It's a sleepy fishing village yet it has a constant flow of fishermen coming and going. Our activities won't be noticed. Also, I know a dubious sailor who lives there. He used to stay at the Golden Nugget every time he found gold which was quite often. We are going to have to enlist his services to recruit our crew. I have already spoken with him, and he's agreeable for the right price.'

'Please continue, Mathew; you have obviously given this not only some thought but have taken action,' said George.

'Richard, our man in Port Fairy, will be able to provide us with a fast steamer which we will use to board the ship.'

'Forgive my scepticism Mathew, but I can't imagine a small steamer running down an ocean liner capable of sailing at twenty knots,' said John.

'I couldn't agree more and that is not the plan. If you will allow me to continue…'

'Sorry Mathew, carry on.'

'You, John, and the four newly recruited pirate crew, as well as myself, will purchase tickets on the *Cygnet*. As we approach Port Fairy John and I will shave our beards and dress in our Banshee costumes. We will approach the bridge requesting that the Captain allows two ladies to inspect the wheelhouse. Once inside we produce our revolvers and order the crew to bring the ship down to five knots. This will be when the steamer comes alongside. The crew on board the *Cygnet* will throw down rope ladders for the remainder of the pirates to board.'

'Why five knots Mathew and not a complete stop?'

'I think smoke billowing from the funnels is important. We don't want to alert other vessels. It's a very busy sea route.'

'How will the steamer know the ship has been secured?'

'I will use a torch to signal success, three flashes a pause and another three.'

'So do we round up all the passengers and crew?' asked George.

'No, at least I hope not. Our aim should be to unload the gold without alerting anybody on board. One of the advantages of Port Fairy is the *Cygnet* passes by there at 1 am.'

'Do we know how many strong boxes need to be unloaded, Mathew?

I have a fairly good idea there are 60,000 ounces of gold dust; that's 3750 pounds. Each box can carry 50 pounds, so I estimate there will be 75 boxes.'

'Do you know where on the ship the gold is being stored?' asked George.

'That is a problem. I'm sure it won't be in the hold of the ship, so more than likely it will be in a secure area close to the captain's quarters.'

'How do we ascertain its location?' asked John.

'I'm hoping the captain will tell us without too much persuasion. Once we have offloaded the strong boxes onto the steamer—'

'I'm sorry to interrupt you, Mathew, but how do you propose to get 75 fifty-pound boxes off the ship and onto the tender?' asked John.

'The steamer has a crane and a large rope net normally used during its fishing operations; we'll use that.'

'That sounds like it could work.'

'To ensure no alarm is given we will kidnap the captain, dropping him on the shore approximately three miles from Port Fairy. By the time he reaches the village and notifies the authorities, we will be long gone.'

'That begs the question Mathew; 'long gone' where?'

'The steamer will rendezvous with *Mary*, George's yacht, which has been anchored two miles astern of the *Cygnet*. The gold will be transferred, and the steamer taken back to port by Richard.'

'Where do we go? Back to Melbourne?' asked John.

'No John, that would be too dangerous. My plan would be to sail to Lorne further down the coastline. It has a working pier, and unloading the strongboxes won't bring undue attention.

'Transporting the gold back to Melbourne and then storing it seems risky to me,' said John.

'I agree, John. I have rented a small cottage near Lorne. It is quite isolated, and therefore it should suit our purpose. I propose we store the boxes there and gradually bring them back.'

'Back to where?'

'I'm not sure yet; we need to devise a plan where we can use the gold to pay our bank debts without causing suspicion.'

'Why don't we use the same method we used to dispose of the gold from the stagecoach robberies? We find an abandoned mine and pretend we've hit gold,' suggested John.

'That's an excellent idea, John, that means the Gold Commissioner assays the gold and issues a bank draft to the value. Everything becomes legitimate.'

'John, can we ask you to investigate what mines are available as well as look viable?' asked George.

'I don't see why not, George. I'll travel to Ballarat to investigate.'

John caught the train to Ballarat the following day. He called into King's Walden to see Kate who now managed the facility. She reported that all the children bar one were progressing well. The odd kid out was a boy called Malcolm who had run away several times and was currently missing.

The Ballarat goldfields had changed significantly from the time when John was a gold miner. Very few small mines existed now. Most of the gold coming out of the area was being mined by large companies.

He made some inquiries and discovered that a small mining company that had been operating three shafts had recently gone bankrupt. The receivers were willing to sell the company for £1000. John knew this would be an ideal front to launder the gold, so he returned to Melbourne to report his discovery to his two partners. It was agreed by the three pirates to purchase the Eldorado Gold Mining Company.

Now they were ready to embark on their pirating careers they had ticked all the boxes and had three days up their sleeve to finalise their plans. An intricate part of the final plan was recruiting men that could not only be trusted but were capable of completing the tasks assigned to them by a faceless master; Mathew.

Four men came on board the *Cygnet* with Mathew and John. Not that they knew either man; it was important that Mathew and John could not be identified by anyone including their gang.

The written instructions were that when they felt the ship slow down, they were to go out to the starboard deck and look out for the steamer. Once it was sighted, they would then lower the rope ladders, allowing the remainder of the gang to come aboard.

They were to wait for instructions as to where the strong boxes were located and then unload them onto the steamer. Once that task was completed they would join their comrades on the steamer heading for the coast with the *Cygnet*'s captain on board. Finally, they were to rendezvous with the yacht and unload the treasure. Each man would receive £1,000 for his effort.

Treasure

Chapter 25

October 2, 1893

The *Cygnet* was moored at the Port Melbourne wharf taking on passengers who would be embarking on the long and sometimes dangerous voyage to Liverpool, England. The cargo had been loaded on the previous day including seventy-five steel boxes, which had been stored in the ship's brig. The Captain was the only one with a key and kept it on his person at all times.

Two of the passengers were travelling under assumed names Mathew had become Francis Spencer, and John was now Samuel Becket. Both Francis and Samuel were in first-class while the other gang members were in third class.

The two first-class passengers went straight to their cabins and stayed there until the assigned time when they would emerge as Mrs Spencer and Mrs Becket.

Mathew checked his watch. It had just turned midnight and it was time to play dress ups with the wig, bonnet and a long dress with a bustle. Both men had shaved their beards as soon as they entered their cabins.

At 12.30 am, Mathew and John met in the alleyway outside their cabins, making their way to the top deck where the bridge was located. Mathew knocked on the wheelhouse door and a seaman opened it.

'Can I help you, madam?'

'We were wondering if you could ask the Captain if it would be possible to have a tour of the bridge?'

Captain Forsythe overheard the conversation and welcomed the two ladies to enter the wheelhouse. 'Well, ladies, you are up very late.'

'We couldn't sleep, Captain.'

'I see, well this is the nerve centre of the *Cygnet*. It is where we steer the ship as well as navigate her course.'

'That's fascinating, Captain. How many of you are on the bridge at any one time?'

'Normally five but tonight we have the full complement of eight considering it is a very dangerous coastline.'

Mathew and John looked at one another; that was the signal to pull out their British Bulldog Double Action Revolvers.

British Bulldog Revolver

'Everybody put your hands up high, so we can see them. Don't try any funny business or you'll be shot.'

'What do you think you're doing, ladies? This is piracy!' said the Captain.

'It certainly is Captain, now tell us where you have the gold stashed, and we'll be on our way and nobody gets hurt.'

'I'm afraid you've picked the wrong ship. There's no way I will reveal where the gold is.'

Mathew approached the Captain, gun in hand, pointing at his head. 'Are you married, sir?'

'What's that got to do with anything?'

'Do you have children?'

'Yes, I do; three. Why are you asking me these questions?'

'If you don't tell us where the gold is hidden I will shoot you. Captain, this is not your gold. It's the British Government's gold. Are you willing to sacrifice your life and subject your family to such grief for the sake of some gold that doesn't even belong to you?'

A look of inevitability passed over the seafarer's face. He knew this female pirate was right. He unclipped the key from his belt and explained how to reach the brig.

'Thank you, Captain, now, please pass me the key to the wheelhouse, instruct the First Officer to reduce speed to five knots and maintain a steady course.'

The two pirates tied up the ship's crew in the Captain's cabin. Only the First Officer was left in the wheelhouse.

Mathew and John found the brig on one of the lower decks. They had signalled to the others to follow them. It took two hours to haul the boxes onto the top deck and lower them down onto the steamer.

The rest of the operation went without a hitch. All the boxes had been loaded and the Captain had been dropped off at a beach just three miles from Port Fairy. By the time he was able to alert the police the Banshees would be well on the way to Lorne where the treasure would be stored.

The final instruction Mathew and John gave to the First Officer was to maintain the five-knot speed for at least two hours. If he disobeyed, the Captain would be shot.

The steamer made a successful rendezvous with George's *Mary*, the strong boxes were transferred, and the three Banshees sailed to Lorne where the gold would be stored and transferred gradually to Eldorado Gold Mine in Ballarat.

The following day *The Age*'s headline was *Pirates' Huge Gold Haul*. The front page was dedicated to the daring raid by female pirates. One journalist noted it was similar to the Banshee stagecoach robberies years ago.

The retired Police Commissioner, Francis O'Connor, sitting in his conservatory reading *The Age* wondered if the Banshees had come out of retirement. I still remember those eyes, he thought.

The three friends headed back to Ballarat with three of the strong boxes which they placed in a secure area deep below the ground in one of the horizontal shafts. It had been decided it would be John who would operate the mine as Mathew and George were required back in Melbourne to run their business. The Eldorado Gold Mining Company, however, had three shareholders all of whom would benefit greatly from the new gold discoveries from the mine.

The Gold Commissioner assayed the gold discovered in Eldorado in batches, and a bank draft was issued for the assayed amount. The Banshees were soon able to pay back their bank debts and secure their properties.

Of the initial £12,000,000, each Banshee received £3,000,000 after paying their outstanding debts.

John opened three more homes; two in Melbourne and one in Geelong.

George expanded his retail empire, opening another department store in Bourke Street and calling it Mary's in honour of his late wife.

Mathew was already a very wealthy man. He was also very cautious; he decided that if anything went wrong and arrest was imminent, he would escape to San Marino, a small country in northern Italy. San Marino had no extradition treaty with any other country. He transferred £3,000,000 to the Bank of San Marino where he had opened an account. A portion of the money went to purchasing a large villa with an olive grove and vineyard. He called it his retirement home.

England April 1895

Lord Abernethy was in ill health. At the age of eighty-six, he had been diagnosed with pneumonia. He was having trouble breathing and had to endure long and painful coughing fits. His wife Julia sent a telegraph to her son Mathew, informing him of his father's condition. Mathew was the sole heir to the Abernethy estate as a consequence of his brother Joseph dying some years earlier.

Mathew made arrangements to sail to England. He knew he would not arrive before his father passed away, but he needed to take over the management of the estate.

Emma, his adopted daughter, had been involved in the business for some time, running the hotels. She had two very experienced mentors in her father and George. It was Mathew's intent to pass the baton to Emma. She was more than capable of managing the business. He arranged to dine with his daughter and inform her of his plans.

Mathew arranged for the restaurant to deliver their dinner to his apartment in the Windsor Hotel.

'Emma, my father is on his deathbed. I don't expect him to live for very much longer.'

'Oh, that's sad. I enjoyed his company when we visited him and Grandmother all those years ago.'

'Yes, I love and respect him very much even though I haven't seen him much over the years.'

'Are you going to go over there?'

'I am, but not just for a visit. I will be the new Lord Abernethy and with the title goes the responsibility to run the estate.'

Mathew explained his plan for Emma to take over the business.

'Father, I have something to tell you that could affect the timing of your voyage.'

'Oh, and what might that be?'

'George intended to see you tonight to ask for my hand in marriage.'

Mathew stared at her. 'George? My good friend George?'

Emma nodded.

'But he's old enough to be your father!'

She smiled composedly. 'Yes, he's much older than me. Mind you, at thirty-seven, most women are married with three children.'

'That's true. I should be happy for you. In fact, I am glad for you.'

'Thank you, Father. Both George and I have experienced tragedies in our lives and I think we deserve to be happy. So now you see our dilemma. We need to marry before you depart. Father, I want you to give me away.'

'How soon can we organise a wedding?' asked Mathew.

'I don't know, but I'll let you know shortly.'

Father and daughter hugged each other they then sat down to a superb meal. They discussed both the wedding plans and the business plans.

The wedding date was set for May 30 at St Mary's Church Carlton. It was not the spectacular event Mathew had envisaged for his daughter's wedding, but they had to be practical. Mathew was booked to sail to England on June 3. The reception for the one hundred guests would be held in the Grand Dining Room at the Windsor.

Emma decided on a simple wedding this time. She had one attendant; her maid of honour Sarah, who had been her nanny when she was a baby. Sarah was now sixty-three and the mother of two boys.

George asked John to be his best man considering the other choice was already busy as the father of the bride.

The weather was good considering winter was just around the corner. There were blue skies with the maximum temperature hovering around 60 degrees Fahrenheit.

The small bluestone church was full, with not a spare seat anywhere. George and John stood nervously in front of the altar and after a short wait the bridal march began playing on the church organ. The congregation all turned to see Emma resplendent in a white dress walking slowly towards the aisle. George had a tear in his eye when she took her place next to him.

The minister was an old friend of John's, Edward Kelly. He was no relation to the infamous bushranger.

The ceremony reached the point where Reverend Kelly said; 'I am required to ask anyone present who knows a reason why these persons may not lawfully marry, to declare it now.'

Emma and George held their breaths, but there was no response from the congregation.

The Reverend Kelly then pronounced them husband and wife. They kissed and departed from the church, greeting their friends as they walked along the aisle.

The reception was enjoyed by all the guests. Mathew made available the Windsor's finest wines including Krug champagne.

The bride and groom said their goodbyes and retired to the honeymoon suite located on the top floor of the hotel. They intended to have a short honeymoon at Phillip Island once Mathew had departed for England.

Time to Pass the Baton

Mathew briefed Emma and George on all aspects of the business. George was an active partner in the hotels and therefore, he knew most of what was required. Emma was allocated 25% of the shares while George retained 24%, leaving Mathew with a 51% controlling interest.

June 3, 1895

The *HM Himalaya*, the most modern ship to sail under the P&O Line at that time, was moored at Port Melbourne waiting to take on 500 passengers. The ship's destination was Liverpool England.

Mathew's carriage carried his large sea trunk secured on the roof. Necessity determined that most of his possessions remained in his house in Ballarat.

Emma, George and John arrived in a separate carriage. All were sad to say farewell to their good friend and father.

'Goodbye, old and dear friend. I'll endeavour to travel to the mother country to visit you before too long,' said John.

'I sincerely hope so, John. When you do, I'll make sure we will have a wonderful time. Your mother would also love to see you. It's a pity your father passed away last year. I am sure both of them would be very proud of you.'

He turned to his son-in-law. 'Goodbye George, you just make sure you take care of my princess.'

'Don't worry Mathew, I will.'

'Well, my love, it's goodbye but not for long. I look forward to your visits.'

Mathew and his beloved daughter had said their farewells at the Windsor where he stayed on his final night.

Once boarded, the businessman made his way to the state room on the first-class deck. It was to be a very comfortable journey as long as the seas were calm.

First Class Cabin

Lord Abernethy went out onto the promenade round about the location he and the other Banshees plundered the *Cygnet*. It seemed an age ago, yet it was barely two years.

The voyage was going smoothly as Mathew spent a considerable amount of his time reading and partaking in the clay pigeon shooting competition. He became the ship's champion shooter.

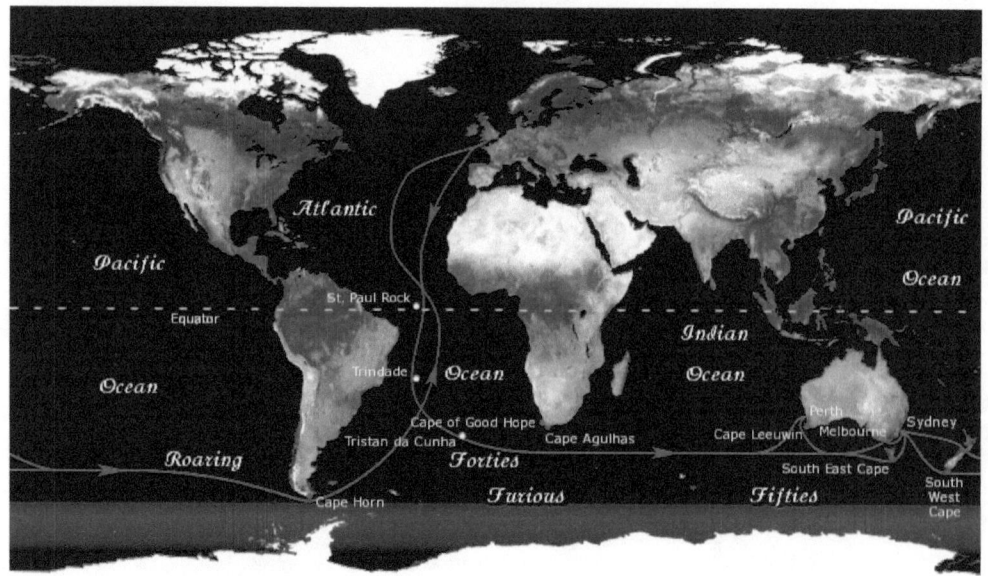

After twenty-six uneventful days at sea, the *Himalaya* was due to round the perilous Cape of Good Hope. The Captain had been notified by the weather bureau located at Cape Town to expect storms and very rough seas. This is what every captain dreaded; he organised his crew to inform the passengers of the inclement weather approaching and to instruct all passengers to remain in their cabins.

The crew then spent the remainder of their time before rounding the cape tying down all loose items on deck.

Black clouds began swirling and although it was the middle of the day, the sun could not be seen. The light was very dim; almost like nightfall.

The seas rose to the point where waves began crashing over the main deck.

Keepsake of Voyage — R.M.S. « HYMALAYA » In stormy weather

Many of the ship's passengers suffered terrible seasickness while two elderly ladies suffered broken arms and would remain confined to their cabins for the remainder of the voyage.

Mathew remained unscathed although he didn't enjoy the experience. The remainder of the journey was smooth sailing and the *Himalaya* docked at Liverpool wharf on August 15.

The butler from Abernethy Manor was waiting on the wharf ready to accompany his Lordship on the four-hour train journey to Gillingham Station in Kent. A carriage was waiting to greet them and take the two gentlemen on the twenty-minute ride to the manor.

Lady Abernethy and her daughter Rosie were standing in front of the mansion when Mathew's carriage arrived.

The family members hugged and kissed. It had been nearly thirty years since they had all seen one another.

Melbourne December 1

Emma and George were having dinner in the Collins Street apartment. They often discussed business over dinner and today was no exception.

'Darling, have you heard what Henry Sutton has installed in his father's music stores?'

'No, I know the man is a genius and he's invented all sorts of things.'

'Have you heard of the telephone?'

'That contraption that American fellow Bell invented. You can talk to someone through a wire or some such thing.'

'That's right. Well, Henry has taken it one step further. He's connected the stores as well as all the various departments within the stores.'

Henry Sutton became a world-renowned inventor. His battery was the first in the world to store electricity and it was acclaimed by Thomas Edison. Other inventions included a facsimile machine and a method of transmitting moving pictures over a wire, which he named the *Telephane*. Twenty years later John Logie Baird used Henry's invention to create the first television.

Henry went on to develop Australia's first motor vehicles, incorporating his invention the carburettor.

In 1908 Henry invented the first portable radio and many other wireless telegraphy systems. The Australian, American, Japanese and British navies later used his inventions.

'Just imagine having our stores connected by telephone plus the various departments just as Suttons Music have done,' said Emma.

'Going one step further, we could have telephones in each hotel room, plus throughout the hotel,' pondered George. 'Why don't we contact Henry and arrange for him to assess the size and cost of the project?'

Emma wrote a letter to Henry Sutton, requesting a meeting to discuss their communication plan. Henry responded immediately, suggesting they meet at his Malvern home the following week. The inventor could see the potential with other hotels around the world adopting the same plan.

George and Emma arranged for a carriage to take them to Malvern, a two-hour journey. Once they arrived an enthusiastic Henry Sutton escorted the couple into his extensive workshop.

'So, from your letter, you wish to establish a telephone network throughout the two hotels in Melbourne.'

'Yes, that's correct. We would also be interested in wiring the two Ballarat hotels,' said Emma.

'I'm keen to examine the possibility of having lines in my department stores,' said George.

'Well, it sounds like a great opportunity, so why don't I visit the buildings and assess what would be required? I can then give you a quote for the work.'

'Excellent, Henry! When would you be available?' asked George.

'I can come tomorrow if you like.'

'What time would suit you?' said Emma.

'Shall we say 10 am?'

'That would suit us,' Emma agreed. 'We'll see you at the Windsor at 10 am.'

Henry Sutton was true to his word. He arrived on the dot of 10 am and spent the remainder of the day examining the Windsor and her sister hotel the Grand. His conclusion was both hotels could be networked with telephones in each guest room. He was given the go ahead to begin the project and it was completed two months later. The investment was £2,500 and a further £1500 was invested in wiring the department stores. No other hotel group or retail chain in the world had such a sophisticated telephone system.

The Lord of the Manor

Chapter 27

Mathew had almost forgotten just how beautiful Abernethy Manor and its surroundings were. He was walking in the grounds reflecting on the news that his father had passed away just two weeks before he arrived back in England. He was deeply saddened; all that knew his father, including his family, held him in high esteem.

Mathew was now Lord Abernethy, lord of all he surveyed. He was aware that he would miss Australia and his daughter and friends, but he had no other choice but to accept his inheritance and the responsibility it entailed.

The history of the Abernethy family dictated that only a male could inherit the estate and he had no male heir. This he knew was a problem, which needed to be solved. His sister Rosie and her husband David lived on the estate in a large apartment contained within the manor. They both took an active role in managing the estate and would be invaluable to Mathew in enabling him in to manage the property effectively.

Mathew decided to consult his mother about finding a suitable wife considering he was now sixty-two and had never married.

'Mother, may I ask for your advice?'

'Certainly, son; regarding what?'

'I'm concerned I have no heir to pass on the title and estate.'

'Yes, that certainly presents a problem.'

'I've decided to marry and hope to father a son.'

'Wonderful, who's the lucky lady? Do we know her?'

'No, I've got no idea who she might be. I was hoping you may be able to suggest someone.'

'My goodness, Mathew you are putting pressure on me, darling.'

'I just thought you might know of a suitable lady in the county.'

'Leave it with me, son.'

'Thank you, Mother.'

Lady Abernethy sat in the front parlour with a cup of tea. 'Who do I know who would be suitable? She must be of childbearing age and from a proper family.' As much as she thought about it, no one came to mind, so she decided to consult her close friend Lady Arlington.

The following day she called on her driver to prepare the carriage for the ten-mile journey. She arrived at the Arlington Estate at 11 am, just in time for tea and cake.

After the preliminary greetings, she broached the subject with her hostess. 'Caroline, I have a problem I was hoping you may be able to assist me in solving.'

'I'll try Julia… what's the problem?'

Julia explained the conundrum to her friend.

Lady Arlington smiled. 'Julia, do you know the Earl of Cambridge?'

'I've met him a few times, but I wouldn't say we were on close terms. Why?'

'He has a daughter, Anne, who I believe is twenty-one. Apparently she's quite beautiful.'

'Do you think such a young woman would be interested in a sixty-two-year-old man?'

'He's not just a sixty-two-year-old man, Julia, he is Lord Abernethy, one of the wealthiest men in England. Not only that but he is still quite handsome and charming.'

'How do we arrange an introduction?'

'Leave it to me, dear; I'll get in touch with you when an introduction has been arranged. James, the Earl, and I go back a long way.'

'Thank you, Caroline I knew you would be able to help.'

Lady Abernethy returned to the manor full of hope. She informed Mathew of her meeting over dinner that evening. He seemed quite happy with the result and looked forward to meeting the young lady.

Lady Abernethy and Lady Arlington conferred, and it was agreed that Caroline make contact with the Earl via a hand-delivered letter.

Dear James,

I hope you and your family are well. I am writing to you on behalf of my very good friend Lady Abernethy. Her son, Mathew, has recently returned from Australia where he established a large business empire. Lord Abernethy, his father, recently died leaving the estate to Mathew who is now regarded as one of the wealthiest gentlemen in Britain.

Mathew is single and is seeking a wife to provide him with an heir. The purpose of this letter is to propose a meeting between your daughter Anne and Mathew to determine if they are suited to each other.

I look forward to your response.

Yours Sincerely

Caroline

The Earl read the letter with interest Anne was his only child. Her mother died in childbirth and he never remarried. His desire was for Anne to marry into the right family but more importantly to be happy in her married life. The Abernethy family certainly satisfied his first criteria and an introduction to the young man would determine if she would be happy.

He replied to Caroline's letter, suggesting he and Anne make the journey to Abernethy Manor to meet Mathew. At no stage in the communication was Mathew's age mentioned.

September 1, 1895

James Hathaway, the Earl of Cambridge, and his daughter Anne, boarded the train at Cambridge Station. The journey to Gillingham Station was expected to take three hours. Mathew had arranged a carriage, the estate's best, to meet the visitors.

Lord Abernethy was feeling nervous. He hadn't felt so pensive since he partook in the first highway robbery in Victoria.

He was waiting in the front parlour, sitting in a chair by the bay window which had an expansive view of the long driveway leading up to the mansion.

At last, he saw the carriage approaching. He checked his attire and ensured his white hair was groomed and he was now ready to greet his visitors.

Mathew had retained his good looks despite his sixty-two years; his eyes were just as blue, and his skin was a light honey olive. Overall, he was a very handsome distinguished gentleman.

Julia entered the room and she could see her son was nervous. 'Come on Mathew, I'll accompany you when you greet the Earl and his daughter.'

Julia put her arm through her son's arm and together they walked out to the front of the manor just as the carriage pulled up.

The driver opened the carriage door the Earl disembarked first, greeting Mathew and Julia. Anne did not follow for what seemed to Mathew an eternity and when finally, she left the carriage, Mathew was aghast. He had never seen such a beautiful young woman before. Anne was tall and very elegant with jet-black hair and stunning blue eyes.

In contrast, Anne was shocked to see Mathew looked as old as her father. He was in fact two years older than the Earl.

Mathew and Julia invited their visitors into the manor house where tea and cake were to be served in the conservatory. Mathew could tell Anne was expecting a much younger man and he felt quite uncomfortable in consequence.

After they had completed their morning tea Mathew suggested to the beautiful young woman that she accompany him on a walk through the estate's gardens. She agreed.

As they walked in the magnificent gardens, Anne began to warm to Mathew. His obvious intelligence and charm had begun to have the desired effect.

When the couple returned to the manor, they found the Earl and Lady Abernethy in deep conversation.

The time came for the visitors to depart Abernethy. Mathew quietly asked Anne if she would permit him to see her again and she agreed.

Over the next nine months, Mathew travelled to Cambridge twice a month, courting the young beauty. She was soon infatuated with the sophisticated man courting her.

May 1, 1896

Mathew embarked on the familiar train trip to visit Anne in Cambridge. This visit was to be different from the others, as this time he intended to ask the Earl of Cambridge for the hand of his daughter. He was feeling apprehensive as he had no idea what the Earl's response would be.

After the usual tea and cake in the conservatory, Mathew asked if he could speak to the Earl privately. Anne knew the purpose of the meeting and quietly retired.

'So, Mathew, what is it you wish to speak to me about?'

'Sir, I would like to ask you for Anne's hand in marriage.'

'So, there is no preamble? Just straight out with it?'

'I'm sorry, sir. I'm very nervous.'

The earl smiled. 'There's no need. I give you my blessing. By the way, you can call me James, after all, I'm younger than you.'

'Thank you, sir; I mean James. Would you excuse me, so I can inform Anne?'

'Yes, of course, I'm sure she's very keen to hear your news.'

Anne was euphoric. They could now start planning their wedding day.

The wedding would take place in the Arlington family's place of worship, Cathedral Ely in Cambridge on 15 July. Over two hundred guests were invited; the wedding breakfast would be held in the Grand Banquet Room at Arlington Estate.

The "Isle of Ely" is so-called because it was only accessible by boat until the waterlogged fens were drained in the 17th century. Still susceptible to flooding today, it was these watery surroundings that gave Ely its original name the 'Isle of Eels', a translation of the Anglo Saxon word 'Eilig'.

Ely Cathedral

The couple decided to embark on a grand tour of Europe for their honeymoon. They departed from Dover, sailing to Ostend in the Netherlands. Mathew hired a very comfortable coach, which took the married couple to Paris. They discovered the city of lights for the next three weeks and both enjoyed the museums and art galleries as well as the magnificent restaurants.

The next city they visited was Geneva in Switzerland and then went on to Lausanne where they stayed for a week. The most dangerous section of their travels was crossing the Alps into Northern Italy. The honeymooners then changed their mode of transport to train and headed for Florence where they stayed for four days before moving on to San Marino. Mathew was keen to view the villa and orchard he had acquired a few years before.

Both Mathew and Anne were impressed with both the villa and the acres of olive groves and vineyards surrounding the estate. If the worst did happen and he and Anne were forced to flee England, Mathew felt comfortable that they could lead a very comfortable and happy life in San Marino.

He arranged a meeting with the manager of the estate who resided in a villa on the estate some distance from the main house. His name was Bruno Romano. He had lived in the valley all his life and was regarded as an expert orchardist. The yield from both the olives and grapes had increased each year since Mathew initially purchased the property.

'Bruno, I am well pleased with the way you have managed the estate. The yields are pleasing, and we have been fortunate with the prices we have been achieving. Do you have any recommendations to further improve the profitability of the orchard and vineyard?'

'Well My Lord, I do have a few ideas.'

'Please don't be so formal, Bruno; call me Mathew. So what are these ideas you have?'

'We are currently selling the crop to processing plants who turn our olives into virgin oil. Similarly, we sell the grapes to the local wine makers who then ferment our crop to make fine wine.

'If we could establish processing facilities on the estate, we would increase our profits dramatically.'

'What sort of investment would be required, Bruno?'

'I would need to do some more research. Would you mind if I got back to you in say a fortnight?'

'Anne and I will be travelling back to England in a couple of weeks, so leave it until we return. Make it next month… there's no hurry.'

Mathew and Anne bade Bruno farewell and proceeded to Venice where they checked into the luxurious Centurion Hotel. Mathew noted telephones were not installed in the rooms.

They enjoyed exploring Venice with its labyrinth of canals; Anne particularly liked the traditional gondoliers. After five days it was time to move on to Florence where the famous museums were of great interest and then to their final destination, Rome. The couple stayed in the ancient city for six days then embarked on the *Cedric*, White Star Line's newest and most modern cruise ship, for their journey home.

The *Cedric* took ten days to sail the route, docking in London Port on 25 November 1896. A carriage from Abernethy Estate was waiting for them. The journey took an hour. Mathew and Anne had enjoyed their European tour but felt a sense of home sweet home as the carriage wound up the tree lined driveway to the manor.

Julia, Emma and David were waiting for them in the conservatory, the family's favourite room.

After the greetings were over, the family sat down to a splendid lunch. Many questions were asked and answered during the course of the meal.

It wasn't long before Mathew became heavily involved in the management of the estate. His plans included increasing the sheep flock and introducing Angora goats. Anne used her time riding her Arabian horse Sultan along the horse tracks dotted throughout the estate and assisting Julia in running the household.

One day, Mathew returned from the far fields and noticed Anne was not in the parlour or the conservatory where she would normally be to greet him at the end of the day. He climbed the staircase to their bedroom where he found her lying on the bed.

'Hello, darling, aren't you feeling well?'

'Hello, sweetheart. No, I feel a little queasy.'

'Would you like me to call the doctor?'

'No, don't be silly. I'm sure I'll be fine. I just needed to lie down for a little while. You go down for drinks, and I'll join you for dinner.'

'Are you sure? It's better to be safe than sorry.'

'I'm sure darling. Now give me a kiss, and I'll join you later.'

Mathew made his way downstairs to the conservatory where the rest of the family were already enjoying a gin and tonic. He explained Anne's situation to them.

'You, don't think she might be pregnant do you, Mathew?' asked Emma.

'My God! I didn't think of that. I really should call Doctor Thomas, shouldn't I?'

'Well, it wouldn't hurt would it?'

Mathew instructed one of his servants to ride into the village and fetch the family doctor. The physician was able to come immediately and arrived at the manor at 6 pm. He went up to the bedroom and examined the young woman. After about forty minutes he returned downstairs and addressed Mathew and the family.

'There is absolutely nothing to worry about Mathew. A woman of your wife's age and health will have no problem carrying the baby full term. What she's experiencing now is normal for a three-months pregnant woman.'

'That's marvellous!'

Mathew climbed the stairs as fast as he could manage, and upon entering the bedroom he saw his beautiful Anne laying serenely on the bed.

'Congratulations, darling, you are going to be a mother.' The excited husband went over to the bed and kissed his wife.

She smiled up at him. 'Congratulations to you too, sweetheart; you're going to be a father.'

'We'll have to start thinking about names,' said Mathew.

'I think we should wait until we know what sex the baby is, don't you?'

'Yes, of course, I suppose I'm getting a little carried away. How do you feel now?'

'Much better thank you. I'll come down for dinner. Just give me a few minutes to freshen up.'

Dinner was a happy occasion. The family's lives had turned for the better since Mathew and Anne had arrived from Australia, and now they had a baby to celebrate.

August 1897

Anne was asleep when she felt her waters break. She woke Mathew who jumped out of bed and began pacing around the room.

'So what happens now? What do I need to do?'

'You need to alert the midwife to come quickly.'

The couple had arranged for a very experienced midwife to stay at the manor during the last month of Anne's pregnancy.

The midwife, Lucy Best, arrived soon after Mathew alerted her. She looked over Anne, and said, 'Lord Abernethy you need to ride into the village and inform Doctor Thomas to come quickly.'

The doctor arrived an hour later, taking over the proceedings with the support of Lucy. Anne was in labour for twelve hours, and finally a baby girl was born. They named her Beatrice Julia. Although Mathew was ecstatic, he still did not have an heir to the family name and fortune.

Beatrice was a delight for both parents. Mathew always looked forward to the end of the day when he could play with his beautiful daughter. Although Anne had appointed a nanny and a wet nurse as soon as Beatrice was born, she spent much of her day playing and attending the baby's needs.

When little Bea turned one Anne announced she was once again with child. Naturally, both parents were delighted.

The pregnancy proceeded without any real problems, and after nine months and two weeks a little heir apparent was born to Mathew and Anne. They named him Samuel Mathew.

Both parents agreed their family was now complete as Mathew was now sixty-five and not keen to father more children.

Mathew missed his life in Australia, but he was in constant communication with his daughter and her husband—his good friend George. The turnover figures for both the hotels and the department stores were very encouraging. He also relished being Lord Abernethy and living in the magnificent manor with Anne, his beautiful wife, and their two children. Despite his love for Australia he couldn't see himself living anywhere else.

May 1, 1902

Samuel and Bea were running around the maypole in the village square. May Day was always a happy time celebrating spring.

Mathew and Anne looked on proudly. Bea and Sam were developing into wonderful happy children.

The following day, Mathew was going through some paperwork in his office. The office was located on the west side of the manor and had a large bay window overlooking the vast manicured lawns where he often saw his children playing.

A knock came at the door.

'Enter,' he called.

'Sir, you have received a telegram,' said the servant.

Lord Abernethy took the envelope and ripped it open. He didn't particularly like telegrams. They usually brought bad news in his experience.

Your Past Will Always Catch You

Chapter 28

Careless Whispers
Easter 1902

John was attending an Easter Service at St Paul's Cathedral; something he did each year.

Archbishop Goe conducted the service, and towards the end he asked the congregation to pray for Francis O'Connor the retired Police Commissioner and church elder, who was on his deathbed at his home in Ivanhoe.

John felt a heavy weight on his shoulders. He had never been able to come to grips with the fact he had shot and killed a police officer. As he prayed for his long-term adversary, he decided he would try and atone by visiting the man who for forty-three years quite rightly accused him of a heinous crime.

Tuesday, April 17, 1902

John approached the white colonial house. People were standing on the front veranda; he approached a distinguished looking gentleman.

'Hello, sir, my name is Reverend John Davies. I've known Francis for many years and I was hoping I would be able to say a last goodbye.'

'I'm pleased to meet you, Reverend; I'm Francis's brother, Roy. I'm sure we can allow a short visit. Follow me into the house.'

John followed Roy until they reached Francis's bedroom. It was a very large room with a bay window overlooking magnificent gardens, but the curtains had been drawn, making the room quite dark.

'I'd ask you to keep your visit short, Reverend. My brother is very frail.'

'I will, Roy. I just want to say goodbye and offer a blessing.'

Roy departed, leaving John and Francis alone. John approached the four-poster bed. Francis looked very pale and was having trouble breathing.

John bent over the dying man. 'Hello, Francis; do you know who I am?'

The policeman looked up, indicating that he knew who this man was. 'What are you doing here? Have you come to see me die?'

'No, Francis, I'm here to confess to you. You were right; it was me who shot Constable Reilly. There hasn't been a day in the past forty-three years when I haven't felt guilty and ashamed.'

'I always knew it was you. You were one of the Banshees, weren't you?'

'I was.'

'Who were the other two?'

'I'm sorry, Francis. I can't divulge that.'

'So, did you pirate the *Cygnet*?'

'We did.'

'Why? A reverend becoming a common criminal doesn't make sense.'

'I can assure you I had my reasons. If it's any consolation, all my share of the loot went into establishing homes for street urchins. I've had great success in turning these kids into responsible citizens.'

'I'm afraid the ends don't justify the means. Now, if you'll excuse me, I'm feeling very tired.'

John took his leave, uttering a blessing as he left. In the darkened room he wasn't aware of a police officer sitting on a chair at the back of the room. He heard every word of the conversation.

The retired Police Commissioner died that night and the young constable reported to his superior officer what he had heard in the dying man's bedroom.

'Good work Constable! I will follow this up immediately.'

Sergeant Ross asked to see his superior officer, Captain Flannery. He related what the young officer heard in the Commissioner's bedroom.

'I think we need to pursue this. I was a young constable when Constable Reilly was murdered by those bitches.'

'Yes, sir although it seems the bushrangers weren't really women. That was their disguise.'

'Well, they did a bloody good job. Most of the blokes at the station were more than happy to give them one before they locked them up.'

'Do you want me to ask the magistrate for a search warrant before we arrest the bastard?'

'Yes, I think so we're going to need all the corroborating evidence we can get against this fellow.'

The sergeant called on the magistrate requesting the warrant; he had no hesitation in issuing it.

April 19, 1902

John was in the kitchen enjoying a cup of tea with a few of the King's Walden children when he heard a loud knock on the front door. David, a boy of fourteen, volunteered to answer it. He returned with two very grim looking policemen.

'Are you John Davies?'

'Yes, that's right officer. Is one of my kids in trouble with the law?'

'No, you are. I'm arresting you on suspicion of murder and highway robbery. It is my understanding another charge of piracy will be forthcoming. I'd ask you to hold out your hands.'

One of the officers placed handcuffs on his wrists.

John was led away and placed in a cell at the notorious Melbourne Gaol.

While John was languishing in his tiny dark cell, the police began their search for further evidence. The first place they searched was King's Walden, but they failed to discover anything that could incriminate the accused. The police captain ordered his men to search the Eldorado Gold Mine. A constable was lowered down the main shaft. He had a miner's lamp on his head but despite the light it was still difficult to see. He came across a shaft that ran perpendicular to the main shaft and was able to enter it. He moved along the shaft about thirty feet, and here he discovered a pile of strong boxes. He hauled one out. Upon reaching ground level, the captain examined the box and was sure it belonged to the *Cygnet* gold shipment.

The public prosecutor William Anderson decided there was sufficient evidence to charge this so- called pillar of society formally. A date for the initial hearing was set for April 29.

April 20, Abernethy Manor, Kent

Lord Abernethy was seated at his mahogany desk in his office going over the latest estate accounts when a knock on the door disturbed him.

'Enter.'

His butler entered handing Mathew a yellow envelope. Mathew took it and dismissed the servant.

April 20, 1902

Dear Father,

Terrible news.

John Davies has been arrested on charges of murder and robbery.
The police have a search warrant for Abernethy House and the
apartment in the Windsor. Please tell me you are not implicated.

Love

Emma

Mathew sat there reading and re–reading Emma's telegram it was if he was in
some sort of trance. It was a knock on the door that brought him back to reality.

It was the butler, again holding an envelope. He handed it to his bewildered
master and left the room.

Mathew was hesitant to open it but knew that he must, so he ripped open the
envelope and read the telegram.

April 21, 1902

Father,

The police came today and went through the entire house. The only
thing they took away was your treasured sea captain's trunk.

What is this about?

Love

Emma

Immediately Mathew knew what he must do. He went searching for Anne and
the children and found them on the front lawn playing bocce.

'Anne darling, I need to speak with you urgently. Leave the children with
Nanny.'

'Darling, what on earth is the matter? You look like you've seen a ghost.'

'Anne, please, I'll explain what's happening when we get inside.'

Mathew ushered his wife into the library adjoining his office. 'You'd better take
a seat, my love. What I'm about to tell you will sound unbelievable, but I can assure
you every word is true.'

Mathew recited the entire story from the first robbery through to the act of
piracy; he also explained the reasons why he turned to a life of crime.

'The police will be coming here to arrest me soon, so I need to leave England
and travel to our villa at San Marino. There is no extradition treaty between the two

countries, so they can't touch me there. I would dearly love you and the children to follow me but I will understand if you wish to remain here.'

'Mathew, you are my husband. I married you for better or for worse. This situation definitely falls in the worse category but I know I couldn't live without you and neither could Bea and Sam.'

'Thank you, darling. I intend to leave tonight. I'll find a ship at the Port of London which will get me to Italy. You and the children can join me later when things have settled down.'

Lord Abernethy arranged for a carriage with four fast horses to take him to London where he found a ship the *Santa Maria*, which was due to sail for Genoa that same night.

April 22, 1902
Russell Street Police Station Melbourne

Mathew's trunk arrived at police headquarters, having been transported from Ballarat. Captain Flannery was present to ensure all went well. A constable tried initially to lever the lid open with a crowbar, but the heavy lock ensured it remained firmly shut.

Captain Flannery took his police revolver from its holster and shot two bullets into the lock. With further prying, the lid opened.

The police officers all looked on in awe. The trunk contained several wigs, women's clothing, revolvers and various other artefacts including what they assumed were fake breasts. They had uncovered indisputable proof that Mathew Abernethy was a Banshee, guilty of robbery and murder.

Captain Flannery contacted the chief prosecutor the following morning requesting the British police serve an arrest warrant on Lord Abernethy. He agreed to contact his British counterpart via telegram.

April 23, 1902

Two police officers from Maidstone arrived on the doorstep of Abernethy Manor at 9 am demanding to see Lord Abernethy. Anne invited them into the front parlour.

'Lady Abernethy, we have an arrest warrant for your husband. Can you inform him we are here?'

'I'm sorry but he's not here. He left the manor three days ago. I have no idea where he's gone.'

'Surely you have some idea where he is? After all you're his wife.'

'I have told you I have no idea where he has gone. Now if you will excuse me I have children to attend to.'

'Excuse me for being forward, but I find it strange you haven't inquired what the warrant relates to.'

'I assume it's for not paying a fine or some such thing.'

'Lady Abernethy, when we find your husband we will charge him with murder and highway robbery. Enquiries are also taking place in Australia which may link him to piracy.'

Anne stared. 'That's preposterous! I can't believe it! He is a respected man in the community. It is his intention to take up his seat in The House of Lords next year. Now, I would ask you to leave.'

'We'll be keeping an eye on the estate in case he returns so don't be concerned if you see the police watching over the estate. We bid you goodbye, ma'am.'

Melbourne, April 23, 1902

Captain Flannery was sitting on the other side of the Chief Inspector's desk at Melbourne Police Head Quarters discussing the Banshees case.

'Captain we've identified two of the so-called Banshees. One we have in our cells and the other I'm sure our English counterparts will find and arrest. Do you have any idea who the third bushranger would be?'

'We do, Chief Inspector. His name is George Griffith.'

'I know him; he owns the department stores my wife frequents.'

'Yes sir, that's the same man. In fact all three suspects were regarded as wealthy philanthropic pillars of the community. Mathew Abernethy was invited by the Premier to run for the seat of Melbourne with the promise of a cabinet seat. Ironically the portfolio promised was Minister for Police.'

'Why didn't he accept?'

'His father died, he inherited the title and the estate and returned to England.'

'So, what are you doing about our infamous shopkeeper?'

'We now have a search warrant. A raid on his Collins Street apartment is planned for early tomorrow morning.'

'Excellent. Let me know the result.'

'Yes, sir, may I take my leave?'

'Yes, Captain, good work.'

George was in Ballarat meeting with his two shop managers when the police called on his Collins Street address. Emma was preparing to leave for a meeting at Mary's Department store when she heard loud knocking on the apartment front door. She opened it only to find six policemen staring at her. The police officer in charge introduced himself as Sergeant Ross and presented Emma with a signed search warrant.

'What exactly are you looking for, sergeant? My husband and I have nothing to hide.'

'We will be the judge of that, ma'am. Now if you could stand aside and let my men do their job...'

The policemen entered the apartment and began their search. The officer assigned to searching George's office found a diary in a locked drawer of a red cedar desk. He brought it to Sergeant Ross.

'So, what have we here, constable? A diary could be incriminating; record it on the sheet and we'll take that back to the station for examination.'

The search took a few hours but the only item of interest was the diary. Emma had no idea of the significance of George's diary as she didn't even know he kept one.

Emma was not aware that John had been arrested and therefore knew nothing of the charges against him and how George may be implicated.

When the police vacated the apartment, she sat down on the sofa and tried to ascertain what the police were looking for and why George was a suspect for an unspecified crime.

George returned to Melbourne the same afternoon and when he walked into the apartment he was bombarded with questions from his wife. When Emma informed him that the police had confiscated his diary he immediately sat down with his head in his hands.

'Emma, sit down. I need to tell you why the police are pursuing me.'

George recounted the entire story to his shocked wife including her father's involvement. He had just completed the story when they heard a loud knock on the door. They looked at one another, knowing full well they might not be together ever again. They kissed then George answered the door.

'My name is Sergeant Ross. Are you George Griffith?'

'Yes, I am.'

'I have a warrant for your arrest on suspicion of murder and robbery.'

'I understand. Would you permit me to say goodbye to my wife?'

'Yes, but make it quick.'

'Goodbye, my love. I'm so sorry it's come to this.'

'I love you darling; I'll make sure you get the best available barrister.'

The police officer clamped handcuffs on George's wrists and led him away.

The journey to the Melbourne Gaol in the police vehicle took only ten minutes. The driver steered the horses through an ominous archway into a courtyard.

Entrance to Melbourne Gaol

Two prison officers were waiting to greet George and show him his new home. They led him up some stairs to a first storey cell.

George was unfamiliar with such a cold and stark environment, as his had been a life of privilege and wealth.

Unbeknownst to George, John occupied the cell next to him. It was in this environment they would live together and possibly die together.

April 29, 1902, Melbourne Supreme Court

The Public Prosecutor decided to try both defendants at the same time as after all the charges were the same. John and George were taken from their cells and as they left their miserable accommodation they were able to see each other for the first time in many months. They were instructed by the guards not to communicate but a nod of the head meant everything to the old friends.

The trip to the Supreme Court building took fifteen minutes. Both accused had handcuffs and leg irons fitted making it difficult to climb the steps to the dock.

This was to be a preliminary hearing where the judge would hear the prosecutor's evidence against the accused and then decide if they should go to trial. The hearing took four hours and the judge had no hesitation in committing the two men to a trial on May 30, 1902.

Trials and Tribulations

Life had been very difficult for Emma Griffith. Her husband George would soon be going to trial on murder and highway robbery charges, not to mention piracy at sea, and she knew the chances of him being found innocent were minimal.

Her father was just as guilty but was hiding in San Marino where the British and Australian authorities couldn't touch him. And then there was poor John! A kinder more caring person could not be found in Melbourne, yet he would die by the hangman's noose, just like her beloved George.

Emma had the responsibility of managing the department stores, plus the hotels; not an easy task for a woman on her own.

The young woman decided to adopt a girl and a boy from King's Walden. With John no longer involved she felt that would be the least she could do.

Emma visited King's Walden and after speaking with several children she decided to adopt a ten-year-old girl named Anna and a twelve-year-old boy named Tom. Despite the charges against her husband, the adoption agency approved the adoptions.

Supreme Court Melbourne
May 30, 1902

The courtroom was packed. The people of Melbourne were intrigued by the cross-dressing bushrangers who were regarded as pillars of society.

George and John were manacled, sitting in the defendant's dock. Emma had secured Victoria's most successful defence barrister Mr Albert Turnbull. It was agreed he would represent both defendants although, based on the compelling prosecutor's evidence, he wasn't particularly optimistic.

The clerk of the court instructed everybody to stand while the judge, Sir Eric Bloomfield, entered the court.

Once everyone was seated, proceedings began. The first task was to choose the jury and after some potential jury members were rejected by both the prosecution and the defence, a jury of twelve men were selected.

The trial was expected to last a week, but with the skilful cross-examination of prosecution witnesses by Mr Turnbull it continued for an additional two weeks.

Finally, the jury retired to make their decision. They returned after four hours with a guilty verdict.

The judge adjourned the court to reconvene two days later when he would pass sentence on the two felons.

John and George had no doubt what the sentence would be; it was just a matter of time before they both would meet their maker.

The prisoners were marched out of their cells and taken to the Supreme Court for sentencing. Once again, the courtroom was packed.

All rose as Justice Sir Eric Bloomfield entered the court. He read to the court his judgement, condemning the two men for their cowardly and criminal deeds. He then placed a black cloth on his head and pronounced the death penalty.

George and John were led away to await their appointment with the hangman. They didn't have to wait long. A date was set for August 1, 1902.

August 1, 1902

The Governor of Melbourne Gaol, William Jones, made the decision to hang John in the morning and George in the afternoon.

A Church of England Minister, Francis Baker, who was known to John, came to visit the condemned man and offered solace and prayers. George also received a visit by the holy man.

At 10 am two prison guards came for John and marched him to the gallows; the same gallows where Ned Kelly was hanged twenty-two years previously.

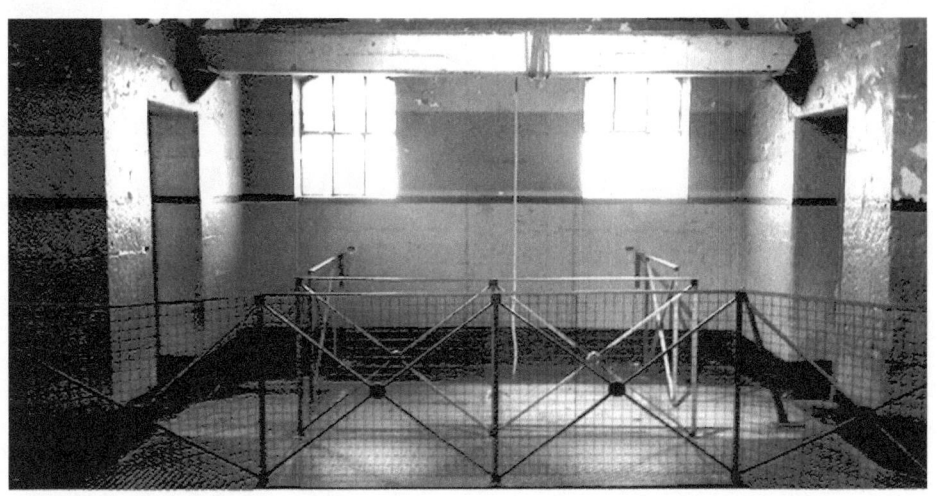

At 10.15, the hangman pulled the lever and John dropped to his death.

John was sixty-six years old when executed. The average life span for a male in Victoria at the time was fifty-five years.

At 2.15 George followed John to meet his maker.

George was sixty-seven years old.

Gordon read an article describing the crimes and subsequent execution in the *London Times*. He couldn't believe his benefactor and mentor had committed such crimes and had been executed. He was devastated.

Mathew too was devastated. Now there was one.

Part Two
The Banshee's Daughter

Emma, a Woman of Substance

The Beginning of a New Life

Chapter 30

August 1, 1902

Emma sat in the lounge room of her Melbourne apartment. It was a beautiful room, expensively decorated without being too opulent. She usually had a whisky poured, waiting for her husband George to arrive home at the end of the day. Emma would pour herself a sherry, and the two of them would discuss the day just gone and plan for the day ahead.

Husband and wife were directors of a retail chain encompassing Georges and Mary's in Melbourne Central, plus a store in Ballarat. They also owned a half-share in two hotels in Melbourne, the Windsor, and the Grand.

They were regarded as one of the wealthiest couples in Victoria.

This afternoon was different. Emma was distraught, despite the fact that it was her birthday.

Her beloved husband George had passed away; not by natural means, but at the end of a hangman's noose.

Emma retired to bed, hoping to get some sleep but it turned out to be a very long night.

The following morning the widow bathed and dressed in black despite the fact there was to be no formal funeral. George was buried in an unmarked grave in the prison grounds on the day of his execution.

During her sleepless night, Emma had decided to devote her life to building a business empire second to none and to raise her two adopted children, Anna and Tom, to the best of her ability.

Both children began their lives in the Ballarat Orphanage; a life not many children would envy, as apart from the tiresome workload they were constantly mistreated and on occasion sexually abused. Anna found some comfort through her strong friendship with Jane McInerney.

When the Reverend John Davies chose Anna and Tom to enter the King's Walden Home for Gifted Boys and Girls, there were only two places available and poor Jane was left behind. It wasn't long before Emma adopted the brother and sister.

Her first action was to call the staff together at each of the hotels and stores, assuring them their positions were safe, and the business would continue to flourish and grow despite the loss of George.

Emma knew it would take a significant amount of her time to manage the empire. With this in mind, she appointed a governess to ease the pressure on her time as well as to aid the children with their schoolwork. Her name was Elizabeth Hathaway and she was a retired schoolteacher.

Anna was enrolled at Methodist Ladies College (MLC), regarded as the premier girls' school in Melbourne.

MLC

Tom had been enrolled in Melbourne Grammar School, regarded as the school of choice for boys of good standing in the city.

In 1902, Melbourne was still the largest city in Australia. As a consequence, it was chosen to host the new Australian Parliament when the six colonies federated in 1901. Parliament House in Spring Street was lent to the Parliament of Australia, while Victoria's Parliament found temporary accommodation in the Royal Exhibition Building.

Exhibition Building

Emma's business empire was affected by the roller coaster ride the Melbourne economy was experiencing. In 1902. The economy was suffering from a recession, but in 1903 there was a revival, and in 1904 the economy began to grow again.

Despite her father living in San Marino, Emma kept constant contact with him via letter and the occasional telegram. Initially, she blamed her father for her husband's fate, but over time Emma accepted the fact that the three Banshees were responsible for their own decisions to become bushrangers.

I am Woman

Trust in God – she will provide. Emmeline Pankhurst

Chapter 31

Throughout the history of the world, women have been denied the right to vote and to participate in politics. New Zealand became the first nation to grant women the right to vote in 1893, but they were not permitted to take a seat in Parliament. Australia, in 1902, was the first country to not only allow women to vote but also to run for parliament.

The suffragette movement developed out of the first wave of feminism in the 19thcentury, when women began to fight for women's rights and equality in public life. They argued for political and civil rights equal to those of men and for the emancipation of women from traditional roles that placed restrictions on their lives. Women began movements throughout the world, promoting the advancement of women's rights and began lobbying for the right to vote, becoming known as the Suffragettes.

The Australian Suffragettes

In Australia, the Suffragette movement began with the determination of women's groups and organisations that advocated for women's right to vote. The Victorian Women's Suffrage Society was the first women's suffrage society, formed in 1884 largely due to efforts of Henrietta Dugdale, a significant activist in the suffrage movement. The suffragettes began to organise across different colonies, publishing leaflets, running debates and public meetings and engaging with members of parliament to push for women's suffrage.

Emma Griffith was seen in Melbourne society as an unusual woman capable of living in a man's world. Most women were seen as frail creatures, whose sole role in life was to bear children and care for their husbands' needs.

Politics was for men only; many feared that allowing women to enter political debate could result in the introduction of 'feminine' attitudes and 'weakness' to public life.

Women suffrage campaigners travelled around the nation, literally knocking door to door to gather signatures in support of women's suffrage on two important petitions. Gathering over 40,000 signatures, these women's efforts resulted in around 1% of the entire population of Australia signing, which was a huge achievement at a time when the idea of women being involved in politics was widely ridiculed.

Emma contributed significant funds to the suffragette movement but did not divulge her support.

A petition was compiled in 1891, which sought to gain support for the claim that Victorian women should be able to vote on equal terms with men. It was known as the Monster Petition due to its enormous size. It measured two hundred and sixty metres, and it took three people three hours to unroll it from end to end. Without Emma's support the movement would not have been able to travel the length and breadth of Victoria to collect the signatures.

With the support of tens of thousands of Victorians, the petition was presented to Parliament, but the Victorian Upper House refused to give women voting rights.

The South Australian suffragettes followed a similar process, collecting close to 12,000 signatures. The South Australian Government granted women the right to vote and sit in Parliament in 1894.

The South Australian legislation was a momentous achievement on both the national and international level as the legislation was the first in the world to grant women's suffrage as well as the right to stand for Parliament.

The success for suffrage in different state elections was the result of the determination of suffrage and women's rights groups and a long, difficult fight to challenge resistance from governments and those in society who opposed women's enfranchisement. After the success of South Australia's suffrage movement, Western Australia granted women's suffrage in 1899, followed by NSW in 1902. Tasmania and Queensland followed, and then in 1908, Victoria finally granted women the right to vote.

In 1902, as an outcome of the relentless lobbying of Australian suffragettes and women's groups, Australia granted women – *except for Indigenous women* – the right to vote in federal elections passing the *Commonwealth Franchise Act*. Along with suffrage, the Australian Government also gave women the right to be elected to federal parliament.

June 30, 1903

Emma received a letter from Mathew, her father. He informed her that he had taken the decision to assign his shares in the two hotels in Melbourne over to her. The two hotels in Ballarat were wholly owned and would also be transferred to her name. Mathew was independently wealthy, still owning the Abernethy Estate in Kent. He was precluded from visiting the estate due to a warrant for his arrest but could receive funds from the estate's vast agricultural holdings.

Emma would now be the owner of the hotel empire which would enable her to grow her business significantly.

Despite her father's reputation, Emma was now regarded by Melbourne society as a woman of wealth and distinction.

The first significant decision she made was to investigate re-opening Eldorado Gold; the same mine that was used to launder the gold from the *Cygnet*, the ship pirated by the Banshees off the coast of Victoria.

Emma appointed the preeminent geologist Mr Francis Hancock to conduct a survey of the three shafts, which had lain dormant for several years. His assessment would determine if Emma would invest the necessary funds to restart mining operations.

Mr Hancock requested a meeting with Emma at her Hotel Windsor office once he had completed the survey.

'Good morning Mr Hancock, please take a seat. Can I order you some coffee or tea?'

'Thank you, Mrs Griffith, tea would be nice.'

Emma rang through to room service and ordered tea and cake.

When they were settled, Hancock motioned for her attention. 'Now Mrs Griffith, I have conducted a thorough survey of the shafts. My assessment is that all three have the capacity to be excavated an additional six hundred feet.'

'Is that good?'

'Not for the sake of digging, but I believe if we went down to that level there is an excellent chance we would discover major gold seams.'

'I know there are no guarantees in mining for gold, but I would like an assurance that I wouldn't be throwing money down a very deep pit.'

'As I intimated earlier my assessment is there is a high chance Eldorado would be a substantial gold mining operation. Indications are there are significant quartz seams which would result in a high yield of gold.'

'Excellent, Mr Hancock. I know it is outside your field of expertise, but do you have any idea what size investment would be required to re-establish the mine?'

'You're right I'm a geologist, not a mining engineer, but I can recommend an excellent man who could determine the investment required.'

'What's his name?'

'Samuel Simpson. He's regarded as the most experienced mining engineer in Victoria. I can arrange for him to contact you if you like.'

'Yes, please do. I'm keen to get started.'

Samuel Simpson arranged to meet with Emma the following week. He agreed to Emma's offer of employment and began work on July 1. His first task was to determine the cost for extending the shafts. Part of the agreement was to include a group of four miners who had worked with Samuel for five years. He knew he could rely on these men.

Samuel and his team worked tirelessly in the shafts, digging rock and bringing it to the surface for geological assessment. After four weeks, the mining engineer had arrived at a figure, which he could present to his employer.

He requested a meeting with Emma, and she was keen to hear Samuel's estimate for the mine extension. The meeting was set for 10 am Friday, August 15 in her office at the Grand Hotel.

'Mrs Griffith will see you now Mr Simpson,' said Jane, Emma's assistant.

'Thank you.'

'Good morning, Mr Simpson. I trust you have brought a favourable report.'

'Madam, I have brought you a report. It's up to you whether you deem it favourable or not.'

'So, in essence, what investment am I looking at?'

'I think it's important to understand the cost involved in transforming the mine to an efficient safe operation. Using modern mining techniques will require an initial sum of £5000. This would entail installing a cage lift system to protect the miners when being lowered down and ascending to the top. The shafts would be dug using hand drills to drill holes and dynamite placed in them with a slow fuse. This would not only make the digging safer it would speed up the excavation.'

'The £5,000 would be required for each shaft I take it?'

'That's correct ma'am. It's a substantial investment.'

'Is there one particular shaft that shows more promise than the other two?'

'I believe shaft three looks the most promising and the geologist, Mr Hancock, agrees with me.'

'Well, I think that's where we start. If shaft three lives up to expectations we can move on to the others.'

'Yes, ma'am, so you authorise me to begin work on shaft three?'

'I do, and you will need to present me with a running cost statement each week.'

'Thank you, Mrs Griffith, I look forward to working with you.'

'As do I with you, Mr Simpson.'

The Midas Touch

Chapter 32

October 1903

Simpson and his mining team began work on shaft three of the Eldorado Mine on 16 October. The first task was to install the safety cage lift system. The lift was manufactured by Johns and Waygood in South Melbourne.

Once the cage system was installed, the drilling and blasting could commence; this phase had an estimated time frame of six months. Simpson and his team completed the extension of the shaft to the required level of six hundred feet by March 4, 1904.

Emma was delighted with the way the project was progressing and she now waited eagerly for the assessment of the quartz seams, which contained the gold they all sought. Emma wasn't disappointed. The initial gold yield was deemed high and by June the Eldorado mine, shaft three, was in full production.

December 1904

Emma arranged a meeting with her mining engineer, Mr Simpson, and the geologist, Mr Hancock, to decide whether Eldorado should extend shaft two. The fact that shaft three had now produced 1000 ounces of gold in the first six months of operation made it one of the most productive mines in Ballarat.

All three agreed they should move to open shaft two immediately beginning the work in early January 1905.

The extension of the shaft followed the same procedure as number three but instead of completing it early it ran two months over the schedule due to the hardness of the rock they were required to blast.

August 1905

In the first few weeks of mining in shaft two, the indications were the gold yield was poor. Samuel Simpson recommended they continue mining in the hope they would discover significant gold seams. After a period of six months, the decision was taken to close down the shaft as the amount of gold produced was less than 200 ounces.

September 1905

Emma called for Mr Simpson and Mr Hancock to meet with her in her Windsor Hotel office.

'Thank you for coming, gentlemen. I called this meeting to discuss whether we should open shaft one or should we continue with shaft three and forget the other two.'

'Ma'am, I know it's very disappointing that shaft two has failed to produce anywhere near the gold we had hoped for, but shaft three is one of the most productive shafts ever in the Ballarat area. Number one could be as good as three; extending the shaft is the only way we'll ever know.'

'Yes, I understand what you're saying Mr Simpson, but it was me who just lost £5,000 on a worthless hole in the ground. I may be considered wealthy, but if I keep investing in projects such as this I'll be begging on the streets of Melbourne.'

'If it makes any difference to your decision, ma'am I believe we can salvage most of the equipment from shaft two and re-employ it into shaft one.'

'How much money will that save me?'

'Well, instead of £5,000 it should reduce the cost down to £2,500.'

'Are you sure?'

'I'm relatively sure.'

'What are your thoughts, Mr Hancock?'

'I tend to agree with Mr Simpson, ma'am. We've come so far now it would be a shame not to complete the project.'

'I hope you're both right. I give you permission you to commence work on shaft one.'

Work on the final mine shaft began in October. The equipment, including the cage, had been dismantled from shaft two and reassembled in the new mine.

The deepening of the shaft by a further six hundred feet was completed by March 30. The yield was poor in the first three months of mining and it began to look as if the mine would need to be closed.

Emma received a telegram from Samuel Simpson on April 15 requesting she visit the mine in Ballarat as soon as possible.

She arranged to travel by train on April 18, fearing Simpson and Hancock would recommend she close the mine. The first shaft, number three, was no longer providing the yield it once was.

Simpson met her at the train station and transported her to the Eldorado Mine office. He would not divulge the purpose of the meeting, saying Mr Hancock needed to be present.

When Emma entered the office, she noticed a large trunk in the middle of the room.

'Well gentlemen, you summoned me, and here I am. What have you to say to me?'

'Ma'am, we felt that you might be interested in what we found in shaft one a few days ago.'

'So, show me.'

Mr Simpson approached the trunk and opened it.

'Would you care to look inside the trunk, ma'am?'

Emma rose from her chair and moved over to the trunk. 'Oh my God I don't believe it. How much does it weigh?'

'We've weighed it twice to verify it, ma'am. It weighs 2900 ounces.'

'That would have to be one of the largest nuggets found on the Ballarat goldfields.'

'We believe it's second only to the *Welcome Stranger*, ma'am.'

'Does this indicate the shaft will produce a significant amount of gold?'

'It's hard to know. This nugget may be the only significant find, or it could be the tip of the iceberg,' said Hancock.

'Well, I suppose there is only one way to find out. We keep the shaft going.'

'What are you going to call the nugget, ma'am?' asked Simpson.

'*The Eldorado*; that seems like an appropriate name.'

'May I suggest you maintain it as a nugget and not melt it down? I believe it would be more valuable in its original form.'

'I'll take your advice on that Mr Hancock. We will need to have it locked in a bank vault for security reasons. I'll contact our bank in Ballarat and arrange to have it transferred,' said Emma.

Shaft one proved to be more productive than shaft three, yielding 1000 ounces a month, but no more large nuggets were discovered.

Telephone for You Ma'am

Chapter 33

Emma and George had commissioned Henry Sutton, the great inventor, to install telephone networks throughout the hotels and stores; the first time this had been done anywhere in the world. When Alexander Graham Bell, the telephone's inventor, visited Australia in 1910, he visited Georges Department Store and the Windsor Hotel to inspect Sutton's network; he was impressed.

Emma suggested to Bell that he stay at the Windsor while in Melbourne so he could experience the telephone network first hand, and he gratefully accepted her offer.

Mr Bell returned to America where he sang the praises of Henry Sutton and Emma Griffith to all who would listen.

Henry Sutton and Emma became close friends and it was through this friendship that they decided to form a company to manufacture some of Henry's inventions. The company was named Sutton Innovations; Emma held 50% as did Sutton and the seed capital was provided by Emma, with an initial £10,000.

The first product they released was a telephone network based on the model Henry had installed in his father and mother's music stores and Emma's hotels and stores. The subsidiary was named Austral Telecommunications.

The Victorian Government was the first major client, installing Austral telephone networks in all the major Government Departments including the Police Force.

Several large businesses also installed the Austral networks including Amcor, AMP, Arnott's, BHP and David Jones.

The next direction for Sutton Innovations was wireless technology and radio transmission. Sutton met Nikola Tesla in London at a conference where Tesla gave a series of lectures on wireless energy. Henry had already invented a method of sending facsimile images over radio.

Upon Sutton's return to Australia, he erected a radio tower in the backyard of his Malvern home. It boasted seven hundred metres of steel cable. It was from this tower that Sutton Innovations claimed the world's longest radio transmission.

Twelve months after this transmission the Government granted Sutton the county's second radio license, allowing him to transmit up to four hundred kilometres.

Other successes followed for Emma and Henry, such as the world's first portable radio transmitter with a range of four hundred and sixty metres, which was released to the market in 1910. Sutton Innovations was awarded a contract by the Australian Navy to assist them in developing top-secret long-range radio technology. The company went on to be a roaring success for the two entrepreneurs both in Australia and overseas.

March 1910

Emma decided it was time to visit her father in San Marino. It had been ten years since she had last seen him, although they kept in touch regularly via letter and telegram.

Anna, Emma's adopted daughter, was now eighteen while her son Tom was twenty. Neither had met their grandfather. Emma thought it would be an excellent opportunity for them to meet and get to know her father.

Emma was also looking forward to meeting her father's children Beatrice and Sam. It seemed ridiculous to her that Bea was now thirteen and Sam eleven and she hadn't seen them since they were toddlers.

Anna had been accepted at Melbourne University to study medicine while Tom had enrolled at the recently opened Duntroon Military College to study and become an army officer. They applied for a one-year postponement to their studies and their request was granted, partly due to Emma's influence. She was a close friend of Brigadier General William Bridges, the first commandant of the college. She was also a significant donator to the University and had received an honorary doctorate for her contribution along with Henry Sutton for their development in wireless technology.

Emma and her two children boarded the *SS Osterley* bound for Southampton, England, a voyage that would take thirty-five days.

The voyage was completed without incident although Anna did meet and have an on-board romance with a young Navy officer named Lieutenant James Townsend.

ORIENT LINE TO AUSTRALIA
HEAD OFFICES—FENCHURCH AVENUE, LONDON, E.C.

s.s. "OSTERLEY," 12,129 TONS, 14,000 H.P.

Once the *Osterley* docked at Southampton, the family of three disembarked. They were met by Rosie, Mathew's sister, and transported by train to Abernethy via train and coach.

Anna and Tom were in awe of the magnificent manor house surrounded by beautiful gardens and meadows.

Emma intended to stay at Abernethy for a few weeks then travel to San Marino with Anna and Tom to visit her father. Mathew's mother Julia had died in May 1900, leaving her daughter and her husband to manage the estate. The property still belonged to Mathew and would be passed down to Samuel upon Mathew's death.

The siblings were both keen horse riders, taking the opportunity to ride some of the Abernethy fine Arabian steeds over the estate's trails.

While the family was dining together on the visitors' third day, Rosie raised the subject of an upcoming foxhunt.

'You are all visiting at a very opportune time. The annual Abernethy foxhunt is due to be held on Sunday week. Would you be interested in taking part?'

'I would! Father was the Master of Foxhounds at the Melbourne Foxhunt Club in Victoria. In fact, he was the founder of the club and responsible for importing the first foxes into Australia,' said Emma.

'Yes, I'm aware of his love of the hunt. The last time he was at Abernethy in 1868 he took the role of Master of Foxhounds. I was appointed Lady Master of Foxhounds two years ago. So, what about you two? Will you be joining us?'

'Well, I'm only speaking for myself, but I'm unsure whether I could watch the hounds rip a fox apart,' said Anna.

'I can understand your trepidation Anna, but the fact is it is highly unlikely we will catch a fox. If you saw what a fox could do to a newborn lamb, you may think differently. However, it's up to you.'

'I'd be honoured to take part, Rosie,' said Tom.

June 28, 1910

At 11 a.m. a hundred and twenty riders assembled, including Rosie, Emma and Tom. Anna had decided not to ride. Accompanying them were over forty hounds.

When Rosie was satisfied all was in order, she instructed the huntsmen to lead the pack of hounds out over the estate's meadows.

Yet again the fox eluded the hunters, and the riders and hounds returned to the manor house empty-handed. Waiting for the group was Anna; pleased the riders were outfoxed. The usual banquet of food and drink on the lawns of Abernethy Manor was consumed by all and sundry.

July 3, 1910

Emma walked into the manor's conservatory, hoping to make herself a cup of tea. Rosie was already sipping a cup, so Emma poured from the teapot and joined her aunt.

'Aunty Rosie, did Father ever discuss with you the reasons for his illegal pursuits?'

'Not really.'

'As you know I now own his businesses, and therefore, I've been able to look at the books around the time of the robberies. It seems he was making significant profits from the hotels.'

'It doesn't make sense does it?'

'No, it doesn't. I'm hoping he will open up when we visit him next week.'

July 9, 1910

Emma, Anna and Tom caught the train to Southampton where they boarded the Italian ship *Padrona* bound for the port of Rimini. The voyage took six days, mostly spent reading books from the ship's library.

The ship docked at the busy port, but Emma could not see her father amongst the sea of people on the wharf. Finally, she heard her name being called. Mathew approached his daughter, hugged her and kissed both cheeks.

'Father, you look so well! It must be that suntan.'

'I put that down to clean living in paradise.'

'I'll get Anna and Tom. They've being looking forward to meeting you.'

Emma made the introductions and Mathew was very impressed with both Anna and Tom. Brother and sister were tall and very good-looking.

The trip to the villa took an hour in Mathew's new Fiat motorcar along very rough roads. Finally, the car turned a corner and Mathew pulled over.

'Why don't we all get out? I have something to show you.'

Emma and her children did as they were told, and Mathew gestured widely.

'As far as the eye can see is my property. You can view the villa where you will be staying.'

'It's magnificent, Father. No wonder you don't want to leave here.'

Mathew sighed. 'As you know I couldn't if I wanted to, but living here makes it tolerable, Emma.'

The group continued on down to the villa where Anne, Mathew's young wife, greeted the group at the front door. Mathew showed his three visitors their rooms, all with a beautiful vista over the property.

'May I suggest you all rest up after your journey? Dinner will be at 7 pm. As it's such a beautiful day, I think we should eat alfresco on the terrace,' Mathew said.

'Thank you, Father, I believe we are all a little tired.'

The family met on the beautiful terrace at the specified time. The entire outdoor area was covered in grape vines with a mature olive tree growing in each corner.

Bea and Sam served a glass of ORO Chianti wine to each member of the group. After taking a sip they all agreed it was excellent.

'How did you choose the name ORO Grandfather?' asked Tom.

'It's Italian for gold; something that has had a major effect on my life.'

Maria, the cook, brought to the table a large antipasto and panini bread. Mathew ensured there was sufficient wine to complement the dinner, including a Pinot Grigio for those who preferred white wine.

Bea placed a large bowl of Spaghetti Marinara on the table, Sam brought out a large plate of Osso Bucco. Finally Scaloppine di Vitello completed the main course.

'My God, how on earth are we going to eat all this magnificent food?' asked Emma.

'We always eat well in San Marino, yet you would have to look hard to find an overweight person,' said Anne.

'I would like to propose a toast; to my family. May we always have a loving and supportive relationship,' said Mathew.

The table raised their glasses and drank.

'So, Anna, what do you intend to do upon your return to my beloved Australia?' asked Mathew.

'I am enrolled at Melbourne University to study medicine.'

'Wonderful! So we will finally have a doctor in the family. What about you, Tom? What's your ambition? To follow in your mother's footsteps?'

'I'm afraid her shoes are far too big for me to wear. I've enrolled at Duntroon Military College with the intention of becoming an army officer.'

'Well done, I had similar ambitions when I was a young man. I'd be keeping a watchful eye on Germany if I were you. They seem to be building far too many battleships for my liking. They've also increased the size of their army.'

'Yes, sir I'm aware of the danger; Britain is building even more battleships than the Germans. There seems to be an arms race taking place.'

'What about you Bea? What are your ambitions when you finish your schooling?' asked Emma, turning to her young sister.

'I intend to complete a degree in Viticulture so I can become a winemaker working for ORO.

That would be excellent Bea. Where do you intend to study?'

'Milan University.'

'What about you Sam? Do you have any great ambitions?'

'I'm afraid my future is preordained when Father passes away I inherit his title and the Abernathy Estate.'

'Well that doesn't sound too bad to me.'

'Don't get me wrong Emma; I'm more than aware how fortunate I am.'

'Well, that's enough of discussing future plans; tomorrow I'll take you on a tour of the winery and the olive oil distillery.' said Mathew.

'Thank you for a very enjoyable dinner, Father,' said Emma. 'But I'm not sure if I'll be able to eat another meal for a day or two.'

'You wait, I'm sure you will be eating a hearty breakfast tomorrow morning.'

'We'll see.'

The hosts bade everybody goodnight.

You Can't Change History

The next morning the family came together in the large kitchen/casual dining room. Her father was right; Emma ate a hearty breakfast, as did the rest of the group.

Mathew was the last person to be seated at the table, arriving some twenty minutes later than the agreed time.

'I do apologise for being late. I was called out by our head winemaker who was concerned about one of the vats.'

'Is everything under control now?' asked Anne.

'He assures me it is, my love; as you can imagine if an entire vat of wine were ruined the financial implications would be significant, to say the least.

'It seems everybody else has finished their breakfast so may I suggest we meet in front of the villa in fifteen minutes?'

When the group assembled at the meeting point, they were met by a red Ford Model T pickup, furnished with bench seats in the back.

'In you get! I'm afraid it will be a rough ride, but we don't have to go far,' said Mathew.

The pickup started down the dirt road, heading to the winemaking facility. Mathew was right; the trip took only five minutes. Once they arrived, Mathew led them into the building.

'Let me explain the five stages of winemaking; obviously harvesting the grapes is the first step in the winemaking process. Do this right, and you will produce a delicious wine.

'Grapes are the only fruit that has the essential acids, esters, and tannins to consistently make natural and stable wine. Tannins are textural elements that make the wine dry and add bitterness and astringency to the wine.

'The moment the grapes are picked determines the acidity, sweetness, and flavour of the wine. Determining when to harvest requires tasting the grapes by the winemaker. The acidity and sweetness of the grapes should be in perfect balance, but harvesting also heavily depends on the weather.

'The harvesting is done by a combination of ORO staff and casuals from the village. Once the grapes are taken to the winery, they are sorted into bunches, and rotten or under ripe grapes are removed.

After the grapes are sorted, they are ready to be de-stemmed and crushed.

Then the fun begins crushing the grapes with our feet until all the juice is extracted.

For white wine, we quickly crush and press the grapes to separate the juice from the skins, seeds, and solids. This is to prevent unwanted colour and tannins from leaching into the wine.

Red wine, on the other hand, is left in contact with the skins to acquire flavour, colour, and additional tannins.

After crushing and pressing, fermentation begins. The juice can commence fermenting naturally within six to twelve hours when aided with wild yeasts in the air. However, our winemaker adds cultured yeast to ensure consistency of the wine.

Fermentation continues until all of the sugar is converted into alcohol and dry wine is produced. Fermentation can take anywhere from ten days to one month or more.

Once fermentation is complete, clarification begins. Clarification is the process in which solids such as dead yeast cells, tannins, and proteins are removed. We then transfer the wine into oak barrels.

The next step is fining; this occurs when we add clay any unwanted substances will adhere to the clay clarifying the wine. Filtration occurs by using a filter to capture the larger particles in the wine. The clarified wine is then transferred into another vessel and prepared for bottling or future ageing.

And now the most satisfying stage occurs ageing and bottling this is the final stage of the wine making process. We have two options available to us; bottle the wine right away or give the wine additional ageing. Further ageing can be done in the bottles or oak barrels.

After ageing, wines are bottled and corked.

So, there you have it the wine you drank last night came from this exact process.'

'How much wine do you produce each year sir?' asked Tom.

'Currently, we produce 200,000 cases, but our ambition is to increase production to 300,000 within the next three years. When Bea joins the team fulltime I am sure we will reach our target.

'What percentage of the wine is red?' asked Emma.

'Fifty percent. The balance is obviously white. Is that all the questions you have? Let's move on to the olive oil distillery. It's about a ten-minute drive down the hill.'

Mathew drove through the olive grove between the rows of trees, which seemed to go on forever.

Finally, he parked outside the distillery, a large timber building reminding Emma of the whisky distilleries in Scotland.

'Let me explain the distilling process. We naturally have to pick the olives first. As you saw we have a large orchard.'

'May I enquire as to how many trees you have in the orchard, Grandfather?' asked Anna.

'We have approximately 500,000 Anna. Our intention is to increase that to 700,000.

'The picking process is very laborious. The pickers use ladders which they rest against a branch and pick the olives. The fruit is dropped down onto a silk sheet then placed in shallow baskets and transferred to the press as swiftly as possible to avoid the olives deteriorating.'

'Do the olives go off that quickly?' asked Emma.

'Yes, as soon as they are picked. The olives are washed to eliminate impurities then they are taken to the crushing room. Come, I'll show you.'

Mathew led the way.

Tom stared around. 'My God, it's huge, sir! Do you have any idea how much the wheel weighs?'

'Not exactly Tom, but it would be several tonnes. It's made of granite. Once the olives are ground for a half hour or so, the paste becomes oily. We take the paste and scoop it into the presses to extract the oil.

Olive Oil Press

Once the paste has been pressed we leave it to rest; this process separates the water from the oil. We store the oil in either oak or cherry casks for up to twelve years our below ground storage facility holds up to 100,000 casks storing 2 million litres of the finest ORO olive oil. The final stage is bottling the oil.'

'Grandfather, how many litres of oil does a tree produce?' asked Anna.

'On average, about 3.5 litres, Anna.' He smiled. 'I hope you all enjoyed the tour and learnt a little about what we do at ORO. Now I suggest we head back to the villa and sample some of our produce.'

The family group returned to the villa where Anne greeted them with a cold limoncello, gratefully accepted by all.

At 7 pm they met once more on the terrace and devoured another delicious dinner prepared by Maria with a selection of the vineyard's wines to compliment the meal.

Most of the family decided to retire early after such a busy day. Emma decided to take a walk before turning in. The night sky was magnificent, and it never ceased to amaze her.

Upon returning to the villa, she noticed a light emanating from Mathew's office. When she peeked in, he was sitting at his desk going over some papers. 'Hello, Father do you mind if I join you?'

'No, not at all darling.'

'I've wanted to catch you alone, but it seems almost impossible.'

'Yes, it's been a busy time; I must say I'm very impressed with Anna and Tom. They do you proud.'

'Thank you yes, I am very proud of them. They both started out in life with very little love or attention.'

'Can I offer you a French Cognac? It's over a hundred years old.'

'Well, how can I resist a such an offer?'

While Mathew was pouring the cognac, Emma looked around the room which was lined with what seemed to be hundreds if not thousands of books.

'Have you read all these books Father?'

'Not all of them, but most.'

Mathew passed the brandy balloon to his daughter and they both sat down on the Chesterfield lounge, similar to the one he had in his home in Australia.

'Father, I can't thank you enough for what you have done for me, particularly in recent years with the transfer of the hotels.'

'I love you, darling, it was the least I could do for my elder daughter.'

'May I ask you some questions relating to your so-called life of crime?'

'Yes, I was expecting you to query why I did what I did.'

'What I don't understand is this. You were a wealthy man, well respected in the community, when you participated in the first robbery. Why did you do it?'

'You're correct. I was quite wealthy, but my good friend John, whom you know well, had been cheated by a card sharp in a high-stakes poker game in my hotel. He lost everything; £5,000 in all. I suggested to him that we hold up the Cobb & Co coach with this fellow, I think his name was Harmsworth, travelling onboard and take back John's hard-earned money. No other passengers were robbed, just the fraudster. The money was the foundation capital to establish King's Walden.'

'I believe you dressed up as women?'

'Yes, I'm afraid that was my idea. When I purchased the Golden Nugget I inherited a trunk with women's wigs and clothing. I thought it was an ideal disguise.'

'I can understand why you it did once, but why three more times?'

'The second robbery was to help out your husband.'

'Why did George need the money?'

217

'Did he ever tell you how he was tricked out of his share of one of the largest nuggets ever found on the Ballarat goldfields?'

'No, I had no idea.'

'George and his partner Henry Baynes discovered a nugget which was worth at the time over £10,000. The two partners decided Henry should take the nugget to the bank in Melbourne and convert it to cash. Well, he certainly did that, and he also withdrew the partnership's savings of £2000 and sailed back to England where he established himself in high society, became a peer and now sits in the House of Lords.

'George was left destitute. John and I decided to partake in what we thought would be our last highway heist. The money we received established George in his first store in Ballarat and of course later in Georges and Mary's in Melbourne.'

'You said you thought that would be the end of it, yet you committed a third robbery.'

'I must admit we committed the third out of sheer greed and the rush you receive from being a bushranger. Unfortunately, this was the heist where the poor policeman was shot. He fired first, hitting George; John reacted on impulse.'

'George was shot?'

'Yes, just a flesh wound.'

'So Father I would have thought that was the time to quit.'

'Yes, I agree, and we did quite for many years. Then the depression of 1893 combined with being defrauded of £150,000 by two so-called esteemed business people who I thought I knew brought us back to a life of crime. John wasn't affected by the fraud, but the banks were close to liquidating him. He couldn't bear to think of all those children he cared for being thrown out on the street.'

'So George was in a similar situation, I take it?'

'Yes, George was my partner in the investment and he stood to lose his business empire as I did.'

'But you all retired after the piracy episode?'

'Yes, we went back to a simple life of business – if you can call business simple.'

'How did they catch George and John?'

'The Police Commissioner of Victoria, Francis O'Connor, was riding in the coach when we committed our first heist. It was during this robbery that the policeman got killed. Apparently, O'Connor could remember a criminal's eyes forever. He remembered John's and harassed him for many years. John discovered the Commissioner was on his deathbed and decided to make a full confession before the fellow died. What John didn't know was in the corner of the room was a policeman keeping guard, and he heard the entire confession.'

'Did John implicate you and George?'

'No, he refused to name his accomplices.'

'So how did the police know about your and George's membership of the Banshees?'

'John, George and I purchased the Eldorado gold mine for the purpose of laundering the stolen gold. The stolen strong boxes were discovered in our mine. The police were granted a search warrant of both George's and my house on the suspicion we were the other Banshees. They were right.'

'Well, isn't it ironic. You thought the Eldorado was a barren mine and I've turned it into the richest gold mining operation in Victoria. My bonanza proved to be your demise.'

'I suppose you're right, my love.'

'Father, would you mind if you went back to this Henry fellow who stole all of George's wealth?'

'What is it you want to know, Emma?'

'You mentioned he had been appointed a Lord and sits in the Upper House.'

'Yes, that's correct. He's done rather well for himself considering he's a crook.'

'The same could be said about you, Father.'

'Oh dear, yes, I suppose I deserved that comment.'

'Sorry, Father, that was cruel. Do you think I could expose this villain for what he is?'

'Lord Baynes is very much part of English establishment. He's friends with the Prime Minister and has been known to mix with royalty. The only way to bring him down would be through the press, and I'm sure they wouldn't touch him for fear of retribution.'

'That may be so, but this man is ultimately responsible for George's death. I don't intend to give up.'

'If there is anything I can do to assist please let me know.'

'Thank you, Father; I also appreciate your openness in recounting your escapades.'

'My tales of woe and misdeeds. Goodnight Emma, sleep well.'

'Goodnight.'

Harmony Seldom Makes a Headline

I Fear Three Newspapers more than a 100,000 Bayonets
Napoleon

Chapter 35

The following morning Emma announced a change in her original plans to travel to Venice and then Rome before returning to London with her children.

'I won't be going to Venice and Rome with you, Tom and Anna. I have some important business to take care of in London. You two continue and I will see you back in London in a couple of weeks.'

'That's a shame, Mother,' Anna said. 'We can go with you if you like. Venice and Rome aren't that important.'

'Thank you darling, but there's nothing you can help me with. It's a business matter.'

'When are you leaving, Mother?' asked Tom.

'Not for a few days, in the meantime we can all explore San Marino.'

San Marino is a mountainous microstate surrounded by north-central Italy. Among the world's oldest republics, it retains much of its historic architecture. On the slopes of Monte Titano sits the capital, also called San Marino, known for its medieval walled old town and narrow cobblestone streets. The Three Towers, dating to the 11th century, sit atop Titano's adjacent peaks.

Guita Tower San Marino

August 2, 1910

Emma said farewell to her father and stepmother, Anne, and her two young half-siblings, Beatrice and Sam. Mathew drove her to the port of Rimini where she boarded the *Parrona* for the return journey.

August 8

Emma checked into her hotel, Claridge's in Mayfair. Although the room was beautiful she didn't stay and relax as she had an appointment with her banker, Mr Lamont, at Westminster Bank.

The Australian businesswoman was shown to the anteroom of Lamont's large office. David Lamont only dealt with the wealthy, and even then, he was selective as to whom he accepted as clients.

'Good afternoon, Mrs Griffith, please take a seat. May I offer you tea and biscuits?'

'Yes, thank you, I've only just arrived from Italy this morning and I'm feeling rather tired. A cup of tea I'm sure would pick me up.'

'So, while we wait for our tea, let me ask you— how's business down in Australia?'

'Very good. The four hotels' occupancy rates are high thus all are profitable, the Eldorado Gold Mine is producing excellent yields with the promise of significant growth, and finally the retail division is going from strength to strength. All in all, business is good.'

'I must say you are doing extremely well, particularly for a woman.'

'I don't know what being a woman has to do with it but thank you for the compliment.'

An ornate tea trolley was wheeled into Lamont's office carrying a silver teapot and Wedgewood cups and saucers. The tea was poured by a young bank employee. There was a selection of cakes to choose from. When they were served, Lamont turned to Emma.

'So, Mrs Griffith how can I help you?'

'I have three transactions I wish you to pursue on my behalf.'

'And they are?'

'I wish to invest in a hotel in London.'

'Excellent decision, hotel space is at a premium in this city.'

'I have chosen the hotel I wish to purchase.'

'Really, which one?'

'Claridge's.'

'Well, you've certainly gone for the top shelf as it were. Do you have any idea what investment you would be required to make?'

'I have an idea, but what I would like is for the bank to approach the current owners and establish their selling price.'

'We can do that.'

'I also wish to purchase a London newspaper; one that needs to boost its circulation.'

'You have quite a shopping list, ma'am, so what's the third transaction?'

'I wish to list the Eldorado Gold Mining Company on the London Stock Exchange.'

'I take it you want to raise capital for future growth?'

'Exactly.'

'Well, ma'am may I suggest I make the approach to the hotel and get back to you with their answer in due course.'

'I would like you to contact them promptly. I'm only in London for another ten days then I shall sail back to Australia. The same goes for the newspaper. I understand the float will take some time.'

August 13

Emma returned to her hotel room after an afternoon shopping in Bond Street. As she opened the door of her suite, she noticed an envelope on the floor. She placed the parcels on her bed and retrieved the envelope. In it was a handwritten letter from David Lamont.

> *Dear Mrs Griffith,*
>
> *Please contact my office to make an appointment as soon as possible.*
>
> *Best Regards*
>
> *David Lamont*

Emma telephoned the bank, arranging to see David Lamont the following day at 10 am.

She arrived at the bank fifteen minutes early keen to learn if Lamont had been successful, and he greeted her promptly.

'Good morning Mrs Griffith. Please come in and take a seat. Can I offer you tea or coffee?'

'No thank you, Mr Lamont, I'm keen to hear your news.'

'I see, well, regarding Claridge's, there is good news and possibly bad news.'

'What's the good news?'

'They are willing to sell the property.'

'Excellent. And the bad news?'

'They want £2 million for it.'

'My goodness, that's a lot of money.'

'It certainly is; do you think it's more than you're willing to pay?'

'Not necessarily. Do you think I would achieve a reasonable return on my investment?'

'Not on the hotel's turnover at the moment, but the capital gain on the building could be very lucrative.'

'Is there any room for negotiation?'

'I'm afraid not; they made that very clear.'

'Let me think it over. What about the newspaper?'

'Yes, we have discovered the *Sunday Times* is in a spot of trouble. The circulation has dropped significantly. As a result, we believe you could purchase the paper for £100,000.'

'Do you know why the circulation has dropped?'

'Our firm belief is that the current editor Francis Baker is taking the newspaper in the wrong direction. He has made the paper highbrow, and the ordinary reader has abandoned it.'

'Therefore, if I find a suitable editor and staff I should be able to turn the paper around?'

'We at the bank firmly believe so.'

'I would ask you to make an offer of £80,000.'

'Yes, ma'am, I think that might be enough.'

'Finally, the stock market float; does the bank believe it would be adequately subscribed?'

'We do; in fact I wouldn't be surprised if it were oversubscribed, as gold stocks are very attractive at the moment.

'May I ask you to appoint a broker and get things moving?'

'Certainly, Mrs Griffith.'

'Allow me a day to cogitate over the Claridge's deal if you will.'

Yes, ma'am.

Emma left the bank with a scorecard of two out of three; not exactly what she was hoping for.

She returned to Claridge's, the hotel she hoped to purchase. Upon entering her suite, she sat at the desk and began playing with some figures. Her conclusion was she would have to borrow £500,000 to make the purchase. Her asset base would cover the debt several times over, but Emma would have to make the decision whether she wanted to borrow that kind of money.

Having had a fitful sleep, Emma woke with the decision that she would borrow the money and purchase the hotel. After breakfast, she telephoned David Lamont, informing him she would proceed with the acquisition.

Lamont was pleased, and he also informed Emma that the *Sunday Times* had accepted her offer and she was now the proud owner of a major newspaper.

Westminster Bank agreed to loan Emma the £500,000 for the Claridge's purchase using the Windsor and the Grand hotels as collateral.

There was now only five days before her departure. Anna, and Tom were due to arrive in London in three days and she had many things to organise before they arrived.

Emma's research had told her the best editor in London was Richard Grey of the *Times*, so she telephoned him and arranged to meet with him in Claridge's in the Foyer and Reading Room restaurant.

Richard arrived at midday and they sat at a corner table. After the usual pleasantries, Emma broached the subject of coming over to the *Sunday Times*.

'With the greatest respect Mrs Griffith why would I leave the best newspaper in Britain to join a Sunday rag?'

'I agree, the *Sunday Times* needs to improve its content, but if you had control over the entire operation and owned a slice of the newspaper, I believe it could be a premium paper.'

'You mentioned a slice of the paper… what exactly do you mean?'

'I mean you would own initially 15% which could rise to 25% based on performance.'

'I must admit that sounds tempting.'

'Richard, do you mind if I ask what salary you are paid at the *Times*?'

'Not at all, it's £6,500.'

'I am offering you £10,500 plus equity.'

'Mrs Griffith, you are certainly making it difficult to say no.'

She gave him a straight look. 'I need an answer by tomorrow. Think it over and get back to me here at Claridge's. By the way, I have just purchased this hotel.'

Emma received a telephone call from Richard Grey the next day accepting her offer.

'I'm very pleased, Richard. I'll arrange to get your employment contract drawn up I'll contact you when it's ready to sign.'

'Thank you, Mrs Griffith, I'm looking forward to the challenge.'

'Now that you are my editor, Richard I would like you to address me as Emma.'

'Thank you. Goodbye, Emma.'

'Goodbye Richard.'

When Emma hung up the telephone, she realised she didn't have a London solicitor, so she decided to search the telephone book. As she flipped the pages, a name stood out; "Gordon Huston & Partners."

She just stared at the name for what seemed like an eternity. Memories of her past came flooding back, and she began to weep. Gordon her only true love, her brother.

What was she to do? Contact her long lost brother; her long lost lover, or let sleeping dogs lie?

She picked up the telephone and dialled the number.

'Gordon Huston & partners. Can I help you?'

'My name is Emma Griffith. I wish to speak to Mr Huston please.'

'May I enquire what it's in relation to?'

'Yes, I have completed a number of large commercial transactions. I require him to draw up the legal paperwork.'

'Just one moment please.'

Emma waited for three minutes, which seemed like thirty, and then she finally heard Gordon's voice.

'Hello, Mrs Griffith it's Gordon Huston here. How can I be of assistance?'

Emma didn't say a word. She froze.

'Hello, Mrs Griffith. Are you there?'

Emma cleared her throat and responded. 'Yes, Mr Huston, I'm here. I wish to make an appointment.'

'When would you like to see me?'

'I'm travelling back to Australia in a few days so as soon as you can see me please.'

'I thought I detected an Australian accent. I'm originally from there myself. I can see you at 3 pm tomorrow if that's convenient?'

'Yes, I'll see you tomorrow.'

'Excellent. I'll see you then. You'll be able to bring me up-to-date with what's happening in Australia.'

'Possibly. Goodbye.'

'Goodbye, Mrs Griffith.'

Emma hung up the phone but didn't move. Could she cope with seeing Gordon again? Should she cancel the appointment and find another solicitor?

Emma decided that she needed to find closure. It all ended so abruptly all those years ago.

She had another restless night, thinking about the following day's meeting on the one hand and the excitement of purchasing the hotel and newspaper on the other.

In the morning, Emma walked to Bond Street and bought a new outfit for she wanted to look her best. She had her hair coiffured at London's best hairdresser and then returned to Claridge's.

The day seemed to go slowly but at last it was 2.30 pm, time for her to begin her fateful journey to Gordon's office.

Upon arrival Emma was instructed by a secretary to sit in the anteroom of Gordon's office. She waited there for twenty minutes. She was at the point when she was ready to depart when Gordon opened his office door.

'I'm so sorry for keeping you, Mrs Griffith. I had to attend to an urgent matter for a client. Please come in.'

Emma walked slowly into Gordon's office, analysing every feature of the man as she went. He was now forty-eight years old, as indeed was she. He was still very handsome, and his deep voice still resonated.

'So Mrs Griffith, it's very nice to meet you,' said Gordon holding out his hand.

It was at this point, when their eyes met, that Gordon realised who was in his office. 'Oh my God, Emma, is it really you?'

'Hello, Gordon. It's been a long time.'

'What are you doing here? I mean in London?'

'Are you going to invite me to sit?'

'Oh, I apologise yes please take a seat Emma. I think we both need a strong coffee. I'll order some.'

He did so, and then turned back to her. "I can't believe it's you, Emma! You've hardly changed… still as beautiful as ever.'

'Thank you, Gordon. You were always one to flatter. I must say you seem to be in rude health.'

'Yes, fighting fit.'

'Did you ever marry?'

He smiled. 'Yes, I've been married twenty-three years to Sarah and we have two sons. Adam is twenty and Luke is eighteen. By the way, I'm sorry to hear George passed away Emma.'

'How did you know that?'

'The trial was reported here as was the final verdict.'

'Maybe we should discuss the business I need your legal assistance on.'

'Of course, but before we do I want you to know there hasn't been a day in the last twenty-seven years that I haven't thought about you.'

'I can assure you the same applies to me. I don't think it helps if we keep talking about it though. What happened was tragic, but we've both moved on.'

'Yes, I agree. What is it you wish to discuss with me?'

Emma briefed Gordon on what she required. He agreed to take on the brief and have the completed documents to her by the end of the week.

Their business completed, Emma rose out of the chair, ready to depart.

Gordon cleared his throat. 'Emma, we should never forget that we are brother and sister – family. Let's stay in touch even though we live half a world apart.'

'Yes, I agree Gordon; I'll see you on Friday.'

Emma returned to Claridge's. She felt relieved that the reacquaintance went without any real drama albeit being stressful for both parties.

The settlement for the hotel was due in thirty days and she would be on the high seas at that time, so Gordon would represent her.

The *Sunday Times* would settle the day before she departed. A telephone call to Richard Grey ensured he would meet her at the hotel on Saturday morning to review the employment contract and sign the document.

August 27

Emma was eagerly waiting to see her children. Anna and Tom were due to arrive in London that afternoon. The siblings caught a taxi from London Dock to Claridge's Hotel, which would be owned by their mother on September 23; a fact they were unaware of at that time.

The brother and sister asked at reception for their mother and the gentleman behind the receptionist desk telephoned Emma in her suite to get her permission to send them up.

Emma answered the doorbell and gave both her children a hug and kissed them on both cheeks. 'So you two... how are the happy wanderers?'

'We're great thank you, Mother. We had a wonderful time in Venice and Rome. The only disappointment was you weren't with us,' said Anna.

'Yes, I'm sorry I had to miss it.'

'Did you get your business done?'

'I did and I'm very excited about it. I'll bring you up-to-date over dinner. I've booked a table in the Fera restaurant in the hotel. Why don't you two check in and freshen up and meet back here at 7 pm?'

Over dinner, Emma described the business transactions she was able to close and her plans for the future, particularly for the *Sunday Times*. Anna and Tom were both as excited as their mother.

There was another important task Emma had on her list before her departure. She had employed a private investigator, Mr Ryan, to find Henry Baynes. Her intention was to confront him face to face and assure him his criminal past would be exposed.

Ryan informed Emma Henry's residence was at 13 Howick Place Westminster. Emma caught a taxi to the address. Mr Ryan accompanied her; his intention was to stay out of view and only intervene if needed.

Emma knocked on the front door. A maid opened it and showed Emma into the front parlour. She was kept waiting a few minutes before Lord Baynes strode into the room and greeted her.

'I don't believe I know you, Mrs Griffith. How exactly can I be of assistance?'

'You are correct, Lord Baynes; you don't know me; however, you knew my late husband very well.'

'Did I? What was his first name?'

'George.'

The look of shock on Baynes' face was obvious. 'Mrs Griffith, I paid your husband a sizable amount as compensation for my actions all those years ago. If you are here to demand even more, I can assure you I will not pay another penny.'

'Lord Baynes, I can assure you I'm not here to demand money.'

'Good, so why are you here, madam?'

'I am an independently wealthy woman; therefore, your money holds no interest to me. I have just purchased the *Sunday Times* and will be investing a considerable amount to make it one of London's best and most influential newspapers. Once I have achieved that milestone I will be instructing my editor to conduct a long and protracted campaign against you. I hold you responsible for my husband's death. I have obtained evidence of other illegal acts committed by you over the last twenty years. You, sir will pay for your misdeeds. Goodbye.'

Emma departed the house. She and Ryan caught a taxi back to her hotel and she smiled to herself. 'Well, that certainly put the wind up him.'

The final task was to meet with Richard Grey. Before she could do that, she required the employment contract from Gordon. She instructed the taxi to call by the offices of Gordon Huston and asked Ryan to collect the contract which was waiting for him at the receptionist's desk.

With the contract in hand, she called Richard and arranged for him to meet her at the hotel's coffee shop at 4 pm.

He read the document and agreed to sign it. The *Sunday Mail* had a new editor and Emma had a powerful weapon, which she intended to use ruthlessly.

Return to the Lucky Country

Chapter 36

August 30

Emma, Anna, and Tom said their farewells to Rosie at the railway station where the family boarded the train that would be transporting them to Southampton Dock. There, they would board the *Osterley* bound for Melbourne.

The journey was to take thirty-five days, all going well. They filled their days playing deck games such as quoits and skittles. Tom and Anna also took part in the clay pigeon shooting. Both were skilled shooters; consequently, they became the ship's champions.

A large part of Emma's day was spent writing business plans for her newly acquired businesses.

Having observed how efficiently Claridge's had been run while she stayed as a guest, Emma had no hesitation in keeping the management team and staff in place.

Richard would decide who stayed and who would be fired at the *Sunday Times* and the new publisher had total confidence in his judgement.

Emma did take the time to read the recently published novel by E M Forster entitled *Howard's Way*. She found it engrossing.

The *Osterley* sailed into Port Phillip Bay on October 5 and all three members of the Griffith family were glad to be home in Melbourne.

Anna was due to begin her first semester in the first week of February, giving her time to see her friends and relax before the arduous four years of medicine began.

Tom was due to begin his officer's course on December 1. He too would use his time catching up with friends in both Melbourne and Ballarat.

December 1, 1911

Emma and Anna accompanied Tom to the Spencer Street Railway Station. He would travel to just outside Sydney and transfer to the newly constructed Canberra line.

'Goodbye darling, take care of yourself. I'll look forward to seeing you next Christmas.'

'Bye bye, brother, don't shoot yourself in the foot.'

'I'll try not to, sis. Good luck at Uni.'

Tom boarded the train, finding the first-class carriage he had booked and settled in for the long journey. Emma had given him a book to read. It was *My First Summer in the Sierra* by John Muir and he was well into the first chapter before the train had left the metropolitan area.

After three days of travelling, Tom arrived in Canberra, which would soon be the capital of Australia.

Duntroon had arranged army trucks to transport the recruits to the Royal Military College and once they arrived, an officer allocated them their barracks.

Duntroon Barracks and Parade Ground

Each barracks held twenty recruits in very basic conditions. The Commandant of the college lived in slightly more salubrious accommodations at Duntroon House.

AUSTRALIAN WAR MEMORIAL   126544

During the first week of the four-year course the trainee officers completed twenty hours of marching and twenty hours of academic study. The second week also comprised twenty hours marching and twenty hours of academic study. This regime was maintained for the first month.

More variety was introduced over the coming months, but the academic component remained constant over the course of the program.

The trainees were taught leadership skills, military communication, weapons training and physical training.

The comradeship between the recruits was strong and many lifelong friendships were developed.

Tom recalled the conversation he had with Mathew when he was in San Marino relating to the likelihood of an arms war. Despite his desire to become an army officer he wasn't particularly looking forward to fighting in a war.

Unbeknownst to Tom, a confidential report had been received by Senator Edward Millen, the Minister for Defence. The information contained in this document would determine Tom's future.

July 1st, 1912

Confidential Report to Senator Edward Millen
Minister for Defence
Australia

Dear Minister,

I have begun to accumulate some useful intelligence, which I believe
could be useful to you. I would like to firstly address the history of the
various alliances that exist in Europe.

Triple Entente:

French and Russian diplomatic relations gradually developed
through the late 1890s, and the Franco-Russian alliance of 1894
strengthened ties between the two countries. Anglo-French rivalry
ended and cordial terms were established between Britain and France
in 1904, when the two countries signed the Entente Cordiale. Britain
and Russia signed the Anglo-Russian Entente on August 31, 1907, at
Saint Petersburg, Russia, ending traditional territorial conflict and
defining the boundaries of Afghanistan, Tibet, and Persia. The
alliance between France, Britain, and Russia that crystallized out of
these three pacts is referred to as the Triple Alliance. It forms the
backbone of the Allied Powers.

Triple Alliance:

The Dual Alliance as you would be aware was the treaty signed by
Austria-Hungary on October 7, 1879. The alliance promised mutual
support in case of a Russian attack. Italy, having lost the rivalry with
France with regard to establishing the colony in Tunis, joined
Germany and Austria-Hungary to form the Triple Alliance in 1882.
Italy viewed the alliance as a guarantee against the invasion of

Austria–Hungary, a rival nation. Italy also signed a guarantee of neutrality with Britain and later signed a similar guarantee pact with France.

In 1902 Britain made a naval treaty with Japan.

All the countries in the two alliances are building their armed forces at an alarming rate.

Germany 2,200,000 soldiers 97 Warships

Austria-Hungry 810,000 soldiers 28 Warships

Italy 750,000 soldiers 36 Warships

France 1,125,000 soldiers 62 Warships

Russia 1,200,000 soldiers 30 Warships

Britain 711,000 soldiers 185 Warships

Some military analysts believe in a time of war these countries with the help of reservists could dramatically lift their numbers. An estimate is:

Germany: 8.5 million men

Austria-Hungary: 3 million

Great Britain 1.5 million

Russia: 4.4 million

France: 3.5 million

There is no possible reason for such a build-up other than to wage war. I firmly believe the Triple Alliance is on a war footing looking for an excuse to invade France.

Yours truly,

John Foster

Australian Military Attaché London

February 6, 1912

Anna placed the books she had recently purchased from the University bookshop into her Gladstone bag, they included:

Gray's Anatomy for Students.

Atlas of Human Anatomy.

Human Genetics and Genomics

Janeway's immunobiology

Principles of Neural Science

Anna had spent some time browsing through the books. She had to admit to herself these subjects looked daunting and she hoped she would be able to cope.

The medical student caught a tram from her Collins Street apartment on the top floor of Georges Department store to the university in Parkville on the other side of the city. She had been to the campus a few times, but this was different. She would be spending most of her time here over the next four years.

Melbourne University

Anna's first commitment was to attend the Dean's welcoming speech in Wilson Hall where she would join sixty other medical school students all as nervous as she was.

Wilson Hall

July 2012

Emma was well pleased with the trading results from the hotels, the department stores and in particular Eldorado Gold Mining in her absence.

A telegram arrived, informing her that a stockbroking firm, Potter & Partners, were keen to manage the float of Eldorado. In their opinion, the float would be oversubscribed.

Emma was equally pleased with the successful management of King's Walden Home for Gifted Boys and Girls. Kate Morgan had managed the home since John's demise and she had achieved great success, guiding the children to become valued citizens in the community. Tom and Anna were two examples of her success.

Gordon had also contacted her, informing Emma the settlement of Claridge's Hotel had been concluded.

The hotel manager, Mr Francis Armstrong, was required to report to her monthly but she requested Richard Grey to report weekly until he had turned the newspaper around.

January 1, 1913

Emma had decided to hold a New Year's party to welcome in 1913. The Windsor Hotel was the venue she naturally selected.

Over one hundred invitations were sent out and she expected at least a hundred and eighty guests to attend, including her own family.

The Victorian Symphony Orchestra provided the music and the grand ballroom was awash with music and champagne.

The Victorian Premier, Mr W Watt, and his wife attended, as did the Governor, the Rt Hon. John Fuller and his wife.

The Grand Ballroom Windsor Hotel

At midnight the ballroom erupted with *Happy New Year* and a hundred and eighty guests singing *Auld Lang Syne*.

Emma was delighted with the function and she decided this would be an annual event at the Windsor.

May 1, 1913

Potter and Partners listed the Eldorado Gold Mining Company on the London Stock Exchange at £1. It was oversubscribed by a factor of five and at the end of the first day's trading the share price was £1.70.

Emma received a telegram with the result and naturally she was well pleased. She arranged for a bottle of Dom Perignon to be delivered to her Windsor apartment to be shared with Anna. Unfortunately, Tom couldn't join them.

The remainder of the year remained uneventful. Anna passed her first-year medical exams in the top ten percent and Tom also achieved outstanding results at Duntroon.

January 1, 1914

Emma once again hosted the New Year's Eve ball at the Windsor. The new Governor, Sir Arthur Stanley, attended, as did the newly elected Premier William Watt.

None of the guests could have guessed what would unfold in the coming year. They all made their New Year resolutions and hoped 1914 would be a happy healthy and prosperous year.

Events on the other side of the world would put paid to their expectations.

I Don't See Any Borders Do You?

Chapter 37

Events Leading Up to the Assassination of Prince Franz Ferdinand and his wife Sophie

Bosnia and Herzegovina were provinces south of Austria which had until 1878, been governed by the Turks. The Treaty of Berlin settled the disposition of lands lost by the Turks following their disastrous war with Russia. Austria was granted the power to administer the two provinces indefinitely.

Primarily four groups populated Bosnia: Croats predominantly Roman Catholic; ethnic Serbs; Serb-Orthodox and Muslims.

There was a strong desire by the Bosnian Serbs to amalgamate with Serbia.

The Annexation

On 6th October 1908, Austria annexed Bosnia and Herzegovina directly into the Austro-Hungarian Empire. The reasons were twofold.

Annexation would remove any hope the Turks might have for reclaiming the provinces. Full inclusion into the empire would give Bosnians full rights and privileges.

The annexation caused concern to a number of Europe's powers. The move was regarded by some as illegal. Russia was particularly concerned by the move despite previously giving approval to the annexation.

After tough negotiations, Austria paid Turkey a cash settlement. This seemed to placate most of Europe.

The Serbs, however, were not happy. They coveted the provinces to expand the Serb empire.

The Black Hand

The Black Hand was established to spread anti-Austrian propaganda within Serbia as well as sabotage, espionage and political murders abroad. This terrorist group included many government officials, professionals and army officers.

The Black Hand became aware that the heir-apparent to the Austrian throne, Franz Ferdinand, was scheduled to visit Sarajevo in June of 1914 – it was decided to assassinate him. Three young Bosnians were recruited, trained and equipped: Gavrilo Princip, Nedjelko Cabrinovic and Trifko Grabez.

The Serbian Government

Because the Black Hand had infiltrated both the government and the army, the plot became widely known. When the Serbian Prime Minister Pasic learned of the assassination plot, he faced a difficult decision. If he remained silent and the plot succeeded, the Black Hand's involvement would be revealed. If the clandestine connections between the Black Hand and the Serbian government came to light Serbia would be put in a very onerous position. There would be a very real chance that war between the two nations would erupt.

His problem was that if he warned the Austrians of the plot, his countrymen would see him as a traitor. He would also be admitting to his knowledge of Black Hand's operations.

A half-hearted attempt was made to intercept the assassins at the border. When that failed, Pasic decided diplomacy should be attempted.

The Serbian Ambassador to Vienna, Jovan Jovanovic, was given the task of warning the Austrians. He was aligned with Black Hand and was not well received by the Austrian Foreign Ministry. He did, however, have a good relationship with the Minister of Finance, Dr Leon von Bilinski.

On 5th June Jovanovic told Bilinski that it might not be a good idea if Franz Ferdinand went to Sarajevo.

'Some young Serb might put a live rather than a blank cartridge in his gun and fire it.'

Bilinski, unaccustomed to subtle diplomatic innuendo, completely missed the warning. 'Let us hope nothing does happen,' he responded good-humouredly.

Jovanovic knew that Bilinski did not understand, but made no further effort to convey the warning.

Preparations

The three Black Hand assassins secretly made their way to Sarajevo a month before Franz Ferdinand was due to visit. A fourth man, Danilo Ilic, had joined the group and on his own initiative recruited three others. Vaso Cubrilovic and Cvijetko Popovic were seventeen-year-old high school students. Muhamed Mehmedbasic, a Bosnian Muslim, was added to give the group a bipartisan appearance. Officers from the Serbian army supplied four Serbian army pistols and six bombs.

Prince Franz Ferdinand and Sophie's Royal Visit

Franz Ferdinand accepted the invitation of Bosnia's governor, General Oskar Potoirek, to inspect army manoeuvres outside Sarajevo. The Archduke's role as Inspector General of the Army made the visit logical. It had also been four years since a prominent Royal had made a goodwill visit to Bosnia.

The visit would also coincide with his fourteenth wedding anniversary. Security during the visit was not particularly tight. Franz Ferdinand disliked the presence of secret service men. Nor did he like the idea of a cordon of soldiers between the crowd and himself. The Bosnians welcomed Franz Ferdinand warmly. Sarajevo was not seen as hostile territory; the normal police guard was present, nothing more.

28 June 1914

At approximately 10:00 am the Austrian party left Philipovic army camp, where Franz Ferdinand had performed a brief review of the troops. The motorcade, consisting of six automobiles, headed for City Hall where a reception was to be hosted by Sarajevo's mayor. The chosen route was a wide avenue, Appel Quay, which followed the north bank of the River MilToma.

In the first automobile rode the Mayor Fehim Effendi Curcic and the city's Commissioner of Police, Dr Gerde. The second automobile was a 1911 Gräf & Stift Double Phaeton. It had its top folded down and was flying the Royal Hapsburg pennant. This was the vehicle, Franz Ferdinand, Sophie and General Potoirek were travelling in. The car's owner, Count Harrach, rode on the car's running board acting as a bodyguard for the Royal couple.

Minutes before the Assassination

The third automobile in the procession carried the head of Franz Ferdinand's Military Chancellery; Sophie's lady-in-waiting; Potoirek's chief adjutant; Lieutenant Colonel Merizzi; the car's owner Count Harrach and his driver. The fourth and fifth automobiles carried other members of Franz Ferdinand's staff and assorted Bosnian officials. The sixth automobile was empty, a spare should one of the others break down.

The morning was sunny and warm and many of the houses and buildings lining the route were decorated with flags and flowers. Crowds lined the Appel Quay to cheer the imperial couple. Amid the festive crowd lurked seven young assassins. They took up their assigned positions, all but one along the riverside of the Appel Quay. First in line was Mehmedbasic, to the west of the Cumurja Bridge. Near him was Cabrinovic. The others were strung out as far back as the Kaiser Bridge.

The Bomb

The motorcade approached and the crowds began to cheer. As Franz Ferdinand's car passed Mehmedbasic, he did nothing. The next assassin in line, Cabrinovic, had more resolve. He took the bomb from his coat pocket, struck the bomb's percussion cap against a lamppost, took aim and threw the bomb directly at Franz Ferdinand.

In the short time it took the bomb to sail through the air, many small but significant events took place. The car's owner, Count Harrach, hearing the bomb being struck against the lamppost thought they had suffered a flat tyre. The driver apparently saw the bomb flying. He reacted quickly, accelerating away from the scene. As a result of the driver's quick thinking, the bomb would not land where intended. Franz Ferdinand raised his arm attempting to deflect the bomb away from Sophie.

The bomb glanced off Franz Ferdinand's arm, bouncing off the folded car top and into the street behind them. The resulting explosion injured a number of spectators. The third car was hit by shrapnel and stalled. Merizzi received head injuries. Others in the party received minor cuts. The first and second cars continued on for a hundred metres or so, then stopped while they assessed who was injured.

The Aftermath

Cabrinovic attempted to commit suicide but the cyanide capsule was well and truly past its use-by date – he just vomited, then jumped into the river hoping to drown. This proved futile, as the river was only a few inches deep.

He was seized by the crowd and arrested by the police. The motorcade continued on to City Hall, passing the other assassins on the route. Not one of them attempted to assassinate the Royal couple.

At City Hall, a furious Franz Ferdinand confronted the Mayor.

'Mr Mayor, one comes here for a visit and is received by bombs! It is outrageous!'

The Mayor was either completely unaware of what had happened or naïve.

'Your Royal and Imperial Highness! Our hearts are full of happiness...'

By the end of the Mayor's speech, Franz Ferdinand had regained his composure and thanked his host for his cordial welcome.

'There is no chance, no destiny, no fate that can circumvent or hinder
or control the firm resolve of a determined soul.'
Ella Wheeler Wilcox

Discussions were held as to whether to abandon Franz Ferdinand's schedule. The Archduke did not wish to cancel his visit to the museum and the lunch at the Governor's residence. One change he wished to make was to include a visit to Merizzi in the hospital: he was very concerned for Merizzi.

The motorcade set out once again along the Appel Quay, but neither the Mayor's driver nor Franz Ferdinand's driver had been informed of the change in schedule.

The young Black Hand assassins had counted on succeeding on the first attempt. With no assurance that Franz Ferdinand would follow his original itinerary, the remaining assassins took up various other positions along the Appel Quay. Gavrilo Princip crossed the Appel Quay and strolled down Franz Josef Street. He stepped into Moritz Schiller's food store to get a sandwich. As he emerged, he met a friend and engaged in light conversation.

Fate Plays its Part

The Mayor's car, followed by Franz Ferdinand's turned off the Appel Quay and onto Franz Josef Street, as originally planned, to travel to the museum. General Potoirek leant forward.

'What is this? This is the wrong way! We're supposed to take the Appel Quay!'

The driver applied the brakes and backed up. Franz Ferdinand's car stopped directly in front of Schiller's store, five feet away from Princip, the assassin.

An Opportunity Too Good to be True

Princip was quick to recognise what had happened. He pulled the pistol from his pocket, took a step towards the car and fired twice. General Potoirek happened to look directly at Princip as he fired.

Both Franz Ferdinand and Sophie were still sitting upright. Potoirek, thinking the shots had missed, ordered the driver to drive directly to the Governor's residence at speed.

Princip then turned the gun on himself but was mobbed by the crowd. Police were able to arrest him. Princip also attempted suicide by swallowing cyanide. He too was violently ill but did not die.

Mortal Wounds

As the car sped across the Lateiner Bridge, a stream of blood shot from Franz Ferdinand's mouth. He had been shot in the neck. Sophie, seeing this, exclaimed: 'For Heaven's sake! What happened to you?'

She sank down in her seat. Potoirek and Harrach thought she had fainted and were trying to help her up. Franz Ferdinand, knowing his wife better, suspected the truth. Sophie had been shot in the abdomen and was bleeding internally.

'Sopherl! Sopherl!' he pleaded. '*Sterbe nicht! Bleibe am Leben für unsere Kinder!*' ('Sophie dear! Sophie dear! Don't die! Stay alive for our children!')

The cars rushed to the Governor's residence. Sophie died before they arrived. Franz Ferdinand died shortly afterwards.

The Horrific Result

On 23rd July the Austro-Hungarian Ambassador to Serbia delivered an ultimatum:

'The Serbian government must take steps to wipe out terrorist organisations within its borders, suppress anti-Austrian propaganda and accept an independent investigation by the Austro-Hungarian government into Franz Ferdinand's assassination, or face military action.'

Serbia appealed to Russia for help; the Czar's government began mobilising its army, believing that Germany was using the crisis as an excuse to launch a war in the Balkans. Austria-Hungary declared war on Serbia on 28th July. On 1st August, after hearing news of Russia's general mobilisation, Germany declared war on Russia. The German Army then launched its attack on Russia's ally France through Belgium, violating Belgian neutrality and bringing Great Britain into the war.

Australia declared war on Germany the same day as Britain, August 1914.

However, most Australians were unaware that neither the Australian Parliament nor Australian Government had any role in decisions about their soldiers' deployment.

In 1914 Australia, like New Zealand, Canada and South Africa, was a dominion of the British Empire. This meant that although Australia had a constitution, which gave the Australian Parliament the power to make laws for Australia, Britain still controlled Australia's foreign affairs and the power to declare war rested with the King. Neither the Australian Government nor the Australia Parliament made the decision to go to war in 1914.

The atmosphere at Duntroon was electric. The young men from Tom's year were due to graduate in six months; but the Chief of Army, Brigadier Joseph Gordon, decided the graduation should be moved forward which meant Tom and his year would be graduated in October 1914 instead of January 1915.

The young officers would get the chance to lead men in a real war situation; a very exciting prospect they all thought.

The graduation ceremony was held on the parade ground at Duntroon House. The newly commissioned officers looked resplendent in their dress uniforms. Their families were obviously very proud of their warrior sons although pensive about what lay ahead on the other side of the world.

None were prouder than Emma and Anna; Tom had been awarded the Sword of Honour, which is awarded to the cadet who displays "exemplary conduct and performance of duty" throughout their course.

Once the young officers threw their caps up into the air, they were allowed to mingle with families.

'Congratulations, Tom. I'm very proud of you,' said Emma.

'Yes, well done, Tom. Winning the Sword of Honour is something special. I'm sure you're very proud,' said Anna.

'Thank you both and yes, I am very happy to have graduated let alone winning the sword.'

'So Tom, do you know what happens next?' asked Emma.

'Well, I would imagine we'll all be shipped overseas to fight in the war. The word is it will be over by Christmas so the likelihood of arriving in France and coming straight home without a bullet being fired is on the cards.'

'At least you'll be safe, son.'

'Yes, Mother, but that's not why I joined the army.'

The newly commissioned officers would be platoon leaders once they reached the front.

Duntroon Graduates 1914

Australians Arise

Chapter 38

November 1, 1914, Albany Western Australia

The day had arrived where 30,000 young Australians and New Zealanders departed from Albany in Western Australia on board a flotilla of ships bound for Egypt and the battlefields of the Great War.

They had never heard of Gallipoli or the Somme, but they were cognisant of the fact that many would never return home.

ANZACs Aboard *The Ceramic*

Tom Griffith was a Lieutenant in the 8th Battalion, having arrived from Victoria on the HMAT *Ceramic* the same ship that would take the Australian troops to Egypt.

The voyage was uneventful although the soldiers were aware of the threat from German U-Boats. The greatest threat was death from boredom. The officers, including Tom, organised training drills for the men. The most popular activity was playing two-up; a gambling game played with two pennies.

087872

Troops Playing Two-Up

The Australian Flotilla in the Suez Canal

December 2, 1914

After six weeks at sea, the *Ceramic* berthed at the Alexandria wharf in the early morning. It was mid-afternoon before all the troops had disembarked. The heat was stifling, and the smell of body odour was overwhelming. The 8th Battalion was loaded onto a train for a hot smelly three-hour journey to Cairo. On arrival they were given a meal of bread and cheese. They were then marched ten miles to Mena Camp in the shadow of the pyramids and at 1 am they were able to retire to their tents to get some well-earned sleep.

Mena Camp Egypt

For the next four months, Tom was required to march his men in full pack across the searing desert sands. There was some relief with the odd cricket match against the New Zealanders and inter-battalion Australian Rules Football matches.

At night, they were permitted to go into Cairo and enjoy some of the delights the city had to offer. Despite constant warnings, some of the diggers contracted VD.

March 15, 1915

Four of the Duntroon graduates were playing cards in Tom's tent when the conversation turned to where and when their battalion would be deployed.

'I would have thought France is the most likely. That's where all the action is from what I understand,' said Lieutenant Frank Baker.

'Yes, I think you're right, Frank,' agreed Lieutenant Christopher Armstrong.

'The Turks are in this up to their necks. I wouldn't be surprised if we have to take them on.'

'I hope not. I hear they put up a bloody good fight at the Suez Canal last month,' said Tom. 'Well, either way, I think we are all ready for some action. The men are getting restless and to tell you the truth so am I,' he added.

They wouldn't have to wait long.

April 9, 1915, Egypt

Frank Thomas entered the tent of his good mate Wally Sheppard. John Reeves was also there, reading a heartfelt letter from home. The three soldiers were members of Lieutenant Tom Griffith's platoon.

'Hey, have you heard the news? We're being shipped out tomorrow. Finally, we're going to see some action,' said John.

'Great, it's about fucking time, I'm sick of this bloody sand and heat,' said Wally.

'Do you know where they're sending us to, mate? I suppose it'll be France,' said John.

'The rumour is it won't be France— more likely it will be Turkey.'

'Oh shit.'

'Don't worry Frank; we're up for it, Turks scream just as loud as Germans when they get stuck by a bayonet,' Wally said.

Tom entered the tent, having overheard the conversation as he passed by. 'Good afternoon, boys, enjoying the heat?'

'Not really sir, to tell you the truth we're all a bit sick of it,' said Wally.

'Well, I can confirm that we will be shipping out tomorrow so make sure your packs are in order and your rifle's clean and don't forget to polish your bayonets.'

'Beauty! Where are we going, sir?'

'I'm afraid I can't tell you right now, but you'll know soon enough.'

The Anzacs didn't sleep well that night and they used the time to write letters and postcards back to their families and loved ones.

Reveille was at five am. They ate breakfast; same old, and then marched to the train station where they boarded a train bound for Alexandria. The three-hour trip was hot and cramped.

Two troop ships were waiting at the dock; the HMAT *Seeang Bee* and the *Australind*. Lieutenant Griffith's men boarded the *Australind*. It was dusk when they finally set sail heading for Moudros on the island of Lemnos; this would be their staging point before landing at Gallipoli.

Moudros Camp

The diggers were allotted their tents, and the waiting game commenced. Each day passed slowly without a word about when they would finally experience some action. Wally and his two mates hoped they would be fighting the Turks before the war was over.

Each day the diggers were required to exercise and partake in rifle and bayonet practice as well as marching, more fucking marching.

Two weeks passed then, just when they thought they would never get off the island, they received orders to assemble at dockside.

Tom was just as anxious as his men to get off the island and take on the Turks. It had been nearly six months since they left Australian shores.

Tom's platoon marched down to the wharf and embarked onto the *Australind* where they were packed in like sardines. Although it wasn't summer quite yet, it was still 90 degrees.

They set sail for Anzac Cove, and an experience none would forget.

The 8th Battalion was assigned to be part of the second wave; they would be joining their Anzac comrades from the 9th, 10th, and 11th Brigades in the initial morning invasion. The three Australian mates watched from the *Australind* as the landing boats, full to the gunnels with Anzacs, were towed towards the shore carrying the 3rd Brigade to secure the beachhead.

High Command was unsure to the level of defence the Turks would mount against the invasion; they'd soon find out.

Anzacs being towed to Shore

It wasn't long before the Turks started to shell the Cove. Shrapnel ripped into Anzac flesh and bullets were also doing their fair share of damage. The retaliatory shelling from the Allied armada made for a horrifying light show. Men were dying before they hit the sand, some drowning under the weight of their heavy packs, others being ripped apart. Anzac Cove turned red.

Turks Defending Gallipoli

'Fucking hell those poor bastards from the 3rd don't have a chance,' said Wally.

'Don't worry mate, they're Anzacs. We'll lose far too many that's for sure, but I bet we'll win the day,' Frank reassured.

'I don't know about you blokes, but I count myself lucky we weren't in the first group,' said John.

'Do you reckon we'll be okay? I mean those poor bastards have taken the worst of it and by the time we get ashore things may have calmed down,' said Wally.

'I wouldn't bet on it, Digger. I think we'll get a similar welcome,' said Frank.

Five am came around, and the officers on board informed the nervous soldiers they'd be boarding the landing craft at 5.30 am.

The time came when they were ordered to assemble at the side of the ship where they would be required to climb down rope ladders and into the landing boats.

Anzac Troops Preparing to Board

The officer in charge of the boarding operation was Captain Humphries, a senior officer who had fought in the Second Boer War. He had a pretty good idea what these young men would face and couldn't help wondering how many would survive the landing.

It was time for Wally and his mates to descend the ladder. The landing boats were waiting.

'All right men down you go, and keep your heads down,' Tom ordered.

One by one the soldiers climbed down into the small craft and took their seats. Wally was assigned an oar while the other two sat in the middle, hoping they were in a safe position protected from bullet and shrapnel. Tom sat at the bow of the boat, ready to lead his men onto the bloody beach.

The steamboats towing the diggers took off towards what would become known as Anzac Cove. The noise from the battlefield was deafening.

'Bloody hell, John, this is all a bit scary,' said Wally.

'We'll be right, mate, just keep your head low, and listen out for bullets coming your way.'

'How the fuck will I know bullets are coming my way?'

'Don't worry son, you'll know.'

About four hundred metres from the beach, the steamers cut the row boats loose, and Wally and the other oarsman began to row. They were now close enough for the Turkish machine guns to cause havoc amongst the Anzacs.

Frank hadn't said anything since entering the boat, which was unusual for him.

'Hey Frank, are you all right mate?' asked Wally.

'Yeah, I'm okay, just a little scared.'

'We all are mate, don't worry about that; fucking hell how could we not be.'

As the boat neared the shore, Tom looked around at the diggers from his platoon. He couldn't believe it! At least five of the forty who started out on the short journey had been killed, and at least another five or six had severe wounds. He'd been so intent on the landing he wasn't aware some of his men had been hit.

Lieutenant Tom Griffith gave the order to disembark and run for the bottom of the cliffs where the first wave had established a beachhead, albeit vulnerable to Turkish attack.

Lieutenant Griffith was the first to jump out. He disappeared under the water, which was about five feet deep. The weight of his pack made it very difficult for him to make his way. He finally found a footing and waded towards the stony beach. Once on dry ground, he ran as best he could with a wet uniform and a pack that weighed over forty pounds dry; God knows how heavy it was wet. He made it to the cliff without being shot. John and Frank and most of the platoon also made it safely.

The same could not be said for the rest of the 8th Battalion. Over one hundred men either died in the boats or on the beach, cut down by a ferocious Turkish defence.

The 8th were instructed to move to the left flank of the beachhead and then to move inland to support their comrades from the 3rd who had landed in the early morning. By the time they began to climb, darkness had descended over the beach bringing a dark curtain over the dead and wounded.

Tom led his troops up the steep cliff face, though the crumbling rock made it difficult to climb. The constant shellfire also contributed to the difficulty of the task.

'For fuck's sake, Frank, this is getting a little ridiculous. Every time I take one step up I fucking slip back two. How in the hell are we going to make it to wherever the fuck we're supposed to be going?' complained Wally.

'Mate, we're all in the same fucking boat so just keep going. There's no going back now.'

Finally, the platoon made it to a valley, which would be given the name "Shrapnel Gully" by the Anzacs, and for good reason.

For the next eight months Tom and his platoon suffered horrendous conditions, as did the other allied troops who landed at Gallipoli.

The never-ending sound of battle, the disgusting sanitary conditions, rampant disease and the stench of dead bodies, both Anzacs and Turks, made Gallipoli an unendurable hell hole to be. What made it even worse were the terrible food, lack of sleep, shortage of clean water and the constant awareness of comrades being killed in battle.

Tom and his men were literally clinging onto the edge of a cliff with the sea at their backs and the Turks were constantly firing on them from the higher ground. The Anzacs were forced to dig trenches to protect themselves and these became a filthy living and working environment.

The disastrous Gallipoli campaign conceived by Winston Churchill was eight months of hell for the Anzacs and the other countries involved. Over 8,000 Australians died during this ill-conceived campaign.

Lieutenant Tom Griffith survived, as did Wally and Frank.

The decision was made by high command including Lord Kitchener to evacuate the troops from the Gallipoli peninsular as they finally realised it was a futile exercise.

The question was, could the Anzacs retreat, unseen? There was a view that any evacuation would result in heavy casualties but, in the event, there were virtually none. At Anzac and Suvla, an Australian staff officer, Lieutenant-Colonel Charles Brudenell White, devised a plan to gradually withdraw men and equipment while convincing the Turks that everything was normal. 'Silent stunts' were instituted, where nearly all firing from Anzac ceased, in order to make the enemy think preparations for winter were under way. After the end of these stunts, an irregular rifle and artillery fire, of the sort to be expected by the Turks, was kept up. Although much equipment was taken away by night, during the day material was still brought ashore at the piers at Anzac Cove and North Beach.

On 17 December, just two days before the final evacuation, a famous game of cricket was held at Shell Green while Turkish shells passed overhead.

The Gallipoli campaign was over. Gallipoli cost the Allies 141,000 casualties, of whom more than 44,000 died. Of the dead, 8709 were Australians and 2701 were New Zealanders.

The 8th Battalion, or what remained of it, was shipped back to Egypt but not for long.

'On 13 July 1916 Australian General Iven McCay received word from high command that the 5th Australian division would be participating in operations intended to prevent the Germans moving their reserve troops to the Somme front.

General Mackay

The operation was close to a small town called Fromelles in France.

The 5th were shipped off from Alexandria and disembarked at Marseilles where they were loaded onto trains heading for northern France.

Apparently, there were some serious doubts as to whether the Fromelles action would achieve its objectives by not only various officers but also General Haig himself. One Australian officer, Brigadier Harold 'Pompey' Elliot, commander of the 15th Division was racked with doubts.

Pompey spotted Major Howard who was on General Haig's staff. 'Excuse me Major Howard,' called Pompey. 'May I speak with you for a moment, please?'

'Yes sir. How can I help?

'I'm very concerned that this attack is not only going to fail but will become a slaughterhouse. I would like you to come me and see for yourself.'

They both crawled into no man's land. On viewing the terrain they realised the tremendous risks facing the Australian and British troops if the attack went ahead.

Howard was shocked by the three hundred and fifty yards of totally exposed land that the Australian and British troops would have to cover before they reached the German trenches.

Pompey asked Major Howard to return to headquarters and convince General Haig that there wasn't a hope in hell that this operation would be a success.

Major Howard agreed with Pompey's assessment and he returned to General Headquarters and requested a meeting with General Haig.

'Sir, I have just completed a recognisance of the battlefield. I'm very concerned this operation could be a bloodbath. Our men will be mowed down by the German gunners, as there is no cover apart from the odd shell crater and the distance they are required to cover is over three hundred and fifty yards.'

'I appreciate your concern, but, General Haking assures me it will be a success.'

'General Haking, Major Howard and some other officers are very concerned that if we go ahead with the attack our troops will be destroyed. What are your thoughts?'

'I totally disagree; we have enough men and ammunition to drive the Germans out of their rat holes. In fact, I would be surprised if there were many Germans left alive once our artillery is finished with them. Not only that, the troops are well and truly worked up to it; any change in plan would have a devastating effect on their morale.'

The battle would proceed.

It was obvious from the time the first digger climbed over the parapet that the battle would be lost.

The generals delayed the withdrawal, causing even more bloodshed. When General Haking was told that the British forces suffered 1,547 casualties and the Australians lost 5533, Haking responded, 'I thought it did both the British and Australian Divisions a lot of good.'

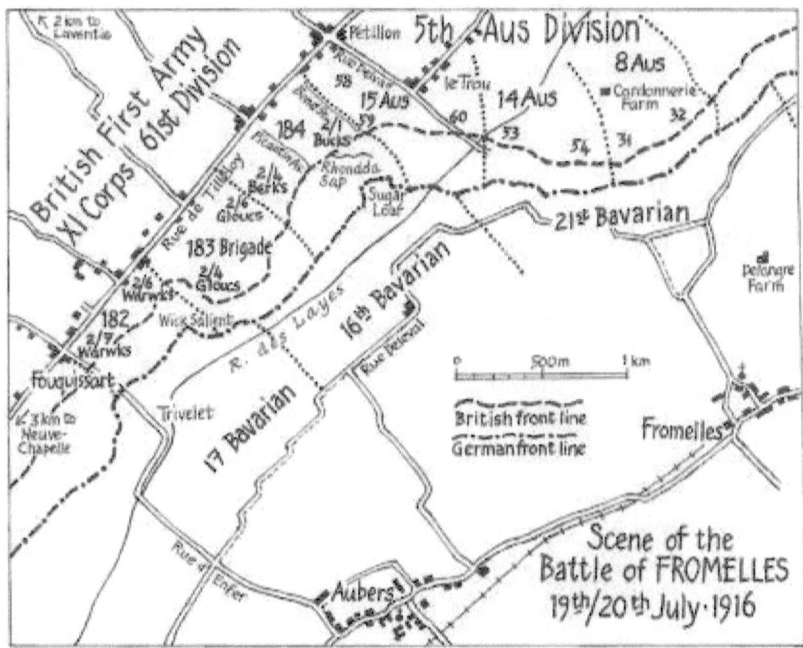

Tom and the 8th Battalion were on the northernmost sector of the battlefield called Cardonnerie Farm.

July 1916

Tom was in the trench with his platoon from the 8th Battalion. They had been hearing the bombardment of the German positions for hours now. He listened to his men's banter.

'Geez, I hope Pompey was right; this bombardment should knock the shit out of Fritz. Just a quick sprint and we take the German trenches,' said Wally.

'You're bloody mad, Wally it's not gonna be that easy,' said Frank.

'I was only joking Frank, I don't really believe we'll skip over no man's land and capture all the Krauts that aren't dead. As a matter of fact, I think we're in deep shit. Are you scared, Frank?'

'Fucking oath mate, I really don't want to die here, I was rather hoping I would die in my sleep when I'm about fucking ninety.'

'Yeah, me too,' said Wally. 'Did you hear what happened to Bruce Cook?'

'No, what happened?'

'He copped a fucking shell in the trench.'

'How do you know?' asked Frank.

'The runner told me. You were having a bit of a kip. Fucked if I know how with all this bloody noise.'

Tom and the other officers and NCOs started to move along the trenches, informing the diggers they were due to go over the top in thirty minutes. They instructed them to check their equipment, most importantly their rifle bayonet and grenades. It had been reported that inexperienced troops were forgetting to pull the pin on their grenades before hurling them, which made them fairly ineffective.

Tom took the time to write a quick note to his mother, back home in Melbourne.

> *Dear Mother,*
>
> *I have been told we are going over the top very soon. I know what that is like from my time at Gallipoli and it's hell on earth. I survived Gallipoli and I have no doubt I will survive here with the help of God.*
>
> *Have you been informed where Anna has been posted? I was hoping to catch up with her while on leave.*
>
> *I will put this letter in my pocket and if anything does happen to me, my cobbers will find it and send it on to you.*
>
> *I want you to know that I love you.*
>
> *Well, I said a quick note and there's the five-minute whistle, so I'd better sign off.*
>
> *Love*
>
> *Tom*

'Well mate this it, I'll see you in Fritz's trenches soon,' said Wally.

'See you there, cobber,' responded Frank.

Lieutenant Griffith checked the time on his gold pocket watch, a present from his mother.

He blew his whistle and yelled out to his men, 'Give them hell boys over you go. I'm right here with you.'

Tom's platoon all clambered over the top and started to run heading for the German trenches.

Machine guns were firing from all directions. Tom could hear the bullets tearing through the flesh of the diggers from his platoon running beside him. He found a shell crater and jumped in, only to find a soldier's body lying in a pool of filthy water at the bottom.

So this is what they call Anzac soup, he thought.

Tom knew he could not stay there long so he clambered up the slope and starting to run again. He had not fired a shot from his revolver yet; a bit useless this far away.

He could feel his heart pumping furiously. The adrenalin was rushing through his veins like a river torrent; the noise of the guns and shellfire was deafening.

He identified Wally and Frank through the smoky haze and slithered over to them. 'Are you boys all right?'

'Yes sir. I know a few of the other lads copped it but we're okay,' said Frank.

'See that pill box ahead?'

'Can't fucking miss it, sir.'

'I'm going to blow the bastard up. I need you both to cover me while I get close enough to hurl a couple of hand grenades through the firing slit.'

'Yes, sir.'

Tom slowly made his way to the concrete fortification as the two diggers fired madly at the pillbox, careful not to hit their platoon leader.

Finally, Tom was close enough to throw his bombs. The grenades had a ten-second fuse. He pulled the pins of two simultaneously and waited eight seconds, then threw them in. He rolled away, hoping to avoid injury. The grenades exploded, and Tom waited to ascertain if the explosions had killed the inhabitants. He heard nothing, so he made his way to the entrance and found four German soldiers, all dead.

Tom signalled to Frank and Wally to join him at the destroyed gun emplacement.

'Okay, lads we now have a clear passage to the German trenches. We need to see if we can rustle up the remainder of the platoon,' said Tom.

German Pill Box

The three diggers waited impatiently and eventually they were joined by ten comrades.

'Listen up, men, we're going to capture the trench immediately ahead. When I give the signal we run as fast as we can, weaving the whole way and firing our rifles. Is that clear?'

The twelve men nodded their understanding of the order.

'Right men, let's go.'

The platoon did as they were ordered and as a consequence they made it to the enemy's trench where fierce hand-to-hand fighting took place. After half an hour the Australians had killed or captured thirty Germans.

Frank looked to Tom for his approval but couldn't find him amongst their group. Another digger, Sam Williams, noticed Tom at the far end of the trench, lying down holding his chest. He had been shot.

Wally decided to go back to their own line to find an ambulance team. He hadn't travelled far when he spotted one. He approached them, explaining the situation. The team followed Wally back to the German trench and quickly assessed Tom's wound. It was decided that even though the lieutenant had a slim chance of survival it was worth a chance. The six-man ambulance team took Tom back to the Allied line under enemy fire. He was transferred by ambulance to the Wessex Farm Advanced Dressing Station for initial treatment.

Call Me a Doctor

Chapter 39

February 15, 1915

Anna had begun her final year and although she was excited to be graduating at the end of the year, she was concerned that the war with Germany didn't look like ending anytime soon. She had made a promise to herself that if the war was still going by the time she graduated, she would enlist in the army as a medic.

Final year medicine is never easy. Anna devoted every waking moment to her studies. When the final exam results were announced, she didn't achieve dux of the faculty, but she was runner-up.

January 6, 1916

The graduation ceremony was held in Wilson Hall where her life at Melbourne University began four years before.

Emma attended. She was very proud of her daughter and they both felt Tom's absence, hoping he was safe and well.

At the time Anna received her Medical Degree, her brother was back in Mena Camp, Egypt, having been evacuated from Gallipoli on December 19.

He wrote to his mother:

> *'I was extremely angry, as I had for a long time cherished the hope that I would leave this inhospitable graveyard defiant and with my head held high. I could not admit, even to myself, that we had been beaten after the sacrifice of so many men … to desert our fallen comrades and sneak away in the dark without a fight is a revolting thing and the thought of it nauseates me.'*

At the conclusion of the ceremony, Emma approached her daughter with the suggestion they dine at the Windsor.

They arrived at Emma's magnificent hotel where several of the staff congratulated Anna on her achievement.

'Well, darling, have you decided where you will do your internship?'

'Yes, I have, Mother; a field hospital on the Western Front.'

'No, you can't be serious! I already have Tom in the firing line… not you as well.'

'Our boys in Europe need doctors. I thought you would be proud of me.'

'Darling, I'm very proud of you but I can't stand the thought of losing you.'

'I'll be out of the danger zone in a field hospital well behind the front line. Don't worry.'

'I will worry, but it's obvious you've made up your mind so there's little I can do about it.'

'No, there's not, I've already enlisted, and I leave March 1.'

'Oh my God, that doesn't give us much time together. We should make the most of it. I have just purchased a grazing property called *Ercildoune*. I used to go fox hunting on the estate with my father… it's only twenty miles from Ballarat. Why don't we stay there for a week or so and go horse riding? There are beautiful trails spread over its twenty-thousand acres.'

Ercildoune Homestead

Anna laughed. 'Mother, I can't keep up with your growing business empire! Why a sheep grazing property?'

'Don't forget the wheat, darling, there are five hundred acres, making it one of the largest crop farms in Victoria. It has a reputation for the best rams in the country and the sheep are highly prized for their fine wool. It's a good investment, Anna.'

'What do you know about growing wool or wheat, though?'

'Not much, but I will have excellent staff to manage the farm. I didn't know much about hotels or department stores or newspapers for that matter, but if you hire the right staff the chances are you will be successful.'

February 7, 1916

Mother and daughter were driven to the homestead mid-morning and after dropping off their luggage they walked around the lavish gardens.

'These gardens are magnificent. No wonder you bought the property,' Anna said, looking about with delight.

'Yes, they are rather beautiful, but not the reason I invested as you know.'

The women spent the week riding over the estate, eating good food, drinking fine wine and talking, lots of talking.

The time came to leave Ercildoune as Anna had things to organise before boarding the *Kanowna* and sailing to France.

March 1, 1916

H.M. Australian Hospital Ship "KANOWNA."

Of the fifty-five interns who graduated alongside Anna, ten enlisted in the army as medics and these all sailed with her to France.

The doctors didn't play two-up or other games during the journey. Instead, they honed their skills in surgery, particularly amputations, using dummies.

May 15, 1916

Anna and her comrades landed at Marseilles; from the beautiful port city, they caught a train travelling eight hundred kilometres to Havre. She and her comrades were then transferred to a double decker bus normally used as a troop carrier and driven to the Advanced Dressing Station at Essex Farm where she would be stationed for a large part of the war.

Essex Farm Advanced Dressing Station

She would soon experience the horrors of war.

Initially, the Dressing Station received sporadic casualties as there were no major battles taking place within the vicinity.

German artillery and trench mortar activity began to intensify at Vimy Ridge, the front-line trenches were badly damaged, and casualties began to pour into the Dressing Station. Anna amputated her first limb; the leg of a young British soldier. This would be the first of many amputations.

May 21, 1916

A German bombardment on the Berthonval sector intensified. It continued for several hours. It not only concentrated on the front-line trenches, but it hit the rear artillery positions also. Some shells exploded eight miles back from the front line. The enemy also employed tear gas; over 70,000 shells fell in a four-hour period. The casualties were extremely heavy.

Anna once again worked for eighteen hours straight. She completed eight amputations as well as extricating shrapnel from several young soldiers.

After eight weeks of working in the Dressing Station Anna was granted four days of leave. Her initial desire was to go to Ypres, but one of her colleagues showed her a recent photo of the town.

Ypres June 1916

She decided to visit Poperinge instead, but after one night in the town she decided to cut short her leave as the town was full of drunken soldiers, intent on relieving their frustrations with any female they could find.

July 20, 1916

Dr Griffith began to examine a badly wounded soldier. There was no doubt he was near death.

'Nurse, clean him up as best you can. I can't determine the extent of his injuries with so much blood and dirt.'

The young nurse began to wipe the soldier's face, cleaning away the caked blood and grunge.

'Not his face, Nurse, his chest!'

Dr Griffith returned to the young soldier. She looked at his battered face and froze. She did not move or utter a word.

'Doctor, are you all right?' asked the nurse.

'He ... he's my brother.'

'Oh my God! Well stop staring and start saving him for goodness' sake.'

The nurse's words prompted Anna into action. She immediately classified him 'priority one'. An ambulance was waiting outside the dressing station within the minute and sped Tom and Anna off to the field hospital five kilometres away.

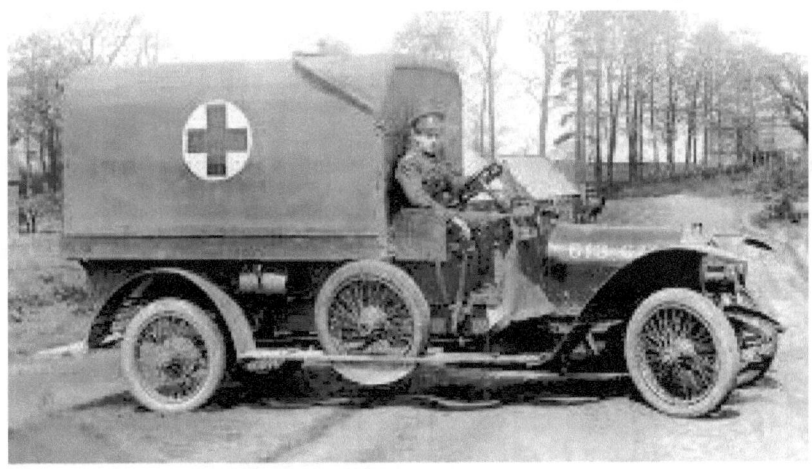

The first thing Anna organised was a chest x-ray.

At the beginning of the war, chest injuries caused by bullets or shrapnel were bandaged and left to heal, usually resulting in infection and or death. With the advent of x-rays, doctors behind the front lines were able to locate and remove foreign objects successfully.

Anna was able to determine a piece of shrapnel had penetrated the chest wall, puncturing Tom's right lung. If she did not operate immediately he would die within the hour.

She called for two nurses to assist. Only one was available. She requested the help of a senior surgeon. None was available.

Dr Griffith and Nurse Jane Flanagan would have to cope with the resources at their disposal. Nurse Flanagan administered the ether to Tom. Once he was anaesthetised, Anna made a cut down his sternum and spread it wide enough for her to extract the metal from his chest and his right lung. She closed him and immediately called for an ambulance to speed him away to the nearest base hospital where he would be further treated and monitored.

Anna did not have the luxury of accompanying him, as she was needed back at the dressing station. The wounded were pouring in from Fromelles.

My God, war is cruel, she thought as she rode back in the cabin of the ambulance.

Dr Griffith worked another twelve hours. She amputated three legs, two arms, and tried to arrest the bleeding of a young soldier with a severe groin injury – she was unsuccessful, and he died.

Anna tried not to think about Tom but that was an impossible task. When her shift finally ended, she hitched a ride in one of the ambulances going to the base hospital.

Initially, Anna couldn't find him. He had been registered as being admitted but he was not in the ward. After asking several hospital staff, she discovered he was undergoing a second operation. The surgeon, having been told Anna was the patient's sister, sought her out.

'Are you Tom Griffith's sister?'

'I am, Doctor. How is he?'

'I believe you are also a doctor? The same doctor that performed the first operation?'

'Yes.' Anna waited for the admonishment.

'Well, I can tell you that if you hadn't operated when you did your brother would be dead. There was still some bleeding in the chest cavity, but we have been able to stem the flow. Your brother is a very lucky man. My assessment is he will live to fight another day. I would envisage he would be sent to England for his convalescence. Hard to know at this stage for how long.'

'That's wonderful. Thank you so much.'

'No, thank you– you're the one that saved his life.'

'When do you think I will be able to see him?'

'I'd leave it until tomorrow.'

'Thank you once again.'

'Stop thanking me. Thank your medical training.'

Anna left the hospital, relieved but still concerned. She knew things could still go wrong. She slept fitfully for four hours before she began her shift again.

Dr Griffith's day was once again filled with amputations and treating burns from mustard gas. She could not stop thinking about Tom and when her shift ended, she hitched another ride to the base hospital.

Anna approached Tom's bed slowly. He was asleep. She grabbed a chair and sat next to him, holding his hand.

An hour and a half went by and then he opened his eyes. He looked at Anna, but his vision was blurred.

'Hello, nurse. Can I have some water, please?'

'I'm not a nurse. I'm a doctor, thank you.'

'I'm sorry, doctor. I'm not seeing too well at the moment.'

'Yes, that's obvious. You don't even recognise your little sister!'

'Sis! Is that really you?'

'Yes, darling! It's me.'

'How did you know I was here?'

'I brought you here, Tom. You were admitted into the dressing station where I was working. I didn't recognise you at first. You were in a right state. I treated you initially then organised for you to come here.'

'I don't remember what happened to me – one minute I'm in the German trench and next thing you're sitting beside me.'

The surgeon who completed the second operation on Tom walked up to the bed.

'Well Lieutenant, you're looking a lot better than when I saw you last. My name is Dr Simmons. I completed the additional surgery on you yesterday. How are you today, Dr Griffith?'

'Better for seeing my brother alive and well, thank you, Doctor.'

'Thank you, Doctor,' said Tom.

'Thank your sister; if it wasn't for her quick thinking and her skill as a surgeon you wouldn't be here.'

'You operated on me, Anna?'

'That's what I'm meant to do, Tom. I'm a doctor.'

'Thanks, Anna I can't thank you enough.'

'Enough, Tom.'

Tom was transported by a hospital ship to England where he was admitted to Harefield House Hospital in Middlesex. Harefield House had been the residence of Australians Mr and Mrs Charles Billyard-Leake who were resident in England. They donated the house to the AIF to be used as a hospital for wounded Australian soldiers.

Harefield House

Tom had been a resident for a month and had healed to the point where he could take short walks through the magnificent gardens. He was on one such a walk when an Australian colonel, James Wilson, approached him.

'Captain Griffith may I have a word please?'

'It's Lieutenant Griffith actually, sir.'

'Not any more, you've received a promotion as a result of your outstanding leadership during the battle of Fromelles.'

'My goodness! Well thank you, sir, I'm honoured.'

'Speaking of honour, Captain you have been awarded *the Distinguished Service Medal* for blowing up the German gun emplacement under heavy enemy fire, so congratulations.'

Captain Tom Griffith, despite the treatment he received at Harefield, did not fully recover from his wounds. His lungs would never operate at full capacity, and as a result, he was dispatched back to Melbourne at the beginning of 1917. He received an Honourable Discharge. His mother was much relieved, as was his sister.

It's Not That Quiet on the Western Front

However, it is at Ercildoune Station

Chapter 40

May 1917

Tom arrived back in Melbourne via South Africa. Emma arranged to meet him at Port Melbourne Wharf and her driver was permitted to drive up to the RMS *Omrah* in her recently purchased Rolls Royce. Emma commanded quite a bit of respect in the city.

PB0651

The soldiers returning home from the war were a pitiful site; some were wheeled down the gangplank with a leg missing, others with both legs gone. There were diggers with horrible facial injuries while others were insane. They left the same wharf two years before as brave and fearless soldiers on an adventure of a lifetime to fight for King and country. Most returned without a future.

Tom was one of the lucky ones. He hadn't lost a limb or been mutilated. He just breathed with half the lung capacity he had when he left the fatal shore.

Emma caught sight of him descending the gangplank and she asked the driver to blow the car's horn to get Tom's attention.

The vision of a shiny black Rolls Royce beeping its horn not only got Tom's attention, but that of everybody on the wharf. Tom felt embarrassed but nevertheless he was pleased to see his mother waving frantically at him. He approached the car and got into the back seat, giving Emma a huge hug and kiss.

'Tom darling, it's so good to see you. How are you feeling?'

'I'm fine, Mother. Better than most of the blokes that got shipped back with me.'

'Yes, I saw some of the poor blighters. It must have been terrible over there.'

'It wasn't good, Mother.'

'Well, let's get your luggage and we'll be on our way.'

'I have my luggage, so we can go.'

'What, that little bag is that all you have?'

'There was no need for luggage over in France, just a uniform and some bathroom items and a revolver.'

'Right then driver, to the Windsor, please. I have organised a beautiful suite for you to stay in until you decide what you'd like to do with yourself, Tom.'

'Thank you.'

Emma hadn't exaggerated; the apartment was superb with two bedrooms, two bathrooms, and a large formal lounge and dining room.

'You're spoiling me, Mother.'

'Well, if I can't spoil my son the hero who can I spoil? May I suggest we dine in the restaurant tonight? I've got so much to ask you.'

'Yes, why not? What time?'

'Say 7 pm.'

'Excellent. I'll see you there.'

Tom entered his bedroom. On the bed was a beautiful dark blue double-breasted suit, a linen shirt and silk tie. A pair of brogues completed the outfit.

She thinks of everything, he thought.

Tom took a long warm bath and after drying himself, he put on the white robe and lay on the bed. He soon fell asleep. He woke at 6.45 pm.

Frantically, he dressed in his new clothes and caught the lift down to the first floor. He walked into the restaurant at 7 pm, gasping for breath. Emma was seated at her usual table at the far end, and the headwaiter showed Tom to his mother's table.

'Tom, are you all right?'

'I apologise, I fell asleep, and I had to race to be here on time. My lungs just can't handle it I'm afraid.'

'You've got to take care of yourself, darling. It wouldn't have mattered if you were late.'

'My strict army training, I'm afraid. Rule number one; don't ever be late.'

'Speaking of the army, Tom, have you had any thoughts regarding what you're going to do now?'

'I have naturally thought about it, but at this stage, I have no idea. I always wanted to be in the army, as you know. When I graduated from Duntroon I thought the military would be a lifelong career. Now, well— I just don't know.'

'Was there ever a chance that you could remain in the army, darling?'

'They offered me a desk job in Logistics but the thought of spending the rest of my life ordering and distributing nuts and bolts didn't appeal.'

'I can understand that. I have a suggestion which might suit you.'

'What's that?'

'I purchased a large sheep and wheat station just outside Ballarat. It's called *Ercildoune*. It has a beautiful homestead and magnificent gardens. You could be General Manager.'

'I appreciate your faith in me, but with my condition, I would have difficulty with the physical work required to run a suburban backyard let alone a large station.'

'You won't have to worry about that. I have two farm managers living on site. Eric Jones manages the sheep farm, and the wheat farm is managed by Ernie Wicks. They would report to you.'

'Can we go out there and inspect it? I must admit the proposition sounds appealing.'

'Of course! We can go out there tomorrow if you wish.'

'That would be splendid. I certainly don't have anything else on.'

Emma and Tom drove the one hundred miles from Melbourne to the property in the Rolls. Tom drove; it made him feel useful.

They arrived at Ercildoune at 1 pm. Emma had arranged for the kitchen at the Windsor to prepare a picnic lunch. Rather than eat in the homestead, the two of them laid a rug down under a large oak tree with a view over a valley below.

'This is beautiful,' said Tom. 'We could be in England, what with all the oaks and elms and the like.'

'Yes, it is beautiful. Wait till we ride out through the paddocks! The countryside is superb. You are able to ride, aren't you Tom?'

'I think so. I must admit I haven't attempted to get on a horse since being wounded.'

'We'll see how you go after lunch. There's no pressure, son.'

Emma and Tom enjoyed their lunch of freshly baked bread, cheese, and ham washed down with apple cider.

Afterwards, Emma guided Tom to the substantial stables where six horses were housed, three Walers as used by the Light Horse Brigades, and three Arabian thoroughbreds.

'So, Tom, choose your mount.'

'I think the chestnut Waler will suit me.'

'Good choice Tom, I suppose you've ridden a few Walers whilst serving in the army.'

'I did. They are a great breed.'

'Right, well I'll take my usual mount— the white filly.'

'Has she a name?'

'Yes she's called Blossom.'

'How cute, and what about mine?'

'I believe he's called Puck.'

'That's a strange name.'

'Yes, some fellow who wrote *A Midsummer Night Dream* named one of his characters Puck.'

'William Shakespeare, you mean?'

'Yes, him.'

Emma instructed Eric, the farm manager, to saddle up both horses. He led them outside and tied them to the hitching rail.

'Do you need help mounting Puck, darling?' asked Emma.

'I'm not a cripple.'

'Sorry. I'm just concerned for your welfare.'

Mother and son rode out of the homestead grounds heading for the far paddocks where the majority of the sheep were grazing. They rode for over an hour and when they reached their destination all they could see were sheep, thousands of sheep.

'How many sheep are you running here?' asked Tom, staring about in wonder.

'About twenty thousand, more or less.'

'That's an awful lot of sheep.'

'Yes, it is. The shearing season is quite frantic as you can imagine.'

'How many bales does the station produce in a year?'

'Last season we got a hundred and ten bales.'

'You have no problem securing shearers?'

'No, not at all. Despite the war there seems to be plenty of able-bodied men available.'

'I suppose that's good and bad.'

'What do you mean, Tom?'

'Well, we have thousands of men and women putting their lives on the line for the King and country while these fellows are making a killing of their own.'

'Tom, the country needs men to stay back and keep the economy going. The war is costing the government an enormous amount of money and if the economy goes into recession everybody loses.'

'I suppose you're right. You're thinking like a business woman, as I would expect.'

'Don't get me wrong. I'm a true patriot and I support our war effort totally.'

'I know you do.'

'Come on, we need to keep moving if we want to see the wheat crops before returning to the homestead.'

It took another hour's riding to reach the extensive wheat fields, where Tom and Emma dismounted and walked amongst the golden sheaves. Looking out as far as the eye could see, they observed a golden carpet of wheat.

'This is very impressive,' Tom said. 'I thought the sheep flock was amazing, but this seems even more so.'

'It could all be yours eventually, Tom.'

'I could be so fortunate.'

'You could be. We need to get moving. I don't want to be out here after dark.'

The station's cook, Mrs Vardy, had prepared a lamb roast for their dinner. They ate the meal in the formal dining room.

'Would you care for a red wine with your meal?' Emma asked.

'Yes thank you, I'll pour it. Goodness me, it's ORO! Grandfather's wine; excellent.'

'Father shipped over several trunks of wine, both white and red. So, Tom, I take it from your reaction today you are impressed with Ercildoune?'

'How could I not be? It's a magnificent station.'

'Would you like to take it on as General Manager?'

'I'd be lying if I told you I was full of confidence in taking on the role, however, with my officer training and experience I'm confident I can manage the station staff. With Wicks and Jones supporting me, I do believe I can handle it.'

'Well then, that's settled. When can you move into the homestead?'

'I suppose there's nothing stopping me from moving in immediately.'

'In that case, I'll head back to Melbourne in the morning and leave you here to get organised. I'll come back with some papers to sign, giving you access to the bank account. We haven't discussed your salary, Tom, I suggest £2,000 per year plus your food and board.'

'That's very generous Mother. Thank you.'

'Excellent. I'm going to bed. I've got a full day tomorrow. I need to attend a board meeting for Sutton Innovations in the afternoon.'

'Goodnight Mother and thank you for all you are doing for me,'

'No need to thank me, Tom, I needed a General Manager I can trust.'

Tom didn't take long to settle into the way of life at Ercildoune. Jones and Wicks were a great support to the novice farmer. They admired Tom for his bravery during the war and ensured that he didn't overstretch his physical capability.

Despite Tom being invalided out of the army, he was still seen as a dashing handsome ex-army officer who had been highly decorated. This made him an attractive proposition to the young women of Ballarat and Melbourne.

One particular young lady had taken Tom's fancy. Her name was Charlotte Web, she came from a pastoral family whose holdings were similar to Ercildoune.

The Mayoral Ball was the social highlight of the year in Ballarat and it was always held in the Town Hall.

Ballarat Town Hall

Tom had decided he would invite Charlotte to the ball as his partner. He wrote to her and she replied in the affirmative.

July 31, 1917

The night of the ball had arrived. All the woman were dressed in beautiful ball gowns and the men were resplendent in their dinner suits. The orchestra was playing the *Vienna Waltz* when Tom and Charlotte arrived. Both knew it would be a wonderful night.

Halfway across the world in the Belgian village of Passchendaele, soldiers from the British Empire, including Australia, were waiting to go over the top to partake in one of the bloodiest battles of the war, just as the young couple were completing their first waltz.

Passchendaele

Chapter 41

Australian forces involved in the Polygon Wood battle were the Fourth and Fifth Divisions, which, as well as the infantry, included artillery, engineers, medical personnel and the hundreds of men involved in supply and transport. All essential war material had to be brought forward by wagons along roads and tracks exposed to heavy shelling. Horses and drivers suffered greatly. While a cratered road was repaired, drivers had to sit and wait, controlling their horses as the shells fell around them.

They belonged to the finest class their nation produced, unassuming, country-bred men. They waited steadily until the break was repaired or some shattered wagon or horses dragged from the road, and then continued their vital work. No shellfire could drive them from their horses. The unostentatious efficiency and self-discipline of these steadfast men was as fine as any achievement of Australians in the war.   *(Charles Bean)*

The Battle of Passchendaele, fought July 1917, is sometimes called the Third Battle of Ypres. For the soldiers who fought at Passchendaele, it was known as the 'Battle of Mud'. Few battles encapsulate World War One better than the Battle of Passchendaele.

The attack at Passchendaele was Sir Douglas Haig's attempt to break through Flanders. Haig had thought about a similar attack in 1916, but the Battle of the Somme occupied his time in that year. However, one year later, Haig felt able to launch such an attack. His main aim was a breakthrough to the coast of Belgium so that German submarine pens could be destroyed. Admiral Jellicoe had already advised both Haig and the British government that the loss of shipping (primarily merchant) could not be sustained and that Britain would face severe problems in 1918 if such losses continued. Haig's plan, to sweep through Flanders to the coast, did not receive support from Britain's Prime Minister, David Lloyd George, but as the Allies had no other credible plan, he gave his agreement for Haig to implement his plan.

Wally and Frank had survived Gallipoli and Fromelles and they were now waiting in a muddy trench about to face their biggest challenge.

'Hey, Frank I heard one of the officers say we'd have tank support. He's got to be fucking joking! There's no way a tank could get through this shit. It would sink up to its gun turret without moving an inch.'

'Yeah, I agree; half these jokers haven't fired a gun in anger. I wish we had Tom Griffith with us.'

'Yes, mate, he was a good man. I wonder what he's up to now?'

Tom was up to his third dance with Charlotte and quickly falling in love.

'Hey Frank, can you hear that?'

'What? I don't hear anything.'

Exactly, the bombardment has stopped after ten fucking days.'

'You know what that means… they'll throw us over the top pretty bloody soon.'

'Yeah, brace yourself mate.'

The atmosphere in the trench was tense to say the least. Some diggers were looking at photos of their families and sweethearts, others were saying a quiet prayer, while others were just silent waiting for the whistle.

They didn't have to wait long. The officers moved through the trenches informing the soldiers that they would be going over in a few minutes. They also reassured their men that it was highly unlikely that they would meet much resistance after the relentless bombardment of the German lines.

'Right mate, we stick together and keep our heads low,' said Frank.

'Too fucking right, mate. We know how to survive.'

The platoon leader, Lieutenant Samuel Mooney, checked his pocket watch and noted they had one minute to go. He extracted his Hudson whistle, placed it between his lips and at 5 am blew it loudly.

Hudson Whistle

Frank looked over at Wally and nodded.

Frank and Wally and the remainder of the Brigade clambered up the ladders and began their advance through the quagmire. They were met with a hail of bullets. Many diggers fell and others got caught up in the wire. As the sun rose Wally and Frank could observe the carnage surrounding them and they knew the Krauts had won the day. Those soldiers remaining slid into water-filled shell holes waiting for nightfall when they could hope to return safely to their line.

Passchendaele Field

A soldier from their platoon popped his head up over the shell hole to try and ascertain if it was safe to leave cover. His head was blown off his shoulders, and his mangled body remained in the hole with Frank and Wally.

As nightfall enveloped the battlefield, Lieutenant Mooney ordered the platoon to leave their cover and slither back through the mud and corpses which were already being devoured by the ubiquitous rats.

Frank could see their line about fifty yards ahead. In his eagerness to be on friendly ground he began to run in a crouching manner. A German sniper hit him in the left buttock, bringing him down. Wally observed what had happened and immediately went to his mate's aid. Together they made it to their own trench.

Once safely in the trench, a stretcher bearer team was called to carry Frank to the Dressing Station.

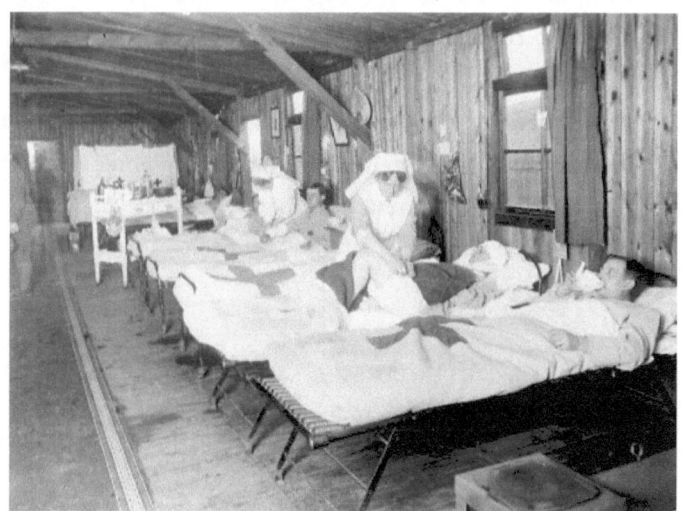

Australian Clearing Station

At the Clearing Station, Doctor Anna Griffith who would be responsible for extracting the German bullet from Frank's arse examined him.

'Well private, you've got yourself a nasty wound.'

'It could have been worse, Doctor. I could have been attacking, not retreating.'

'Yes, I see what you mean. What Battalion are you with?'

'The 8th. At least, I hope I'm still with the 8th.'

'My brother was with the 8th. You'd know him, Captain Tom Griffith.'

'I did, although he was a lieutenant when he was my platoon leader. When did he get promoted?'

'Just before being shipped back home.'

'He is a bloody good man and a bloody good officer. Sorry ma'am I shouldn't have sworn.'

'I assure you soldier I've heard a lot worse.'

'He's a station manager in Victoria now.'

'If I ever get back home I'll look him up.'

'The name of the station is *Ercildoune*. I'll write it down for you. Now, to more pressing matters. We need to extract that bullet.'

Anna used a scalpel to dig out the German souvenir. Frank was under an anaesthetic, a recent development in medicine, so he felt no pain. Anna gave him the bullet so that he could show his family and friends back home.

Frank was transported to a Field Hospital where he recovered and after three weeks he was back on the front line.

Both Frank and Wally survived the war and were shipped back to Australia in April 1919. Wally applied for and was granted a soldier settlement farm allotment in Gippsland Victoria. Frank became unemployed.

Young Doctors in Love

Chapter 42

Passchendaele was a cruel campaign. Over 220,000 Commonwealth troops became casualties including 38,000 Australians.

The Casualty Clearing Stations and the Field Hospitals operated around the clock. Anna, along with the other doctors, managed to survive on an average of four hours sleep.

One of the doctors, Geoffrey Turner, was British. He was seconded to the Australian Medical Corp and he and Anna would operate together on many occasions. They both respected one another's medical skills.

Working so closely together encouraged a physical attraction and it wasn't long before the two doctors became partners in more ways than one.

A typical day would begin with the wounded being transported by ambulance from the battlefield.

Anna and her colleagues would examine the wounded and determine the extent of their wounds. Some would be assessed as critical while others were near death. It was up to the doctors to decide who would receive treatment and who would be left to die.

The most amputations performed in a single day by Anna and Geoffrey was fifteen. They were both exhausted having no sleep for twenty-four hours.

The Medical Corp didn't get much respite once the Canadians finally captured Passchendaele, but they did get a week of leave. Anna and Geoffrey decided to stay in Poperinge as she decided it would be safe in the company of her lover.

They spent their time there eating in excellent restaurants, reading at the Talbot Club and making love in their hotel room at every opportunity.

They had never had the opportunity to discover each other's background and family history while stationed at the clearing station; the time in Pops gave them that time.

'Anna, you talk about your mother and how successful she is, but I've never heard you talk about your father.'

'No, I never met him. He died before I was—'

'Born?'

'I'm an adopted child, Geoffrey. I have no idea who my real parents were. I lived my first seven years in an orphanage until I was enrolled at King's Walden Home. My mother adopted my brother Tom and I and raised us to adulthood. My mother's husband, George, was a very successful businessman who also robbed gold shipments and pirated a ship carrying gold back to England. In one of the stage robberies a policeman was killed. Many years later, George was convicted and hanged.'

'My God, that's an amazing story Anna!'

'Do you still love me?'

'Of course I do.'

'What about your family? Any dark secrets hidden away in the family closet?'

'I'm afraid not, my dear. It's all pretty boring compared to yours. I was born and raised in York as you know. My father is a doctor who established York Hospital and was given a title for it. He is now known as Lord Turner of York and my mother is referred to as Lady Turner.'

'Does that mean you will inherit his title?'

'I'm afraid not. It's not a hereditary title.'

'Was your family always from York?'

'No, we're Scottish.'

'So when did the family move south?'

'It's a long story… are you sure you want to hear it?'

'Yes, I'm sure, family history intrigues me, I suppose because I don't know my own.'

'Okay; the Turners belong to the Lamont clan.

The Lamont clan descends from the original Scots who crossed the sea from Ireland, where their original name meant 'lawgiver', to found the kingdom of Dalriada. The kindred of Comgall is mentioned as one of the three principal kindreds in the ancient 'Account of the Men of Scotland'. Its territory, Cowal, still known by that name although once stretching to Bute and Arran, had in the year 1200 a chief called Fearchar. His sons Duncan and Malcolm granted lands to the monks of Paisley.

'The name Lamont was formed from that of Malcolm's son Ladman. Duncan and Malcolm established their chief seats at the strong Castles of Toward and Ascog.

The powerful Campbells, neighbours of the Lamonts, had steadily encroached on the Lordship of Cowal and after Montrose's great victory at Inverlochy in 1645; the Lamonts seized the opportunity and laid waste to Campbell territory at Kilmun.

The next year a powerful Campbell army invaded, taking Toward Castle and Ascog Castle. After being promised fair terms for himself and his people, Sir James Lamont surrendered. However, the dishonourable Campbells then slaughtered over two hundred Lamont men, women and children.

One tree was said to have carried thirty-five bodies from its branches. Elsewhere thirty-six men were buried alive. The two castles were destroyed and Sir James was thrown into a dungeon for five years.

A precious national heirloom, which has survived from 1464 till today, is the Lamont Harp. It is the oldest existing example of Scotland's earliest musical instrument. It measures thirty-eight inches by sixteen inches and resides with the Robertsons of Lude in Perthshire.

The last clan lands were sold in 1893.

'So there you have it; the Lamont's scattered near and far and changed their names to Brown, White, Green etc. The Turners moved down to Yorkshire where we have resided since.'

'Goodness me, you must hate the Campbells.'

'It was a long time ago, Anna. In fact one of my best friends at school was a Campbell.'

The week went all too quickly and when they returned to the Clearing Station they had little time to settle back in. The Germans had mounted a gas barrage upon the Anzac troops and the injuries were horrific.

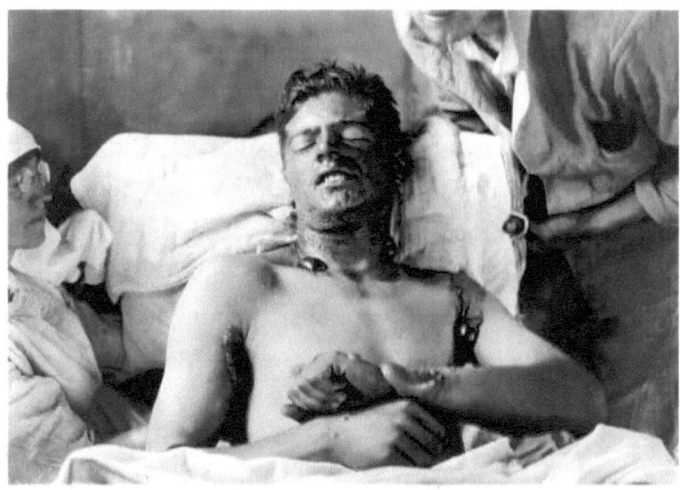

Villers Bretonneux became a major battleground for the Australian diggers. Where there is a battle there are casualties, and where there are casualties there are Casualty Clearing Stations manned by dedicated doctors and nurses. This was where Anna and Geoffrey found themselves.

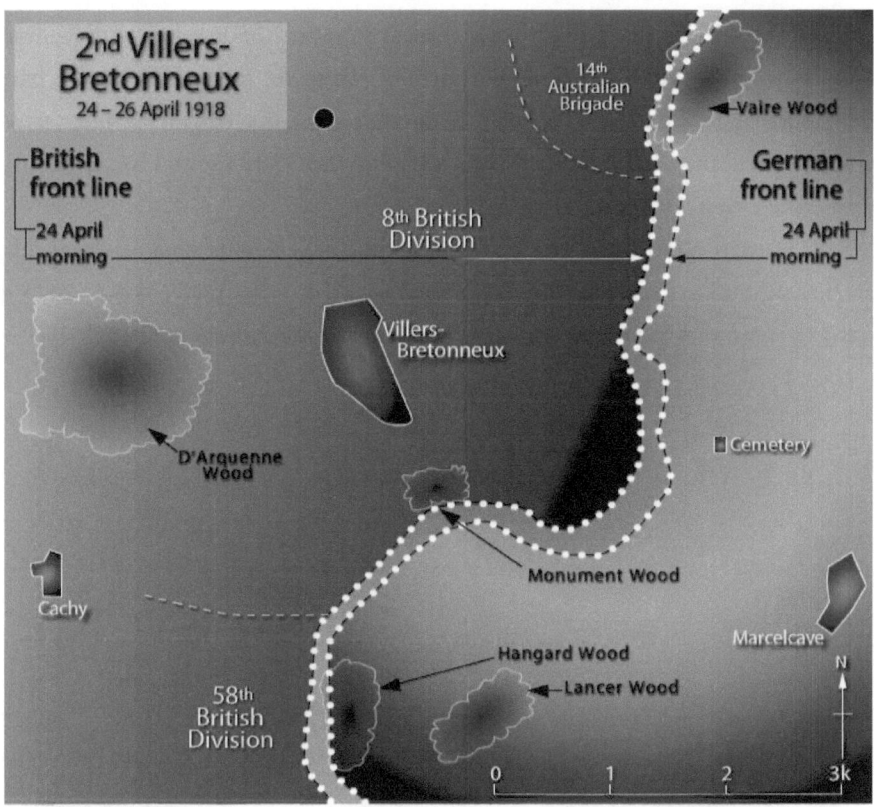

2nd Villers-Bretonneux
24 – 26 April 1918

14th Australian Brigade

Vaire Wood

British front line
24 April morning

German front line
24 April morning

8th British Division

Villers-Bretonneux

D'Arquenne Wood

Cemetery

Monument Wood

Cachy

58th British Division

Marcelcave

Hangard Wood

Lancer Wood

N

0   1   2   3k

The German Attack

The First and Second Battles of Villers-Bretonneux were a part of the Kaiserschlacht (Kaiser's battle), a series of German attacks along the Western Front. The German aim was to win the war before the enormous material and manpower resources of the United States, which had declared war on Germany in April 1917, could be brought to bear. The Germans also had a short-term advantage in numbers as Russia had made peace in 1917, allowing 48 German divisions to be moved to the western front. Beginning on 21 March 1918, the German offensive was the most successful one on the western front to date by either side. In April the Germans planned to take Amiens, 15 kilometres west of Villers-Bretonneux. Through Amiens ran the main north-south rail line in northern France. Cutting the line would seriously limit the British ability to move troops and supplies.

On 4 April, in the First Battle of Villers-Bretonneux, the Germans had narrowly failed to capture the town, but in the second battle on 24 April, they succeeded. Breaking through the British 8th and 58th Divisions, with the assistance of 15 tanks they drove the British back three kilometres. Australian involvement on the first day of the battle was limited: The 14th Brigade, near Vaire wood, bent the southern end of its line back to keep in contact with the British as they retreated, while a troop of the Australian's Corps cavalry, the 13th Light Horse, scouted to determine the extent of the German advance.

The German attack also resulted in the first tank versus tank battle in history. Three British tanks took on three German ones in the fields south of Villers-Bretonneux. One German tank was knocked out and the others retreated.

Villers Bretonneux After the Battle

Both young doctors worked tirelessly and on the few occasions they could rest, that's exactly what they did. There was no time to talk, just sleep.

By the time the battle was over both Anna and Geoffrey were absolutely exhausted. They were given a week's leave and this time they travelled to Paris by train, a three-hour journey.

They booked into the Hotel Elysées Palace, regarded as one of the best hotels in the city of lights.

The five days spent there was taken up by visiting the Louvre and the Musée d'Orsay and other museums and art galleries. They ate in fine restaurants and rediscovered their love for each other.

The war continued. Anna and Geoffrey were obligated to return to the Western Front to continue their duties in the various Casualty Stations dotted around the front.

The Hundred Day Offensive by the allies had begun.

The Hundred Day Offensive was a series of major battles that took place in the final phase of the Great War on the Western Front between August and November 1918. Following the Allied counter-attack at the Second Battle of Marne (15 July – 6 August 1918), the British, Belgian, French and American armies mounted a series of offensive operations that drove the German army from their great gains of the spring and forced the German Government to seek peace. Beginning at the Battle of Amiens on 8 August and continuing at varying levels of intensity until the Armistice of 11 November, the Hundred Days – actually only a total of ninety-five days – marked the final, climactic campaign of the First World War.

Celebrating war's end in the Streets of Paris

Post War Australia

Chapter 43

June 1919

The Great War hadn't done Emma's business empire too many favours, with the exception of Ercildoune. The demand for wool and wheat had continued to grow. Wool was required for uniforms and wheat to feed the hungry masses.

The Windsor and the Grand hotels operated well below normal occupancy but continued to break even, as did the Ballarat hotels.

Although the Eldorado Gold Mine continued to produce gold the demand had flattened. It was only after the war when the Bank of England took steps to re-establish London as the centre of the gold market that things improved.

It was in London where the "fix" was set each day, based on supply and demand. Eldorado, being a publicly listed company on the London Stock Exchange, benefited greatly. The stock price began to rise in 1919 and continued to rise for several years. Emma was the largest stockholder, therefore, her wealth continued to grow.

Claridge's Hotel maintained a high occupancy rate throughout the war as many governments housed their diplomats in the luxury hotel.

The *Sunday Times* increased its circulation throughout the war years and was now regarded as one of the mainstream newspapers in England. Emma's initial motivation to purchase the paper was to destroy Lord Henry Baynes, but the peer died in 1918, just before the armistice.

Sutton Innovations was virtually on hold for much of the war until several navies commissioned the company to build them a wireless network. In 1919 the company was hiring staff and expanding its operations.

Emma's wealth was now estimated at £5,000,000 making her the richest woman in Australia and one of the richest in the world.

While Emma enjoyed her wealth, Frank was destitute on the streets of Melbourne begging for enough money to buy him the one meal a day he needed to survive. His country asked him to answer the call and fight the Turks and the Huns and he did so willingly. He was wounded in action and still felt the pain.

Now, in a dirty AIF uniform, he wandered the streets, not knowing where his next meal would come from or where he would sleep that night.

Frank was sitting on a park bench in the Botanical Gardens when a smartly dressed man passed by. He stopped and returned to where Frank was seated.

'Excuse me, cobber, you wouldn't be Frank Thomas would you?'

'That depends on who's asking me. Who the fuck are you?'

'Albert Wilkie. I was in the 8th Battalion with you.'

'Bloody hell, yeah, I remember you.'

'Mate, it looks like you've fallen on hard times.'

'Yeah, you could say that. I can't find a fucking job for the life of me. I think I was better off over in France. At least I got three meals a day. You're obviously doing all right for yourself mate, what are you up to?'

'I work for a bloke called Squizzy Taylor. He's Melbourne's most notorious gangland boss.'

'So you're a professional crook?'

'I suppose you could say that. I can tell you, mate, I'm earning a pretty penny and the work is not hard.'

'Sounds all right. Does he need any more ex-diggers to join his gang?'

'He might. I'll tell you what, I'm seeing him tonight. I'll ask him. Where can I find you, Frank?'

'If it's past 4 pm I'll be right here.'

Carlton Melbourne July 1919

Albert arrived at Squizzy's favourite gambling house located in Barkly Street, Carlton, to receive his instructions for a robbery in central Melbourne in a few nights time. Several of the gang was present, drinking and playing poker. Squizzy was more concerned with Lucy Burn, a beautiful prostitute who dared not charge the gangland boss for her expert services. Once Squizzy had finished his games with Lucy he turned his attention to business.

Albert told him about his old army mate who was down on his luck.

'So Bert, you reckon I can trust him?'

'Yeah, boss, he's a fair dinkum bloke. He can fight as well.'

'All right, bring him around to the Fitzroy house tomorrow and I'll have a gander at him.'

'Thanks, Squizzy I think you'll be impressed, although he looks ragged at the moment.'

'Go buy him a suit and make sure the bastard's clean. I don't want a rag and bone man fronting up to the house.'

'Yes, sir. I'll make sure he looks the part.'

'Good, now you're right for the robbery on Saturday night?'

'Everything is organised, Squizzy. It should be a piece of cake.'

'Okay, I'll see you tomorrow at the house with your mate. What's his name?'

'Frank.'

'Right, I'll see you then.'

Albert knew he wouldn't find Frank at his normal squatting place in the morning but he decided he would purchase the suit, shirt, tie and shoes with matching socks and underpants at his favourite men's clothing store, Leviathan in Bourke Street.

Albert figured Frank was around his size, which proved to be correct.

He carried the new outfit in a large paper bag to the Botanical Gardens, where Frank was sitting on his park bench.

'G'day, Frank, I've bought you a present mate.'

'It's not me birthday.'

'It doesn't have to be your birthday to receive a present.'

'Fair enough, what did you get for me?'

'A new outfit; we'd better get you cleaned up and dressed up before you meet the boss.'

'I'm not sure how you're going to get me cleaned up, Albert.'

'Don't worry; I've got it sorted. We're going to take a visit to the Melbourne Baths. You'll be able to shower there and put on the new clobber.'

The two friends caught a tram to the baths and once Frank was showered and clothed in the suit, he looked a proper spiv.

The two dapper gentlemen caught a tram to Fitzroy and then walked the two blocks to Squizzy's house. Albert knocked on the door and it was opened by the gangster's wife Lorna. She showed them into the front parlour and offered them a glass of beer, which they both accepted.

Squizzy entered the room and sat in his leather chair without introducing himself to Frank.

'So, Bert tells me you want to join our band of thieves.'

'Well, yes I do, if you'll have me.'

'Why do you think you would be any good?'

'Albert will testify that I was a good soldier and I figure if you can survive in the hell holes we came across you should be able to survive in your world.'

'Are you a good shot?'

'I was considered a crack shot with a 303 rifle, but I must admit I've never fired a pistol in anger.'

'Well, what's your name again?'

'Frank, Frank Thomas.'

'Okay, Frank Thomas, I'm willing to give you a go. Albert, take him with you on Saturday night. He can act as the lookout.'

Frank proved himself on the first robbery and over the following months became an integral member of the gang.

From Left, Squizzy, Frank and Albert

The Sailors Arms Hotel

Squizzy met up with his rival Henry Stokes who headed up the Fitzroy Gang. Squizzy now lived in Richmond and was known as the boss of the Richmond Gang. They decided to join forces and rob the biggest jewellery store in Melbourne, Kilpatrick's. The plan was to walk into the store in broad daylight and force the jeweller to hand over all the diamond rings under threat of shooting.

Squizzy, Albert and Frank represented the Richmond Gang while Henry, Ted Whiting and Long Harry Slater comprised the Fitzroy Gang.

The gangsters entered the store with guns drawn and shouted to staff to hand over the diamonds, worth £1500 in all. The robbery went well, but the three Fitzroy boys were identified and later arrested. The remainder of the Fitzroy Gang became suspicious that someone from the Richmond Gang had tipped off the police. Their suspicion increased when Frank became a prosecution witness in exchange for immunity.

The three men were found not guilty, but outside the court a brawl broke out and Squizzy was badly beaten.

This incident was the catalyst for what became known as the "Fitzroy Vendetta".

Attack and counter attack occurred for some time. Many were injured but nobody got killed.

The Melbourne newspapers reported each incident, yet no charges were laid due to members from each gang refusing to testify.

Ercildoune Station

Tom Griffith was reading the *Argus* newspaper which had been recently acquired by his mother. A story about the Fitzroy Vendetta caught his attention and he recognised a photo of Frank Thomas. He had been one of the best soldiers in the platoon, and not only that, he was a bloody good bloke.

What in the hell is Frank hanging around with Squizzy Taylor for? He'll end up in prison or, worse, he'll be shot dead, Tom thought.

Tom made the decision to travel into Melbourne and endeavour to locate Frank and convince the veteran to return to Ercildoune with him.

He always stayed with his mother when visiting Melbourne and it gave him the opportunity to report on the continued success of the station as well as catching up with all her news. It seemed she had either purchased a new business or created a start up every time he saw her.

Tom told Emma the reason for his visit and she suggested she contact the Police Commissioner, Sir George Steward, who was ironically a close friend.

'George will know where this fellow hangs out. He knows the whereabouts of every gangster in Melbourne.'

'Thank you, Mother, I appreciate your support.'

Emma contacted the Commissioner and as she had predicted he knew the address of Frank Thomas; it was 33 Duke Street, Richmond.

Frank arrived home at 6 pm. He had a busy day completing odd jobs for Squizzy; none of them particularly savoury.

Frank noticed a figure sitting on the steps leading to his veranda. Unexpected visitors made him nervous, particularly while the troubles with the Fitzroy gang were going on. Frank felt for his Colt revolver under his coat, but as he got closer, he recognised the man immediately.

'Lieutenant Griffith! Well I'll be fucked.'

'Captain Griffith to you, Frank.'

'Yeah that's right. I'd heard you'd been promoted. In fact, it was your sister who told me.'

'So you've met her, have you?'

'Yeah, I know her intimately. She extracted a German bullet from my arse.'

'I see. Are you going to invite me in, Frank?'

'Yeah of course. Come on in mate.'

'It's a nice little place you've got here, Frank. Are you renting, or do you own it?'

'If anybody else asked me that I'd tell them to mind their own business, but seeing it's you I'll tell you. I own it.'

'So, you're doing all right for yourself mate?'

'Yeah, not too bad.'

'I came down to Melbourne to talk to you, Frank. I'm concerned about the company you've been keeping.'

'You mean Squizzy and the boys?'

'By all accounts, he's a mean little bastard who takes no prisoners.'

'Tom, I was on the bones of my arse when Squizzy brought me into his gang. My home was not a pretty cottage in Richmond, it was a bench in the botanical gardens. I begged in the street just to get enough dosh to buy one meal a day. Now I wear a good suit, I can eat out in any restaurant I choose, and I'm respected in the community.'

'There's a big difference between respect and fear, Frank.'

'So what do you expect me to do? Give it all away and live on the streets again?'

'No, what I'm proposing is you return to Ercildoune Station with me I'll provide you with a cottage and you work on the farm and learn the ropes. I'll pay you well and before you know it you'll be leading hand.'

That's very generous of you. Do you mind if I give it some thought?'

'By all means, but I return tomorrow, and all bets are off once I go back.'

Frank didn't sleep much that night. He weighed up his options. If he stayed with Squizzy and the boys he'd continue to make good money, but he ran the risk of being gaoled or worse, killed in action.

If he accepted Tom's offer he could end up being leading hand as well as living in the country, something he'd dreamed of for a long time. He could also live to a ripe old age. He could even get married and have some kids.

By the time the sun rose next morning, Frank had made his decision. He would go to Ercildoune with Tom.

He needed to tell Squizzy that day. The gangster lived close by, enabling Frank to walk to his house. He knocked on the front door and Squizzy's wife new wife Dolly answered the door.

Squizzy Taylor's Richmond House

'Hello Frank, I suspect you'd like to speak to Squizzy? He's in the kitchen eating his breakfast. Come on in.'

Frank entered the kitchen feeling very nervous as the last thing he wanted to do was upset his boss.

'G'day Frank, I don't remember asking you to come around this morning. What's up mate?'

'Squizzy I've had a job offer from my old boss in the army. He runs a big sheep and wheat station near Ballarat. I've decided to accept.'

'What the fuck do you know about fucking sheep, Frank?'

'Not much I admit, Squizzy, but he'll teach me.'

'Okay, Frank, I suppose I wish you well, but you'll be sorely missed. Have you told Albert?'

'No, not yet. I wanted to tell you first.'

'He'll be pissed off. After all it was Bert who introduced you to the gang.'

'I intend to go to his place when I've left here.'

Squizzy stood up and held out his hand. 'If things don't work out on the farm, Frank, you are always welcome back here.'

'Thanks Squizzy. I appreciate it.'

Frank left the house and walked the three blocks to Albert's house.

Albert had a similar reaction to Squizzy. He wished his old army mate well and he held no animosity.

Frank then informed Tom of his decision and naturally he was delighted.

One of the gang members Archie Duggan rented Frank's house for a reasonable amount.

Thank God I'm a Country Boy

Chapter 44

Frank arrived in Ballarat by train. Tom met him at the station and then drove him to Ercildoune Station. Frank was impressed with the homestead, though it was not his accommodation. After lunch, Tom showed his friend the cottage, which would serve as his home for the foreseeable future.

Frank was delighted. The cottage was about the same dimension as his Richmond house.

'This is great Tom. I know I'll be more than comfortable living here.'

'I'm glad you like it, mate why don't you settle in? Come up to the homestead at 6 pm for dinner. We've got a big day tomorrow. We'll be riding up to the far paddock to see how the lambing is going.'

'Oh, there is one thing I neglected to tell you, Tom, I've never been on the back of a horse.'

'You can't ride?' Tom stared at him.

'No, I was brought up as a city boy, mate.'

'Well, the first thing we need to do is teach you to ride. Don't worry, it's not that hard. I'll choose a docile mare for you to learn on.'

The next morning Tom selected a horse he thought would be suitable for the novice rider, a mare called Star. Tom helped Frank mount Star and once firmly in the saddle he was taught the correct way to hold the reins and position his feet in the stirrups. They walked around the perimeter of the homestead and a little beyond before returning to the holding yard.

'That's enough for your first lesson. We'll ride again tomorrow. I still have to ride out to the far paddock, but in the meantime, I have a job for you.'

Tom led Frank to the large wooden shearing shed.

'Right Frank, take this instrument. You place it between the floor boards and pick out the sheep dung so that when the sheep arrive for shearing they'll have sufficient grip.'

'So I'm a shit picker?'

'I suppose you are. I should back around dusk and I'll check how you've got on.'

Frank worked hard over the next six months. He became a competent horseman and learnt sheep husbandry, including crutching, a task second only to shit picking on his most unpleasant jobs list.

Frank was drinking a cold beer and reading the newspaper on his veranda after a hard day in the paddocks when a headline attracted his attention.

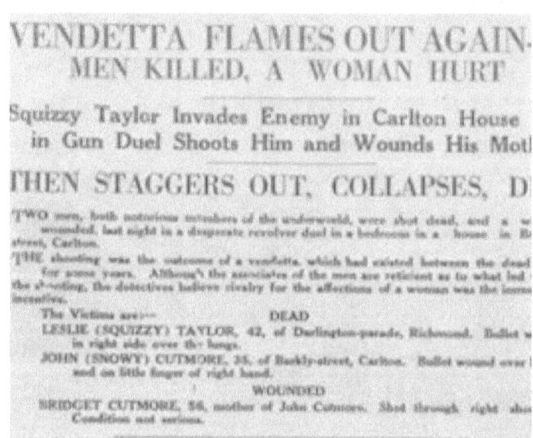

Frank was shocked. His former boss was one of those people who were expected to live forever.

Frank approached Tom to ask whether he could take a few days off as he wished to visit Melbourne to catch up with some friends.

Tom had no hesitation in granting Frank's request, as his new recruit had been putting in the hours.

His old mate Albert was first on the list. Frank caught the train from Ballarat and arrived at Spencer Street Station in the early afternoon. He then caught a tram to Richmond and walked the two blocks to Albert's house.

Frank knocked on the front door and Albert opened it, greeting his old friend warmly.

'How the fuck are you me old mate?' said Albert.

'All the better for seeing you cobber.'

'Well don't stand there like a shag on a rock— come in.'

The two men entered the kitchen.

'Can I interest you in a cold beer, Frank?'

'Now you're talking, Bert It was fucking hot walking here from the tram stop.'

Albert reached into the icebox and extracted a bottle of Victoria Bitter from which he poured two glasses.

'Come out to the front veranda, mate, and you can bring me up-to-date with all your news from the country.'

The two friends settled into their large cane chairs.

'I was shocked to hear that Squizzy bought it, mate.'

'Yes, although if you live your life like he did it's pretty inevitable you're going to die a violent death.'

'Well, mate, it's the life you lead.'

'No, it's different if you lead the gang; us foot soldiers tend to be left alone.'

'I hope for your sake you're right. I know when I ran with Squizzy there were a few hairy moments.'

'Anyway, the little bastard took out Snowy Cutmore before he died.'

'Yeah, that's one consolation.'

Albert and Frank noticed a black Buick pull up outside Albert's house, but before they could react a burst from a machine gun ripped both of them apart. The Buick sped off, never to be seen again.

The police called it a revenge killing. Nobody was charged with the double murder.

Frank had left his life of crime. It was just an unfortunate coincidence that he happened to be in the wrong place at the wrong time.

Back to Old Blighty

Chapter 45

France November 11, 1918

Geoffrey and Anna were sitting in Anna's tent drinking French Cognac given to Geoffrey by an appreciative soldier. It tasted even better now they were at peace with the world.

'Darling, have you thought about what you're going to do now this horrid war is over?'

'Well, I suppose I'll return home to Australia and take up a post at a major hospital in Melbourne.'

'I have an alternative plan.'

'Do you? What's that.'

'Why don't you return to England with me?'

'Why would I do that, Geoffrey?'

'So you could marry me and live happily ever after.'

'Is that a marriage proposal?'

'Well, yes, I suppose it is. Will you do me the great honour of marrying me, Anna?'

'I'm taken aback; let me think. Yes, of course, I'll marry you. I love you more than life itself.'

The two lovers embraced and despite the frenetic activity outside the tent made wild passionate love.

The two doctors in love were shipped back to Old Blighty on January 3, 1919. They had spent two months since the Armistice treating soldiers who had contracted Spanish Flu, a horrendous infection that ended up taking more than double the lives lost in the war.

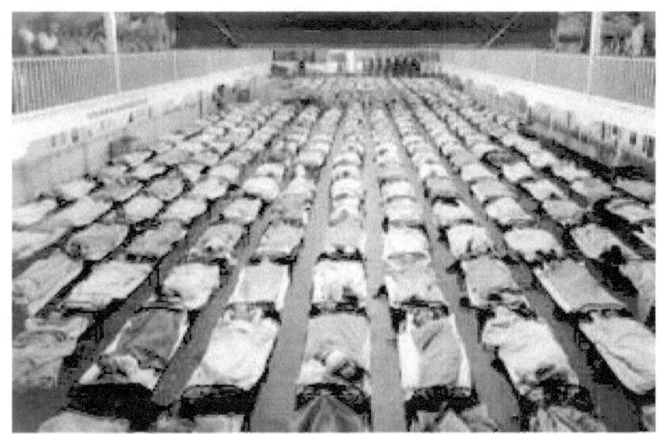

Spanish Flu Patients

Spanish Flu hit the world in the summer of 1918. The Great War was coming to an end with the death rate approaching twenty million people. By the time Spanish Flu disappeared in 1919, it had claimed between seventy and one hundred million people.

No one really knows where Spanish Flu began; some say China, others claim the Middle East. There is also conjecture as to why it was called "Spanish Flu". Again, some say because of the high mortality rate in Spain, others say it was because Spain was neutral and therefore had a free press, which could report what was really happening.

More current thinking places the beginning of the pandemic in the United States.

The pandemic eventually had a disastrous effect on the Germans and its allies, inflicting massive casualties through sickness which they could ill afford as the British and its allies were having significant success on the battlefield.

Military convoys became breeding grounds for the virus. Many died on the ships, as the symptoms were a brief fever rapidly followed by death. The virus caused uncontrollable haemorrhaging that filled the lungs, and patients would drown in their own blood. It was nearly impossible to isolate the patients from the rest of the troops in such a confined space.

The reasons for the pandemic essentially remain unknown. The deprivations of a world war are held responsible by some scientists, although the virus similarly swept through non -war affected countries like the USA, India and much of Europe.

For example, four hundred and fifty thousand civilian deaths occurred in the United States. The majority of deaths were in the twenty to forty age groups. In Britain some two hundred and twenty-eight thousand civilians died and four hundred thousand in Germany. Hardest hit, however, was India with a reported sixteen million casualties alone.

Each nation at war went to great lengths to conceal the extent of losses suffered through the virus, concerned that such reports would serve to encourage their enemies. In reality, each was suffering as badly as the other.

Curiously, in mid-1919, the pandemic withered and died abruptly without a treatment having been found. Scientists continue to believe that a repeat of the pandemic, albeit in a varying form, could find modern science equally as unprepared to meet a repeat of the flu challenge.

January 15, 1919

The hospital ship *Aquitania* with her cargo of armless, legless, blind and insane, docked at Liverpool wharf early in the morning. Unlike the regular troop ships, there were not the crowds of well-wishers waving Union Jacks on the jetty, just a few family members looking for their crippled sons, a look of sadness on their faces.

The exception was Lord and Lady Turner, waiting to greet their son Geoffrey and his fiancée, Anna.

Lady Sonia was the first to see her son coming down the gangway and she began waving and calling his name.

'Look, darling, there's my parents… they both look older somehow.'

'Well, it's been four years since you've seen them. I'm sure we have both aged considering what we've been through.'

Geoffrey and Anna made their way to where Lord and Lady Turner were standing. Lady Sonia hugged her son and only released him on the suggestion of her husband who gave his son a firm handshake.

'Father, Mother may I introduce you to my fiancée, Doctor Anna Griffith.'

'Hello, Anna pleased to meet you dear. Geoffrey has told us so much about you in his letters.'

'Very pleased to meet you Anna and welcome to the family,' said Lord Turner.

'Well, I'd better collect our luggage and we can be on our way,' said Geoffrey.

Once the cases were loaded into the Rolls Bentley's boot, they began their journey to Turner Manor in Bramham, West Yorkshire, a journey that would take them two hours.

The journey was filled with conversations relating to the two doctors' experiences during the war and the return on investment from the estate's livestock.

They arrived at the manor at midday and Anna was impressed.

Turner Manor

Lady Sonia showed Anna her room. It was beautiful, with had a large bay window overlooking the back garden.

'I'll leave you to settle in and have a rest for a couple of hours, and then maybe you'll join the family in the conservatory for pre-dinner drinks.'

'That sounds wonderful, My Lady. I didn't sleep well on the voyage from France and a rest would do me the world of good.'

At five pm, Anna navigated her way through the large manor house to the conservatory at the rear.

Geoffrey and his parents were sitting at a wrought iron table sipping a glass of white wine. Geoffrey smiled at her. 'Darling, I was just about to get you. You've done well finding us.'

'I must admit there were a few wrong turns.'

'Can I get you a glass of wine?'

'Yes, that would be lovely thank you.'

'So, Anna you intend to leave the sunburnt country and become an Englishwoman,' said Harold Turner.

'Yes, a daunting prospect I must say.'

'Why do you say that my dear?'

'I suppose you miss what you know. Mother lives in Melbourne so seeing her will be a rare occasion. Don't get me wrong… I'm looking forward to living and working here.'

'Well, we'll make sure you feel at home.'

'Thank you, I'm sure I will enjoy living here; the most important thing is being with Geoffrey.'

Geoffrey returned with a bottle of wine and poured her a glass. 'Father suggested that you and I take two of the estate's horses and ride around the grounds so that you get a perspective of the size.'

'That would be great! When were you thinking?'

'Tomorrow.'

'I'll look forward to it; I haven't ridden a horse since I left Australia.'

The family dined in the informal dining room and the table talk was pleasant and constant.

Geoffrey walked Anna to her room and as he kissed her goodnight, he whispered in her ear. 'Maybe we can find a secluded spot to make love when we go riding tomorrow.'

She smiled. 'Maybe.'

After breakfast, Geoffrey and Anna approached the stables to inspect the horses. Geoffrey chose a sixteen-hand dapple-grey called Prince, while Anna's steed was a fifteen-hand chestnut with a coat that shone in the sun. Her name was Victoria.

Geoffrey led the way, heading towards the far fields where the sheep were lambing. Anna was captivated by the Swaledale sheep for they looked so different to the merino sheep her mother kept on her station in Victoria.

'Darling, their wool looks too coarse to shear and the colour is quite dark.'

'Swaledales are bred for their meat, not their wool, darling.'

'Oh, well that makes sense. They are ever so cute though.'

'Come on, there's lots more to see, Anna.'

The two lovers rode for thirty minutes until they came across a paddock with a sheer cliff backdrop. The estate's belted galloways were grazing peacefully.

'I can see why they are called *belted*. The white belt is quite distinctive.'

'There's a stream just a little way ahead,' said Geoffrey. "I think it would be a perfect picnic spot. The kitchen prepared a delicious lunch for us.'

'That sounds like a marvellous idea.'

The couple found a beautiful spot beside a stone bridge and here they laid out a tartan rug and unpacked the basket the kitchen had prepared. They ate chicken sandwiches and drank a French wine.

Anna looked at her fiancé with a wicked glint in her eye and began to unbutton her blouse. Geoffrey responded by helping her with the task and before long they were both naked, kissing and fondling passionately. They made love as only two people madly in love can do.

They returned to the manor in the late afternoon and both took a nap before dinner.

Over dinner, Anna announced that her mother Emma would be making the journey from Australia to attend the wedding. Geoffrey and his parents were delighted.

The family then discussed the appropriate time for when the wedding should be held and the decision was made for July 1.

The venue for the service would be York Minster, the cathedral where Lord and Lady Turner were married forty years earlier.

Dying Can Be Expensive

Chapter 46

San Marino 1919

Mathew was in the crushing room of the olive distillery. One of his workers had reported that the crushing wheel had developed a crack. To replace such a wheel would be an expensive proposition and he hoped it wouldn't be necessary. As he approached the large granite wheel, he felt a sharp pain in his chest. He fell to his knees, clutching his chest and then died.

He had suffered a massive heart attack. He was 86 years old.

Anne began to worry when Mathew did not arrive for their pre-dinner drinks on the terrace; an event he never missed. She waited for forty minutes then decided to look for him. She went to the winery initially but couldn't find him, so she then walked down to the olive distillery. She found him lifeless on the crushing room floor. She dropped down beside him and felt for a pulse but there was none. She began to scream, alerting two of the distillery workers. They confirmed that Mathew had died.

Mathew's funeral was held in the village church and a wake was held at the house.

Anne sent a wire to Emma's ship, which was about to enter the Suez Canal, with the news of her father's passing. She was devastated. The reason for her journey was not only for Anna's wedding, but to see her father for what she thought would be the last time.

Tom would have liked to attend his sister's wedding but his responsibilities at Ercildoune and his own imminent marriage to Charlotte precluded his attendance. He and Charlotte did agree to postpone their wedding until Emma returned from England.

Mathew's funeral was a small affair with just forty people attending; all locals from San Marino. Anne had her husband cremated as per his instructions. The ashes would be returned to his birthplace at Abernethy Manor in Kent. At last the Banshee could return to his place of birth and his ashes were placed in the family mausoleum in the estate's grounds.

Anne waited for Emma to arrive from Australia before arranging Mathew's memorial service.

Emma's ship the *Cunard Berengaria* docked at Southampton June 1 where she was met by Anna and Geoffrey. After the normal greetings, they drove to Abernethy Manor, Anne, Mathew's widow and her two children Beatrice and Sam greeted them. The memorial service would take place on June 5.

Despite Mathew departing Britain's shores so many years ago, over one hundred people attended the service. A reception was arranged on the manor's lawns. Since it was beautiful sunny day, it was the perfect venue.

When all the guests had departed, the family gathered in the library for the reading of the will. Gordon, Emma's brother, had been retained by the family to manage the estate.

The first item listed in the will was the vineyard and olive grove in San Marino; Mathew's 50% share was bequeathed to his daughter Beatrice who was now ORO's chief wine maker. His wife Anne retained the balance.

Mathew had transferred all his Australian assets to Emma some years before.

Anna received a cash payment of £50,000.

Rosie, Mathew's sister, received £30,000 and an apartment in the south wing of the manor for life. She had managed the estate in Mathew's absence and would continue to do so on Sam's behalf for an annual salary of £2,500 indexed.

The final and most significant asset was Abernethy Estate. This was left to Sam his son in accordance with family tradition.

Tom had been gifted Ercildoune Station by his mother, Emma the previous year he also received £25,000 from Mathew's estate.

Abernethy Manor

The estate included two thousand acres of prime agricultural land, which produced a sizable income.

Under British law, death duties would need to be paid by Sam when he became of age. Gordon estimated a sum of £500,000 would be the amount owing.

Anne was taken a back. There was no chance Sam could raise that sort of money. The only way he could manage it would be to sell a significant parcel of the estate's farmland, which would diminish his revenue, or sell the estate in its entirety. One other option crossed her mind, but she would need to discuss it with her son. The family's attention focussed on the ensuing wedding, now Mathew was resting comfortably at Abernethy mausoleum.

Anna, Geoffrey and Emma caught the train to York where they were met by Geoffrey's parents and driven to Turner Manor. Anna and Emma were impressed by the manor house with its beautiful gardens and stables.

The family met in the conservatory to finalise the wedding plans. Anna would have only her mother and aunt attending, where the Turners were having difficulty restricting their guests to one hundred.

They decided the guests would understand that Anna came from Australia and therefore her friends would be unable to attend. Naturally she would have preferred Tom and Charlotte to attend but leaving Ericildoune for that amount of time would be impossible, at least Sam and his mother would travel to York from San Marino.

York Minster

The reception would be held in the great hall of Turner Manor.

Grand Hall Turner Manor

July 1, 1920

William Cosmo Gordon Lang, 1st Baron Lang of Lambeth, Archbishop of York, conducted the ceremony. It was a beautiful service. Anna's wedding gown was white lace and satin with a long train. Geoffrey's two nieces acted as flower girls. William Davis, Geoffrey's closest friend, was best man while Rosie, Anna's aunt, was matron of honour.

The guests made their way to Turner Manor in an assortment of motor vehicles including ten Rolls Royce.

The wedding breakfast included pheasant, lamb and beef, which was piped in by the local Scottish band. All the food including the vegetables was produced on Turner Estate.

The young married couple stayed the night at Turner Manor and the next morning they were driven to the train station by Geoffrey's parents. Their destination was London. They both decided a honeymoon in Europe was unwise, as the war had destabilised much of the continent. They decided instead to tour around Britain using the train network.

Emma had arranged for the newlyweds to stay in the bridal suite at Claridge's for three days before traveling to Devon and Cornwall. Anna was intrigued by London with its historical buildings such as St Paul's Cathedral and Westminster Abbey.

Geoffrey arranged tickets to the most popular musical playing in London at the time, *Irene*, at the Empire Theatre.

The cast included: Edith Day (Irene Dare), Pat Somerset (Donald Marshall) and Robert Hale (Mme Lucy).

The popular songs included: *Alice Blue Gown, The Talk of the Town, To Be Worthy of You, Castle of Dreams, Sky Rocket, The Last Part of Every Party.*

They both enjoyed the show immensely and they returned to Claridge's where a bottle of Dom Perignon champagne was waiting for them in their suite, chilled to perfection and ready to pour into the crystal flutes.

Over the remainder of their honeymoon they travelled to Cornwall, Wales, the Cotswolds, Oxford and Cambridge. They spent two days in the Lakes District, returning to Yorkshire 16 July.

Both doctors had been offered positions in York Hospital. The fact Geoffrey's father, Lord Turner, had founded the hospital was quite inconsequential.

Anne had requested Gordon to write a letter to Sam explaining the situation regarding his inheritance of Abernethy Manor.

July 21, 1920

Dear Sam,

As Mathew's only son and heir you are entitled to your father's estate; namely, Abernethy Manor including 2,000 acres of prime farmland. You are also entitled to inherit the title of Lord Abernethy. However, there is a down side, the British Government has increased death duties since the war. The duty on Abernethy is £500,000.

I would ask you to think seriously about what you would like to do, if you commit to taking over the estate, and living in Kent your mother has indicated she will pay the death duty.

The alternative option is to dispose of the estate.

Yours sincerely,

Yours Gordon

Sam gave the prospect some deep thought and consideration. He would become of age the following year, which meant his inheritance, would be available to him. He was reluctant to leave San Marino however he knew Abernethy should remain with the family as it had been since Henry VIII's reign.

He asked for a meeting with his mother who was due to return to San Marino at the end of the week.

'Mother as much as I appreciate you offering to pay the death duty on Abernethy Manor and Estate I'm concerned you will be left short.'

'Don't worry Sam your father held significant cash in a numbered Swiss bank account. I assure you I have sufficient funds to live comfortably for the rest of my life.

Sam now had no hesitation in becoming Lord Abernethy and all that it entailed.

The Aristocratic Siblings

Chapter 47

Emma departed Southampton on 25 July 1920, on the Cunard Line *RMS Laconia,* a newly completed passenger ship. She enjoyed all the luxuries of a first-class passenger.

The *RMS Laconia* berthed at Port Melbourne Pier on September 1, 1920.

Tom and Charlotte were on the pier ready to welcome her home. Emma's favourite motor vehicle, a black Rolls Royce, was the transport of choice. Once Emma, her son and his fiancée were reacquainted with one another, they drove to the Windsor Hotel where Emma's accommodation was located.

There were many topics of conversation during the journey, including Mathew's funeral and Anna and Geoffrey's wedding. Once the matriarch of the family got settled into her penthouse apartment an agreement was made to eat in the hotel restaurant at 7 pm as the wedding arrangements needed to be discussed.

Emma reserved her usual table. Tom and Charlotte arrived a few minutes before seven and Emma, a few minutes later.

'So, you two you must be excited… getting married and living at Ercildoune Station.

'We're both looking forward to it Mother,' said Tom.

Are you organised for the wedding? After all you only have a couple of weeks.'

'Yes, Saint Mary's church in North Melbourne is confirmed for September 23.'

'I know that church. It's lovely. How many people do you expect?'

'We've sent out one hundred invitations and we expect most will accept.'

'That's a good number. Of course, we have the ballroom reserved at the Windsor and a hundred will fit nicely.'

They ate their dinner, complimented by Mouton Rothschild, one of the finest French wines in the hotel's cellars.

October 7, 1920

Charlotte was getting ready for her wedding in her parents' house. They lived in Ivanhoe, her two bridesmaids, Judith Young and Rebecca Hall, were aiding her.

A knock on the bedroom door heralded Charlotte's father, Andrew. 'Hurry up, ladies. The cars are waiting to take you to the church.'

'We shan't be long, Daddy. Tell the driver fifteen minutes.'

'Very well, but not a minute longer.'

'Charlotte do you have something old something new something blue?' Rebecca asked.

'What's that all mean anyway?' asked Judith.

'Something old represents continuity; something new offers optimism for the future; something borrowed symbolises borrowed happiness; something blue stands for purity, love, and fidelity; and a sixpence in your shoe is a wish for good fortune and prosperity,' said Rebecca.

'You've been studying up, haven't you darling?'

'No, my mother told me. Possibly in the hope I'll marry a rich prince one day.'

'Well, I have it all, including the sixpence, which means I'm ready. Come on ladies, we all have a wedding to go to.'

Charlotte and her father occupied the first limousine, and the two bridesmaids, the second. The journey from Ivanhoe to North Melbourne took twenty minutes. Charlotte wasn't sure who was more nervous, her or her father.

Once they got organised at the entrance of the beautiful blue stone church, the organist began playing *Here Comes the Bride*.

Tom, his best man, Bill Edwards, and his groomsman, John Baker, both Duntroon graduates, waited to greet the wedding party.

Charlotte looked absolutely beautiful and, thought Tom, truly radiant.

Once the ceremony was complete, Lord Abernethy and Lady Abernethy rode in a white Rolls Royce to the magnificent Windsor Hotel where the hundred guests would welcome and greet the happy couple.

It was a wonderful night. The orchestra hardly stopped playing and the French and ORO wine flowed like a river. The food was magnificent and once the speeches and toasts were over the bride and the groom retired to the Windsor's honeymoon suite.

After a brief honeymoon at Lorne on the Victorian coast, they made their way to Ercildoune Station and a wonderful life together; well that was their expectation.

A Long and Winding Road

Chapter 48

Jane missed her best friend Anna terribly. Until Anna was sent to the Home, they'd done everything together, and kept a watchful eye out for any looming threat; particularly from Mr Pitt the dormitory master. All the girls in the dormitory called him Mr Creepy. He had a reputation for sneaking in at night and selecting a girl to molest.

Jane was ten when Anna left the orphanage, and despite getting on with most of the orphans of her age she could never replace the friendship she had with Anna.

1904 Ballarat

Jane was sleeping soundly but she was woken by a cold hand touching her left breast. It was Mr Creepy. Up until now, he had left her alone but now she had begun to develop a women's figure, he was attracted to her. He insisted she leave her bed. Once she was up, he grabbed her arm and led her roughly into his room, which was at the far end of the dormitory.

'Right girly, take off your nighty,' he growled.

'No I won't. Let me go or I'll scream.'

'Silly bitch, you can scream all you like. No one will hear you in here. Now take it off or I'll rip it off you.'

Jane reluctantly removed her nighty and stood naked in front of the evil little man.

'What are you going to do to me?'

'As if you didn't know.'

The headmistress of the orphanage's school, Mrs Roberts, had long suspected that her colleague had been molesting her children. She decided on this particular night to check on the dormitory. As she approached, she could hear what was going on in Pitt's room. She burst in and snapped, 'Leave that girl alone, you horrible little man or I'll call the police.'

Pitt turned to stare at her, managing to look injured and innocent. 'I'm not doing anything wrong ma'am. Young Jane was complaining of aches and pains so I thought I'd try and help. Isn't that right Jane?'

'No, you dragged me out of my bed and touched me where you shouldn't.'

'Lying bitch! You know that's not true.'

'I've heard enough,' Mrs Roberts said. 'Collect your things and leave the orphanage immediately Mr Pitt.'

'But ma'am, I have nowhere to go.'

'Well, you should have thought about that long ago. Get out.'

Jane knew she was not the only girl or boy who had been molested at the orphanage and she decided it was time to go living on the streets it had to be better than living in this dangerous environment. Pitt might be gone, but whoever replaced him might be just as bad.

She planned her escape carefully. A milk cart delivered milk every second day and her plan entailed hiding in the cart amongst the milk crates while the driver delivered the orphanage's milk. The day after the incident with Mr Creepy was milk delivery day. She waited behind a hedge in the courtyard, and when the horse and cart pulled up and the driver carried in the milk to the kitchen, she opened the rear doors and climbed in. It was cold but bearable.

The driver returned and continued his deliveries. There was only two more stops after the Ballarat Orphanage.

Jane waited until the horse was unhitched from the milk cart. She now knew they were at the dairy. When the driver opened the door to the cart, Jane bolted. She ran as fast and as far as she could before resting against a backyard fence. She was free.

The young orphan had no idea where she was as Ballarat was foreign to her. She just kept walking towards the tower she could make out in the distance. The tower belonged to the town hall; therefore, Jane was heading for the centre of town.

She reached Sturt Street and was amazed at the activity. Trams were travelling down the streets, motor vehicles were everywhere and people, lots of people.

Jane soon realised she would be noticed in her orphanage clothes. She decided to continue walking and eventually she discovered the botanical gardens. This looks like an ideal place to hide and sleep tonight, she thought.

Ballarat Botanical Gardens 1904

The runaway found a place which seemed ideal; a park bench deep in the gardens. There was one problem, though, she didn't have a blanket. She collected some palm fronds and laid some down on the bench. The remainder of the fronds she placed over herself, hoping they would provide some warmth.

Jane finally fell asleep, only to be woken by a gruff voice.

'What do you think you're doing, girl? This is my bench— has been for over a year.'

Jane sat up and peered blearily at the dim shape in the night. 'Oh. I'm sorry. I had no idea it was reserved. I just thought it was just an ordinary park bench.'

'Well, it's not just an ordinary park bench. Everybody in the park knows it's mine.'

'It's my first night in the park so please don't be angry. I'll move.'

'Where are you from?' The voice sounded mollified and Jane felt less frightened.

'I ran away from the orphanage today.'

'I was there for a while… horrible place.'

'Yes, it is.'

'What's your name, girl?'

'Jane.'

Look, Jane, you're pretty skinny and so am I. Maybe we can share it tonight and try and find you a permanent spot tomorrow.'

'Oh, that would be great, thank you. What's your name?'

'Everybody calls me Ginger on account of my hair.'

'Thanks, Ginger.'

The two street kids snuggled up on the bench and soon fell asleep.

The next morning Ginger showed Jane where they could get scraps from a baker's shop and fruit the hospital discarded each day. It wasn't much of a breakfast, but it was food.

Another park bench close to Ginger's was found for Jane. This became her new home. Ginger also introduced Jane to the rest of the street kids, about twenty in all.

She became a fully-fledged Ballarat street urchin, stealing from rich people, using all sorts of tricks and sleight of hand to do so.

After she had spent six months surviving on the streets, Ginger approached her with a proposition.

'Jane, I've decided to move to Melbourne. I was wondering if you'd like to join me?'

'Why Melbourne? Don't you like Ballarat?'

'It's not that I don't like it here, it's just that Melbourne is much bigger, therefore, more opportunities. The botanical gardens are three times as big as Ballarat's, so they should have plenty of sleeping accommodation.'

'When are you thinking of going, Ginger?'

'Pretty well straight away. We just need to jump on a freight train and in two hours we'll be there.'

She shrugged. 'All right, why not?'

Ginger and Jane were able to sneak onto a freight wagon. They hid among the wool bales and when the train pulled into Spencer Street Station, they ran for their lives, avoiding guards collecting passengers' tickets.

Neither of the runaways knew Melbourne, but somehow managed to find the botanical gardens.

They chose a rotunda to sleep in as it looked as if it was going to rain. It wasn't long before the Melbourne Street Arabs kicked them out. Melbourne may have been bigger than Ballarat, but it had many more street kids.

They found a park bench at the far end of the gardens and once again shared.

A few months passed. Ginger and Jane survived by their wits and pickpocketing skills and eventually the leader of the Arab pack approached them, offering membership of his gang. His name was King Rat. None of the kids knew his real name and he wasn't about to divulge it as Nigel Featherstone.

Melbourne 1908

Jane was now sixteen. She had developed into a beautiful young woman, albeit dressed in shoddy clothes and not particularly clean. She decided to enter the Melbourne CBD and try her luck begging in Bourke Street.

She took a detour through Flinders Lane to approach the middle section of Bourke Street where most of the shoppers congregated.

As she made her way she passed a blackboard sign; it read:

Wanted

Apprentice Seamstress

Apply within

Jane knew if she applied looking as she did she would be rejected, but what could she do? She looked in her purse. A single shilling was all she possessed in the world. Jane made the decision to walk to Melbourne Baths and pay sixpence for a shower. At least I'll be clean, she thought.

The walk up Swanston Street took thirty minutes. She paid the attendant her 6d and received soap and a towel. Jane hadn't showered for several weeks so she gave herself a good scrubbing.

Once she was out of the shower and had dried herself she noticed a very nice dress hanging on a clothes hook. It had matching shoes. She looked around but could see no one. Jane took the opportunity, quickly dressing in the new outfit, which fitted her perfectly, as did the shoes.

After exiting the dressing room quickly, Jane made her way back to Flinders Lane hoping the vacancy hadn't been filled. She breathed a sigh of relief. The sign was still outside the building.

Jane climbed the steep stairs, arriving at a dimly lit waiting room. She noticed a sign saying, *ring for service*. She rang the bell but it seemed to have no effect. She rang again and a very handsome man of about forty appeared.

'Yes, can I help you, young lady?'

'I've come to apply for the job.'

'Have you now? Well you'd better come into my office.'

Once in the man's office, Jane looked out a wall of paned windows at what must have been thirty women busily sewing on mechanical machines.

'What's your name, miss?'

'Jane, sir.'

'Do you have a surname, Jane?'

'Jane McInerney, sir.'

'How old are you, Jane?'

'I'm sixteen, sir.'

'You can call me Mr Jacobson.'

'Yes, sir, oops, I mean Mr Jacobson.'

'Why do you want to be a seamstress, Jane?'

'I think it is a very honourable profession.'

'Do you now and why is that?'

'I'm not sure. I just do.'

'All right, Jane let me tell you about what we do here. Jacobson's Fine Apparel makes clothes for Melbourne's best-dressed women. We have even made a ball gown for the Governor's wife. Do you think you would like to be a part of that?'

'Yes, Mr Jacobson very much so. I promise you if you select me I'll work hard for you.'

'Where do you live?'

'Birdwood Avenue, South Yarra.'

'That's a nice part of the woods.'

Jane smiled to herself for the address was that of the Botanical Gardens.

'I tell you what I'll do. I'll start you on a three-month trial and then assess your progress. How does that sound?'

'Thank you, Mr Jacobson. I can promise you won't regret it.'

'We'll see. I can pay you £1 a week. It will increase until you are a fully qualified seamstress when you will be paid £5 a week. We work six days.'

'Thank you, I appreciate the chance to prove myself.'

'You can start next Monday.'

Jane left Jacobson's office and nearly fell down the stairs, such was her excitement. She made her way to the gardens to search for Ginger and tell him the good news. She found him counting the day's take from his illicit activities; 20d.

'Ginger, I've got some exciting news.'

'Where did you score the new dress and shoes from?'

'Never mind about that… I've got a job.'

'A job doing what?'

Jane described her day and how she was to become a seamstress.

'So, you intend to live with the gang in the gardens and go off each morning to work in a clothing factory?'

'Yes, that's right.'

'How do you intend to shower and look as sweet as a daisy each day?'

'I won't shower every day, but I will every second day at the baths.'

'Well, good luck. I hope it works out.'

'You don't sound very happy for me, Ginger.'

'I am. It's just that I don't want to lose you.'

'Don't worry Ginge, I'm not going anywhere.'

You Reap What You Sew

Chapter 49

Jane arrived at Jacobson's Fine Apparel at 7.45 am, fifteen minutes early. Mr Jacobson was in his office sorting the day's sewing list.

She knocked on the office door.

'Come in, Jane! Good to see you're early. I suppose you would like to know what your duties will be? Initially, you will be keeping the sewing floor free of debris and delivering rolls of cloth to the seamstresses. Do you think you can handle that?'

'Yes, Mr Jacobson, I will do my best.'

'I'm sure you will, Jane. I see Mrs Fagan our head seamstress is on the floor. Come with me and I'll introduce you.'

He led Jane down to the floor, approaching Mrs Fagan who was already at her sewing machine.

'Hello, Mrs Fagan. Let me introduce you to our new apprentice, Jane.'

'Hello, Jane welcome to our sewing workshop.'

'Thank you, Mrs Fagan, I hope I can make a contribution.'

'Well if you work hard and are diligent I'm sure you will. I have your uniform ready for you together with your name embroidered so the other ladies will know who you are. Why don't you go into the staff room and try it on? It's a size 10 which should fit you.'

Jane did work hard; in fact, some of the seamstresses told her to slow down. After six months of sweeping and keeping the rolls of cloth up to the workers, Mr Jacobson decided it was time for her to learn to sew, using one of the machines. Mrs Fagan was in charge of her training. After three months, the head seamstress reported to Mr Jacobson that she was delighted with how fast Jane had learnt the skills and recommended she tackle more complex sewing tasks.

Jane no longer lived at the Botanical Gardens now she was earning a wage. It was sad leaving Ginger and the gang, but she knew she needed more suitable accommodation. She found a room in a lovely house in St Kilda. The owners, Mr and Mrs O'Brien, were very friendly and she ate with the family each night. The other benefit of living there was a large porcelain bath, which she soaked in each day after work.

Mr Jacobson, whose first name was Maurice, kept a very close eye on his protégé. It was not just her work ethic that interested him…he was attracted to the young lady.

When Jane had been working at the establishment for eighteen months, he called her into his office. Jane was pensive, not knowing what to expect. Was he going to fire her?

'Sit down, Jane. I have a few things to discuss with you. Firstly I believe you will be turning eighteen shortly. Is that correct?'

'Yes, on the 1st of next month.'

'I think it's time to increase your wages, not just because of your age but because the quality of work you're producing. Your salary will now be £2 a week.'

'Mr Jacobson, that's wonderful! I don't know how to thank you.'

'No need to thank me, Jane, you've earned it. There's one other thing I need to discuss with you.'

'Yes, what might that be?'

'I'd like to take you out to dinner.'

She stared at him, nonplussed. 'Dinner?'

'Jane, I know I am much older, but I'm very attracted to you. Since my wife Martha died six years ago I've lived a very lonely existence.'

Jane considered, and then stumbled out a reply. 'Well, yes, I'd be delighted to go to dinner with you Mr Jacobson.'

'Please call me Maurice, Jane, although not on the floor.'

'When were you thinking, Maurice?' It came surprisingly easily.

'Are you available this Saturday night?'

'Yes, I can make that.'

'Excellent! Give me your address and I'll pick you up at 7 pm.'

Jane left the office in a daze. She was ecstatic about her raise and confounded yet excited about her date with Maurice.

She had trouble thinking about anything else but her pending dinner date with Maurice, but finally Saturday night arrived. Jane had used her new skills and made herself a new outfit. The mirror told her she looked beautiful. When Maurice knocked on the door of the Edwardian house and Jane answered it he just stood there and stared.

'Forgive me, Jane, but I'm taken aback… you look absolutely beautiful.'

'Thank you, Maurice,' she said demurely. 'You look very handsome yourself.'

'Well, shall we go to dinner?'

Maurice's car was parked in front of the house. It was a Packard he'd imported from America. Jane was suitably impressed and once she was settled in, Maurice drove his pride and joy to Florentino Restaurant in Bourke Street, regarded as Melbourne's best.

They entered the crowded restaurant the headwaiter approached them immediately.

'Good evening Mr Jacobson, your table is ready.'

'Thank you, Roberto.'

The couple followed Roberto to the back of the restaurant where the waiter seated them both and placed napkins on their laps. Jane had never experienced such service, in fact, she had never been in a restaurant before.

'Maurice this is beautiful! I can't believe I'm here.'

'I can assure you, Jane, the food matches the décor. Would you care for a wine?'

Jane had no idea whether she would or not, as she'd never tasted it.

Maurice took her hesitation for indecision and continued smoothly, 'May I suggest a Cabernet Sauvignon? Or would you prefer a white a Riesling perhaps.'

'I'll let you decide. This is all very new to me.'

'Well, Florentino is famous for their steak, so I suggest we order the red.'

'Sounds good.'

Maurice leaned forward and smiled at her. 'So Jane, tell me your life story.'

'Not much to tell really.'

'Come on, Jane, you must have a story to tell.'

She shrugged and said cautiously, 'I'm an orphan.'

'What happened to your mother and father?'

'I'm not sure I want to talk about this, Maurice.'

'I'm sorry. Let's just leave it. Do you want to hear my story?'

'Yes, I'm sure your life is much more interesting than mine.'

'I'm not sure about that, but maybe one day I'll find out. I was born in Russia in 1868, the same year as Nicholas II. My parents were Jews. There were and in fact, there still are, laws which are anti- Semitic in Russia. My mother and father decided to immigrate to Australia when I was ten.

'They were in the rag trade in Russia, so they decided to continue on in Melbourne. It was they who founded my business.'

'Are they still alive?'

'Alas, no.'

'You mentioned your wife dying some years ago.'

'Yes, that was a great tragedy in my life. She succumbed to cancer; she was only thirty-five when she died.'

'Do you have children?'

'No, Martha had a stillborn baby two years before she passed away.'

Jane sighed. 'Your story is so sad.'

'Yes, but I know things are on the up for me. I can feel it.'

'Let's talk about something bright and happy.'

'What do you suggest?'

'I don't know... how about football? What team do you support?'

He laughed in surprise and, still chuckling, said, 'Carlton.'

'Oh dear. I follow Collingwood your team's mortal enemy,' said Jane, also laughing.

Maurice countered, 'How about picnics? Do you enjoy them?'

'I don't know, Maurice. I've never been on one.'

'You've never been on a picnic? We'll have to fix that! Why don't we go on a picnic to Ferntree Gully in the Dandenongs?'

'That sounds wonderful! When?'

'What about tomorrow? Sunday's a perfect day for picnics.'

'Yes why not?' Jane felt very grown up. 'What time will you pick me up?'

'Let's make it 10 am.'

He nodded, evidently as pleased with her as she was with him.

The next day, Maurice drove to Ackland Street in St Kilda and purchased some cheese, salami and ham from the delicatessen and a large French loaf from the bakery. His final stop was the fruiterers where he bought some apples and grapes. He added these to a bottle of wine from his home cellar. He then drove to where Jane lived and then up to Ferntree Gulley.

They had a very enjoyable day for despite the difference in age and station, they enjoyed each other's company.

Over the next two years, Jane and Maurice were partners. It was sometimes difficult to balance work and pleasure, but they managed.

December 31, 1912

Maurice had booked a table at the Florentino Restaurant to celebrate New Year's Eve. The couple arrived at 8 pm. Maurice ordered a bottle of Dom Perignon as soon as they were seated at the table.

The meal was magnificent, beginning with quail in red wine sauce followed by chateaubriand and finally a dessert of crème brûlée. On Jane's dessert, a decorated small box had been placed on the plate.

She peered at it and prodded it with her spoon. 'Why do I have this decoration on my crème brûlée and you don't, Maurice? You should call the waiter over.'

'Why don't you open it?' he teased. 'Maybe there's an exotic chocolate inside, especially for a lady.'

Jane lifted the beautifully decorated box from the plate and opened it. Inside was a magnificent three-carat diamond ring.

'Darling, what is this?'

'Will you do me the honour of marrying me, Jane?'

'I don't know what to say, Maurice.'

'Say yes.'

'Yes, of course, yes.'

He smiled. 'Then I propose a toast to a long and happy life as Mr and Mrs Jacobson.'

They leant over the table and kissed. Unbeknownst to the engaged couple the restaurant patrons were an interested audience to the proposal. They began clapping. Jane was very embarrassed but ecstatic.

The happy couple were married in a private ceremony six months later.

Jane became not only Maurice's life partner but also an equal partner in the business.

August 4, 1914

Germany had been preparing for war long before 1914. In fact, Germany had started drawing up a plan for war - the Schlieffen Plan - in 1897. It took nine years to finalise, but it was based on the theory that Germany would be at war with France and Russia at the same time. It did not prepare for many of the events that occurred in July and August 1914. It was based on the belief that, if the country went to war, Germany would be faced with a war on two fronts with France and Russia.

The plan assumed that France was weak and could be beaten quickly and that Russia was much stronger, but would take longer to mobilise its army.

The plan began to go wrong on 30 July 1914, when Russia mobilised its army, but France did not. Germany was forced to invent a pretext to declare war on France (3 August 1914).

Things got worse when Britain declared war on Germany on 4 August 1914 because, in a Treaty of 1839, Britain had promised to defend Belgium.

Maurice and Jane were fiercely patriotic, supporting Australia's war effort completely.

For King, Country and Profit

Khaki Looks Nice

Chapter 50

October 1914

Maurice and his wife Jane were going through the forward orders in their office on the first Monday of the month, ensuring they had sufficient cloth to complete the jobs.

A very distinguished gentleman dressed in an officer's uniform knocked on the glass door and entered.

'How can we help you, sir?' asked Maurice.

'My name is Lieutenant Colonel John Bunting. I was wondering if I could have a word with you both?'

'Yes, of course, please sit down. Can I organise a cup of tea for you?' said Maurice.

'That would be splendid, thank you.'

Despite Jane being an equal shareholder she went out to the lunchroom and made a pot of tea.

'So what is it you wish to discuss, Lieutenant Colonel?' asked Maurice when Jane returned.

'As you know, we are at war with Germany and her allies Austria and Turkey. It is the intention of the Australian Government to dispatch over 50,000 young men to the battlefields in the first six months. Depending on how the conflict transpires, many more may be dispatched. The army is required to clothe these soldiers in AIF uniforms. You have a fine reputation as a clothing manufacturer, therefore, the army would like to appoint your company as a key provider of uniforms.'

'Well, Lieutenant Colonel, we can assure you we would be honoured to be involved in the war effort. We would need to agree on a pricing schedule but I'm sure we can come to an agreement,' said Jane.

The army contract proved to be very profitable. Over the course of the Great War Jacobson's produced 100,000 uniforms.

AIF Light Horse Uniform

1920

In 1920, Jane and Maurice became the proud parents of a baby boy they named Levi. He had tight curly hair and an olive complexion, like his father. Maurice had always wanted a son, but his child with his first wife had been stillborn.

Maurice and Jane decided to purchase a larger house in Toorak to accommodate the family. It was not only a large Georgian house, but it had a sizable back yard, perfect for Levi to play in when he became older.

They had to borrow a large amount from the bank, but this was not a problem as the business was thriving.

The next ten years were enjoyable healthy ones. The business continued to grow and Maurice, Jane, and Levi were very happy.

October 1929
The Great Depression

The Great Depression was an economic slump which began in North America, it soon spread to Europe, and other industrialized countries of the world including Australia. The Great Depression began in 1929 and lasted until about 1939. It was the longest and most severe depression ever experienced by the industrialized Western world.

The Great Depression begun with a catastrophic collapse of stock-market prices on the New York Stock Exchange in October 1929. During the next three years stock prices in the United States continued to fall, until by late 1932 they had dropped to only about 20 percent of their value in 1929. Australia's stock exchange also collapsed, as did the price of gold, wool, and wheat the country's major export commodities.

In 1932, the official unemployment level reached a peak of 32 per cent. Hundreds of thousands of Australians were out of work.

The immediate effect was on individuals and families: children with not enough to eat; men, the traditional breadwinners, humiliated and powerless; women scrabbling to hold families together.

Suicide rates increased dramatically. In the absence of unemployment insurance, charity groups became the only source of relief but were unable to feed the overwhelming numbers of hungry.

National income declined by a third. More than 40,000 men moved around the country looking for work: setting up shantytowns on the edges of communities and camping in parks. The few jobs that did become available were cruelly fought over.

By 1932, more than 60,000 men, women and children were dependent on the susso, a state-based sustenance payment that enabled families to buy only the bare minimum of food. One Queenslander commented, 'Many spend more on a dog'. This was not unemployment insurance and was only available to people who had been without work for an extended period of time and who had no family assets.

For families still recovering from the pain of the First World War, the Great Depression was a cruel blow that scarred people for decades to come.

1931

Maurice and Jane had closed their clothing business. They had no real choice; the bank had called in their loans. The most difficult exercise was letting all their loyal and hardworking staff go; some had been working at Jacobson's for twenty years.

Jane was cooking the evening meal for the family. Levi was due home from Melbourne Grammar any moment. She heard the back door open and close and called out to her son.

'I'm in the kitchen, son, would you like a glass of milk and a biscuit?'

'It's not Levi, darling, it's me,' said Maurice. Maurice entered the large kitchen and gave his wife a kiss.

'You're home early. I thought you had a meeting with the bank manager,' said Jane.

'I had the meeting, but it didn't take as long as I thought it would.'

'How did it go, darling, will they support us for another year?'

'I'm afraid not, Jane. We've lost the house. In fact, we've lost everything.'

'What that can't be true. We've banked with them all these years; they told us we were one of their best customers.'

'Apparently, past loyalties mean nothing to them. We have two weeks to vacate.'

'Where are we going to live?'

'I don't know Jane, but we'll work something out I'm sure.'

Jane looked at him sadly. 'Well, I'm glad you're confident. Levi will have to leave Grammar no doubt.'

'Yes, I'm afraid so.'

Jane began to weep. 'I can't believe it! We used to be wealthy business people living in a beautiful house and now we'll be homeless. I will be back to sleeping on a park bench again.'

Two weeks passed. The date for eviction had been extended by a week. Jane was packing boxes although she had no idea where they would be stored or if she would ever be able to use the dinner set, or anything else the boxes contained, again.

She heard a knock on the front door and got up off the floor to answer it. Standing there were two policemen.

'You're early,' she said sourly. 'We don't have to vacate for a further six days.'

'We're not here to evict you, ma'am. May we come in please?'

She stood back for them to enter, then said, 'So, why are you here?'

'We're very sorry to inform you your husband Maurice Jacobson was found under Princes Bridge with a self-inflicted gunshot wound to the head.'

Jane was stunned. '*No!* You're lying… it can't be.' She fell to her knees and sobbed uncontrollably.

'Mrs Jacobson, he left a letter addressed to you.'

Jane rubbed her eyes. 'Put it down on the bench. I'd like to be alone if you don't mind.'

'Of course ma'am. Goodbye and God bless.'

Jane waited for some time before opening the envelope. In it was a short note from her beloved Maurice.

> *My Darling Jane,*
>
> *I'm so sorry it's come to this, but I feel I am a failure to you and Levi.*
>
> *Please forgive me.*
>
> *I've left what little money I had left in the biscuit barrel.*
>
> *Love Maurice*
>
> *xxxx*

Jane began to cry again. She didn't care about wealth. All she wanted was her husband back.

Levi came home from school only to find his mother weeping at the kitchen table. 'What's wrong Mother? Why are you crying?'

Jane had the unenviable task of explaining what had happened to his father. They hugged each other and cried for what seemed an eternity.

Mother and son slept in the same bed cuddled close for consolation.

Next morning, Jane looked inside the biscuit barrel. It contained £100, a significant amount, but hardly enough to sustain both of them for long. The young widow knew the only alternative for her and her son was to rent a shack at Dudley Flats.

1927 York England

Lord Harold Turner and his wife Lady Sonia were driving home from a University of Edinburgh dinner where Lord Turner had been the guest speaker at the medical school graduation ceremony the previous night. The morning was extremely misty. As Lord Turner approached a particularly sharp bend in the road the Jaguar skidded off and careered down a steep embankment before hitting a large oak tree. Both husband and wife were killed instantly.

Geoffrey and Anna were in the stables grooming their favourite horses in preparation for a ride out to the far fields to inspect the merino sheep when a police motor vehicle entered the courtyard and parked outside the manor house. Geoffrey and Anna heard the car and went to investigate.

'Hello officers, how can we help you?'

'I'm Sergeant Coombs and this is Constable Smith. May we have a word inside, please?

'What's the matter, Sergeant?' asked Geoffrey.

'If we could go inside sir, I'll explain.'

The policemen, Geoffrey and Anna entered the house and Geoffrey led the way into the library. The officers explained what had happened. Both Geoffrey and Anna were devastated.

Geoffrey was the only son, and he would inherit the entire estate, but Inheritance Tax would make it difficult to retain the property. The funeral was held in York Minster; the same cathedral where Geoffrey and Anna were married nine years before. William Cosmo Gordon Lang, 1st Baron Lang of Lambeth, Archbishop of York conducted the service, and over three hundred people attended the funeral. Geoffrey delivered a heartrending eulogy.

Geoffrey arranged to visit the family solicitor in York to determine the tax the government would place on him. His solicitor, Mr Humphries, informed him the tax based on the recent valuation conducted by the government would be £300,000. He left the solicitor's office bemused and depressed as he knew there was no way he would be able to raise such a sum.

On arrival at Turner Estate, he called Anna to discuss their predicament.

'How draconian! Who could raise such an amount without selling the estate?' said Anna.

'The King, possibly.'

'What do you think we should do, darling?'

Geoffrey shrugged. 'Our accountant might be able to suggest the right course of action.'

Geoffrey made an appointment with Hopgood and Gannet, the family accountants in York, for the following Monday. He and Anna arrived at the professional officers in Miklegate at 9.45 am, a little early for the 10 am appointment with Mr Hopgood. They waited in his anteroom feeling anxious. At 10 am a middle-aged secretary asked them into the firm's meeting room. Horace Hopgood was already seated at the large rosewood table.

'Good morning Mr and Mrs Turner, can I have Penelope get you a cup of tea?'

'No thank you, Mr Hopgood, we're rather anxious to discuss our situation in relation to the inheritance tax on my parents' estate.'

'Yes, I'm sure you are, and it's quite understandable. Well, I've examined your situation and I believe you have a number of alternatives; none of them all that appealing.

'The first option would be to sell the estate. After paying the tax, the balance remaining would be a considerable sum.

'The second option would be to demolish all the buildings, leaving only the land. That would decrease the value significantly. Once the reduced tax is paid you could construct a less grand house retaining the surrounding farmlands.

'The third and final option would be to subdivide the estate, leaving the manor and its outbuildings on a few acres for your use. The money raised from the subdivision should cover the tax.'

Geoffrey sighed. 'You're right. None of the options are particularly attractive but I know we need to be realistic. Anna and I will discuss the alternatives and get back to you in due course.'

The journey back to Turner Estate was subdued with the couple in deep thought.

On arrival back at Turner Manor, Geoffrey attended his newborn calves in the great barn while Anna went to the study to re-examine the estate's books.

They met again at the dinner table that night ready to discuss their plight.

'What thoughts do you have, my love? Have you a preferred option?' asked Anna.

'I would hate to lose the manor. It's been in my family for over three hundred years. Maybe the third option would be best since that way we get to retain the manor. After all, we both earn good money as doctors and we don't have to rely on the farm's income.'

'Yes, I agree with you. If we subdivide the five thousand acres into hundred-acre lots we should be able to sell the sheep and cattle to the new owners.'

'So, that's decided. I'll contact the land agents in the morning informing them we will have fifty hundred-acre lots for sale. I'll also instruct Mr Humphries to prepare the subdivision papers for approval.'

It took over a year to get the subdivision approved by the council and the fencing erected around each allotment.

Finally, everything was organised and in order ready to sell the land…but then the 1929 crash occurred. The Great Depression meant that very few people had the resources to purchase the allotments at £3000.

Geoffrey and Anna tried their hardest, but after twelve months only two allotments had been sold. The government and the bank foreclosed. Turner Manor remained vacant following their eviction.

Geoffrey and Anna rented a cottage in York, continuing to practise medicine at the York Hospital.

Abernethy Manor 1929

Sam was more fortunate than Geoffrey and Anna in that he carried no debt. Anne had paid the inheritance tax on Sam's behalf when Mathew died.

The young Lord still had to watch the estate's finances very carefully. The price of wool and wheat had dropped significantly during the ten years of the Great Depression, which meant reducing the workforce by a significant amount.

Sam spent all day tending the stock. He now only had two farm hands working with him as opposed to the twelve prior to the depression.

Despite the extra workload Sam was content with his life. The only thing missing was a wife.

Emma Griffith née Abernethy: Melbourne, Australia 1929

After the Wall Street crash, Emma knew she was in for a very tough time for a few years. Even she hadn't predicted the Great Depression would continue for ten years.

One of Emma's companies, Eldorado Gold mining, in which she held a majority shareholding, performed extremely well, rising from $65/share in 1929 to $373/share in 1933, a gain of 474%.

The company increased its dividend from £3 to £7 in the same time period.

The hotels also suffered badly during the depression. Emma sold the Golden Nugget in Ballarat at a price well below its value prior to 1929. She also disposed of the Grand Hotel in Melbourne but she was able to retain the Windsor Hotel where she lived in a large apartment.

Claridge's survived, albeit with much reduced occupancy rates.

Her joint venture with Henry Sutton, Sutton Innovations, was retained but placed on the back burner until economic conditions improved. It became viable once more in 1936 producing advanced wireless technology for the Allies.

The *Sunday Times* continued to produce a quality newspaper, but advertising diminished.

All in all Emma was able to keep her business empire fairly insulated from the ravages of the Great Depression.

Not everybody was so fortunate.

Unfortunately; wool prices dropped steadily from the mid-1920s and wheat fell precipitously from 1930. The value of Australia's wheat and wool exports halved in 1929 and 1930 reducing Tom and Charlotte's income to dangerous levels.

Dudley Flats

A Long Way From Toorak

Chapter 51

February 6, 1931

Jane carried a suitcase, as did her son Levi. These contained their worldly goods. They both looked back at what was once their home; a beautiful Georgian house in the exclusive suburb of Toorak in Melbourne.

The journey in front of them, five miles in all, would take them several hours due to the weight of the suitcases. Jane was determined to carry a few of her treasures, including a silver service tea set, to her new home at Dudley Flats on the western fringe of the city. The flats were actually located on a rubbish tip bordering on a coal canal.

They arrived at Dudley Flats at 3 pm, unsure who they should approach to organise accommodation.

A woman and a young boy standing in the mud with suitcases by their sides with a bewildered look drew the attention of one kind soul.

'Good afternoon, madam. My name is Joe Wilson. You look as if you could do with some help.'

'Hello, my name is Jane, and this is my son Levi. We're looking to rent a house.'

'A house! No houses here, Jane, just shacks constructed with anything we can find on the tip. I can recommend you speak with Joan. She has a few shacks for rent and she's a good stick.'

'Where can I find her?'

'You're almost standing on her front step. She lives just there.' Joe pointed to a shack right in front of them. 'Just bang on her door and tell her you're looking to rent one of her shacks.'

Jane did as Joe had suggested and a woman in her fifties answered the door.

'Hello, my name is Jane, and this is my boy Levi. We require lodgings, and I believe you may have a shack available to rent.'

'Yes dear, I do, it's next door to this one. I charge five shillings a week in advance.'

'All right Joan. I'll take it, thank you.'

'Don't you want to look at it first?'

'I don't think I need to.' Jane handed over £1, being a month's rent in advance.

Jane and Levi entered the shack which was as Jane expected; very rudimentary but clean. There was a wood fired stove in the small kitchen, but only one bedroom so Levi would have to sleep in the living area.

As the weeks went by, Jane and Levi settled into slum living. Many of the people they met had come from similar backgrounds. The Great Depression seemed to treat everybody the same – harshly.

View Over Coal Canal Dudley Flats

Levi was due to turn twelve on October 12. He had made friends with other boys around about his age, and the game played in winter was Australian Rules. There was an oval not far from Dudley Flats and that is where the games would take place. Levi played on the forward line due to his accurate kicking.

One of his friends, Frank, approached Levi one Saturday morning at football. Frank had been rummaging through the tip and discovered an old sewing machine and wondered if Levi's mum would be interested in paying the young boy one shilling.

Jane asked to inspect the machine. It had obviously been in the tip for some time and had developed a fair amount of rust. Over all, she felt it could be restored to its former glory. She agreed to Frank's price if he cleaned it up first. The deal was done. Frank delivered the sewing machine the following week and it almost looked like new.

Jane was able to purchase odd rolls of fabric from the Victoria Markets. She made these into dresses of various shapes and sizes. She then in turn sold the garments at the Victoria Markets and made a tidy profit.

Jane and Levi were seen as successful inhabitants of Dudley Flats. Jane added nick knacks to the shelves and covered the cushions and sofa with new material, which made the shack warm and homey.

In 1936 the *Argus* ran a story covering the inhabitants of Dudley Flats. The article featured Jane and Levy and Jane's sewing business. Quite often the *Sunday Times* would pick up an *Argus* story and print it in England, as after all both papers were owned by Emma Griffith.

Doctor Anna Turner read the story, and she recognised her friend from the orphanage in Ballarat. Anna was determined to get in contact with Jane and help her out in some way.

12, December 1936

Emma retired at the usual time of 9 pm. At seventy-eight, she no longer kept late hours. However, her workload was almost as strenuous as it was when she was forty, although it had been a while since she made any new acquisitions.

She continued to reside in the penthouse of the Windsor. It suited her with plenty of dedicated staff to take care of her needs.

He personal maid, Lucy lived in one of the bedrooms, enabling her to be available when needed. Lucy set the breakfast table on the morning of the 13th December and when Emma hadn't appeared at her usual time, Lucy assumed her mistress had decided to sleep in. When the clock ticked over to 9.30 am, she decided she should enter Emma's bedroom and check to make sure everything was all right. It wasn't. It was obvious to Lucy that her mistress of forty years had passed away in her sleep.

Emma's personal assistant Patricia Jennings telephoned Tom and Charlotte and Anna and Geoffrey in England, informing them of Emma's passing. The tyranny of distance made it impossible for Anna and Geoffrey to attend the service. Tom and Charlotte would obviously attend.

The funeral was held at St Pauls Cathedral in the centre of Melbourne on the corner of Flinders and Swanston Streets. The Archbishop of Melbourne, Frederick Waldegrave Head, conducted the service. Emma had donated many thousands of pounds to the church in the past and was regarded as one of the great benefactors to the church and its parishioners.

View of St. Pauls Cathedral
Melbourne, 1930s

From: The State Library of Victoria
Creator: Victorian Railways

Five hundred people attended, including Governor Gipps and his wife and the Victorian Premier Mr Albert Dunston and his wife Sarah. The who's who of the business world paid Emma their respects.

An old family friend and business associate, Henry Sutton, read a eulogy written by Emma's son Tom at the service.

A wake that everybody knew Emma would have loved was held in the ballroom at the Windsor Hotel. Two hundred friends attended, with over a hundred bottles of Dom Perignon consumed.

Two weeks later the will was read at the chambers of Emma's long-standing law firm, Corr & Corr.

The Windsor Hotel, Melbourne and Claridge's, London were left to her daughter Anna. The *Sunday Times* was left to Tom, her son. The *Argus*, Melbourne went to Anna. Emma's shares in the Eldorado Gold Company were transferred to King's Walden Home for Gifted Boys & Girls. Emma's half share in Sutton Innovations was transferred to Henry Sutton. The two department stores established by her late husband, Georges and Mary's, were evenly distributed. Georges was to go to Emma's granddaughter Kate Turner and Mary's Department Store to her grandson Harry Turner. Ercildoune Station was left to Tom.

Anna and Geoffrey created a Trust to administer and manage the two department stores in Melbourne for their children Harry and Kate when their grandmother died. The Trust comprised Mr Irving from Baker & Wilson, Mrs Isabel Cohen a well-known and respected Melbourne retailer, Mr Alan Wilson the store's chief financial officer and Mr Solomon Lord, a wealthy businessman and close friend of Emma's. Under their management Georges and Mary's continued to prosper. Emma had established a cash fund to encourage her grandchildren to immigrate to Melbourne and run the stores for at least five years. Their inheritance would ensure both children would be wealthy for the remainder of their lives.

York 1936

Anna and Geoffrey were eating breakfast in the conservatory at Turner Manor.

'Darling, now that we are outrageously wealthy I'd like to help an old friend I knew in Ballarat many years ago. What with this horrid depression and all she's fallen on very bad times.'

'Were you thinking of throwing her some money?'

'No darling, not at all. If I know Jane she'd throw it right back at me. She was a director of a very successful clothing company with her husband. He died, leaving Jane and her son without a penny as it were. I'd like to invest in her to start up a new company. She was successful before and I'm sure she will be again.'

'Well, my dear, it's your money after all. If you think your investment will be safe I'll support your decision all the way.'

Anna, through her Melbourne-based solicitors Baker & Wilson, undertook some research regarding Jane and her son Levi. She was horrified to learn where they had lived for the past five years but she was pleased to learn Jane had begun a home-based sewing operation, which seemed to be doing well.

It appeared Levi was not only an intelligent young man but also an accomplished sports person.

The solicitors also discovered that Jacobson's Clothing had won a substantial contract to produce army uniforms during The Great War. Although Australia was at peace, the army and in fact the other services still needed uniforms. Having established an excellent reputation during the Great War would certainly help a revived Jacobson Clothing win another military contract.

Anna decided it was time to make contact with Jane. She sent her friend a telegram asking her to go to Baker & Wilson's offices to receive a telephone call from Anna in England.

Jane was sitting at the sewing machine as usual when the postman knocked on her door and handed her a telegram. Jane was surprised. Telegrams were not a usual occurrence in Dudley Flats. She read the message several times. Anna Turner? She couldn't recall the name but then the penny dropped. Anna Turner was Anna Pittman, her friend from the Ballarat Orphanage! She'd been adopted by a rich woman and Jane and she had lost contact.

Why would Anna want to talk to her after so many years? Oh well, it would be nice to catch up again.

2, October 1936 Melbourne

Jane arrived at Baker & Wilson's officers in upper Collins Street on time at 3 pm. She introduced herself and was asked to wait for Mr Irving who would arrange the telephone call from Anna in York, England.

She felt quite nervous. She was about to speak to a girl she hadn't seen since she was ten. Why?

A middle-aged gentleman entered the waiting room. He introduced himself and signalled Jane to enter the firm's meeting room.

The telephone call was due at 3.30 pm and precisely at that time the telephone rang. Mr Irving answered and began a conversation with the caller. Eventually, he handed the telephone receiver over to Jane.

'Hello, this is Jane.'

'Hello, Jane it's Anna. Do you remember me?'

'Yes, Anna, we were friends at the Ballarat Orphanage.'

'That's right, we helped each other cope living in that horrible place.'

'They are memories I've been able to erase from my mind, Anna. Let's not discuss that place right now.'

'You're right! Let's talk about other things. I've been very fortunate in my life. A very caring lady who also happened to be wealthy adopted me. The same woman adopted my brother Tom. I studied to become a doctor and he was an officer in the army.'

'It sounds like a privileged life,' Jane said flatly. 'I ran away and lived on the streets. I was fortunate to get a job as a seamstress and married the owner of the business. Then the depression hit and Maurice, my husband, took his own life. And so here I am today living in a Melbourne slum.' She waited for Anna's reaction, but when it came, it wasn't sympathy or pity, but something else entirely.

'Jane, I would like to invest in a new business with you. Your old premises are still vacant, and the sewing machines are still on the floor. I will fund the employment of seamstresses and provide working capital for twelve months. What do you think?'

'I don't understand. Why would you want to do that?'

'I'm a businesswoman as well as a doctor. Your record in the industry convinces me you would be a sound investment.'

Jane might have been living in the slums for five years, but she still had her intelligence. She asked, 'How much of the company would you want?'

'Thirty percent.'

'Will you let me think about it, Anna? I'd like to discuss it with Levi.'

'Yes, that's not a problem Jane, but don't take too long. I would like to get this underway.'

'I'll get back to you in a couple of days.'

'Excellent Jane. Goodbye. It was wonderful speaking to you.'

'Goodbye, Anna.'

Jane knew she should accept Anna's offer as it was the one and only chance she would have to get back her old life, albeit without Maurice. She discussed the offer with her son Levi who was very enthusiastic; after all what could possibly go wrong?

Jane got back in touch with Mr Irving at Baker & Wilson's and informed him she would be happy to accept Anna's proposal. He said that any other decision would be foolish in his opinion. Anna was informed via a telephone call made by Mr Irving and she was delighted.

The first significant action was to take out a three-year lease on the old premises in Little Collins Street. When Jane first inspected the building, it was like going back in time. Apart from the prolific cobwebs and dirty windows, nothing had changed in the seven years that had gone past.

Jane and Levi worked hard to clean the place up ready for the seamstresses to begin work. Most of the original workforce was rehired, including the head seamstress Mrs Fagan.

Jacobson's Workforce 1936

Jacobson's Clothing Company had been operating for three years successfully. The forward orders were encouraging, and Jane was very confident that the company would continue to grow.

She and Levi had moved out of Dudley Flats and moved into an apartment in St Kilda. All was going well then...

It was déjà vu for Jane. She was sitting at her desk going through the forward orders on the first Monday of the month, ensuring there was sufficient cloth to complete the jobs booked.

A very distinguished gentleman dressed in an officer's uniform knocked on the glass door and entered.

'How can I help you, sir?'

'My name is Lieutenant Colonel Graham Bader. I was wondering if I could have a word with you?'

'Yes, of course, please sit down. I'll organise a cup of tea for you,' said Jane.

'That would be excellent thank you.'

Jane went out to the lunchroom and made a pot of tea. 'So what is it you wish to discuss Lieutenant Colonel?' she asked upon her return.

'As you know, we are at war with Nazi Germany and her allies. The Defence Department is required to clothe our military personnel in uniforms. You have a fine reputation as a clothing manufacturer going back to the First World War, and therefore, the government would like to appoint your company as a key provider of uniforms.'

'Well, Lieutenant Colonel, we can assure you we would be honoured to be involved in helping in the war effort. I assume a price per unit would be agreed upon.'

'Yes, I have a schedule for your perusal.'

'I will examine it and determine if we can meet your expectations.'

The Army contract proved to be very profitable. Over the course of the war Jacobson's Clothing Company produced over 100,000 uniforms.

Anna was delighted as her investment was proving to be very lucrative.

May 1940, Abernethy Manor, Kent, England

Sam was sitting in his study sipping a fine malt whisky. The open fire was blazing, and he was reading an article in the *Times* regarding Germany's invasion of France. He knew this could be the beginning of the end for Great Britain.

May 1940

The campaign against the Low Countries and France lasted less than six weeks. Germany attacked in the west on May 10, 1940. Initially, British and French commanders had believed that German forces would attack through central Belgium as they had in World War I, and as a consequence rushed forces to the Franco-Belgian border to meet the German attack. The main German attack, however, went through the Ardennes Forest in south-eastern Belgium and northern Luxembourg. German tanks and infantry quickly broke through the French defensive lines and advanced to the coast.

Belgium and the Netherlands surrendered in May. More than 300,000 French and British troops were evacuated from the beaches near Dunkirk across the English Channel to Great Britain. Paris, the French capital, fell to the Germans on June 14, 1940.

As part of the armistice agreement France signed with Germany on June 22, Germany occupied northern France and France's entire Atlantic coastline down to the border with Spain. A new French government was established in the town of Vichy, which was in the unoccupied southern part of France. The Vichy government, under Marshall Henri Petain, declared neutrality in the war between Germany and

Great Britain but was committed by the armistice provisions to cooperation with Germany.

The Germans viewed the defeat of Britain's Royal Air Force (RAF) as a prerequisite for an invasion of the British Isles. When the German air force failed to win air superiority over south-eastern England in 1940, Hitler postponed the invasion until the spring of 1941. After the first operational order for the German invasion of the Soviet Union was issued in December 1940, the German invasion of Great Britain was postponed indefinitely.

Sam had been courting a young woman from the adjoining estate to Abernethy, Tabley House her name was Georgia Tabley she was considered the most beautiful woman in the county. After two years Sam plucked up the courage to ask her father for Georgia's hand in marriage. Lord Tabley agreed without hesitation.

Tabley House

The young couple were married in the historic Canterbury Cathedral in front of one hundred family and friends.

Canterbury Cathedral

The war prohibited Sam and Georgia from embarking on the grand tour as was the norm for newly married couples of their standing. They had a week in St Ives Cornwell.

1940

Georgia entered the study and sat opposite her husband in a leather wingback chair. 'You look concerned, Sam. I understand the reason, but there's nothing you or I can do about it. War's a soldier's game.'

'It's no game, my love, but I know what you mean.'

'All we can hope for is that the evil little man and his cronies are defeated and Europe can get back to normal.'

'Yes, I think you're right Georgia.'

Georgia departed from the study, leaving Sam to contemplate his future. He was forty-one with no military experience. However there must be a role he could play in aiding Great Britain to win this war. He knew some high-ranking officers in the services from his London club, he decided to approach one or two and elicit their advice.

Sam arranged to have lunch with Alan Brook at the Army and Navy Club situated in Pall Mall.

Alan Brooke (July 23, 1883 - June 17, 1963) was a Field Marshal and a senior commander in the British Army. He was Chief of the Imperial General Staff during World War II and later promoted to Field Marshal in 1944. Brooke was the foremost military adviser to Winston Churchill, and is regarded as one of the chiefs architects of the Allies victory in 1945.

'Thank you for meeting me, Alan,' Sam said after shaking hands. 'I appreciate it, considering the demands on your time at the moment.'

'That's all right, Sam. I always have time for you. What is it you wish to discuss with me?'

'I would like to join the war effort in a support role of some sort. If I can contribute in some way to get rid of Hitler and his band of thugs, I would be happy.'

'Damn good of you Sam. Leave it with me. I'm sure we can use your expertise to help defeat the Germans.'

The two friends ate their lunch, washed down with a bottle of French wine.

One week later, Sam received a call from Alan Brook informing him that he had identified an important role for Sam in a top-secret project. He was instructed to report at Army Headquarters in Hampshire on July 15, 1940.

Sam chose the right time to disclose his decision to Georgia. It was while dining at the Savoy. Once Sam explained that it would be an administration role she accepted the news graciously although with some reservations.

It's an Enigma

Chapter 52

Lord Abernethy attended a meeting at Army Headquarters in Andover, Hampshire in his first week of service. His superior officer, Colonel Daniels, met him in the foyer and led him into a small briefing room.

'Welcome aboard, Lord Abernethy. Your reputation precedes you.'

'Thank you, Colonel please address me as Sam I don't think my title is appropriate in this environment.'

Yes, that's fair enough.'

'I've got some very confidential news. Could turn the course of the war.'

'My God! What is it?'

'One of the Enigma machines used by the German Navy has been acquired from a captured U-Boat. If we can determine how it works, we will be able to decipher the coded messages being sent. We believe the Polish and British are close to breaking the code on the primary Enigma. If we can break both, it would put us in a very strong position. British command has requested your involvement. I want you to move to Bletchley Park in Buckinghamshire by the end of this week.'

'Yes, sir. Colonel, where will I sit as far as the level of command?'

'You will report to me but the officer heading up the operation is Commander Alastair Denniston. He's our top code-breaker. He heads up the Government Code and Cypher School (GC&CS).

'You mentioned the Polish— why they are involved?'

'The Germans, specifically Albert Scherbius, invented the Enigma back in 1919. It was patented and further developed by the company Gewerkschaft Securitas after they purchased the patents from Scherbius. The German armed forces initially rejected Enigma but eventually saw merit in adopting it for encrypting messages. The Polish customs service discovered one being smuggled into the German Embassy in Warsaw. They embarked on a program of re-engineering to determine how the machine worked. Determining the exact wiring of each of the three rotors became the Polish cryptanalysts' first task. To accomplish this, Poland's cypher bureau tested and hired three mathematicians in 1932: Marian Rejewski, Jerzy Rozycki, and Henryk

Zygalski. They painstakingly analysed the intercepted encrypted messages searching for clues. Rejewski eventually determined a mathematical equation that could determine the wiring connections. However, the equation had too many unknown variables. He was able to finally make the initial breaks into the wiring sequence only with the aid of a German traitor.'

'So how did we get involved, sir?'

'On 25th July 1939, in Warsaw, the Poles initiated French and British military intelligence representatives into their Enigma-decryption techniques and equipment, including the Zygalski sheets and the cryptologic bombe, and promised each delegation a Polish-reconstructed Enigma machine. Without these gifts of techniques and technology from Polish military intelligence, decryption of German Enigma messages at Bletchley Park would not have been possible.'

'Well, it sounds like an incredible project, sir. I hope I can make a contribution. I am sure once I am ensconced at Bletchley Park I will have a better understanding of the challenges ahead. It would be my intention to rent a suitable property close to Bletchley and move my wife Georgia down here. Is that acceptable?'

'I don't see that as a problem. She may want to work at BP in a civilian role. If she's interested I'll have one of the WRENs talk to her.'

Georgia warmed to the idea of working at Bletchley Park as it would mean she was close to Sam and not be bored staying home all day. Although the house they rented was very nice it wasn't Abernethy Manor.

Georgia was appointed a clerk in Hut 8 while Sam was Logistics Officer for the entire operation.

What Did He Say?

Chapter 53

Bletchley Park

When Sam arrived at BP, as everyone called Bletchley Park, he was impressed with the grand manor house set in beautiful gardens. I can work here, he thought.

He entered the main entrance, a gothic structure with a gryphon on either side guarding the doors to the impressive foyer. At the reception desk sat a very pretty young lady, one of the ten thousand who was either working or had worked, at Bletchley Park during project 'Ultra'.

'Good morning, my name is Sam Griffith. I have an appointment with Commander Denniston.'

'Yes, sir I'll let his secretary know you are here.'

A tall man who looked more like a university professor than a commander entered the waiting room.

'Hello,' said the commander, extending his arm to shake hands rather than a salute.

'Good morning, Commander.'

'Please, we are very informal here. Have to be actually. Some of the brightest people working on this project are civilians. Now, would you like a tour of our establishment, Sam?'

'Thank you, Alastair. I'm keen to see what you and your team are up to.'

Commander Denniston was Operational Head of GC&CS from its formation out of the Admiralty's Room 40 and the War Office's MI1B in 1919, until 1942. On the day that Britain declared war on Germany, he wrote to the Foreign Office about recruiting 'men of the 'intellectual type'.

Personal networking was used for the initial recruitment, particularly from the universities of Cambridge, Oxford, and Aberdeen. Reliable and trustworthy women to perform administrative and clerical tasks were similarly recruited by personal contacts. This has been characterised as recruiting 'Boffins and Debs' or 'Dilly's Fillies' (Dilly Knox), and the indexing section where many of the women worked was called 'The Deb's Delight'.

Cryptanalysts were selected for various intellectual achievements, whether they were linguists, chess champions, crossword experts, polyglots or great mathematicians. GC&CS was ironically referred to as 'the Golf, Cheese and Chess Society'. In one instance, the ability to solve a *Daily Telegraph* crossword in less than twelve minutes was used as a test. A newspaper was asked to organise a competition, after which each of the successful participants was contacted and asked whether they would be prepared to undertake 'a particular type of work as a contribution to the war effort'. FHW Hawes of Dagenham in Essex finished in less than eight minutes and won the overall competition.

New entrants were given a basic grounding in code breaking at the Inter-Service Special Intelligence School set up by John Tiltman. Initially, at an RAF depot in Buckingham, it moved to an ex-Gas Company showroom in Ardour House, 1 Albany Road, Bedford, which was known locally as the 'Spy School'.

Working in three shifts or 'watches' over twenty-four hours was inaugurated by the Air Section in Hut 10 under Josh Cooper, and the practice soon became universal. The shifts were 4 pm to midnight, midnight to 8 am and 8 am to 4 pm. Staff had a six-day week and rotated through the three shifts. Thirty minutes was allowed for the meal in the middle of the shift.

The irregular working hours affected workers' health and social life, and the private homes nearby where most of the staff was billeted. The work was tedious and required concentration, some 'girls' collapsed and required extended rest. The staff got one week's leave four times a year.

Nine thousand armed services personnel and civilians were working at Bletchley Park at the height of the code-breaking project in January 1945 and over twelve thousand worked there at some point during the war, eighty percent of them women. A relatively small number of men were also employed on a part-time basis, typically for one shift each week when they were used for their Morse code or knowledge of the German language.

Alan Turing

Alan Turing is widely considered to be the father of computer science and artificial intelligence.

Turing worked for the GC&CS at Bletchley Park. For a time he was head of Hut 8, the section responsible for German naval cryptanalysis. He devised a number of techniques for breaking German cyphers, including the method of the bombe, an electromechanical machine that could find settings for the Enigma machine.

Hut 8

Puzzle

Sam and Alastair made their way out of Bletchley Park's main entrance walking down a gravel path with timber huts on either side.

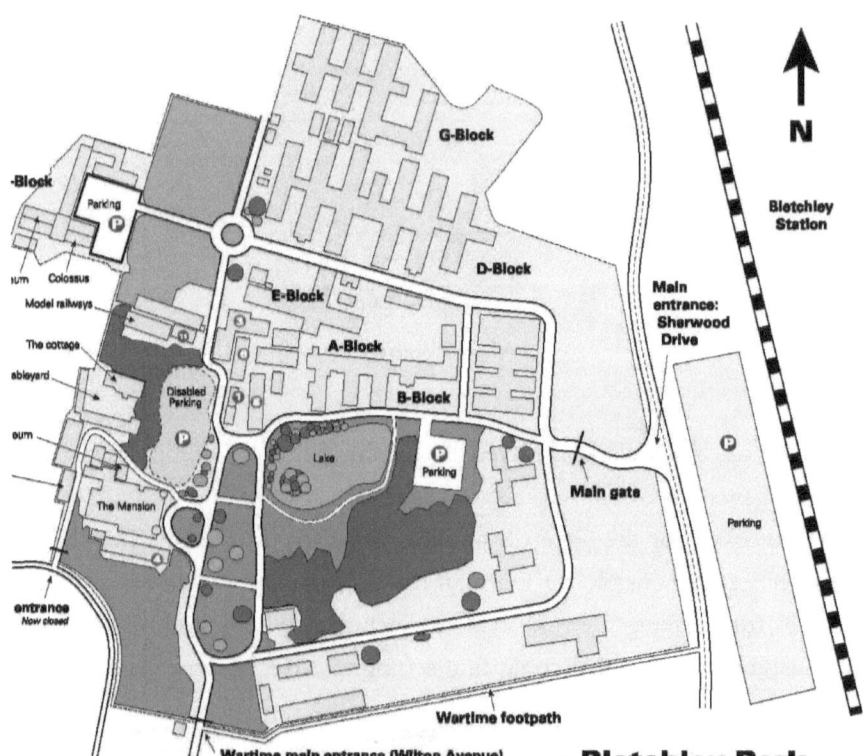

Bletchley Park's Grounds

'As you can see, Sam, the grandiose mansion overshadows the huts where the actual work is done. Let me briefly explain what is taking place in each hut.'

'This is Hut 1. We have developed our first bombe (computer) in there. We aptly called it 'Victory'. This is where Alan Turing and Gordon Welchman wove their magic initially. I will introduce you later on.

Here is Hut 2. This is the recreation hut, serving provisions and luncheon vouchers, and Hut 3, over here, is responsible for the intelligence analysis through translation, emendation and sorting of the decrypted Army/Air Force material from Hut 6. It's disseminated to appropriate commands and ministries, and to units in the field.

'The hub of operations in Hut 3 is the Watch Room, where the Watch and Naval, Army and Air advisors work in close liaison. The Central Intelligence Section is responsible for the study and solving of longer-term and highly complex intelligence. Hut 4 houses the section responsible for the intelligence analysis of the decrypted material from the German Navy sourced from Hut 8. It's currently occupied by the German naval section as well as the Italian and Spanish naval sections. The processes of Hut 4 are very similar to those of Hut 3 with the decrypted messages being passed through the various stages of emendation, translation, evaluation, commenting and sign drafting.'

Sam looked about. It was all very organised.

'We will look at the other huts tomorrow, Sam, but I do want to show you Hut 8 where your wife works. That's where you will be working with Alan Turing. He is a brilliant fellow. He's been working on the naval Enigma which by all accounts is the most difficult to crack. He has developed the most advanced bombe to date. I am sure he would be more than happy to demonstrate it to you.'

Alistair and Sam entered Hut 8. It was a hive of activity with WRENs (Women's Royal Naval Service) everywhere typing and analysing documents.

Hut 8 Bletchley Park

Alistair approached a man with a shaggy tweed coat and hair that could only be described as unkempt.

'Hello Alan, I would like you to meet Sam Griffith. He's been assigned to 'Ultra' to assist your project with anything the Defence Department can provide logistically.'

'Pleased to meet you.'

'Please call me Sam. Yes, the Prime Minister has made it very clear to me that I should do anything I can to assist you.'

'That's nice. Would you like to see our baby?'

'Baby?'

'Our Bombe, Sam.'

'Oh, of course. Yes! I would love a demonstration.'

'Follow me.'

Turing led them through to another room attached to the hut. There, sitting proudly with its cogs spinning and whirring was Turing's bombe.

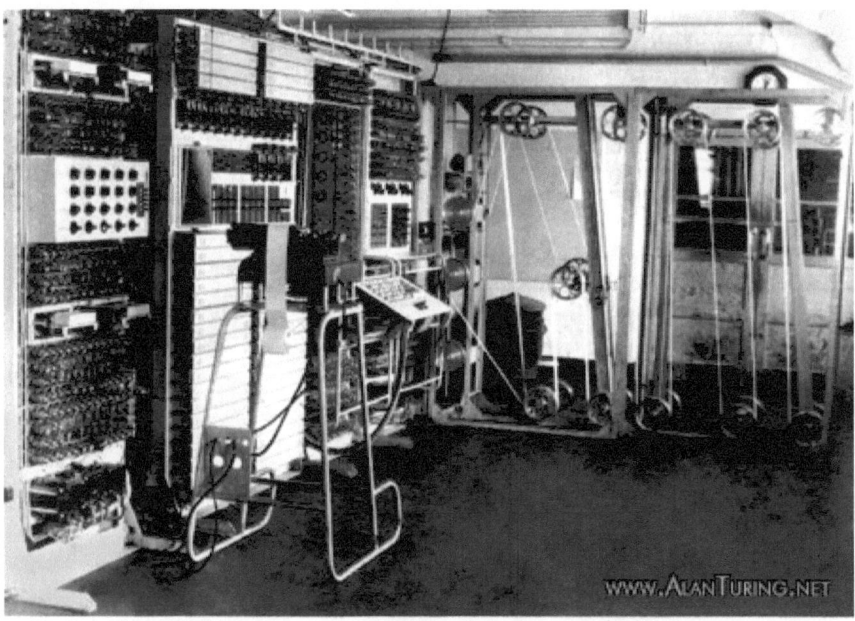

Turing's Bombe

'So, here she is, the machine that is cracking the naval Enigma codes and putting German U-boats where they belong - on the bottom of the ocean,' boasted Turing.

Sam worked at Bletchley Park throughout the war, as did Georgia. Over the next few years they achieved great results, saving the lives of thousands of Allied forces.

The Fall of the Third Reich

Chapter 55

1945

January 1-17 – Germans withdraw from the Ardennes.

January 16, 1945 – U.S. 1st and 3rd Armies link up after a month long separation during the Battle of the Bulge.

January 17, 1945 – Soviet troops capture Warsaw, Poland.

January 26, 1945 – Soviet troops liberate Auschwitz.

February 4-11 – Roosevelt, Churchill, and Stalin meet at Yalta.

February 13/14 – Dresden is destroyed by a firestorm after Allied bombing raids.

March 6, 1945 –Last German offensive of the war begins to defend oil fields in Hungary.

March 7, 1945 – Allies take Cologne and establish a bridge across the Rhine at Remagen.

March 30, 1945 – Soviet troops capture Danzig.

In April – Allies discover stolen Nazi art and wealth hidden in German salt mines.

April 1, 1945 – U.S. troops encircle Germans in the Ruhr; Allied offensive in northern Italy.

April 12, 1945 – Allies liberate Buchenwald and Belsen concentration camps; President Roosevelt dies. Harry Truman becomes President.

April 16, 1945 – Soviet troops begin their final attack on Berlin; Americans enter Nuremberg.

April 18, 1945 – German forces in the Ruhr surrender.

April 21, 1945 – Soviets reach Berlin.

The Battle of Berlin, 1945

The final chapter in the destruction of Hitler's Third Reich began on April 16, 1945 when Stalin unleashed the brutal power of 20 armies, 6,300 tanks and 8,500 aircraft with the objective of crushing German resistance and capturing Berlin. By prior agreement, the Allied armies (positioned approximately 60 miles to the west) halted

Their advance on the city stalled in order to give the Soviets a free hand. The depleted German forces put up a stiff defence, initially repelling the attacking Russians, but ultimately succumbed to overwhelming force. By April 24 the Soviet army surrounded the city slowly tightening its stranglehold on the remaining Nazi defenders. Fighting street-to-street and house-to-house, Russian troops blasted their way towards Hitler's chancellery in the city's centre.

Inside his underground bunker Hitler lived in a world of fantasy as his "Thousand Year Reich" crumbled above him. In his final hours the Fuehrer married his long-time mistress and then joined her in suicide. The Third Reich was dead.

Finally the war in Europe had ended although the Japanese were yet to be defeated in the Pacific.

End of War Celebrations

England is a Nation of Shopkeepers

Napoleon

Chapter 56

January 1, 1946

Sam and Georgia returned to Abernethy Manor at war's end. It didn't take long to fall into the normal routine. Sam commenced a program of rebuilding the sheep flock and cattle herd while Georgia ran the household. Despite trying for some years Sam and Georgia were unable to have children and they decided not to adopt. Sam was more than aware that he would not have an heir.

Anna and Geoffrey were aware that both their children were destined to be wealthy, but they wanted both Harry and Kate to learn the responsibility of life and the lessons it entailed. A work ethic was extremely important to the Turner family.

Harry received a letter from Oxford University accepting him into Law school. He was delighted. The first semester would begin on March 2, which didn't give him much time to get organised.

Kate decided to enrol at Cambridge studying economics. She would begin in March also.

Both children enjoyed their university days. Harry passed his law degree with a high distinction and Kate graduated in economics.

Kate and Harry were summoned to the Turner library soon after their graduation ceremonies. Both thought it would be to receive a graduation present from their parents. They entered the magnificent room to find not only their parents but also the family's lawyer, Mr Humphries and the family accountant, Mr Phipps.

'Take a seat Kate and Harry. We have something important to discuss with you,' said Geoffrey.

Brother and sister looked at one another with a *what in the hell is going on here?* expression. They sat on the leather three-seater lounge.

Geoffrey said, 'When your grandmother died she left a will leaving various assets to her loved ones. You were left a significant asset each. The will states that you were not to be informed of the bequeathment until you both turned twenty-one, which has now happened. I will hand the floor to Mr Humphries.'

'Thank you, Doctor Turner.

'In her will, Emma Griffith bequeathed you, Harold Turner, a department store in Melbourne Australia which trades under the name of Mary's. Kate, you were bequeathed a department store called Georges. Both stores are regarded as the premier retail outlets in Melbourne, turning over £2,000,000 each. Emma also left both of you a cash sum of £30,000.'

Harry and Kate were silent for a moment, then Harry said, 'My God this is amazing!'

The lawyer smiled grimly. 'As with all things, there's a catch.'

'Oh right, here we go,' said Kate.

'I'll hand the floor back to you, Doctor Turner.'

Geoffrey smiled. 'Your grandmother was a very proud Australian as your mother is. To receive your inheritance Emma stipulated that you both go to Australia and live there for a period of no less than five years.'

'Hold on… this sounds like transportation! I didn't even steal a hankie,' said Kate.

'We have just both graduated and you're telling us we have to live in the colonies for five bloody years?' said Harry.

'The will doesn't say you have to work in the stores. You can join a law firm and Kate you could join a bank. Melbourne is a wonderful city and I know you both will enjoy your time there. It's not a life sentence.'

'Well, I don't know about Kate, but I need to think about this for a while.'

'I agree with Harry. This is all too much to absorb at once.'

The meeting ended with an agreement Kate and Harry would get back to their parents with a decision within a week.

Harry and Kate got together in Harry's room to discuss the situation.

'So, what do you think?' asked Harry.

'Well, to be honest, I feel we are being pressured into something neither of us wants to do. I have often thought I'd like to go to Australia for a holiday but not for five years.'

'Yeah, I know what you mean. The other side is how much do we forfeit if we don't go along. Maybe we just accept the £30,000 and forego the department stores.'

'That's got to be an option, and after all, that's still a lot of money.'

'How about we both sleep on it and get back together after breakfast?'

'Done, sleep well.'

'I don't think I will,' said Harry.

Brother and sister had a restless night. They showered, dressed and went downstairs to join their parents for breakfast in the conservatory.

'Good morning you two. How did you sleep?' asked Anna.

'To tell you the truth Mother, not all that well,' said Harry.

'What about you, Kate?'

'Same.'

'Your father and I can understand your trepidation but if you did decide to go to Australia we know you would thoroughly enjoy it.'

'You can always return for a holiday once a year. QANTAS flies to England and it only takes seventy-five hours. The ship took thirty-five days.'

The family completed their breakfast in relative silence. Harry and Kate decided to take their horses for a ride, giving them the privacy they sought.

Once on the trail Harry and Kate began their conversation.

'So Kate, what are your thoughts after a fitful sleep?'

'Harry, I don't want to go. I want to get a job in London and pursue a career in economics.'

'I feel the same.'

'Well, I think we should take the £30,000 and forget Australia.'

'Right, let's go back to the manor and inform them of our decision.'

The brother and sister rode back at speed. They both felt a heavy weight off their shoulders.

They found both their parents in the library.

'Mother and Father, we have made our decision,' they announced in unison.

'And you have decided—what?' Geoffrey raised his brows.

'We're not going to Australia. We understand we forfeit our inheritance of the stores. We will take the £30,000 and leave it at that.'

Geoffrey sighed. 'I think you misunderstand the situation. The £30,000 was available to you to establish yourselves in Melbourne.'

'What do you mean— establish ourselves?' Kate asked.

'Purchase a house and furniture, buy a car and so on.'

'So you're saying we either immigrate to Australia or receive nothing from Grandmother's will.'

'Harry, I didn't write the clauses. It was Grandmother's wishes. The will is a legal document and it must be adhered to.'

'I think we need to think again Kate,' Harry said, with a grimace.

'I agree.'

After much discussion and cogitation the siblings decided to immigrate.

I Now Call Australia Home

Chapter 57

April 4, 1948

Harry and Kate boarded a Lockheed Constellation bound for Melbourne. Along with twenty-seven other passengers and eleven crew, they departed London with stops in Tripoli, Cairo, Karachi, Calcutta, Singapore and Darwin. The plane stopped overnight at Singapore and Cairo. The trip took seventy-five hours.

Tom arranged for a senior staff member from the Windsor Hotel to meet them at the airport and drive them to the hotel. They would stay at the Windsor for six weeks while they settled into Melbourne life. Harry purchased a beautiful terrace house in Parkville a few miles from the Melbourne CBD.

Kate chose a house in Hawthorne, which was also close to the centre of Melbourne.

The siblings were impressed with their inheritance and even though their original thoughts were to find positions in a law firm and bank after they moved into their new dwellings they decided to be active managers in the department stores.

Harry and Kate were quickly accepted into Melbourne society, as, after all, their grandmother, Emma, was regarded as the matriarch of the city. Not only that, but being the proprietors of the two most prestigious department stores in the city carried some weight.

Invitations to functions and society parties came quick and fast.

Their uncle Tom had inherited from his mother Ericildoune, a large sheep and crop station not far from Ballarat. Harry and Kate spent every fourth weekend at the station, riding through the magnificent countryside. After they had made friendships they invited friends to stay at the impressive homestead. These weekends were filled with laughter and good food and wine.

Both department stores were trading profitably. After one year, Harry had increased Mary's turnover to £2,500,000 per annum while Kate increased turnover at Georges to £3,000,000 per annum.

1950 Melbourne

Kate had become friendly with a director of one of Georges suppliers of women's clothing. His name was Levi Jacobson. Levi always made sure it was he that called on Kate to determine the department store's requirements rather than one of his sales representatives.

After two years, Levi finally built up the courage to ask Kate out to dinner and she accepted.

Levi chose his mother's favourite restaurant, Florentino in Bourke Street. It was one of his favourites also.

Levi arranged to pick up Kate at her Hawthorne address in his pride and joy a Daimler Conquest Convertible. It was a balmy evening, so he decided to have the roof down.

Levi parked the car and walked up to the front door. He knocked and almost lost his breath when Kate opened the door.

'Kate, you look beautiful! I've never seen you with your hair up before.'

'Thank you, Levi, I'm glad you like it.' She looked past him. 'Is that your car?'

'Yes, I only purchased a couple of months ago. Do you like it?'

'It's very sporty. Yes I like it, but I hope my hair stays up. Maybe I should grab a scarf.'

Kate quickly got a scarf and placed it over her head.

They headed for the CBD where Levi parked the car and they walked one block to the restaurant.

'Good evening Mr Jacobson, it's good to see you again.'

'Thank you, Giuseppe, it's good to be back.'

'Please, follow me to your table.'

Once seated Kate made the obvious comment. 'Obviously, you invite many young women to this restaurant. They certainly know you well, Levi.'

He hastened to assure her by saying, 'No, I came here regularly with my mother. It was her favourite. It also held fond memories for her as it was here that my father first invited her out.'

'Oh, I see. I apologise for the inference.'

'No need to apologise, Kate.'

'I take it your father is no longer alive?'

'No. Actually he committed suicide during the Great Depression.'

'Oh, that is sad.'

'It was a very difficult time for my mother and me. We lost our house and our business and my father also.'

'How did you survive?'

'We moved into an area called Dudley Flats. It was a slum made up of shacks right next to a rubbish tip. Mother bought an old sewing machine and began making clothes and that was the genesis of the second iteration of Jacobson's Fine Clothing.'

'That's amazing! The business began in a slum.'

'Well, yes, although we did get incredible support from a lady in England who grew up with my mother in an orphanage in Ballarat. Her married name is Anna Turner. I don't know her maiden name.'

Kate laughed, and he looked at her curiously. 'I don't believe it!' she spluttered. 'She's my mother.'

'You can't be serious.'

'I am… talk about a small world.'

'You know she still holds a percentage of our business.'

'No, I didn't know that. I don't really know about Mother's business affairs. She's a doctor.'

The remainder of the evening was spent talking about family and living in Melbourne.

Kate and Levi enjoyed the evening and Kate agreed to go to the theatre the following Saturday to see Gilbert and Sullivan's *Pirates of Penzance*. The courtship had begun, and eighteen months later they married.

Harry remained the confirmed bachelor. He established a reputation for being a ladies' man and he enjoyed his wealth, his fast cars and his women. A keen horseman, he joined the Melbourne Hunt Club chasing the elusive fox around the Victorian countryside, including Ercildoune where the hunt was held four times a year.

Harry's network of business friends centred on the Melbourne Club and his social life centred around the Melbourne Football Club where he eventually became club President. Considering he had never played a game of Australian Rules football his position was seen as unusual.

The Melbourne Club

Kate and Levi flew to England every second year visiting Kate's father and mother in York and also visited Kate's aunt Georgia and Uncle Sam at Abernethy Manor.

Harry visited less frequently.

December 10, 1965

Kate and Harry received a telephone call from their mother, Anna, with the sad news their father Geoffrey had passed away during the night. His passing wasn't expected. He just died in his sleep at the age of seventy-five.

The decision was made that Kate, Levi and Harry would fly over for the funeral to be held on 17 December.

The service was to be held in York Minster Cathedral; the only church that could hold the expected four hundred mourners.

The Archbishop of York, Donald Coggan conducted the service and Harry delivered the Eulogy. Geoffrey was laid to rest in the family mausoleum at Turner Manor. Geoffrey and Anna were able to purchase Turner Manor back from the receivers.

The wake was held in the Turner Estate Great Hall. Over two hundred attended and it was a grand occasion. Anna was as gracious as ever.

The following day, the family gathered in the library to hear the will being read by Mr Abercrombie, the family's legal advisor.

Mr Abercrombie addressed the family. 'As I'm sure you are all aware, the Turner family's tradition is for the eldest son to inherit the estate. That means you Harry. Your father made it clear in his will that his wife Anna shall have the right to live in the manor until her death. Naturally you retain Mary's Department Store.'

' Excellent and I certainly have no problem with my mother living on the estate for as long as she wishes,' said Harry.

'Kate, you retain ownership of Georges Department Store and in addition you have been bequeathed the sum of £50,000.

'Well, ladies and gentlemen, that concludes the reading of the will. Harry, I need to talk to you privately. Everybody else is free to go.'

Once the family departed from the library, Mr Abercrombie and Harry sat down in the leather wingbacks.

'Harry, you have a decision to make. The inheritance tax on Turner Manor will be quite large.'

'What do you call large?'

'It could be as high as £600,000

'What! You've got to be joking!'

'I'm afraid not. Her Majesty's Government like to take their fair share.'

'It's hardly fair. I need to think about this, long and hard.'

'I'm sorry to be the bearer of bad news Harry.'

'I'll get back to you in relation to what I decide, Mr Abercrombie.'

Harry discussed his dilemma with his mother and sister over dinner that night.

'Harry, you would have to sell Mary's to raise that sort of money,' said Kate.

'I know, and I have no intention of doing that. Mary's is a large part of my life.'

'What do you intend to do?' asked Anna.

'I don't know yet. I'm hoping I'll come up with a clever plan.'

Harry thought about his options over the next few days and finally he decided on a course of action.

He planned to contact British Heritage with an offer to donate Turner Manor to the people of England. British Heritage would take possession only after his mother, Anna, passed away.

The land, apart from five acres of garden and lake where the manor house sat, would be subdivided into fifty-acre lots and sold.

No inheritance tax would be due.

British Heritage was delighted. Turner Manor was one of the finest homes in Yorkshire.

Harry was also delighted. It was never his intention to return to England and now he could return to his beloved Melbourne with a clear conscience.

December 22, Melbourne 1965

Jane Jacobson was in the kitchen of her beautiful South Yarra home. She had just boiled the kettle to make herself a pot of tea. As she reached for the packet of Twining's English Breakfast, she felt a sharp pain in her chest. It was the only warning she got. She fell to the floor writhing, and then the pain ceased, as did her heart. Jane, the orphan girl who rose to be one of the most successful businesswomen in Melbourne had died.

Levi, Kate and Harry, oblivious to Jane's passing, were on the long way home from half a world away.

Upon learning the news of his mother's passing Levi was devastated. She had been not only his mother, but his business partner, best friend and advisor.

The first thing Levi did when back in Melbourne was to visit the funeral home to say his final farewell to his mother and mentor. She looked serene lying in the blackwood casket.

Although not born Jewish, she converted to Judaism when she married her husband Maurice. The Jewish religion requires a person to be buried as soon as possible after death. This was not possible with Jane. However, her funeral was held the day after Levi and Kate arrived back. There were two hundred mourners in attendance at the East Melbourne Synagogue.

The Beginning of the End

Chapter 58

Before Tom became the proud owner of Ercildoune, the previous owners were the Wathaurong Tribe a people that had settled the land 25,000 – 30,000 years before.

The men of the tribe would hunt kangaroo and other marsupials while the women would gather berries roots and other edible vegetation. The Wathaurong people lived a predominately peaceful life though, as with all humankind, there was conflict with other tribes. The Wathaurong warriors would roast and eat their fallen adversaries as a tribal ritual.

Tom was riding his favourite horse, a thoroughbred Arabian stallion called Sultan, over the far paddocks. His purpose was to inspect the sheep, which were due to lamb in the very near future. Once he was satisfied all was in order he decided to let Sultan have a free rein. Sultan loved to gallop over the green fields as he reached full speed, Sultan's left front hoof fell into a deep rabbit hole. Sultan fell heavily, throwing Tom head first into a large tree trunk. Tom died instantly. Sultan survived the fall.

Sultan made his way back to the homestead where he was discovered by one of the jackaroos who raised the alarm.

Six station staff mounted their horses and began their search. It didn't take long to discover Tom's body. It was returned to the homestead his distraught wife, Charlotte, made funeral arrangements immediately.

Aftermath
1965

Levi continued to run the clothing business very successfully, while Kate continued to manage Georges. Together they were one of the wealthiest couples in Australia.

Harry had remained a bachelor. Mary's department store continued to flourish under his ownership.

Ercildoune remained the preeminent supplier of fine merino wool and a major supplier of wheat to the UK and Japanese markets. Charlotte was regarded widely as a very successful pastoralist.

Anna and Geoffrey practised medicine at York Hospital throughout the war years, caring for wounded allied soldiers. At war's end, they established a private clinic in York. After Geoffrey's passing, she continued her career in medicine until retirement in 1960.

The End

Bibliography

w History of Melbourne – Wikipedia

Alice Cornwell: Fergus Hume on our myst...

Mining Technology: Overview – Theme – E...

Squizzy Taylor and Other Notorious Austr...

Leslie 'Squizzy' Taylor targeted in brazen ...

Duntroon graduates | Australian War Mem...

ct Duntroon: The class of 1914

Australian War Memorial

The evacuation chain for wounded and sic...

Themes > Pre-war | 1914–1918–Online

(189) Essex Farm, Advanced Dressing Stat...

NZ Passchendaele letter from Leonard Hart | ...

A look at the dark side of Ballarat's streets...

Psychological Wounds of Conflict: The Im...

Full_Experience_Timeline_SpiritofAnzacCe...

Turner (Lamont) Family Crest and History

W What happened here? | Australian Nationa...

Cunard Line Page 2 – Ocean Liner Postcards

Savills | Back Lane, Bramham, Wetherby, ...

1920 – 1929 World History

Women And The Right To Vote | Australia...

The Suffragettes | Rosie

The 1920s, the Roaring Twenties, in Britain

australias-trade-since-federation.pdf

w Alloa Coal Company – Wikipedia

w Dudley Flats – Wikipedia

15 Jul 1949 – Drab Memories of Dudley Fl...

About the Great Depression

w Economic history of Australia – Wikipedia

BBC – History – World War Two: Summary ...

British Generals – Generals of WWII

w Victorian Aborigines – Wikipedia

w Wurundjeri – Wikipedia

Edward Towle | ss Great Britain
W SS Great Britain – Wikipedia, the free ency...
W SS Great Britain – Wikipedia, the free ency...
W Isambard Kingdom Brunel – Wikipedia, th...
Life in 19th-century Britain – Q-files Ency...
Life in the 19th Century
9781420297959.pdf
YOUR HUNTING TRIP – FOX HUNTING TRIP...
The Fox Hunt: From Downton Abbey Back...
Search Results for samuel Willmott – Fami...
Recreating the Polite World: Shipboard Lif...
W SS Great Britain – Wikipedia, the free ency...
Life on board the Great Britain during first...
Everyday life | Ergo
Pictures of Australian Cities, Towns and Vi...
G description of a high rollers poker game –...
W The Eugowra Gold Robbery by Ben Hall an...
W John Francis (bushranger) – Wikipedia, the...
Law_and_Order–14f0i4a.pdf
Genetic Sexual Attraction: husband and w...
Shock for the married couple who discove...
W Life Inside Childrens Homes – Ballarat Dis...
The Lost Gold Ship – No 67 Autumn 2001...
The Journey – by Sailing Ship | Maritime ...
Growing Up in an Orphanage: Tales of Per...
My Story: How Is It Like To Grow Up In An ...
Treatment of Orphans in 19th Century En...
G sutton inventor ballarat – Google Search
Three Australian scientists you've never h...
SUTTON, Henry – Federation University Au...
SovHill–chinesesballarat–notes–ss1.pdf
W History of Chinese Australians – Wikipedia
~ GOLD ~
Walk From Robe Book Scan.pdf
W Tierra del Fuego gold rush – Wikipedia
Cripple Creek & Victor Colorado Mining H...
1890s | My Place for teachers
The Australian Economic Depression of 1...
18 Feb 1931 – BANKING AND FINANCE – ...
Colorado Gold
~ GOLD ~
W Wire transfer – Wikipedia

www.ingramcontent.com/pod-product-compliance
Lightning Source LLC
Chambersburg PA
CBHW022243020726
47496CB00004B/1044